SOLVED

SOLVED

edited by

ED GORMAN and MARTIN H. GREENBERG

Carroll & Graf Publishers, Inc.
New York

CONTENTS

OPERATION TROJAN HORSE*
by David Everson

In the history of unsolved mysteries, the question of the identity of "Deep Throat" remains one of the two or three most elusive. Until now.

"I know Deep Throat," he said.

I stared at him across the bare table. "Yeah, Linda Love-whatever. Love-LACE. I envy you, but so what?"

He sighed, shut his eyes, and squeezed his tennis ball. "Not the porno movie star. I'm talking Watergate," he said. "The Nixon scandal."

"Frank, I *know* Watergate," I said. "All right, you know Deep Throat. I still say, so what?"

"Throat was a double agent for the Company."

"Company?"

"CIA."

I yawned. "So?"

"You know what Throat's doing now?"

"Scope commercials?"

He rolled his eyes, then said, "He's active in the current presidential campaign."

It was February 9, 1988, the morning after the Iowa caucuses. I had just gotten back from Des Moines. I was

* The inspiration for this story comes from Chapter 19, "Throat," in Jim Hougan's book, *Secret Agenda Watergate, Deep Throat and the CIA* (New York: Random House, 1984). Of course, I alone am responsible for the fictional contortions I have made out of the ideas in *Secret Agenda.*

decompressing from a month in a state where voters and politicians regarded issues as ends, not means. I had no way to know it at the time, but I had played a minor role in crippling Mike Dukakis's presidential campaign by helping to pin the rap for giving the Joe Biden plagiarism tapes to the media on John Sasso, Mike Dukakis's closest adviser. Dukakis had been forced to give Sasso—his savviest campaign pro—a sabbatical which lasted until George Bush and his media assault had tattooed LIBERAL on every portion of the Duke's anatomy. Everyone had been saying it was Dick Gephardt who had nailed Biden, but getting the truth out of the reporters Sasso had given the tapes to—after a few drinks—had been as easy as betting against the Cubs to get to the World Series.

Now I was kicking back in the swivel chair in the office of Midcontinental Op and Associate when the phone rang. I answered in my customary professional manner. "Yeah?"

"Miles, get your ass down here," said Alfred "Fast Freddy" Martin. Fast is the guy who delivers the Speaker's bad news. And Fast truly enjoys his work.

"Jawohl, mine furor," I said.

I figured the Speaker wanted a debriefing on Iowa. But maybe it had something to do with the upcoming Illinois primary. We were backing Illinois' favorite son, Paul Simon, even though we knew he had no chance for the nomination. Maybe the Speaker wanted me to find out what Dukakis had been smoking when he had told the beleagured Iowa farmers to switch to Belgian endive.

Who am I? The name is Robert D. Miles, a private eye with a difference. My base is Springfield, Illinois, Lincoln's hometown. It is also the state capital and second only to Chicago as Clout City, Illinois. But we try harder. My specialty is political intelligence—that's not a contradiction if you know the Speaker of the Illinois House of Representatives, a Chicago Democrat and magna cum laude graduate of the Richard J. Daley Academy of Applied Political Science. The Speaker is boss of a statewide political organization second to none.

Call what I do for him opposition research.

The Speaker has files which would have turned J. Edgar Hoover kelly green with envy. The Speaker seldom has to use them. The knowledge that they exist is sufficient to the task.

Today, as usual, the Speaker sat in his royal-blue chair behind an immaculate desk, absently toying with a small silver gavel and staring out the window at the bare Capitol grounds. He turned his ice-blue eyes on me. "Robert, I've set up an appointment for you with Frank Cross tomorrow," he said.

That caught me like a sucker punch, for reasons I will explain shortly. "What in blazes for?" I asked.

The Speaker put down the gavel and made a steeple with his hands. "Cross wants you to carry a message to me."

I took a deep breath. "I'll pass on the reunion."

The Speaker's pale-blue eyes burned for a second. "I need you to do this, Robert."

"Inmates can make all kinds of phone calls these days."

Fast Freddy—standing in the corner in his vanilla ice-cream suit, red suspenders, and red-and-white bow tie— said, "Cross thinks his calls are being trapped."

He meant, "tapped," of course. Fast Freddy believes—as in horse shoes, hand grenades, and hanky-panky—close also counts in English.

"Why doesn't he write you a letter?" I asked.

"They molest his mail," Fast said.

The Speaker picked up the gavel and pointed it at me. "Robert, he wants *you* to deliver the message."

"Why?"

"I don't know."

"I don't like it."

"I don't much care for it myself. Nevertheless, I want you to find out what he wants."

I still don't like it, I thought. But I didn't have much choice. The Speaker accounts for half of Midcon's gross. "I'll do it," I said. "What's it about?"

"Politics," Fast said.

"Thanks for the news update. Film at eleven? Why are we dealing with Cross at all?"

"Cross is a serious player," the Speaker said. "Not a good man, but someone you have to treat with a degree of respect. I suspect he wants to cut a deal. I want to know what he has to trade."

"Have you considered he may be trying to set us both up?"

"Of course."

On the way back to the office, I thought about Frank Cross. He had been the unofficial boss of the state Republican Party and the owner of numerous lucrative properties, eventually purchased at inflated prices by the state, in the Springfield area. He had lived on the luxury floor of the downtown Cap Centre Hotel—of which he was part owner —until he got involved in a basketball-point shaving scandal, a drug deal, and a couple of murders and got sent away to a place we used to call a prison.

His sentence: three years with a chance for parole in eighteen months.

One of the black basketball players who had confessed to taking bribes to shave points had received five years.

That's what we call equal justice in Illinois.

It didn't compute that Cross wanted me unless he was trying to set me up. I had helped get him his membership card in that barbed wire country club. Guys like Frank Cross never forget something like that, even if they suffer from Alzheimer's.

The word around Springpatch was that Cross was connected to fellas who'd as soon slam a drawer shut on your fingers as eat linguini and clam sauce. After Cross had exhausted his appeals and actually went away, I had started getting dead red roses under my office door once a week. Believe me, I twitched each time I started my 1981 Toyota Tercel and flinched when cars backfired.

After the obese guard with the small eyes almost lost in the folds of fat around them patted me down, he showed me into a large room which resembled a drab junior high school cafeteria. There were about a dozen tables. Half of them were occupied by families and prisoners. Off to the side were a set of small conference rooms behind windows. The guard showed me into one of these. For a few minutes, I sat staring at a blank green wall, which captured how I felt.

In a few minutes, Cross came in, dressed in an expensive running outfit and white court shoes. He was squeezing a yellow tennis ball. He was trim, with only a suggestion of a potbelly, had dark-gray hair and sallow skin. I guessed he was in his early sixties.

"You should get a new florist," I said.

He smiled coldly. "No hard feelings, Miles," he said. "I know it wasn't personal."

"Yeah, it was," I said.

He shrugged. "Water over the bridge." He gestured at the window. "This place isn't too bad once you get used to it. I can work out, stay in shape. In the Pacific, I found out you can get used to almost anything. Not that I don't want out. You know what I miss the most?" he said.

"The little mints when the maids come in to turn down the beds?"

He smiled, but his gray eyes were not participating. "Attending the concerts out at the university. Oh, I have a CD player. But it's not the same."

"If you can't do the time, you shouldn't do the crime," I said.

"That's right."

"What's the deal?"

Cross squeezed the ball. "The guy you work for collects political intelligence. It's well known. I have an interesting story to tell. No names yet. I want you to pass it along to your Man."

I waited.

"I know Deep Throat," he said.

I thought back to Watergate. The Ervin hearings. John Dean. The Prussians, Erlichman and Haldeman. Colson.

The revelation of the tapes. The eighteen-minute gap. Then the firestorm over the firing of Archibald Cox. The House impeachment hearings. The "smoking gun" on the tapes. And finally, the resignation.

Cross squeezed the ball. "There's a guy doing time in here who was tight with one of the Watergate burglars. You remember Liddy?"

I nodded. "G. Gordon Liddy. One of the plumbers. A wild and crazy guy. Wanted to terminate Jack Anderson and tap *The New York Times*. Liked to hold his hand to the flame, as I recall. Now on the lecture circuit pulling down big bucks."

Cross said, "A stand-up guy. Anyway, Liddy told my guy the whole deal."

I leaned forward. "Hold it right there. Liddy wouldn't talk. That's why the Feds dropped the hammer on him."

"You're right. He'd never rat to the authorities."

"To anyone. He'd suspect a plant."

Cross shrugged. "Liddy's a blowhard. Take my word for it. Do you want to hear the story?"

I spread my hands.

"When Watergate broke, *The Washington Post* reporters Woodward and Bernstein were hot on the trail and chasing all kinds of leads. Like a couple of bulls in a china shop. They were likely to blunder into some stuff the CIA would rather they wouldn't. Domestic spying. Which was clearly illegal. The people they targeted would have made Nixon's enemies' list look rational. The Company wanted to keep tabs on what Woodward and Bernstein knew, what they guessed, and what leads they were following. So they recruited Deep Throat"—he paused and chuckled—"only they code-named him 'Zapata' and called the operation 'Trojan Horse'—to make contact with Woodward and offer to be an informant."

"Zapata?"

"I'm not sure why that name was chosen. Anyway, Woodward bit on it."

"You're saying Deep Throat/Zapata was working for the other side?"

"Absolutely." Cross stared at me out of his depthless gray eyes.

I rewound the tape in my head again. "As I remember, Deep Throat never gave Woodward and Bernstein a bum steer."

He nodded. "Of course. Double agents must give reliable info to remain credible. Actually, if you read Woodward carefully, all Throat ever did was confirm what they already knew. But Throat's value to the Company was in finding out which direction the investigation was moving and trying to steer it back on course. Understand this, *if* Woodward and Bernstein had ever gotten too close to the sensitive areas, they'd never have lived long enough to get the Pulitzer."

I shook my head. This sounded like a scene from a low-grade espionage thriller. "There's just one big problem with this whole story."

Cross squeezed the ball. "What's that?"

"Nixon bit the big enchilada. He resigned. Ford pardoned him. That's why he has to be rehabilitated."

Cross looked impatient. "Miles, you missed the whole fucking point."

"Oh?"

"You're assuming that the Company's goal was to keep Nixon in the presidency."

"I get it. Okay. Truth or fiction aside, what good is this information now?"

"That would depend on who Deep Throat is, wouldn't it? Here's my deal. When you figure it out, I'll confirm and steer you in the direction of proof."

"What's the price?"

"Something from the Speaker."

"What?"

"He serves as a character witness at my parole hearing."

"No chance," I said. "Why don't you get your pal the Guv to pardon you?"

Cross shook his head. "If asked, he might admit he met me once at a social function. He wants to be Attorney General in the new administration and he doesn't want to answer questions at his confirmation hearings about his relationship with me."

I'm no Archie Goodwin, but I gave the Speaker and Fast Freddy almost a word-for-word account of what Frank Cross had said.

When I finished, Fast Freddy said, "That's all ex post factor. Who gives a rat's ass now?"

But the Speaker made that steeple with his hands. "On the contrary, Alfred, I find it fascinating. Bizarre. Prison has not dulled Franklin's mind. He still has the capacity to surprise. Improvise. Perhaps embellish."

I rolled my head back and forth. "I'll give you that. But for once, I'm with Fast. What difference does it make?"

"He's offering me potential leverage."

"Over whom?"

"Someone highly placed in the next administration."

"Why doesn't he use it directly?"

"That is the question. Robert?"

"Yes?"

"I'm going to assume we're talking about Republican candidates for President and their top advisers." He turned to Fast Freddy. "How many candidates are there?"

"Realistic ones?"

The Speaker nodded.

"Bush. Dole. Haig. Robertson. Kemp. DuPont, if you stretch it."

"Robert, do some background research and narrow the field for me."

"Alexander Haig," I said to the Speaker. "Has to be Haig."

"How did you determine that?"

"I read everything Woodward and Bernstein said in *All the President's Men* about Deep Throat." I glanced at my notes on a yellow legal pad. "This is a direct quote. 'Woodward had a source in the Executive Branch who had access to information at CRP as well as at the White House.' CRP was the Committee to Re-elect the President, popularly known as CREEP. Then I matched what I found against the current presidential candidates and their top advisers. It wasn't hard to get to a very short list of one. Haig was the only one in the Nixon executive branch."

The Speaker shut his eyes for a couple of seconds. "Haig had worked for Kissinger?"

I nodded. "He was a career soldier. He was brought into the White House to help fight the Watergate firestorm."

"What else?"

"At various points in the narrative, Woodward drops some clues about Deep Throat's identity. Heavy smoker. Drinker. Loved to hear his own voice. In love with gossip. He also recounts some conversations that Deep Throat must have observed and some facts which only a limited number of people could have had access to. From what I can determine about Haig's role in the Nixon administration and his personality, it all fits."

The Speaker turned and stared out the window. "Except it doesn't," he said slowly.

"What do you mean?"

"Seems to me I've read speculation that Haig was Deep Throat. And rebuttal."

"So?"

"Cross wouldn't offer to trade damaged goods."

"He wouldn't?"

"Not with me."

"Good point."

"Robert, go talk to him again. Run Haig's name by him and see what he says."

As I left the Capitol, I noticed a headline on a Chicago *Herald-Star* at the newsstand: DOLE LEAD HOLDING IN NEW HAMPSHIRE.

"Haig," I said.

Cross squeezed his ball and smirked. "Wrong," he said.

"Has to be. Couldn't be any other candidate on the basis of what's in *All the President's Men.*"

"I didn't say 'candidate.' "

"No. But Haig fits the Woodward description."

Cross squeezed the ball. "Of *course* he does. That's the point."

"It is?"

"That's all legend."

"Legend?"

"Cover story. Routine tradecraft."

"This is a spy thing, isn't it?"

He nodded. "Look, Woodward promised to protect Deep Throat's identity, right?"

"Yeah."

"After he promises, then he gives all these clues that could only point to one man? Give me a break. Smoke and mirrors. Look, you obviously read the account carefully. It's got misdirection written all over it. But other details clearly point in one direction. Think about it. The clandestine meetings. The signaling systems—the moving of the flower pot and the use of *The New York Times.* Throat's a spook, not a career military guy."

"Couldn't he have been in military intelligence?"

"Forget about Haig. There is clear evidence he couldn't have been Throat. Forget what Woodward says about Deep Throat. That's a blind alley. Concentrate on Woodward. He's the key. Who was *he* that Throat went to him?"

"He was the reporter on the story."

"But not the only one. Why Woodward and not Bernstein?"

"Because Woodward knew Deep Throat?"

"Did he? Or was that just part of the cover? Isn't it more likely that Throat was someone Woodward would instinctively trust?"

I sighed. "Cross, why don't you just cut out the crap and give me the name?"

"That would take away all the fun. Like Throat, I'll only confirm."

It was the morning of February 16. I stood at the dust-streaked window of the Midcon office staring at the dull silver dome of the Capitol down the street. "What do you make of it, Mitch?" I said.

Mitch Norris is my associate at Midcon. Former big-league catcher and my fashion idol. Mitch would rather wear a nose ring than a tie. Today he wore a shocking-pink shirt, bright orange pants, and white shoes. He leaned back in the swivel chair and blew a cloud of cigar smoke. "Bobby, Cross's jerkin' you around."

"I know *that*. Why?"

"Hey, you can only squeeze so many tennis balls. You want me to do the background on Woodward?"

Mitch was the scholar of the office, a graduate of Knox College in Galesburg, Illinois. "Yeah," I said. "Why don't you just do that?"

That afternoon, I gave an update to the Speaker. He thought for several minutes and then said, "Robert, I think I have a faint glimmer of where this is going," he said. "And it's fantastic. In the sense of make-believe. But if it's true . . ." he trailed off.

"I take it you want me to pursue it?"

"Absolutely."

"Do you have a file on Frank Cross?"

The Speaker raised his eyebrows. "Of course. Alfred, get that for Robert."

As I left the Capitol, a headline on the *Herald-Star* said: DOLE LEAD SLIPPING IN N.H.

Back at the office, I read Cross's file. I found I had contributed more than a few items. Mitch came back from Lincoln Library and gave me his report. I pondered for a while and decided to go country-clubbing for the third time.

Cross squeezed his tennis ball. "Well?"

"Robert Woodward. A WASP's WASP. Son of a Republican judge. Registered Republican himself. Yale graduate. Service in the Navy with a high security clearance. Communications officer for the Chief of Naval Operations. Extensive prior contacts through briefings and such with the CIA. Almost a spook." I paused.

"You've done your homework," Cross said grudgingly.

No, Mitch did it, I thought. "Yeah. But I don't know what it means."

Cross bounced the ball rapidly on the table. "It's right in front of you. Once a part of the spook community, always a part of the community."

"You're saying Woodward was Deep Throat?"

Cross chuckled. "How could that be?"

"In the sense that he was a double agent in the ranks of the *Post* for the CIA."

"No. First, there was no way they could know he would be assigned the Watergate story. Second, Woodward is not part of any presidential campaign."

"Okay, Woodward is not Deep Throat. So what are you saying about him?"

"I'm saying that he was a natural choice for the Company to target to aim Zapata at so they could keep track of the investigation and to nudge it in the right direction."

"Which was?"

"Getting Nixon out."

"Why?"

"Détente. And getting their guy in."

"Ford?"

He snorted. "No. They moved their guy around where they wanted him. Congress. The Republican National Committee. The CIA. China. The executive branch. Now they're real close to the brass ring. I've given you enough to work it out."

"Suppose I do? Then what?"

"I'll confirm it. And provide proof."

"Cross, why don't you just use this information yourself?"

"I can't use it without endangering my own life. If I use it directly, it'll blow back on me. Believe it."

"Frank, how old are you?"

"Sixty-one."

"You served in World War II?"

"Yes."

"Navy flier? Pacific? Shot down?"

"That's right. You've been in the Speaker's files I take it."

I nodded. "Where'd you go to college?"

He shrugged. "Out East."

"Yale?"

He dipped his head.

"You graduated in '48?"

He nodded. "With honors. I majored in the Classics."

"Lot of intelligence people were recruited out of Yale during and after the war?"

"That's what I hear."

"What were you doing in 1972?"

"Helping to run the Nixon campaign in Illinois."

"In charge of dirty tricks?"

He widened his eyes and smiled.

"Somebody from CREEP recruit you for the job?"

He didn't say anything.

"I'm taking silence as assent. Am I wrong?"

His expression did not change.

I leaned over and whispered a name to him.

He winked at me.

It was the morning of February 17. I was back in the Speaker's office. I had just given him a replay of the last conversation with Cross. "What do you think?" I asked.

He made that steeple. "I think Cross was having us on. His little joke. A minor form of revenge."

I nodded. "So do I."

"Let me see if I have Cross's story straight. 'Deep Throat' or 'Zapata' had been recruited into covert intelligence by the CIA at Yale after the war. Frank Cross had met him in the Navy in the Pacific and then again at Yale. 'Zapata' drafted Cross for the 1972 Nixon campaign and turned him over to Hunt and Liddy. Cross ran the dirty-tricks operations in Illinois. Many years later, it was Liddy who told Cross directly—not through a third party—that 'Zapata' was 'Deep Throat.' "

"That's the way he tells it."

"So Zapata is a wholly owned subsidiary of the CIA?"

I nodded. "Cross said, 'Zapata was in Iran-Contra up to his eyeballs.'"

"Where's the proof?"

"Cross says 'next time.'"

"If there is a next time."

As I left the Capitol, I stopped at the newsstand on the ground floor. The twin headlines on the *Herald-Star* said: FRANK CROSS CRITICALLY INJURED IN PRISON SCUFFLE and BUSH CRUSHES DOLE IN N.H.

CLOSING THE DOORS
by Rick Hautala

There have been too many early deaths in the history of popular music. Here Rick Hautala takes a penetrating look at one of the most famous of these tragedies.

I'd thought for days—maybe weeks—that someone was following me, but I didn't realize until that last night in Paris that I was haunting myself.

That's why I've come back to the States, back to the New Mexico desert, back to where it all began all those years ago. To sort it all out if I can. To see if I can find that man, that dead Indian I saw out here when I was a kid.

Maybe he has the answers I'm looking for.

I'm keeping this journal to help me remember and to help me work it all through. There have been too many times when things I've written in songs and poems have come too close to the truth.

Much too close.

Sometimes I think I have no control over my life—never have . . . ever since I was a boy and that dying Indian's soul entered my body, replacing . . . whatever was there originally—the *real* me. It's as if I write about things first, and then I have to live them. Now that he's left me, I don't know who I am.

But it's all there in the songs and poems. Listen to "Hyacinth House" on *L.A. Woman*. I give it all away—*everything* that happened in the apartment that hot July night in Paris.

In 1971, Pam and I had gone to Paris to get away from it all, y'know? The media circus that was all part of being a rock 'n' roll star—the "Lizard King." Shit, I was burned out, and we both needed a break. To tell you the truth, we were seriously trying to patch things up between us, to make it good again. Problem was, when Pam wanted to make it better, I didn't; and when I did, she didn't.

The yin and the yang of it all.

Maybe that's why we were so compatible in our incompatibility.

Of course, since coming to the desert, I can see now with a newfound clarity that I never had before that *I* was the one who needed the break.

Oh, sure, Pam had her share of problems. No doubt about it. But I can't help but think, even now, that I was the source of all of her problems. Maybe I'm making myself too important in her life—maybe not.

But yeah, the drinking and drugs had gotten out of hand.

Way out of hand!

And the writing?

Shit! The writing wasn't coming at all. No poetry! No songs! Nothing!

I was looking for inspiration—or escape—in a bottle. Even then, part of me was warning me that I was overdoing it. I've read some of the things written about me since—that I had a death wish—that I was sick of my celebrity and wanted to die because I'd gotten everything I was after and found that it was hollow—that I no longer wanted to be a rock star, just a poet.

Some of that may be true.

You certainly don't make a lunch of a few Bloody Marys and a bottle of Scotch unless you're running away from something.

I see now, though, that I was also running *to* something. Maybe I needed one last hit of LSD that night in Paris to make it all clear to me. Maybe that's when the Indian's spirit left me . . . so I could find out exactly who I used to be.

Who is this person inside me who never got the chance to grow up?

That Friday night, July 2, I'd gone out to the movies—alone—to see *Pursued,* starring Robert Mitchum.

Pretty fuckin' apt title, now that I think about it.

Pam was off somewhere with those friends of hers, no doubt looking for something to shoot into her arm. I'd been drinking most of the day, so I was in no condition to care where she went. After the movie, I wandered down to the Rock 'n' Roll Circus to check out what was happening.

Can't remember much about what I did there.

No idea who was playing that night.

The only clear memory I have was feeling like someone was watching me. I'd been feeling like that for days . . . weeks, thinking I was being followed. I kept looking around, trying to see who it was, but I didn't catch even a glimpse of him . . . not until I got back to the flat.

Shit like that happened a lot back then. People would recognize me and follow me around. The new album had been released in April and had done pretty good. It had some great reviews, and the first single had a good run in the Top Ten. The rest of the band was excited about what we'd do next, but I wasn't ready to come back to the States.

Not yet.

I had to die first.

But shit, I should have been thrilled to have someone recognize me, what with all the weight I'd put on over the past few months. I've lost most of that weight now and feel a hell of a lot better.

One thing I do remember clearly from that night was scoring a hit of acid while I was there. I must have scored a bit of heroin then, too. I think maybe Peter might have given it to me. I took the acid first, and, before long, the music, the people, and the night were all blending together in a riot of sounds and colors.

Like a vision of hell.

Something straight out of a Bosch painting.

After tripping my brains out for an hour or so, I snorted

the heroin to help bring me down. Never could stand to take a needle. Whatever—sometime around midnight, I guess, some friends piled me into a cab and sent me back to the flat.

Pam was there when I finally made it up the stairs. She was sitting cross-legged on the bed, nodding out but looking like she wasn't feeling any pain.

I was.

My head felt like it was encased in cement. The slightest sound was magnified so loud it hurt my ears. I thought I must be going crazy and vowed to stop taking acid. It wasn't doing me any good anymore, anyway. The world seemed so far away, like I was looking through a foot-thick plate-glass window. I thought maybe I'd fallen through some kind of hole in reality. *Maybe*—I remember thinking and laughing about it—*I've finally broken through.*

I went over to Pam, and before I knew what was happening, we were naked and fucking our brains out on the bed. Time and reality lost all meaning. They always did whenever Pam and I connected. That didn't happen enough. Too bad for both of us we didn't realize until too late that it was us, not the drugs, that made us feel that way.

When we were finished—who knows when?—Pam started drifting off to sleep with a contented smile on her face.

God, it breaks my heart to think of how seldom I saw her smile like that! I was still feeling like shit, so I told her I was going to take a bath, thinking that would help bring me all the way down. I ran the water—hot—and eased on down into the tub, feeling every pore in my body open up to the gentle, lapping water.

I was floating in space, dreaming . . . watching the muffled explosions of color behind my eyelids. I have no idea how long I lay there with my head back and my arms resting on the sides of the tub. I might have been there for hours . . . or days, for all I know. It was still dark outside, and the water had turned ice-cold when I opened my eyes and saw myself standing there at the foot of the tub.

For a moment I thought I was looking at my reflection in

the mirror that hung on the bathroom wall. Then I realized that whoever this was—me or someone else—he was
wearing a white button-down shirt, tan chinos, and a pair
of beat-to-shit Frye boots just like I had been wearing earlier that night. I was confused as hell, thinking for a moment that maybe I hadn't yet undressed and gotten into
the tub.

"Hey, what the fuck're you doing here?" I asked.

A small voice in the back of my head was telling me that
this wasn't really me; it was just someone who *looked* like
me. I didn't have enough energy to get nervous or to wonder how the fuck he'd gotten into the flat.

He smiled and said nothing as he stared down at me
lying there in the tub. The acid was still worming through
my brain, so I was having one hell of a time trying to figure
out which was the real me—the one in the tub or the one
standing there beside the bidet.

"Are . . . you . . . me?" I asked, faintly surprised that
his lips didn't move when I spoke.

He nodded his head slowly and answered, "I *want* to be."

"You're the one who's been following me, right?"

Again, he nodded.

"I want to *be* you," he said, running his fingers through
his long dark hair.

I know now that there's a term for something like this.
Schizophrenic dissociation. This guy might not have really
looked like me, but the LSD was twisting reality into all
sorts of new shapes. I finally understood that I wasn't really talking to myself there in the bathroom. This guy—I
never asked his name—was my ultimate fan. For all I
know, he might even have had plastic surgery to alter his
face to look as much like mine as possible. He had long,
curly hair like mine; he was dressed like me; and he acted
like me—even to the point of embracing my supposed
death wish. I sensed that in him right away: that he had
come here either to kill me or to die.

I don't know what possessed me, but I nodded toward the
bedroom door and said, "Pam's in there. If I'm going to die,
go in there and say good-bye to her for me."

He looked at me, momentarily confused. Then his smile widened and he said, "Do you mean, make love to her?"

I rolled my head lazily back and forth, and answered, "Naw! Just fuck her!"

I lay back in the bathtub and listened while he went into the bedroom. I heard him take off his clothes, rouse Pam, and then—for several minutes—all I heard was the squeaking of bedsprings and soft moaning. When he was finished, he came back into the bathroom, his naked body —thinner and stronger-looking than mine—glistening with sweat.

"Here," I said, standing up and stepping out of the bathtub to make room for him. "Why don't you get in?"

Without a word, he walked over to the tub, stepped into the icy water, and lay down.

Dripping water and naked, I leaned over him and stared at his face, unable to rid myself of the impression that I was gazing into a mirror. His dark eyes were large, glistening as he looked up at me.

"Relax, now," I said, caressing the back of his head. "Close your eyes and relax . . . I'm going to die now."

He heaved a deep sigh, closed his eyes, and slumped back against the tub. When I saw that he was completely relaxed, I went over to the sink and took a fresh razor blade from the cabinet. Back at the bathtub, I handed him the blade and said, "If you hold your wrist under water, it won't sting as much."

He did just as he was told.

Gripping the blade between his thumb and forefinger, he carefully, almost lovingly, ran the sharp edge from the heel of his thumb up the inside of his arm. The skin split open like a lizard shedding its skin. His blood spurted into the water in bright red strands that twisted like hair before diffusing. All the while he looked at me, and I saw myself—*felt* myself—dimming as his energy and life flowed from his arm into the cold water.

I caressed his head again, combing back his long hair with my fingers as I watched him. I saw the very instant when the moist light in his eyes changed to an empty, glazed stare.

"Good-bye, Jim," I whispered, leaning forward and kissing him on the forehead.

A soft, angelic smile curled the corners of his mouth.

I hurriedly dried off and got dressed. Making sure I had plenty of cash in my wallet, I left the flat in the predawn stillness. At the time I didn't know that I would never see Pam again. That wasn't part of my plan, but I knew I couldn't have trusted her with my secret. I had faith that she could ride out the emotional storm before I finally dared to come back to her.

As it turned out, she didn't.

The general press reported my death accurately, stating that I had died of heart failure. What do they think is going to happen if you slit your wrist? Of course your heart is going to stop. Perhaps the French doctor who so hastily signed my death certificate and sealed the coffin simply wanted to avoid the scandal of a famous rock star committing suicide in Paris.

There have been other things written about me since that night—that I died of a heroin overdose or a punctured lung from that fall I took out of a hotel window. There's been some speculation that I overdosed in the restroom of a nightclub and was dragged back to the flat, or that I purposely committed suicide. A few investigative reporters have raised concerns that Pam was the only person to identify my body before I was buried in Père Lachaise cemetery, that neither Bill nor anyone else examined the body, that the doctor's signature on the death certificate might have been forged, and that no autopsy or exhumation was ever conducted.

Some of these stories come close to the truth, but none of them ever hit it.

But what about Pam?

I often wonder about her.

I know she took it real hard, thinking that I was dead, but I wonder if she knew or suspected what had really happened. Was she so far gone with grief, or so fucked up on drugs that she actually thought that guy was me? Or did she go along with it, covering up the truth and trusting that I'd eventually come back to her.

Most people believe that I'm dead, and I'm willing to leave it at that. The man who took my place in the bathtub certainly didn't seem to mind playing out the final act for me. Remembering his voice as he died soothes me late at night.

". . . I want to be you! . . ."

There *is* liberation in death!

But now, for the past few weeks as I've been driving through the desert in New Mexico, searching for that dead Indian I passed by so many years ago, I can hear other voices talking to me, calling to me . . . voices inside my head, telling me to . . . to—

—This final journal entry, which ends in midsentence, was found in 1976 in an abandoned rental car several miles south of Albuquerque, New Mexico.

RUBY, RUBY
by William J. Reynolds

John F. Kennedy, Sirhan Sirhan, Lee Harvey Oswald, Robert F. Kennedy, Jack Ruby—five men bound together for all time, with the motivations of Jack Ruby still the subject of much speculation.

IN THE NAME AND BY THE AUTHORITY OF THE STATE OF TEXAS, *the Grand Jurors, good and lawful men of the County of Dallas and the State of Texas, duly elected, tried, impaneled, sworn and charged to inquire of offenses committed within the body of the said County of Dallas, upon their oaths do present in and to the Criminal District Court* __No. 3__ *of Dallas County, at the* __October__ *Term, A. D. 1963, of said Court that one* __Jack Rubenstein alias Jack Ruby__ *on or about the* __24__ *day of* __November__ *in the year of our Lord One Thousand Nine Hundred and* __63__ *in the County and State aforesaid, did then and there unlawfully, voluntarily and with malice aforethought kill Lee Harvey Oswald by shooting him with a gun, contrary to the form of the Statute in such cases made and provided, and against the peace and dignity of the State.*

(SIGNED)
Foreman of the Grand Jury
HENRY WADE
Criminal District Attorney of Dallas County, Texas

November 22, 1991—Long Island
The clouds were low enough to touch, and they spat a gritty, unlovely snow. The old man sat behind the big desk,

in his high-backed leather chair, and watched the weather move in.

He did a lot of that lately, watching, musing, reflecting. It is what people do when they know with certainty that more of their life is behind them than ahead of them. It is what people do when they know with certainty that nearly all of their life is behind them, and very little lies ahead.

Twenty-eight years ago . . . Could it have been that long ago? Could it have been *only* that long ago?

The old man—thin, his colorless, waxy-looking skin stretched taut over his skull, his wispy white hair a floating halo around his head—the old man had for some reason hoped he would make it an even thirty years. Why, he couldn't say. Perhaps only the sentimental daydreams of a dying old man. Perhaps to close out the story.

The story. A thin smile sketched its way across the old man's white lips. All these years later, still the subject of so much debate, so much controversy. He had known, back before the event, that it would loom large in the history of the twentieth century, as large or larger than the Lincoln assassination almost a hundred years earlier. But even he had had no conception of just *how* large the event would be —and how it would seemingly grow larger with every passing year, rather than fade and die as they had all expected.

Not that it mattered. There was no one left who could reveal the truth now, even if he wanted to. There were few enough who knew the whole story, and of that small, elite group, all were long since gone now. Except the old man. And he had no reason to loose the secret he had held for almost a third of a century.

In that time he had frequently been amused at how wildly wrong some of the "conspiracy buffs" had been in their speculations. At other times, he had been almost alarmed at how close to the truth their guesses had been. But he always reminded himself that they were only guesses, and guesses they would forever remain.

Astonishingly, to him, nearly all of the "conspiracy buffs" focused their attention on the first assassin, who was hardly worthy of it, and all but ignored the greater mystery.

The assassin of the assassin.

November 22, 1963—Dealy Plaza
Ancona thumbed imaginary glare from the barrel of the rifle and thought sour thoughts. He didn't like this job, he didn't like a thing about it. Except the money. And Ancona was too much the professional to let himself be tempted by money alone. You don't take jobs that smell bad simply for the money. That's not how you get to be the top trigger man in Vegas, and for five hundred miles in any direction from Vegas. That's not how you stay on top.

But you don't stay on top, either, by turning down Tataglia when he asks you for a "favor." The lawyer spoke for half the families in the east, and he didn't need to tell you which family, or families, he was representing—or if he was representing any of them—when he called you. Tataglia asked a "favor," Tataglia was accommodated. Good things tended to happen to those to whom Tataglia was "indebted." If you couldn't help Tataglia out, well, no hard feelings. Not for long, at any rate.

Tataglia had called Ancona, and now Ancona lay in the grass, in the shelter of a leafy bush, thinking sour thoughts and waiting for the damn job to be finished so he could blow out of Texas forever.

There was fifty thousand dollars in Ancona's Grand Cayman account, with another fifty to follow after the job. And that was fine. It would enable Ancona to "retire" for a year or so. But it didn't do much toward taking away the stink that hung over the whole job. Tataglia hadn't said anything—he wouldn't, and Ancona wouldn't have asked—but the fine hand of the Agency was all over this one. It was too complicated, too fucking complicated. That was the Agency way. That's how they lost Cuba. That's how Cuba was going to stay lost.

Ancona didn't know from Cuba, but he knew this job didn't have to be so elaborate. He'd told Tataglia that much, clear back last summer. *Forget the other guy, send me down there alone,* Ancona had urged. *I'll hide up on that little hill or knoll or whatever they call it, one shot—* fa-zip!—*take the mick's face right off him, be a hundred miles away from Dallas before any of those cowboys even know what happened. Simple, clean, and fast.* That's the way you did a job—simple, clean, and fast. Not too many people, not too many plans, not too much chance for something to get fucked up. In Ancona's long experience, things got fucked up by themselves just fine without having to go out of your way to help them.

But the plan was already "in motion," Tataglia had said. Too late to change now, and too late to cancel. He realized it was not how Ancona usually liked to work, but if he could see his way clear to doing Tataglia this one small "favor" . . .

A buzz, a kind of electric current, went through the people scattered on the grass below Ancona, and he snapped his mind away from the events of last summer, focusing them on the events to come in the next minutes. As he sighted experimentally the pavement below the knoll, Ancona was aware of the sound of the approaching motorcade.

April 10, 1963—New York
Brenner hated New York. It was crowded, it was dirty, and it stank, especially on a day as warm as this one. The worst part, though, was the noise, the steady undercurrent of sound that got under his skin the moment he stepped out of the La Guardia terminal and stayed there until he got away again. There was no escape from the noise. All you could do was try to cover it up with other, different noise. No wonder New Yorkers were so obnoxious.

Brenner consoled himself with the thought that his business would take only a few hours at most, and he would be back in the District by nightfall.

Besides, he told himself, it made more sense for him to come to New York than for Tataglia to come to Washington. For one thing, Tataglia wouldn't have come; for another, there was too great a possibility of their being seen together in Washington, and that was something Brenner couldn't afford. His name was mud at the Agency already, and being seen in the company of Tataglia wouldn't do him any good. In fact, it would probably scotch forever any hope of his regaining his stature.

Traffic was light at that hour of the day, by local standards, at least, and Brenner was settling with the taxi driver in front of the Plaza less than an hour after his plane had touched down. Tataglia always took a suite for their infrequent meetings—for all Brenner knew, Tataglia maintained a suite there for business meetings. Brenner supposed it was safer than his meeting the lawyer at the latter's Long Island house.

He went up.

Tataglia was waiting for him—alone, as always. He looked smooth and sleek, his dark hair brushed away from his tanned and carefully shaven face. He offered Brenner a drink, which Brenner declined. He had been drinking too much, he knew, ever since—Christ, had it been two years already? Yes, two years April 17, a week from today. Two years since fifteen hundred Cubans and Brenner's career went straight into the crapper, thanks to a playboy rich kid on Pennsylvania Avenue.

"Our man has been contracted with," Tataglia said, smashing Brenner's reverie. "He knows his assignment. I assume everything is up to speed on your end?"

"Uh—yeah. We've got the guy lined up, been training him for over two weeks now. He knows how to shoot; he spent three years in the Corps. He's just what we talked about before: a little off center. Lived in Russia for a while, got a Russian wife even. Tried to kill himself over there, but who wouldn't? Self-proclaimed Marxist, Fair Play for Cuba, all that bullshit. Delusions of grandeur, too—we've got him convinced he's the last great hope for mankind. He knows his way around guns, too, like I said. He'll go down like a dose of salts. His name's Oswa—"

"I don't need to know names," the lawyer said.

Brenner shrugged. "You might as well. In six months' time everyone in the world's going to have heard of him."

November 22, 1963—Dealy Plaza
The motorcade was moving in slow motion. Everyone's
eyes were focused on it.

This part of the job was like stealing candy, Ancona reflected, his right eye against the scope mounted to the rifle.
Sunny day, open car, traveling only a couple of miles an
hour . . . He'd have more than enough time to let fly the
two rounds he'd been instructed to fire—one to kill, one for
insurance. Ancona didn't need the second round, but what
the hell. Tataglia—or whoever—was paying the freight.
For what they were paying, Ancona would gladly spring for
the second, unnecessary round.

The motorcade came into range.

November 22, 1963—Texas School Book Depository
Lee leaned out the window and watched the cars approach.
He felt . . . what? Not detached, exactly. Separated. Like
there he was, poised on the edge of the greatest event of his
life—the greatest event of *anybody's* life, the greatest event
of the twentieth century, the event that would change the
course of history from here on in—and yet at the same
time there he was over there, smirking cynically at that
skinny twenty-four-year-old kid at the window, all pumped
up with excitement . . .

Yes, separated, as if there were two of him. One of them
about to alter the world forever, the other mocking him for
thinking his action would make any difference.

Individuals *do* make a difference, Lee told himself
fiercely. Engels, Marx, Lenin. Castro. Kennedy.

Oswald.

Excitement spread across the pavement below like oil
seeping from a jar.

Lee licked his lips and raised his rifle.

June 12, 1963—Long Island
Tataglia put down the phone and rested his head against
the high back of his leather desk chair. They were impatient—the families. They wanted action, they wanted re-

sults, they wanted them *now*. It had, after all, been four years since Batista fell, four years since the easy pickings from the Havana casinos evaporated. And it had been two years since the government's half-baked plan to "liberate" Cuba had sunk to the bottom of the Bay of Pigs. And in all those years—nothing.

The families wanted Cuba back, that went without saying. And they wanted to punish the man they felt was responsible for "losing" Cuba in the first place, and who through a sudden, inexplicable lack of backbone dashed the attempt two years ago to reclaim the country—the man who'd let so many people down—the Agency, the Cuban exiles, and, most important, the families.

The older ones, who usually could be counted on to be reasonable, even philosophical, in this instance had the greatest blood-thirst. Tataglia knew that several of them knew the target's old man back in Prohibition days. To them, the Cuba situation was like being betrayed by an old family friend. They were not inclined to be philosophical. Stung, they were eager to sting back.

More than anything, though, the families wanted to send a message.

The message they had in mind, because of the deadly way they wanted to send it, would reverberate all the way from New York to Havana. Hell, Tataglia thought, all around the world. For the most part, though, the signal was intended for the new President. It was a simple message: Get Cuba back.

And if that punk-kid attorney general learned something from the experience, too, well, so much the better.

Tataglia had had a time convincing the families that patience was called for here. They had wanted to handle the job the way you would handle any hit: Hire the button, go in, do it, go home. They still wanted to handle it that way, and couldn't—or wouldn't—understand why Tataglia wanted to go slow, wanted to muddy things up so. Giancana had wondered aloud whether Tataglia wasn't spending too much time with his disgruntled Agency friends. These were the people who were good at coming up with great ideas like slipping Castro a chemical that would make his beard fall out, and other hot tickets like that. Wasn't Tataglia's elaborate, slow-moving plan beginning to smell like another overblown, unworkable Agency pipe dream?

But Tataglia realized that this was not just another hit. Not because of the target, per se, but rather because of a factor usually all but absent from a regular hit: the public. You can whack a cop, a judge, even a member of congress— depending on the member—and within two weeks the public outcry will have died down to a distant, low grumble. Not so with the target they had in mind. The public would be outraged. Half the people in the country hated the man's guts—half of them had voted for Nixon, after all— but that made no difference. Precisely because the man generated such strong responses from people, precisely because people either loved him or hated him, the clamor following his assassination would be universal, loud, and endless.

Unless the people had someone to blame.

Thanks to Tataglia and Brenner, they would.

August 14, 1963—National Airport
Brenner moved through the airport quickly, but unhurriedly. He had no baggage to wait for; fourteen years with the Agency had taught him to be ready to leave at a moment's notice, perhaps less, and to travel light when he did go. Everything he'd needed for this latest junket was in the carry-on in his left hand, a bag only slightly larger than a briefcase.

He was feeling pretty good. His side of the operation was coming together nicely—better than he had thought it would, in fact, that first time he'd gotten a look at the fish that Fuller and LaFleur had lined up. Oswald was a skinny, sort of twitchy-looking kid, the kind of guy you wouldn't be surprised to learn knocked his wife around because she put the spoon back in the sugar bowl after she stirred her coffee, or something equally dumb. According to Fuller and LaFleur, Oswald did clout his Russian wife every so often. Well, Brenner thought, too bad for her, but all the better for us when that little tidbit hits the fan along with everything else.

He went outside and found a taxi.

The weather was warm, but mild and springlike, not the District's usual late-summer muggy. In the bright sun, the city looked new and clean.

Nipping at the ankles of Brenner's good mood was the recurring thought that maybe Oswald was just a little *too* unstable. Brenner and Tataglia had agreed that the fish had to be convincingly loony, but the problem with someone as off base as Oswald was that you had no way of knowing if you really had him in line, or whether he'd suddenly bolt and fuck you up royally. Oswald *seemed* okay—okay enough for the job, at least—overeager, maybe, but that wasn't necessarily a bad thing. Fuller and LaFleur insisted that they were keeping him reined in tight, but Brenner didn't know. Still, he'd worked with Fuller and LaFleur since the early days of Ike, and they were good men. Like Brenner, they were persona non grata in the Agency after the Bay of Pigs debacle—as if *they* were the ones who, at the eleventh hour, decided to renege on the promised support to the Cuban liberators—so they had as much riding on the plan as Brenner did.

The plan. It had seemed insane when he and Tataglia first started kicking it around, all those months ago. But as it took shape and began to solidify, it began to look to Brenner as if it might actually work—and not just work, but work out the way they wanted. Oswald's pro-Marxist, pro-Castro leanings were a matter of record, and when the job was over Brenner would make sure that that record was well publicized. A wave of anti-Castro sentiment would sweep the country. The new President would have little option but to commit solidly to the ouster of Castro and his crew. Brenner and his discredited colleagues would be redeemed. Tataglia and his clients would recoup their Havana interests. The Sovs would have to look for another foothold in the West.

And the target . . . the target would become a martyr, a

hero, cut down in his prime. It was better than he deserved, Brenner thought hotly. But Tataglia was right: the public would revere him, the public would mourn him, and the public would demand blood in restitution.

They would see to it that the public got what it wanted.

Yes, it would work. Tataglia could be relied on to carry his end—Brenner and Tataglia had worked together more than once in the past thirteen years, and if it was too much to say that they trusted each other, they at least understood each other and relied on the other's professionalism. As for Fuller and LaFleur, they, too, were pros. They knew their fish, they had hooked him months ago, carefully reeled him in, worked with him, trained him. If they said he would do, then he would do.

Brenner worked hard to make himself believe that.

November 22, 1963—Texas School Book Depository
Lee licked his lips and raised his rifle.

He knew the drill, knew it backward and forward. Somewhere—*somewhere*—out there, there was a second shooter. Lee didn't need to know who, didn't need to know where. Lord, hadn't they pounded that into his head over and over and over again. *We work on a need-to-know basis, Lee, that's for everybody's protection, yours, ours, and the other guy's, and you just don't need to know, Lee, all you need to know is where you're supposed to be and when and what to do and when and what to do when you're done.*

Lee knew.

The other shooter, the one out there *somewhere*, the one Lee didn't need to know, he was to fire first. Lee was to wait for that, to be ready, because it would happen right down there in front of him. Only when he heard that other gunman's shot was Lee to fire his rifle, and then only once. The other gunman would fire again, but that was his business. Lee wasn't to hang around waiting for it—"sightseeing," his trainers had called it—but rather was to be well along the prearranged escape route within seconds after getting off his single round.

It sounded like a lot of folderol to Lee, but they'd explained that there was a lot more going on than met the eye. *Need-to-know.* But they did intimate that the idea was to make sure that the target went down, to create enough confusion that the gunners could get away, and to make the ultimate investigation as difficult as possible, ensuring the conspirators' ongoing anonymity and safety.

Lee had rebelled a little at that last part—what was the point of doing this if the world didn't know who was doing it and why? His trainers carefully explained that the world would indeed know, soon enough—but *causes,* Lee, ideals, truths, not individuals.

And Lee had nodded, and was quiet after that.

Now he stood in the window and sighted down the rifle at the cars below, waiting . . . waiting . . .

And then there was a shot!

And Lee—the part of Lee that stood apart and took everything in with a sardonic smile on his face—knew the shot had come from his gun.

September 29, 1963—Dallas
Jack rolled out of bed and wandered unthinking, automatically, to the coffeepot. George, his roommate, was still asleep. Quietly, then, Jack went through the morning ritual of putting the percolator together. That required no conscious thought, so instead he thought about money.

People think about money, of course—it's something people do, like thinking about the weather—but Jack's thinking about money was far more immediate than that. Specifically, he was thinking about the money the IRS said he owed them, and what he was going to do about it.

The IRS. Jeez. Jack was no virgin, he was fifty-two years old, he'd come up the hard way—the Maxwell Street ghetto, foster homes in Chicago, Halsted Street, scalping tickets on the West Side. He'd dealt with some tough customers, he'd lived in that gray area between the world and the underworld, and he liked to think he was pretty damn tough himself. But the IRS . . . Jack didn't mind admitting, at least to himself, that those fuckers scared the crap out of him. Jeez, they were the guys who took down Capone.

The coffee was ready. Jack poured himself a cup, took it over to the rickety little table, and sat down.

Where was he going to get the kind of money it would take to get the IRS off his ass?

Sure, he had friends; Jack was well liked; Jack had friends all over town. Important people, too, a lot of them—cops, city officials, other businessmen like himself. But the IRS wanted forty grand in excise taxes it said Jack owed on his two clubs, the Vegas and the Carousel, plus almost five grand for his personal income taxes. Jack didn't have the kind of friends who could give him fifty thousand bucks, even if they wanted to.

He was fifty-two years old, he was losing his hair, he was putting on a little weight despite his daily workouts, he was trying to run two clubs, a dance club and a strip joint, he was just trying to get by, for crying out loud, and here the IRS wanted to step up and squash him like a bug. Jeez.

Where the hell was he going to get the kind of money it would take to get the IRS off his ass?

October 4, 1963—Long Island
"I assure you, all is going according to plan. Everything is ready, all of the people are in position, it's just a matter of waiting for the target to come to us—as he will, less than six weeks from now.

"Of course. Of course. Yes, he's already running for re-election, so of course he's showing up everywhere. And we could, in theory, take him any time. He himself has said that killing a President is no trick, as long as the killer is prepared to die, too. Which is an important obstacle: most of the hitters of my acquaintance are not inclined toward suicide missions. No, I'm not being flip, I'm being realistic.

"Because Dallas is the perfect opportunity. Our fish has lived there in the past, so it was easy to reestablish him there; it is a city that for some reason attracts political extremists of all stripe; and only fifteen minutes ago it was cowboys-and-Indians country—the people there are used to violence, they tolerate it better. Yes, I do think that matters. I think that how people will respond to this is what matters most. That's why I have been so careful, and why I've urged you and our friends to proceed slowly.

"He can be trusted as much as anyone who is not one of us can be trusted—probably more, since he has everything hanging on this. No, he assures me that his people assure him that the fish will perform as desired. Who knows? The man has to be crazy, that was one of the prerequisites.

"Yes. Yes, I spoke to our friend again yesterday, and he's very clear on this. Resisting arrest. No, our friend's associates in the police department down there will see to it. There will be no trial."

November 22, 1963—Dealy Plaza
Confusion.

When you're not used to the sound, gunfire out in the open sounds like firecrackers. Ancona knew that well, and knew that everyone on the plaza thought that was what they'd just heard, a single, rather pathetic little firecracker pop.

Ancona knew otherwise.

He knew that their fish had blown it, jumped the gun.

Too fucking complicated.

In his scope Ancona saw a red mist envelop the target's head and the target jerk forward. In that fraction of a second, Ancona adjusted his aim and squeezed off his own round. The target jerked backward from the impact. Ancona fired his second shot, if only to be able to say later that he'd followed instructions, and then jammed the rifle into the big green duffel bag on the grass next to him. He closed the duffel and shoved it farther under the bush before scurrying out from under it. Later he would return for it—Ancona didn't like loose ends—but even if someone came upon it and stole it in the interim, it wouldn't make any difference. The rifle couldn't be traced to Ancona, or anyone else, and the duffel was just like any of a dozen you could buy in any Army surplus store in Dallas, exactly as Ancona had.

The main car in the motorcade was speeding up, trying to get the hell away from there. A woman in pink was climbing out the back end of the car, and a man in a dark suit and dark glasses was climbing up from behind the car to help her. Everyone realized what had happened, even if they couldn't believe or comprehend it. A few had sense enough to drop to the ground, but most of them were rushing toward the street, toward the accelerating cars, toward the sudden horror.

Ancona joined them. He didn't want to stand out in anyone's memory as the only guy who acted like he wasn't wondering what the hell had happened.

November 22, 1963—Texas School Book Depository
The noontime sun was harsh. Lee stood a moment, blinking against the brightness, trying hard to marshal some poise.

Mainly, though, he was trying to figure out what the hell had just happened.

There was only one possible explanation, and the part of Lee that stood apart, observing mockingly, had already divined it, although barely a minute had elapsed. Lee had jumped the gun—an expression that was both appropriate and ironic now—and fired the first shot.

Incredible.

Appropriate.

He remembered the time he shot himself by accident, back in the Corps. The derringer really did fall out of his locker and discharge upon hitting the floor; it really was an accident, a dumb accident, like he'd told the court-martial. The bullet had hit him in the elbow. Lee couldn't believe it. He had been sitting there, looking at his arm, when the guy from the next cubicle came rushing in. "I believe I shot myself," he remembered saying.

I believe I shot the President of the United States, his cynical, standing-apart self thought now.

November 22, 1963—Dallas Morning News
Jack always insisted on composing his own ad copy for his clubs. It was the old story: if you want something done right, do it yourself.

He was, as usual, sitting at John Newnam's desk, trying to come up with some classy copy for the weekend ads for the Carousel and the Vegas. It was getting on toward one.

A couple of guys came into the classified-advertising office. They looked white. Jack glanced at them with mild interest, then went back to his labors.

"The President's been shot," one of the guys said.

Jack's head came up with an almost audible snap.

"It happened just a couple of minutes ago. They rushed him to Parkland, but some of the eyewitnesses are saying there's no way he can survive."

Jack felt as if someone had pulled a plug and let all the blood rush out of him. There was a phone on the desk. He groped for it and called his sister, Eva. She sounded almost hysterical. He had a hard time controlling his own voice.

They talked a while, then Jack hung up and left the building. He passed knots of people talking about what had happened, sharing the latest unconfirmed rumor.

If the President died, Jack would close the clubs for a couple of days. That was the only decent thing to do.

He left the newspaper building, got into his car, and drove. It was hard to see, because he couldn't stop crying.

November 22, 1963—Texas School Book Depository
Having made its somewhat obvious observation, Lee's standing-apart self took its sardonic smirk and disappeared, leaving Lee alone, confused, and scared.

He looked at the rifle in his hands, as if he'd never seen it before. What was he supposed to do with it now? He couldn't remember, and he didn't care. He shoved it behind some boxes.

The plan that had been hammered into his head all those weeks included an escape route. Although he had kept his mouth shut, Lee had believed all along that it would be smarter for him to go back downstairs after the event and report for the afternoon roll call of depository workers. Now, however, scared-rabbit impulse told him to run for it, immediately, before the dust settled and people started realizing what had happened.

He fled the building.

There was enough reason left in his swimming head to remember where the car would be waiting. He forced himself not to run. There it was—a black 1959 Galaxie, just like they said. The car would be unlocked, the ignition key would be hidden under the dome-light cover . . .

A cop came around the corner near the Ford. He looked right at Lee. He began to walk toward Lee.

He knew. He *knew!*

I should've brought that pistol with me this morning, Lee thought desperately.

He about-faced and, again willing himself not to run, disappeared into the confusion of the crowd.

November 22, 1963—Long Island
Tataglia didn't care for television, but for today he had had one wheeled into his office. It sat near the big windows, the volume turned low, while a radio on the desk played softly. Tataglia liked radio. It didn't intrude.

But when the first reports came through, Tataglia—with some regret—turned to the television.

The news was sketchy and tentative, as was to be expected. The target had been hit, that much was obvious, but there was no word beyond that. Tataglia had faith in Ancona, though; that was why he had hired him.

Oddly, there was nothing about the fish. Tataglia looked at the brass nautical clock on his desk. Allowing for the hour's time difference . . . yes, their "friend" should have taken care of that by now . . .

The phone burred softly, and a small crease appeared between the lawyer's eyebrows as he reached for it.

November 22, 1963—Dallas

Brenner cradled the telephone receiver. His hotel room was cool, but he was faintly aware of the pools of sweat under his arms and down the center of his back.

Oswald was alive.

God damn.

He rubbed his eyes and willed himself to *think!* Of all the intricate, carefully dovetailing pieces of the plan, that was the *last* thing Brenner had worried about. There was the loose-screw Oswald, he had been at the top of Brenner's things-to-worry-about list, but Oswald had come through. There was the question of whether the moving target could not only be hit, but fatally, and that had worked out. There was the matter of Tataglia's trigger man escaping undetected, and that had happened. All of the tricky parts had clicked just fine.

And then Tataglia's dirty cop goes and fucks up the last part.

There was a bottle in his suitcase that Brenner had planned to save for a little celebratory toot. There was nothing to celebrate now, for damn sure, but he needed the blast anyway. He filled a bathroom glass, half drained it, and then refilled it and took it back out to the other room.

So simple—so *simple.* The fish would be told where to find his getaway car. He'd go to it, and a cop would just happen to be nearby, just happen to think Oswald was acting suspicious. He'd stop Oswald, ask him a few questions, decide to take him in. Oswald would resist. There would be a struggle, in the course of which Oswald would, unfortunately, be killed. By then the rifle on the fifth floor of the depository building would be found, it would quickly be traced to the late Oswald, a leftist, a Marxist, a Castro sympathizer and possible agent . . .

So *fucking* simple.

Now what?

Brenner emptied his glass and went for more, this time bringing the bottle with him.

Tataglia, in giving him the bad news, had told him not to

panic. It had never occurred to Brenner to panic. Swallow a bottle of poison, then throw himself off a building and slash his wrists on the way down, sure—but never panic.

He filled his glass again.

November 22, 1963—Long Island
The clouds looked ominous, but Tataglia doubted they would produce anything. They were, he thought, merely there for effect.

No longer relying on the news media, the lawyer had turned to his own sources for information. The calls were coming fast, on both telephone lines, and the reports were not encouraging. The families' "friend" had blown his part, spooking Oswald, who gave him the slip. Evidently Oswald then made his way back to his boardinghouse, where he had a pistol. Armed now, he had for some stupid reason gone back out onto the streets. Barely forty-five minutes after the hit, he had killed a Dallas police officer.

That was good news to Tataglia. Armed, dangerous, and now a cop-killer, Oswald would not be treated gently if apprehended. There was still a good chance that he would be silenced.

That happy thought had a short life. Just over half an hour later, Tataglia received word that Oswald had been captured in a movie house. There had been a scuffle with the police, but the suspect had only suffered a black eye.

The phone rang again as soon as Tataglia set it down, but when he reached over to it, it was to shut off the bell, not to answer it. He leaned back and looked out at the low clouds.

Tataglia did not believe in making backup plans, because that implied that you expected to fail. Nothing focuses the mind like working without a net. However, only a fool neglects to keep other options, other avenues open at all times.

He picked up the phone, disconnected whoever was on the other end of the wire, and dialed a number.

November 22, 1963—Dallas Police and Courts Building
Jeez, what a day.

Jack walked in a fog. On the one hand, his brain was jumping, misfiring, shot-gunning thoughts in all directions. On the other hand, though, things had seldom been so clear and obvious to him. He had talked to some other club owners about them all closing down for a couple of days in honor of the dead President. He had listened to the reports of the capture of the man suspecting of killing the President and a Dallas cop. He had heard that cops would be working around the clock. And so here he was at 11:30 P.M. bringing a load of sandwiches to his friends on the force.

The police station was a madhouse. Reporters, photographers, radio and TV people. It seemed to Jack that half the cops on duty tonight were there only to maintain crowd control—*in* the building. Jack went right on in, of course. They all knew him; he was in and out of the building all the time.

He had been a petty crook in his time, a ticket scalper, a penny-ante gambler—small-time stuff—and he had two concealed-weapon convictions on his record, but Jack got on well with cops. He liked cops, and they liked him. They were genuinely touched now, when Jack brought them the sandwiches. They appreciated his thoughtfulness, Jack could tell that.

Although he made small talk with a few of the cops and some of the media people he knew there, Jack's heart and mind weren't in it. Partly because he was preoccupied, like everybody, by the day's mad tangle of events; partly because—perhaps because he had neither—he felt terrible for the slain President's wife and kids—and partly because of the phone call he'd had that afternoon, one of several he had placed or received since he'd heard the news.

Jack had barely remembered the guy, from those hard days back in Chicago, after Jack's father disappeared and his mother was committed . . . But the guy had offered details to buttress Jack's faulty memory, and slowly the memory had floated to the surface. The guy had been another Halsted Street floater, like Jack; now he had "business enterprises" in Chicago and other places, he said.

Jack asked the guy why he was calling him now, after all these years. He didn't want to be talking to the guy, he was too distressed over what had happened that afternoon; this was no time for a stroll down memory lane with a guy he hardly knew and barely remembered.

The guy had talked about friends, the importance of having friends and being a friend—all of which Jack readily agreed with; he believed the same thing, and practiced what he believed. The guy had a lot of friends, he said, owing to his "business enterprises." Good friends, he said. He and Jack had some friends in common, he said.

Like who, Jack wanted to know.

The guy kind of slid past that one, and started talking about how these anonymous mutual friends had told him about Jack's money problems. The guy was very distressed, he said. He tried to think of a way to help Jack out. Friends help friends, that's rule number one.

Jack agreed with that, too.

The guy said he thought he had an idea.

November 23, 1963—Long Island
There had been many long nights, over the years, but few as long as this one. The phone quite literally had not stopped ringing yesterday, and when the families started to call, late that afternoon, demanding explanations, demanding to know what Tataglia planned to do now, Tataglia hadn't dared shut off the bells.

Plus he had made a dozen calls in rapid succession early that afternoon, and was anticipating call-backs.

Only now, as the sun made ready to face the day, was the phone blissfully silent. Red-eyed, Tataglia leaned back into his chair and thought. In retrospect, he could see that the Dallas cop who'd botched his assignment should have been better briefed. He should not have shown himself until Oswald was in the car, trying to unscrew the dome-light cap for the ignition key that wasn't there. It would have been much more difficult for Oswald to escape.

But hindsight, in addition to being 20/20, was useless.

Now there was only the future to think of, the very immediate future.

Oswald was a loose cannon. There was no telling whether or when he'd go off, or what he'd hit if he did. Tataglia's sources indicated that Oswald had so far said nothing of importance, that he seemed to be enjoying playing the part of the innocent victim of police brutality. That was fine for now, but it wasn't something to hang your hat on. Oswald had delusions of grandeur, Brenner had said, and such men are dangerous. They're prone to shooting off their mouths. Tataglia knew without having to be told that *Life* and *Look* and the other weeklies would be sniffing around, fat checkbooks in hand, eager to hear Oswald's story as told by Oswald himself. Book publishers would be interested, too. Maybe even the movies.

And there would be a trial, of course. A local trial, Tataglia knew, a Texas trial, since the law that made it a federal offense to kill certain officers of the government somehow managed to overlook the President, but it would still be a media circus. And you never knew how a man like this Oswald, a nobody, a loser, a loner, would react when he suddenly found himself at the center of attention.

There could be no trial—that had been obvious from the start. Tataglia thought that detail had been taken care of in the original plan, but now the plan had to change.

There were certain members of the police department who were considered "approachable," according to Tataglia's contacts. Finding someone to take care of Oswald wasn't the problem—that person finding a way to *do* it was the problem. The Dallas cops weren't dummies, they knew what sort of a powderkeg they were sitting on. The FBI had informed them that they had logged numerous death threats against Oswald in the past few hours. The City of Dallas had sustained one black eye that day already; they weren't looking for another; they wanted no more violence. They were taking no chances.

So a cop was out of the question. So, too, was a professional trigger man: as Tataglia had had to explain to the families, no professional would be willing to take on a suicide assignment, and that's what the Oswald situation had degenerated into.

Men contemplate suicide for a number of reasons, Tataglia believed, chief among them the belief that they had nothing left to lose. There had to be someone, someone appropriate, who fit that description. There was always a right man for any assignment, Tataglia believed. It was usually just a matter of locating that man.

It was then that Tataglia had made his phone calls.

November 23, 1963—Washington, D.C.
Brenner had had a lot to drink in the past twelve hours, but somehow he hadn't been able to get drunk. After a couple of conversations with Tataglia, and a couple more with Fuller and LaFleur, Brenner had gotten the hell out of Texas and come home. Where he proceeded to sit up all night, drinking and not getting drunk.

The whole damn thing was in a shambles, and nothing Tataglia said changed any of it.

There was, Brenner thought, one ray of sunshine: Oswald was nuts. Already that had started to come across, as the media dug into Oswald's history—aided, unknown even to the media, by Brenner and his friends. There was, Brenner had come to believe, a good chance that anything Oswald might choose to say would be taken as the ramblings of a grade-A left-leaning kook. Oswald knew nothing that could come back to Brenner, Fuller, and LaFleur, or Tataglia. As far as Oswald knew, he was working with a group of people, American and Cubans, who were sympathetic to Cuba and who wanted the President eliminated because of his ongoing attempts to interfere in Cuba's business.

Christ, Brenner thought, that even *sounded* crazy. Who'd believe bullshit like that? Who'd believe Oswald would have believed any such thing?

Clearly the guy was a nut case. Leave him alone, Brenner counseled, he'll end up in a rubber room somewhere—where he belongs.

Tataglia, though, would have none of that. His clients

were not people inclined toward hoping for the best. Oswald was unfinished business, and Tataglia was determined to see it finished.

That made Brenner feel a little queasy—or maybe it was all the booze.

November 24, 1963—Dallas
After having not slept at all Friday night and most of Saturday, after having spent most of the last sixty hours in a blur of activity that even he would have trouble giving a good reason for, Jack finally fell asleep in the small hours Sunday morning.

Only to be awakened shortly after nine by the damn telephone.

He half expected it to be his Halsted Street "friend"—again—but it was only his cleaning lady, wondering if she should come and do the apartment, as she usually did on Sundays. Jack was so exhausted he barely knew who she was or what she wanted.

He stayed up then, though, and made a pot of coffee. George had been out doing his laundry. He came back, and the two of them watched TV and drank coffee. Jack was distracted, mumbling. He didn't look so good, but then he hadn't had much sleep the last couple of days.

At 10:19 the phone rang.

It was only Karen, one of his girls from the Carousel. Since the club was closed, she hadn't been able to collect her salary; now she needed some grocery money and could Jack wire her a twenty-five-dollar advance?

Sure. Why not?

Jack went to get dressed.

George could hear him mumbling to himself, pacing, pacing . . .

George had no idea what was going through Jack's mind, but whatever it was, it sure was eating at him.

November 24, 1963—Dallas Police and Courts Building
Jack wired the money to Karen.

On his way to Western Union he'd passed the police station, and noticed a fair amount of activity—as a rule, it was pretty quiet down there on Sunday mornings. Coming out of the Western Union office, curiosity got the best of him. It was less than a block, so he left the car where it was and walked down there.

As a courtesy to the gathered newsmen who hadn't had any sleep since the assassination, the Dallas police had assured them that their prisoner would not be transferred from the city jail to the nearby Dallas County lockup before ten o'clock Sunday. That would enable them to go get some sleep without worrying about missing the transfer, which they all wanted to cover.

Since before ten o'clock, then, the ramp off the basement of the police building had been crammed with reporters awaiting the appearance of the alleged assassin.

Jack joined the mob. As usual, he walked right in, unchallenged. Everybody there knew him.

Jack didn't really know what was going on; nor did he know what he was doing there. His brain was a mad tangle of dissociated and yet interconnected thoughts: the slain President—the Vegas and the Carousel—the IRS and the money they wanted—Jack's Halsted Street "friend" and his frequent calls proposing a way to "help" Jack with his problems—the President . . .

At 11:20 A.M. the jail-office door swung open and the accused, flanked by two plainclothesmen, finally appeared.

He looked like a kid. A smart-ass, snot-nosed kid.

The path to the car that was to take the accused over to County was blocked by TV equipment. They had to go around it. The car's driver, impatient to get going, gunned the engine several times, filling the underground ramp with the roar of the engine and the smell of exhaust.

The detour led straight into the gaze of the television cameras. Right past Jack.

"You son of a bitch!" Jack yelled, and lunged forward.

December 15, 1963—New York
Tataglia handed Brenner his drink, and felt with some certainty that this would be the last time he saw his—was

"friend" the right word? It was a word that was used often in Tataglia's world, and it connoted different things in different contexts, but none of them fit the relationship he had had with Brenner these years.

Still the lawyer felt a twinge of sadness to see how bad Brenner looked, to note how his hand shook as he accepted the drink. Brenner had always been a drinker, but the way he looked now, Tataglia thought, he had to be breaking all his old records. If he lasted another six months, Tataglia would be surprised indeed.

It was the upcoming trial that upset Brenner—ironically, since he had argued in favor of letting Oswald go to trial. Brenner had believed that Oswald's record indicated he was nuts, and that anyone would accept that as his reason for killing the President. But why would anyone want to kill Oswald—that is, why would anyone want to commit suicide by killing Oswald in a police station, on television? Unless he was nuts, too, and Brenner was afraid that the man whom Tataglia's "friends" had ultimately convinced to make the hit just wasn't nuts enough. If there was even the slightest suspicion that he had been recruited for the job . . .

"Relax," Tataglia told Brenner. "No one wants him to go to prison. Hell, seventy-five percent of the people in this country think he's a hero, and the other twenty-five percent plain don't care. They'll have to go through the motions of a trial, of course, but I'd bet even money that he's acquitted. Worst case, temporary insanity, eighteen months in a hospital somewhere."

"But if he talks—"

"Why should he? He knows we'll take care of him. Besides, I understand he's putting together a nice book deal. He stands to come out of this a rich man, a hero—better off than he went in, that's for sure—why would he complain?"

The Agency man was unconvinced, and showed it.

Tataglia leaned across and slapped Brenner's knee in an uncharacteristic gesture of camaraderie. He felt good. He had turned a cock-up into a raging success, from his clients' perspective. In fact, it probably was better that the assassin died at the hands of a citizen, rather than a cop. There was already a lot of loose "conspiracy" talk circulating, and it would only have added fuel to that fire if Oswald had died while "resisting" arrest. Tataglia's people were happy. They had, finally, delivered their message. And the consensus was that Cuba would be reopened by this time next year.

"Listen," Tataglia told Brenner. "In six months, if the trial isn't over by then, it'll be back-page news. Six months after that, unless some citizen group erects a statue of him, nobody'll even remember the man's name. At most, he'll be the guy who gave that rat Oswald what he had coming."

"If you say so," Brenner said glumly.

"I know so," Tataglia said with confidence. "By next Christmas, the whole grisly affair will have slipped into the mists." He made a floating gesture with his left hand. "People have awfully short memories," he said.

WHITE MUSTANGS
by John Lutz

The question of the existence of a conspiracy in the assassination of Dr. Martin Luther King, Jr., has troubled millions of people. Here, Edgar Award-winning author John Lutz provides a startling answer to this important question.

The New Yorker smiled, only barely believing it. "You thought you was gonna just drive away from it and that'd be that, huh?"

Swiveled sideways on his stool, Bo rested his arm on the long mahogany bar and watched him until the smile went away. He said, "Thought I was gonna get paid. That's why I came here with you, remember?"

The smile returned. The New Yorker, who'd said his name was Nychek, was about Bo's age, thirty, only he was a smooth number in a tailored gray suit. He had razor-cut black hair, long sideburns that framed his lean, handsome face. Looked something like a movie star, Bo thought, only there didn't seem to be much behind the prettiness. No. Bo changed his mind. There was something. He could see it now. Didn't like it.

"Well," the New Yorker said, "you'll get paid, all right." He lifted his glass and nibbled at his Scotch rocks. When the expensive gray suitcoat flapped open, Bo caught a glimpse of a black leather shoulder holster. He knew he could reach out his big hand and grab the New Yorker before the gun could come out, then maybe he could handle the guy. Maybe. But whatever happened tonight, it wouldn't make a difference. That much he understood.

They were in a place called Dandy's, where Bo had been told they were coming to pick up his pay. Why should he figure anything was wrong and *not* come? The nigger was dead, right? It had all gone smooth as fried okra.

Dandy's turned out to be one of those little sports bars, the kind with oak-paneled walls and black-and-white photos of old-time boxers and Joe Dimaggio all over the place. It also turned out to be owned by people cooperating with the New Yorker, because it was closed now, nobody here but Bo and the handsome dude with the gun. And the girl waterskiing on the softly illuminated clock-and-beer advertisement behind the bar, her tanned legs together and slightly bent, arms extended far in front of her, back arched, a rooster tail of water arcing away behind her. She was blonde and gorgeous and smiling out at Bo and the New Yorker without a care. She'd never had this kind of trouble and never would.

The New Yorker apparently figured Bo was stupid, but Bo knew different. It was loneliness and Lone Star beer that had brought him here. He'd never really been part of any cause, never bought into the bullshit they'd shoveled at him to convince him to take the job. He'd only pretended. Wanted the money. Wanted to be somebody, even if nobody else would ever find out about it. It didn't look now like he'd even get the money.

A car swished past outside on the dark street. Another world out there. Had nothing to do with what was going on inside Dandy's. The smooth bar was cool beneath Bo's bare arm.

The New Yorker glanced at his gold wristwatch no thicker than a potato chip and seemed to relax. There was plenty of time, his look said, so take it slow, easy. He said, "You wanna know how it is, redneck?"

"I got an idea how it is," Bo said. He might be just a country boy, but the beer had lost its effect on him as soon as he'd realized everyone else in the bar had left and the place was locked tight, shades pulled.

"It's this way," the New Yorker said, obviously liking to talk, liking to brag. "Witnesses say James Earl Ray made his getaway in a white Mustang hardtop. Thing that confuses everybody, including the cops, is there was several white Mustangs driven hell-for-leather away from the area right after the nigger went down. There's some real organization behind this fucking thing, I can tell you, and they got it sanctioned by a higher authority than God. You weren't the only decoy, Bo, old scout. White Mustangs going every which direction."

"I read that in the papers," Bo said, "about the other Mustangs." In the corner of his vision he caught his reflection in the back-bar mirror. Redneck, all right. Big beefy sandy-haired guy with a heart tattoed on his bulging left bicep. He'd been drunk when he'd gotten the tattoo in Galveston, out partying with a bunch of Navy yahoos. Almost had the tattoo artist write 'Mother' under the heart, then figured what was he doing there anyway, and screw the old bitch. So the tattoo was just a heart, like he loved everybody and nobody. He thought again about trying to jump the New Yorker, taking him by surprise. But there was something about the confident, lean man that suggested he'd never in his life been taken by surprise.

"I'm truly shocked you can read," the New Yorker said. "Musta had comic books in your neck of the swamp. Two thousand dollars to drive a car away from where it was parked at a certain time, then leave it someplace. I mean, that musta seemed like a lotta money for a little work to a dirt-poor yokel like you."

"It's a lotta money," Bo admitted.

"Looking back on it, don't you think maybe you shoulda been just a little bit suspicious."

"I was suspicious. But that ain't the same as being sure. Life's a fuckin' risk, you know?"

The New Yorker nodded slowly, looking at Bo now with something like respect. "You got no brains, but you definitely got balls. That was why they hired you."

"Why'd they hire you?" Bo asked.

The New Yorker stared at him, seemed to decide he hadn't been insulted, and said, "I'm a professional. And I believe."

Another car went past outside, tires singing on hot pavement. It was warm inside Dandy's, and it smelled like stale tobacco smoke and spilled whiskey. Bo had himself a sip of beer. It didn't matter now. "Believe what?"

"Believe in the natural separation of the races. That's how God meant it to be." He stirred the ice in his Scotch delicately with a manicured finger. "You know who's behind the nigger getting taken out?"

"Know they're rich, know they're white."

"Some very important business people in the South," the New Yorker said. "I mean corporate and political people. Movers and shakers. They believe in the cause of racial purity and they had the guts to do something about it."

"Folks like that," Bo said, "what they believe in is money, not causes. Anything threatens to upset the way things are, that'd be costly. The nigger threatened the status quo. Threatened big."

" 'Status quo,' " the New Yorker said, grinning. "I like that."

Bo said, "I heard Walter Cronkite say it once."

"I met some of the top people in on this," the New Yorker said. "Take it from me, it's the cause that's uppermost in their minds. Interracial marriages, lost jobs, lost morals, society splitting apart at the seams. They moved to prevent that happening."

"It was the money," Bo repeated. "I know how they are, and in that way they're just like me. It was the money."

The New Yorker laughed. It was a brief, ugly sound. "Not like you, Bo. Not at all. And you're not fooling me. You did this 'cause you hate the niggers, 'cause they're the only ones lower'n you, only ones a poor white like you can look down on. Poor white trash, our mutual employers called you. More balls than brains. They knew you'd drive that car and wouldn't ask why. The money wasn't nothing. Hell, they'd have paid you five thousand if you'd have asked, only they knew they didn't have to. They knew what kinda clockwork was inside your poor honky head."

Bo thought about that. He'd been in 'Nam. Knew some blacks there he couldn't dislike. 'Nam had opened his eyes. Not all the way, but opened them. He said, "I don't hate nobody." Believing it now.

The New Yorker gave his nasty, wise-guy grin.

"But you're right about how the ones that do hate need to look down on the niggers," Bo said. "Only it don't stop there."

The New Yorker said, "Ain't nobody lower'n the niggers. Not even the Jews."

"I ain't talking about how it goes down the ladder," Bo said. "I'm talking about how it goes up. Thinking about the rung where you're at."

A soft glimmer of puzzlement flared in the New Yorker's flat black eyes. Then he seemed to realize what Bo meant. "You trying to cut yourself a deal, Bo?"

"Just laying it out like it is," Bo said. For a moment, despite what he knew, he found himself hoping. "We able to deal for that two thousand?"

The New Yorker shook his head, amused. "Two thousand's nothing like what I'm getting paid for this."

Bo finished his beer. Said, "You'll get paid, all right. Everybody'll get paid but a very few, and they won't have to worry about getting paid, 'cause they're the ones with all the money."

"I'm not gonna hang around afterward like some dumb swamp turkey," the New Yorker said. "I mean, this ain't like pulling some rich guy's weeds and going back next week and see if he wants it done again."

Bo said, "It's just like that."

The New Yorker didn't care to hear that kind of talk anymore. He reached for his gun. Bo lunged at him.

As soon as he moved, Bo realized the beer was slowing him down more than he'd figured. And the New Yorker had barely touched his lips to his Scotch. No matter. Little jerk-off figured to be quick as a snake anyway, drunk or sober.

The gun, a small pearl-handled revolver, cleared the black holster, but Bo slapped it away with his huge hand and heard it clatter behind the bar. He clamped his other hand around the New Yorker's neck. Then both hands.

Didn't see the knife.

He felt it, even heard it, slide between his ribs at an upward angle, seeking the heart. Pain hit Bo as if he'd been hooked to high voltage. His arms were paralyzed. He couldn't breathe.

The room tilted and he was on the floor, staring up at a dirty ceiling and a light fixture shadowed with dead bugs in the bottom of its milky globe. The New Yorker was gazing calmly down at him, rubbing the side of his neck where Bo had dug in his fingers. Then he bent down and wiped the knife blade on the leg of Bo's jeans. Bo didn't care. Could only think of the pain. The pain was all there was in the world.

And when even that began to fade, along with the light, he got scared.

Was dead before the cops broke in.

The New Yorker stared at them. What the fuck? This wasn't the way it was supposed to go.

"Big guy attacked me with a gun," he said, thinking fast. "I got it away from him and threw it behind the bar, then he started choking me."

There were two cops, just inside the door, a fat one with a scar over his eyebrow, a skinny one with a bristly haircut and ears that stuck straight out and were round as half dollars. The cherry light on their patrol car was revolving outside, casting flashes of red on the drawn shades. They hadn't used the siren.

"How'd you guys get here so fast?" the New Yorker asked.

The cops exchanged glances. The skinny one swallowed hard, making his Adam's apple dance. The fat one looked scared but determined.

The New Yorker said, "Hey, no! Listen!"

The cops had their guns out, the fat one already taking

aim. The skinny one said in a choked voice, "We're only doing our job, buddy."

The New Yorker lurched backward until his heels were against Bo's body. He knew that when the bullets hit, he'd fall on top of Bo. One rung above him on the ladder. Just like Bo had said.

The skinny cop said, "What'd you think, you was just gonna do this and drive away from it?"

The floor was slippery under the leather soles of the New Yorker's shoes. Bo's blood, he realized. "Jesus!" he said, not liking how high his voice was. "I know there's a way around this thing if you'll only listen! There's a way around everything!"

The fat cop grinned and said, "Not something this big. Guy like you oughta be smart enough to know that."

His skinny partner started bouncing nervously on the balls of his feet, like he was getting ready for a foul shot in basketball. "Let's goddamn do it, Eddie."

"It's payoff time," the fat one said, still with the grin.

Squeezed the trigger.

SPEEDBALL
by Brian Hodge

The reason John Belushi died seems clear. But even the seemingly simplest explanations, complete with eyewitness testimony, can be wrong, as Brian Hodge shows us in this riveting story.

He had become the same sort of temporal landmark as John Kennedy had once been, but for a generation of cynics. This new breed, disillusioned with politics and nurtured on pop culture. Used to, everyone could answer the same question: *Where were you when you heard that Kennedy's head came apart?* Which is not such a prevalent character trait anymore. *I* certainly can't answer, too young at the time, seven years old and about as cognizant of things presidential as I was of things sexual. Who knew, who cared? Of what possible use are those thoughts to a seven-year-old?

But I remember where I was when someone told me that John Belushi was dead. The memory is etched like the inscription on the back of a locket, to be hung about my neck. Like an albatross.

These things I kept to myself, though, while looking at his grave. I was not alone, and while Shelby and I had kept passionate company this whole autumn trip, there were places I would not let her. Things I would not say. Had that problem a lot. I don't think it mattered to her. I seem drawn to the type to whom it never does.

John Belushi had been buried on Martha's Vineyard, March 9, 1982. Four days after his death; eight and a half years ago. He and his wife had owned a house here, but from what I gather, he spent the bulk of his time elsewhere . . . Los Angeles, New York, movie sets. His loss. A genuine oasis of Atlantean beauty and tranquility, Martha's Vineyard. A mutant triangle of an island, moored south of Massachusetts along with Nantucket and a few other piddly islands. Massachusetts proper hooks back around north into Cape Cod, like a shrimp tail, as if snubbing these lesser pretenders.

Downeast crust and blueblood elitism. I didn't belong here, and in his soul, Belushi never did, either. But here he found peace, a commodity all too scarce for the living.

Massachusetts, the state that gave the country the Kennedys: a dynasty founded on a bootlegger's fortune, rising above that with pride and stoic hope, only to sink into borderline disgrace, awash in scandal and alcoholism. What goes around comes around. Funny, with some people, the way it always comes back to substance abuse. I'm certainly not one to point fingers, not with the very special relationship I have with George Dickel sour mash, but then again . . . I'm not the dead one.

Shelby regarded the grave with a cocked head, one hand cupping an elbow, the other hand at her chin. Studied, classic. Behind large-frame glasses, her eyes were serious. She moved with a cautious ease, black hair knotted in a simple twist over one shoulder, standing very straight. Courtroom posture. I suspected a charm school's influence in her early years, suppressed but not entirely overcome.

Back home in south Florida, she was a public defender, champion of the oppressed and the scum of the earth. My existence was far more ignoble, maintaining that grand old tradition of yellow journalism at its most wretched. *The Vanguard* was the sort of paper generally bought in supermarket checkout lines. I take a bizarre pride in knowing my work is part of the national diet.

No idea what I represented in Shelby's life, not even sure what she represented in mine. Oddly enough, we met while both on the job, at the gonzo bizarro trial of a guy who made videotapes of himself with an Alsatian—porno, of course—then put them in his neighbors' mailboxes at night. The guy showed up in court his first day wearing a Lassie T-shirt. Shelby hadn't had a chance. I always wondered who she'd pissed off to get assigned *that* one.

Maybe I was the sexual court jester she needed to counteract day-in, day-out dealings with those aforementioned oppressed and scum of the earth. No talk of love, of commitment, of anything as far away as next week, even. It was primarily a hormonal thing we had going. Ain't life grand?

So here we were, on vacation from our real lives at the other end of the nation. Mid-October, a leisurely drive through New England to witness its transition into autumn. Last week Shelby had curled onto her side in bed, turning her back on me forever as she watched heat lightning flicker in a humid Florida sky. Finally said she wanted to see leaves changing color. I was a native, and never really missed that. She wasn't, and did, and in that moment it was like watching her peel back years and the mileage of the courtrooms and their great cattle call of justice . . . and find there was still a poetic little girl inside who still marveled at the simple brilliance of oaks and sugar maples.

Shelby was more human to me in that moment than she ever had been. And I wished I could return the favor.

The gravesite, Abel's Hill Cemetery. Belushi's grave was not alone in more ways than one. Yes, it had the company of other stones, but it also bore the attention of those who sought it just as I had. A few trinkets and notes had been left behind. Offerings from pilgrims who had come east, or north, or south, out of a melancholy yearning to see all that remained to be touched.

Shelby looked at it, then at me, and I knew what she was thinking. It was like a little shrine.

"I once saw a piece of pop art," she said. "Someone had painted the NBC peacock and highlighted an axis of feathers so that it looked like a cross. With Belushi in a loin-cloth, nailed to it with syringes."

"Belushi dying for our sins? Now that's a little much."

"It's so easy to deify a dead legend. As long as they die young enough."

"So when's the cutoff point?"

Shelby shook her head. "Don't know, I don't know. But we only indulge the *young* and reckless. Old and reckless is just pathetic. Do you think anybody would deify Frank Sinatra if he was found dead of an overdose? It would never happen."

"Too late, he's working against handicap," I said, grinning. "Frankie's *already* old and pathetic."

She shifted, seesawing her weight back and forth, grinning back, rather lopsided, conceding the point. "Ah, but there was a time, though . . ."

I thought about it, deification, that whole process by which the prematurely dead are kept forever young in the national consciousness. Like some sort of spiritual archive. Maybe it wasn't so much deification as a romanticism, probably of all the wrong things, but the forbidden allure *did* have its own undeniable appeal. Vaudevillian wisdom, carried to the extreme: Always leave 'em wanting more.

I remember reading about a sign someone had tacked up out here shortly after Belushi's death. Some wiser soul, I think, who saw through more bullshit and misguided romanticism than I'll ever recognize: *He could have given us a lot more laughs, but noooooo.*

I knelt to the grave, reached for the offerings left behind. A Quaalude imbedded in clear Lucite, like a paperweight. A little Samurai sword letter opener. A collection of ticket stubs, their dates, printed in a computerese font, years old; tiny capsulized reviews had been scrawled beside the movie names: *Continental Divide: Not bad. The Blues Brothers: Loved it. Neighbors: Sucked big-time.*

And, of course, the notes. Three, at the moment, sheets of paper folded into tight squares. I wondered: did someone come out here periodically to gather these sad little efforts at communication with a dead legend? Were they collected and cared for in some sepulcher? I grabbed one of the notes, looked back at Shelby. "Do I dare?"

"Legally, you're in the clear. I don't know about morally."

I unfolded the note. The needle had snapped off my moral compass a long time ago.

And I read. A few lines of lament, sorry you're gone, man, but you're not forgotten, hope you can see the Samurai sword I left behind, see it from somewhere, and that you like it. Signed simply with initials, L.R.

The next one was a poem, definitely penned by a feminine hand, and young, too. Or hopelessly gridlocked into romantic immaturity. Her i's were dotted with little hearts. Crystal Hemmings, of Pittsburgh. Probably got to know Belushi after the fact. *Saturday Night Live* reruns, courtesy of cable TV.

This was just too fucking sad.

I read the third one. Read it again. And again.

John—

I figure I'm due for Heaven, 'cause I already done my Hell on earth. I thought I could live with this. The only person I could ever lie to was me.

You're dead and I'm sorry. My fault, man. My guilt. Wherever you are . . . forgive me?

Tim

And didn't these scant few lines read just like a confession of sorts? Or was that just wishful thinking, more muck I could rake up and flesh out into a full and sordid tale?

A little of both, probably.

Whoever this Tim was, he wasn't the only one who couldn't lie to himself. And here Shelby and I had said we'd leave our other lives back in South Florida for a while. I tried to pretend I didn't really notice the inevitable disappointment in her eyes as I pocketed the note.

We spent the night on the Vineyard in a hotel that had once been some lofty manor house. We slept with windows open to the night, breathing cool Atlantic air that smelled and tasted and felt far different than it did down home. Like it came from an entirely different ocean. The next morning we took a ferry back to the mainland and set south again. Seeing John Belushi's grave, bunking on an island, these had been spur-of-the-moment ideas the day before. Shelby had seen her New England leaves, hopefully gotten her fill, as far north as Vermont. Real life and careers awaited at the other end of I-95.

These were a lot more certain than what awaited us in the form of one another. But I'm used to that kind of uncertainty. I find it adds a perverse spice to the interpersonal.

We didn't stop for breakfast until Providence, Rhode Island. Shelby indulged me while I set off on foot, and found a shop called The Book Worm. Used stock only; you want new, go someplace else. The door swatted a delicate overhead bell to announce my arrival, and the air within was richly musty with the dry air of old pages. Thousands of them, millions, waiting to be turned.

I pawed through shelves and stacks of nonfiction. In The Book Worm, it appeared that alphabetical order was merely a loose suggestion, nothing to break sweat over. I began in the W's, finally found two copies of what I wanted, one in the T's and the other a few spines away surrounded by U's. I selected the less dog-eared and battered of the pair, filed the other one where it belonged, and paid for my prize.

Carried it outside into crisp October air, just pleasant enough to make me forget that pungent essence of old words. Everything's a tradeoff.

"What did you buy?" Shelby asked when I met her at the car. Nor was she empty-handed herself; she had used the time to browse through an antique store and carried a small brass lamp. Probably half my weekly salary.

So I showed her the paperback. *Wired,* by Bob Woodward. The short life and fast times of John Belushi. I had one at home, read five years before, and a fat lot of good it did me there.

"Research," I said.

She smiled, and it was one of indulgence. I had four years on her, and sometimes in her presence I still felt like a terminal kid, ready to be sent to the principal's office for spitwad warfare. Only in her case, I was ever more willing to bend over and grab my ankles.

"The sleaze-monger lives," she said, and unlocked her car door. I followed, obedient. She drove a Saab. I drove a Plymouth with noisy brakes. Which one would *you* want to take north?

The atlas quoted almost fifteen hundred miles between Providence and home. We'd do it in three days. And Shelby would drive the bulk of it. Which would leave me with a lot of reading time.

Hell, I'd already caught the scenery on the way up.

At some point years ago, a stretch of Florida's southeastern Palm Beach County got tagged with the label of "Tabloid Valley." Seven main supermarket tabs in the country, and six of them are published within less than twenty miles of each other. Not quite as prestigious as California's Silicon Valley, but you do what you can. The intelligentsia's dissenting opinions to the contrary, it still isn't as bad as toxic waste. Go ask the folks living around Three Mile Island which they would rather have.

The Vanguard comes out of Delray Beach. A large, solid building of Spanish architecture, stucco and arched portals and red tile roof. We the inmates call it Taco Hell. My first day back at work after our leaf-viewing field trip to New England, I was in the office of my boss. Janice Fletcher, Celebrities Editor. Affectionately regarded around the building as the world's only known case of permanent PMS.

Janice stared through bifocals at the note I had brought back from Martha's Vineyard. Memorizing? Her salt-and-pepper hair was pulled back into a bun so tight her forehead nearly screamed.

"And for this I should send you to Los Angeles?" She was not amused. "How do you know this isn't some kid from

Boston or wherever, he talks to his TV to old reruns and thinks John Belushi answers him?"

What, like I had a persuasive rebuttal to that one? I let it slide and fired off Exhibit B, tossing my speedily read secondary copy of *Wired* onto her desk. Decorated inside with numerous swathes of yellow highlighter.

"Do you remember anything more than the headlines about Belushi's death?"

Janice looked long and hard at the book's cover. And I knew she was focusing on the author's name. Bob Woodward. Looking up at me from below, then, all grim mouth and condescending eyes. As if to say, *Delusions of grandeur, Mike, is that what's going on here?* She didn't need to remind me that he and Carl Bernstein had won a Pulitzer for *The Washington Post* in 1973 for breaking open a little thing called Watergate. *So you think you could find out something* he *couldn't, is that it?*

In a nutshell, yes. We all have to dream, don't we?

I don't know precisely what her problem with it was. Here at Taco Hell, we didn't exactly operate with standard journalism ethics, two sources to back up every allegation. Give us a whiff of anything, real or imagined, and we'd run with it.

Maybe Janice had a denial of just where she was working, and those delusions of grandeur were her own. At least I *knew* I wrote for a scandal rag that few with more brains than an oyster took seriously. But *The Vanguard* could be a weird place, as if some of the power brokers here secretly longed for respectability. And Janice had this irritating sense of righteous duty from time to time.

But maybe that's why my own inertia had come to rest here. Because so did I. That wistful longing to do something that would truly matter on an informational level. Uncover that dirt, blow the dust off that closeted skeleton, and make a difference for once in my life.

Like I said, we all have to dream.

"Enlighten me," she finally consented.

"Belushi was in L.A. at the time, ostensibly working on a script he had in development, but mostly finding excuses

not to work on it. He was staying at a bungalow at the
Chateau Marmont, off Sunset. But there's only one person's word in the world that says just how Belushi died:
Cathy Smith. Sure, you got a lot of backup support, all
these other people that knew what was going on, those last
days of his life when Belushi was on a binge. The man was
going through thousands of dollars worth of hard drugs.
During his last five days or so, he was mixing cocaine and
heroin and injecting it. It's called a speedball. Or rather,
Cathy Smith was doing it for him. It's mainly her testimony that says how he died. Everything else is just coroner's reports, that sort of thing." I took a breath, combed
for facts. I'd tried memorizing all this last night, earlier in
the morning. Making a pitch for something like this looks
bad enough without crutching yourself with notes. "The
day he died, she shot him his last speedball, say, three-
thirty in the morning. He showered and slept off and on
after that. She checked him around ten-fifteen and he was
okay. Next thing anybody knows, his physical trainer finds
him dead around two hours later."

"Do you think Cathy Smith was lying?"

I shrugged. "It's possible, but maybe that's all she knew.
She took off for Canada, gave this exclusive interview to
The Enquirer for fifteen grand, saying how she was the one
killed John Belushi. Later she denied that. But as far as
anyone's telling, that's the way it happened. Maybe she's
not so much lying as in the dark about something. Hell, she
was a junkie herself, a part-time dealer. An aging groupie
who'd pretty much been chewed up by her own life. Her
priorities would have been . . . limited."

I could see wheels turning in Janice's head. Forge on.

"But all through what Woodward was able to piece together of Belushi's last few weeks, months, there was a lot
of time unaccounted for. Times he would just take off. Nobody could watch him all the time, nobody could keep up
with him. With enough cocaine, the man could keep going
strong for nearly two weeks, no sleep. So who's to say that
at least one of his lowlife friends didn't slip through the
net?"

"Tim," she said, and snapped a red fingernail against the note. "Who went all the way to Martha's Vineyard to try clearing his conscience."

"It's a cry for help," I deadpanned. "I think he wants to unload."

Janice rolled her eyes. Yes, sometimes I tried her patience. "So are you thinking this Tim was just another player in an accidental overdose? Or is your fertile brain tipping all the way into some full-blown conspiracy theory here?"

I just rocked on my heels and let her have that smile I sometimes unleash. That gosh-I'm-so-charming smirk. All I needed was a hat at a rakish tilt.

I explained to her that, actually, there were two film projects in which Belushi was involved, that certain unknown parties might not have wanted made. The first being *Kingpin,* an idea of Belushi's to base a film on the life of a New York druglord named Mark Hertzan with whom he had gotten friendly. The studios weren't interested, but Belushi was gaining more clout, and enough contacts to go outside the Hollywood mainstream into independent filmmaking. Just a month before Belushi's death, Hertzan was gunned down execution-style in his apartment building. File this one under unsolved; Belushi himself admitted it might have had something to do with the *Kingpin* project.

The other film was far more of a definite go, a script called *Moon Over Miami.* Louis Malle was spearheading this one, a story inspired by the Abscam case in which FBI agents posed as Arabs ready and willing to bribe congressmen for favors. Malle's vision was a black comedy that would demonstrate just to what depths spit-and-polish FBI agents would stoop: hiring criminals to incriminate their congressional targets, in order to boost the bureau's public image. Not the most flattering portrayal.

So I pitched it all, I pitched it hard, and I pitched it from as many directions as I possibly could. It's a numbers game. You batter your head against a wall in enough strategic locations, you're bound to smash through eventually.

"Where would you start, once you got out there?" Janice said.

"Rollie Newkirk." I braced, waiting for the bomb to drop.

Rollie Newkirk had spent six or seven years affiliated with *The Vanguard* as a Hollywood contact. Gossip columnist was probably the most apt label to hang on him, but even that didn't seem quite right. Gossip columnist, you think of a certain tacky glamour, Rona Barrett, like that. Rollie didn't come close to even measuring up to her dubious level.

Remember high school? There's usually one kid who saunters into the bathroom and takes a long leisurely piss, then takes forever to wash his hands. Always with a slightly cocked head, tipping that ear for best reception so he doesn't miss any potentially juicy conversations by people who wouldn't ordinarily talk to him on the best day of his life.

Take that kid, add fifty pounds and half as many years, plop him down in Hollywood, and you have Rollie Newkirk.

"I guess he's a start," Janice said, and sighed.

So I had it, just like that. And hadn't even really had to fight that hard. Nor use my secret weapon, a line penned while driving to work, to shame her into seeing it my way . . .

If *The Enquirer* could pay fifteen thousand dollars to a junkie, at least *The Vanguard* could allot me that much to go find another one.

A couple of days later, I jetted cross-country, out of Miami and into the Hollywood-Burbank Airport. Took a cab down to Hollywood, and my hotel, then stretched out on the bed. Luxury, after spending a full workday's equivalent in United coach.

First time I was out here, maybe a dozen years ago, it was a real eye-opener. *Hollywood,* the name alone conjures glamour on an epic scale, but such fancies are an anachronism from a bygone era. The bus station is full of rude awakenings. Runaways and other naive hopefuls, bored by

Kansas or wherever, ready to see their names in lights. They're more likely to have police portraits done in chalk on pavement.

At least it ensures the pimps a steady influx of fresh faces.

New numbers had to be invented for the sleaze factor here. South Florida certainly has no shortage of things sleazy, but it seems different there. South Florida is younger, fresher, its tawdriness taking on more of an adolescent naughtiness. Hollywood has been around longer, lying there between desert and ocean like a whore long past her prime, her cunt dried up like an old gulch. But still tough, make no mistake. Still vicious, still chewing up innocents who come seeking her favors.

Rollie Newkirk was expecting me; I'd called his last known number a few hours after getting the go-ahead from Janice . . . had to give Rollie time to rise and shine. I called him again once I had arrived and we did brunch the next day. Sidewalk cafe on La Brea called Charmaine's. He picked it, and once I saw the prices, I knew why: there was never any doubt but that I was paying.

"Kiss kiss," he said when I got there, joined him at a little square table. Rollie was all in gray, thinning hair combed back into a short limp ponytail, with plump cheeks crinkling into a dimpled smile. He looked like a Buddha after an image makeover. Rollie had been seated on a far perimeter, next to the hedges. A definite nobody. I checked carefully for hornet nests while sitting, and he clucked at my clothes. "Oh, dear, I see you're *still* dressing like an off-duty lifeguard."

"Rollie," I greeted. Tight smile. "And I see you're still ducking that HIV-positive test."

"Vicious, vicious," he said. "You must pick that up from working too long around Janice Fletcher. How *is* she?"

"Mellowing."

I'd been there all of fifteen seconds before some stuffy young ramrod of a waiter arrived with a clip-on tie for me. His name was probably Thad. Gazing with vaguely regal distaste at my blue-and-green shirt; at least it didn't have palm trees on it. Maybe I should have made the effort to tuck it in. He left the clip-on hanging cockeyed, and Rollie eyed all this with bemusement.

"Oh, I didn't *tell* you about dress standards . . . ?"

I shook my head no. "Must have slipped your mind." Rollie, Jeez. He could still be a real bitch.

Menus were a long time in coming. Oh that Thad, being fussy again. When he *did* come back, he wouldn't even tell us his real name, that he would be our waiter this morning. I had no idea we were *that* detestable. I hoped Charmaine's had at least put him on combat pay for dealing with our obviously distasteful ilk.

I saw no point into getting straight down to business right off. Wait until the food came, at least, when most of Rollie's attention would be focused on our table. For the time being, he had to show off for me, or perhaps himself, discreetly waving to select newcomers. They all carried portable cellular phones. None of them I recognized; shows you how much I know about Hollywood politics. But then, a lot of them seemed to have the same reaction to Rollie. After he waggled his fingers and flashed his pinkie ring at one tanned, gray-haired gent, the fellow turned to his companion—a niece or granddaughter, I'm *sure*—and hunched his shoulders.

I pretended not to notice. Let him salvage one or two shreds of dignity.

I found it easy to laugh inside at him . . . for maybe a minute. Then I just felt depressed, watching him try to maintain this facade of his own creation, perhaps trying to outrun that grossly unpopular kid he must have been a few decades ago. Desperately attempting to achieve whatever immortality or notoriety he could, so that when he died, he might warrant more than a standard single-column inch in the *Los Angeles Times* obituaries.

Didn't I want the same thing? And wasn't I scoring about as well?

I hunted for other thoughts to fill the void. Wondering who had worn this tie before me. Maybe some noble eccentric, too talented to consider such trivialities before leaving home. Had I ever seen Spielberg wearing a tie? Maybe Thad would let me keep it as a souvenir.

He brought our food at last, bless him. I let Rollie get a couple of bites down before I got to work.

"How good is your memory?" I said.

"Speak in timeframes, love, timeframes."

"Let's go back eight and a half years. Spring of 1982."

Rollie sat up straighter, tilted his head back. Three chins waggled at me. "Oooo, we *are* dipping back into ancient history now, aren't we? I remember there *was* a 1982. What of it?"

"John Belushi's overdose."

Rollie looked bored, disappointed even. He flipped his chubby hand north. "I do believe there's a dead horse up on Santa Monica, if you'd like to go beat that one a while, too."

"Bear with me, would you? Who's picking up the check anyway?" Mister diplomacy. "Belushi's O.D. Surely there was a lot of talk flying around about it at the time."

"Oh, dearheart, tell me about it." Rollie leaned across the table, eyes wide. Confidantes, that was us. He even forgot about his food; I must have struck a vital nerve. "That man was a frightening legend in his own time."

"You remember hearing anything about anyone he might have been hanging around with at the time, name of Tim?"

Rollie pursed his lips, tapped his fork against the china. Ting ting. "Let's see—"

"I don't have a last name. We're probably talking about a junkie, or close to it."

Rollie leaned back in his seat, sitting taller all of a sudden. He'd dropped out of gossip mode and gone straight to shrewd. It was going to cost me, this much I knew.

"So we're dealing in information now, are we," he said, high and delighted. "Just how much is this worth to you and our dear Janice, so far away?"

I leaned one way, then another, made a show of contemplation. "I can't say offhand, Rollie, but . . . you point me in the right direction, and I can arrange some sort of consultation fee."

He leaned back again, looking skyward, lacing plump fingers and pulling them apart. Repeatedly. "It's a start. Of course . . . I'd have to go through my notes. And this *is* eight and a half years ago we're talking about. This could be a time-consuming process, why, it could take . . ."

I rolled my eyes. The gossiping Buddha had me by the short hairs and he knew it. "And I suppose I could see my way clear to adding a processing fee to speed things along."

"Ooooh, we do speak the same language, don't we." He beamed. "Now, just what sort of context am I looking for, in regards to this Tim-no-last-name? What's he supposed to have done?"

I'd thought about this already: should I tell Rollie the angle I was working? It wasn't the kind of thing you wanted to deposit in a rumor factory like him. On the other hand, he had already dealt himself in for substantial self-interest. If he knew the stakes, he would undoubtedly find them all the more juicy, and work all the harder.

Sure, why not. What's a little scandal-talk among friends?

So I laid it out for him, bare bones. No need for the persuasive arguments that had been necessary with Janice. And the further I went, the more Rollie began to regard me in some new light. I wasn't sure I liked it. It fell dangerously close to an ogle.

When I wrapped it up, Rollie leaned back with hands folded over his ample belly. Happy Buddha. "I always did love the way your mind works. I never told you that, did I?"

I said nothing. I could always take a compliment.

"I can't promise you anything, Mike," he then said, and it was like a completely different Rollie. As if a genuine human being were in there, peeping out for the moment. "Only that I'll check my files and see if I can come up with something for you."

I could ask for no more. So from my wallet I took a business card—*The Vanguard* logo didn't generally impress

people so much as amuse them—and scribbled out my hotel number, slid it across to him. Rollie pocketed it and I
assumed our business this morning was done.

After brunch was eaten, Rollie left first—busy, busy—
and I sat for a while, smoking two cigarettes and lowering
the property values. Never was Thad more attentive, so
close to evicting us, yet so far, one down and one diehard to
go. On his third tight-jawed trip to ask if there was anything else I required, I finally tossed a pair of twenties and
a five onto his tray to take care of the bill.

"One thing," I said. "Can I keep the tie? I've really come
to envy your sartorial taste."

"By all means . . . *do.*" His jaw could have cracked wal-
nuts.

"Great," I said, and rose. I peeled off a hundred-dollar
bill, folded it into quarters, and slipped it into the pocket of
his starched white shirt. "And this is for you, Thad. You've
just been an absolute peach this morning."

He looked down at his pocket, at me, pocket, then me
again. Blinking. I do believe I'd caught him off guard. But
he quickly recovered, and that haughty fusspot countenance returned.

"My name's *Tad,*" he said, as if I were cretin of the year.
I just smiled.

Yeah, I remember where I was when someone first told
me that John Belushi was dead.

I'd followed him ever since the fall of 1975, when *Saturday Night Live* debuted. In college at the time, at Gaines-
ville, and the show quickly became one of those ritualistic
totems for myself and my friends. Gathering in apartments
or houses rented en masse, awash in celebration of the
weekend. Or we'd catch it in bars, places packed and gener-
ating enough noise to rival a factory, but come eleven-
thirty, silence would descend so the TV could be heard. Ill-
mannered louts who persisted in noisy distraction were
quickly dealt with by mob mentality.

Chevy Chase went on to be the first star to emerge out of
the repertory company that made up the Not Ready For

Prime Time Players. One season, then the jump to feature films and leading-man status. I knew he'd eventually drift into comfortable ruts and diminish into mediocrity. He was too smug. And played one basic character: himself.

No, for me, from the very beginning, Belushi was the one I tuned in to see the most. *He* was the embodiment of anarchy incarnate. The bottled outrage, the short fuse, the comedic rhino with a ferocious edge and no restraint. He was the one who defined the true excitement of live TV, because he was a gifted menace to himself and everyone around him, and you never knew what he might do next.

I hated it when he and Dan Aykroyd decided to leave the show after the fourth season. No more weekly fix, but I understood and respected their reasons. Hollywood had opened up to them, and they had outgrown the show. Bigger and better spectacles ahead? I certainly hoped so.

But I noticed something different in those next few years, maybe because I had grown more worldly myself. The nature of the work changed, grew flaccid and safe. And I could watch Belushi giving an interview to some shellacked TV personality profiler, and catch the occasional glimpse of desperation in his eyes—a look wholly removed from any mania of comedic intensity. As if the laughter wasn't enough anymore, or he didn't trust it, or believe it was there at all.

At least, I think now that I did at the time. Maybe I'm just fooling myself with 20/20 hindsight. Wouldn't be the first time.

But I do know this: On Friday, March 5, 1982, I was with friends. Three years out of college and working in Tampa on the staff of an alternative weekly press. No sacred cow was safe from our righteousness, and we fashioned ourselves young journalistic anarchists, devoted to some credo of free expression and liberal anger I can't even fully remember anymore. Fridays we generally knocked off early, and that particular one several of us met at one couple's house and devoted several hours to sensimilla via an ornate bong. Friday afternoon became evening, hazy and mellow.

One of my fellow writers went on a pizza and beer run, came back in twenty saying he'd heard on the radio that John Belushi had fatally overdosed in L.A. I refused to believe until I heard it from Dan Rather's lips during a CBS news update after we'd flipped on the TV. Imagine. Dan Rather. I had refused to believe my friend until he had Rather backing him up.

I knew right then I was a sellout.

But it got worse, as this nosedive evening wore on, injury upon insult. I sat on the floor in this dumpy house, realizing that this was the first true loss of applicable culture I had experienced. The first one to really hit home and *hurt*. Yes, I'd loved Boris Karloff's movies as a kid, and when he died I was sorry, but he could have been my grandfather. Hendrix, Joplin, Morrison . . . they were gone before I was old enough to appreciate their music. And John Lennon didn't count; the Beatles were already history by the time I awakened musically, and by then, newer bands played harder, louder, faster.

And while some would say it was for the best, for the first time I really felt like a full-blown adult.

It's overrated.

Rollie Newkirk called me the day after our brunch, said he had struck out regarding the name Tim. Still, he had a suggestion, gave me the name of a limo driver he had talked to years ago. She had lugged Belushi around on a few occasions, nights of high speed endless thrills, get the limo and go from there. Anything could happen, he could wind up anywhere.

Then Rollie asked if I wanted to join him for an afternoon swim at his apartment's pool. I pictured some crumbling marble depravity, with spouting water nymph statues and free-roaming peacocks, and begged off. Sorry Rollie, forgot my special L.A. trunks. The ones with the stainless-steel codpiece and butt armor.

It took several phone calls to track down Joyce Fulton, the driver. She was apparently a nomad on the limo circuit. Rollie knew her agency as of 1984, and I took it from there, shifting into legal mode. It's a routine I frequently run, introducing myself as the attorney and executor of the estate of some recently deceased philanthropist. In this case, said eccentric philanthropist recalled a particularly pleasant chauffeur named Joyce from a few years ago, and he wanted to remember her with a bequest. Could I please be directed to her next employer?

It couldn't fail. Most drivers, from the longest stretch limo to the lowliest taxi, believe that next passenger might turn out to be another Howard Hughes, earmarking them for future gratitude. Never mind that Howie had fourteen-inch toenails by the end, his money spends just the same. As incentive, I said I'd be sure to tell Joyce who had helped direct me to her. Everyone believes in the possibility of finder's fees, too.

They volunteered the information quicker than if I had used thumbscrews.

Joyce Fulton had driven for four firms since 1984, and when I at last reached her present employer, I shifted out of legal mode and into customer. Ordering a limo for that night, and asking if it would be possible to request her. She had come recommended by a former client of a month or so ago, I explained. They were quite accommodating. The customer is always right.

I had her pick me up around nine o'clock. She phoned my room from the cellular to let me know she had arrived, and was standing at reasonably military erect posture beside an open door once I set foot outside the hotel. I smiled, shrugged, and slid in. The door shut after me with such a gentle clunk it was almost a caress. When Joyce returned to the driver's seat, she seemed so far away we might as well have been in different area codes. The partition between us was wide open; at least I wouldn't have to call her back.

"Where are you looking to go?" she asked.

"I don't know. Anyplace is good."

"Ah, another one of *those,*" she said, though cheerfully enough. "Okay. Got anybody you want to impress?"

"Sure. How soon can we be in Miami?"

"Uh *huh*," Joyce said. "How 'bout *I* pick the circuit?"

I told her lead on, and the limo slid out into traffic like a great maroon yacht. It's quite the decadent sensation. I pilfered the bar right away, clinked bottles around, and fixed a margarita just so I could say I'd used a blender in the back of a moving automobile. I turned the TV on, flipped through some channels, found a titty station that must've been relayed in via satellite feed. This limo company thought of everything. I left it there with the sound off. Looked like a Ginger Lynn video. Ah, the classics.

"You don't have to wear the chauffeur's cap if you don't want to," I said.

"Sorry, company regulations."

I frowned. "I'll give you twenty extra dollars to lose the cap."

"Deal," she said, and whipped it aside.

So, she could be bought. This I took as a good omen.

And I liked her already. Joyce looked to be in her early forties, give or take. Hair dark and not quite shoulder length, with a side part. Her tailored gray uniform fit well; Nautilus workouts, I would have bet. Good tan and just enough faint smile lines for character.

I let her run the tour guide spiel for a while. Here's Mann's Chinese Theater, here are the La Brea tar pits, there goes Century City. That's where D.W. Griffith built his own vision of Babylon in 1915. She went through it all with easy familiarity, and I'd pop in with questions now and then to let her know I was paying attention.

Babylon? What a portent.

"This bar is understocked," I told her an hour into this aimless ride. "There's no George Dickel."

"Well, it's your own fault." By now we were comfortable enough for mild chastisement. "You should have asked for it when you made the reservations this afternoon. It would've been waiting for you."

No problem, I told her, just find a liquor store. Idling in the lot, I tried to talk her into joining me for a drink, but company regs got in the way again. I understood, and needled her long enough into breaking down and letting me buy a couple of bottles of mineral water for her. Twist of lemon. Of course.

"Mind if I sit up front?" I asked when I came back out with sack in hand. "I hate shouting all that distance."

"It's your ride, Mikey. Do what thou wilt."

I brought up a glass and a bucket of ice, and the passenger side front was mine. Joyce wheeled us back onto La Cienega, northbound. Let's go slumming, I suggested, see how Beverly Hills looks these days, so she steered us toward Coldwater Canyon Drive.

"They probably told you I requested you specifically. Didn't they." Time to cut through one layer of bullshit, at long last. I had plenty more to spread.

"Yep. Happens sometimes."

I smiled across the front seat at her. Still seemed too far a distance. "Just so they could meet you?"

That twining road with lots of southern California's prime real estate lost some of her attention. She looked at me with one wary eyebrow cocked. "Just what's going on with you, Mike? Why don't you tell me that right now."

"I'm doing a book," I said, "and I was hoping to interview you. An earlier resource said you might make a good one yourself."

"Oh yeah?" She brightened considerably. Smiling anew.

I expected as much. Say you're from a newspaper, and I don't care if it's *The New York Times* or *The Washington Post,* and as often than not, warning lights go off in the subject's head. Defenses rise. The *60 Minutes* Syndrome, I call it. All of a sudden you're Mike Wallace, barging in with cameras rolling, ready to wreak havoc on lives and careers. But say you're writing a book, and people want to be included.

That longing for immortality again, I imagine. Books don't line the bottom of a bird cage the next day.

"What's it about?" Joyce asked.

"Loosely, about cultural shifts. The way what used to be more underground culture insinuates itself into the mainstream, becomes gradually more accepted. I'm really fascinated by the punk and postpunk culture out here."

Joyce sputtered a laugh. "You don't look like a punker."
"I don't look like a cultural anthropologist, either."
"No, you don't. More like—"
"An off-duty lifeguard, right?"

All at once, Joyce looked straight at me with widening eyes. "Oh Lord, Rollie Newkirk sent you!" she wailed. "Didn't he? That used to be one of his favorite lines."

Mayday, mayday, I'm dying here. I got her through it, though, talked her down, told her hey, he was just a source, I was no more fond of the man than she apparently was, we'd met once at a party, and in his own unctuous way, he *was* one of the more memorable ones there that night. She bought it, and the more the lies rolled off my tongue, the worse I felt about it. Joyce Fulton was a genuinely fine lady, and my bullshit potential was wholly undeserved.

I really should tip heavily a bit later.

She took the limo around onto Mulholland and back down Beverly Glen, and I went on.

"I'm interested in doing a chapter or two on John Belushi. I know he was wanting to do some punk-influenced work that he never got to film. Rollie said you used to drive him some nights. I was wondering where he used to go, who he used to see from that sort of scene." I had no idea if this was the milieu where my unknown complicitor lurked or not, but it made sense. Heroin use is a definite counterculture vice. "And specifically, I'm looking for a guy Belushi would have known, named Tim. I talked to this guy, oh, probably five years ago and made notes—this was even before I ever thought of doing this book—but I lost all the notes in an apartment fire. Psychotic girlfriend, you know how it goes. But that's all I remember: Tim."

Ah, what a silver-tongued weasel I could be.

Joyce drummed fingers on the wheel, thinking. Then, "Just Tim, huh? Big city down there, Mike."

I shrugged. "That's okay." I patted the seat. "Big car."

She wheeled back down into the sleaze factory and started me on a junket of clubs and nightspots whose patrons probably saw the light of day only rarely. Taking a definite walk on the wild side. Following the footsteps of a dead comic genius.

If I've learned one thing at *The Vanguard*, it's that if you really want to know someone's life, you root through their garbage like a pig after truffles. It's all in there. But the problem this time was that the trash had been taken out eight and a half years ago. The best I could do was retrace the man's most likely footsteps and see what turned up.

And this much I knew, John Belushi had been heavily into the underground club scene. By now, lo these many years later, a lot of the places Joyce said she had taken him were gone. They live and die according to whim and trend. This week's fashion is next week's anachronism. But the people? Some grow out of it, some die. But some hang with it year after year after year. The hardcores.

And so with Joyce pointing me in the right direction, then waiting with the limo, I did not go gently into that good night, but I went just the same. It was like a tour of Dante's Inferno, only paved.

They were generally places with all the genteel charm of a broken cinder block. With minimalist decor and music, either live or from a D.J. booth, at airport runway sonic levels. I'd generally work my way to the bar and wait for a bartender who appeared to be a veteran, been at this game a few years.

Typical scenario: I'd order a drink and tip well. Sit there with a folded twenty between my fingers like a cigarette and try not to look like a bunboy or a lech readying for a proposition. And when I had their full attention, however long it would take, I'd leap right in: "How'd you like to get your name in a book?"

Whether or not it worked, I'd at least usually score points for originality. And when it did, we'd talk, I'd hit my litany. Tim, anybody know a Tim, used to be an acquaintance of John Belushi? Sometimes I'd crap out entirely, but sometimes I'd come away with referrals. A tedious business, this. No wonder private detectives charge three hundred per diem for legwork.

I went at it all the rest of that night, until nearly every

place was closed, and had Joyce take me right back out the next night so I could do it some more. Following leads, talking to waste cases whose memories ran the foul risk of being as foggy as an English moor, I actually did get steered toward a couple of Tims who claimed they'd known Belushi. One even had the picture to prove it, a worn and faded shot pulled with care from a wallet. The two of them, one younger, the other still alive, standing in some unknown club, faces cranked up with the intensity of celebration either liquid or chemical.

But neither of these Tims was the one I was looking for. *Humor me*, I'd say to them, then ask for a sample of their handwriting. No match either time, but by then I knew already. It was in the eyes that they had no connection with what I had come here for.

By the end of that second night, I was almost willing to give up, pack it in. Worn out, smelling of sweat and stale smoke; sore of feet and numb of ears. But mostly, overwhelmed by that peculiar noxious sense of failure that sets in around three, four in the morning when you can't sleep. When that fathomless sense of the dead of night comes to call, makes you reevaluate your life. What the hell was I doing out here? It was times like this when I felt like a buzzard, picking the last tattered scraps away from the dead, the dying. Telling myself what the hell, they don't need them anymore, why not take them and put them on display.

The fourth estate. How noble. How constitutionally protected.

Maybe Joyce sensed this in me by the time she got me back to my hotel. Sat there as the engine idled, wearing a light and easy smile—I still hadn't returned to the backseats—and then she did a rimshot with one hand on the steering wheel. "So we gonna do this again tomorrow night, Mikey?"

"Don't know," I mumbled.

Her brow creased, all concern. "Aw come on. You're a fun date. And none of this Dutch treat for *you*, no, you're a first-class guy all the way."

I smiled, leaned back in the seat a moment with burning eyes. "There'll be others, you're young . . ."

She switched off the engine, reached over and smacked me lightly on the shoulder. "Come on. Get out. Walk a minute." And then she was out the door. Seconds later, so was I. I'd long relieved her of the obligation to open doors for me.

Joyce got me scooted along and moving, a slow leisurely amble, the speed preferred by those with nowhere to go and all the time in the world to get there. Moving past a sidewalk gauntlet of shrubs and palm trees, fronds stirring overhead. Not much foot traffic in this neighborhood, this time of night.

"You know," she said, "far be it from me to tell a writer how to do his job . . . but it seems to me you're expending a lot of time, energy, and money to find one minor source for a book. Are you sure this guy's that important?"

"You'd be surprised."

"Or are we," she said, very even, very knowing, but without judgment, "even going to be in a book at all?"

I probably knew it was coming, doubts on her part. In two nights, I'd gotten the sense that Joyce Fulton was as sharp as she was discreet. "Have you been talking to Rollie today?"

"No. And don't worry, I won't ask. I don't even think I want to know. It's . . . easier that way. When you *don't* know. When these lives that cross your own don't leave any traces behind. That way, later, when you hear what's happened to them . . . or what they did to themselves . . . it doesn't hurt."

I said nothing, just walked at her side, listening to her voice, softer now than in the limo. And I wondered about her, who she really was. She'd told me nothing and I hadn't asked. But I had compiled mental stats, just the same. I had her divorced, twice. One kid from the first marriage, a son. Around fifteen, sixteen by now. Splitting time equally between Mom and Dad, and she missed him terribly that other half of the time.

I didn't think I wanted to know how right or wrong I was.

"I genuinely liked him," she finally said. "Belushi. He was just too intense for his own good. He ran me hard and ragged sometimes . . . but in the end, he was always a gentleman."

We had turned around by now, heading back toward the limo. I tried reconciling all those varied John Belushis people spoke of into one package. The addict. The gentleman who could be so sweet and disarming. The tyrant who at times bullied and badgered those with whom he worked. The star who had a weekly per diem living rate of twenty-five hundred dollars built into his movie contracts, even though his accountants paid all his bills . . . the studios and everybody else knew it was for cocaine. Oh, it's just John, it keeps him going in front of the cameras, he needs it.

I tried to picture him his last weeks. Distraught over a script called *Noble Rot* he had worked on that was reviled by Paramount as unworkable. He had nearly alienated himself from almost everyone concerned in trying to ramrod it through into production by sheer force of his will. And speedballing those last five days of his life . . . getting high with a little help from his friends.

How many friends had it taken?

There were so many unknowns here. Cathy Smith's help with procurement and the needle notwithstanding, Belushi's death still went down as an accidental OD. Maybe, maybe not, if there was a wild card named Tim in the deck. But Hollywood is a town that hides its secrets well, right from the very beginning. In the early twenties, when William Desmond Taylor was shot in his home, friends, lovers, and associates swooped down upon the house to rid it of anything scandalous before reporting to the police. When William Randolph Hearst shot producer Tom Ince in the head during a yachting excursion, newspapers and even the San Diego district attorney dismissed the death as due to acute indigestion.

Why should anything change? The two main motives to

kill were still love and money. Apply that to Belushi's two back-burner projects. *Kingpin,* the druglord script? Some unknown player had too much cash at stake to allow that kind of possible exposure. *Moon Over Miami,* the Louis Malle film? The FBI or other conservative factions in those new years of the Reagan presidency loved their image too much to see it tarnished any more.

Or hell, maybe it really was accidental, and Tim was just the street hustler who sold the last doses of heroin to Cathy Smith.

Joyce and I had reached the front of my hotel, and it was one of those oddly awkward moments when I felt I wanted to kiss her good night and had no right to even think it. Maybe all this would look clearer after sleep. Deep and dreamless.

"So . . ." she said. Popping her cap on, the first time since last night. She grinned wryly. "See you tomorrow night?"

And I nodded. "Wouldn't miss it."

There are probably sadder things in the world—in fact, I know there are—but at the time, nothing seemed sadder than an aging punk rocker. It's a persona best worn by youth; the young come by anger naturally. But let a decade or more go by and there comes a time when you can't even remember what it was you once were so angry about.

Tim surfaced on the fourth night, late, after I'd spent hours running a slalom that sent us back and forth over twenty-mile stretches or more. A bouncer here knew a doorman there who thought he'd met a waitress some-where else who remembered meeting a punk musician named Tim Frenzy who might have claimed he knew John Belushi. Or something like that. After so long, this food chain of bottom-feeders tends to blur.

The end of the road, a Culver City club named Nine-One-One. The emergency phone number, I liked that. I wan-dered in as I'd done countless other places these past four nights that seemed a lot longer. Maybe because I'd seen too many desperate people looking for that break they would never get. It nibbles away at you after a time.

The music was loud, barbaric, formless, angry. Didn't *anybody* out here play reggae? I tipped the bartender ten just to point him out, Tim Frenzy, and there he was on-stage. Guitar player, all bones and sweat, flailing away at his axe with a glazed intensity that didn't allow much for tracking the rhythm. He had this kind of little-boy-lost quality that was at definite odds with the lines in his face.

Three thousand miles, several thousand dollars, Rollie Newkirk and Joyce Fulton and a cast of nameless hundreds, and this was the guy? I was seriously underwhelmed. Of course I didn't know at the time, he was just one more contender.

I waited until the band—they called themselves Chili Fart—took a break, then bribed my way to the club's backstage area. An extra beer in hand to break the ice, help Tim replace those precious bodily fluids dripped out front. I flagged him down in a narrow hallway, dim and hot and stale.

"Drink up," I said in greeting, and handed the bottle to him. His other three mates looked irked, as if I'd breached etiquette. Hard old world, guys, sorry. "Talk to you a minute?"

Tim glanced me up and down, eyes flat as a lizard's but less alive. "You from a record company?" Maybe just the tiniest flicker of hope still alive in his voice.

I shook my head. "Sorry. I represent other interests."

I caught a bit of deflation in him, one more pinprick in a dream that must have been losing air for years. He waved the others off, and lingered alone with me in that dismal hallway.

"So what is this, like private shit, or what?"

"Depends," I said. "Did you happen to do any traveling back East a couple weeks ago?"

He was silent, but this time I knew I had something. It was probably easier to detect in him than it would have been in most of the others. *Any* sign of life in a dead face and pair of eyes is cause for note. I reached into my pocket for that folded sheet of paper, and he watched my hands with a dull amazement. And a fatalistic dread.

"Yours, right?" I held it before his eyes. This was no time to innocently question. Questions would tip him off as to just how little I actually knew. *"Right?"*

Tim nodded, leaning against the wall in abrupt exhaustion. Shaking his head like he couldn't believe it, yet at the same time could, wasn't this just his luck, his life? And I looked at this miserable failure of a musician, with the bruises and scars of needles old and new along his arms, and I wondered which of us was the more world-weary. I'll see your arms and raise you my liver.

"You don't look like a cop."

"Doesn't mean I'm still not curious." And then, just to goose it along, "You satisfy that curiosity, I can make it worth your while."

God help us both. He looked more alive in that instant than he had since I'd seen him. The starving dog after the bone.

"There's a room here somewhere," Tim said, looking down the hall, "maybe we should . . . you know, privacy?"

He tried doors and I followed, and from out front, music from some bass-heavy club stereo rattled the floor. Tim opened one door and stepped inside. Scarcely a room, more of a walk-in utility closet. We shared it with mops and buckets, cleansers cruel to the nose. And whatever small creatures scuttled unseen behind boxes.

"I tune my guitar in here." Tim grinned. With his red eyes and soured teeth, he was a walking death's head. "I like it 'cause it reminds me of my first apartment. Takes me back, you know. Nothing like those . . . those first days, right?"

I guess anything can be shellacked with nostalgia and called romantic.

"How'd you *find* me, man? I didn't . . . didn't even sign my last name to that thing, did I?"

"Why don't you tell me *your* story first."

Tim's hands were shaking with the occasional nervous

twitch of his shoulders. I gave him a cigarette to calm him.
Smoking in a closet full of solvent fumes, oh we were
bright boys.

"I don't even know who the fuck you are."

I shrugged. "Does it matter? You went a hell of a long
way to make an apology to a grave."

"Yeah, well, I was in the neighborhood, okay?" Tim up-
turned a large metal bucket, sat on its rusty bottom, took a
long drink and dragged the cigarette into ash. "My dad
died in Boston, okay? Hadn't seen him in eight years, figured I might as well not fuck up my last chance, right?" He
laughed. "And that asshole, you know he didn't leave me a
fucking thing in the will. Just like him, and I could *use* it,
too, could use some cash to cut some new demos, we wrote
some decent stuff this year, you know? Did you hear it out
front?"

I told him yeah, yeah. Gold record debut for sure. But
noncommercial. He liked that.

Tim, smoking, both of us in clouds. He shut his eyes and I
felt the anguish by osmosis. Dead dreams, glimpsed
through that cruel magnifying glass of time. All the accumulated regret of one breed and another.

Tim looked up, and he was ancient. "I killed him and I
was glad to do it at the time. Motherfucker, he said . . .
one time said he was gonna help the band I was in. Get us
on *Saturday Night Live* and maybe a record deal. I mean,
why not, I believed him, he was helping those guys in Fear,
he got *them* on *Saturday Night* for a fucking Halloween
show." He ground the butt beneath a scabrous boot tip, did
a horribly repugnant Belushi parody: "I trusted him to
keep his promise, but noooooo."

"And so you shot him up that last time, yourself?"

"Cathy Smith, she'd already left. I knew where he was
staying at the Marmont, he told me once, said come by,
bring my guitar, we'd write some tunes. I found him in bed
that morning. Man, I don't even think he knew it when I
popped him in the arm." Again with the death's-head grin.
"Junkies give the best shots." And then, something worse

than that grin. The ghost of old premeditation. "That's
what I said to the guy paid me to go in there and do it."

It was like waking up in a whole new world, hearing
that. I leaned in closer. "Who?"

Tim spewed a bitter little laugh. "Think I cared back
then? I was *pissed!* I had a right to be *heard!* Then some
guy hears me talking one night, knows I'm pissed at Belushi for going back on his word on me, he offers me three
grand to do a job like that? Hell yes I'm gonna take it, I'da
done it for nothing if I'd thought it up myself. I didn't ask
who he was . . . I just took the money. And I didn't leave
nothing behind . . ." His voice was losing that bitterness.
His head hung, and I believe if he'd been able, he might
have cried. "I shouldn't have done it, you know. I mean
. . . he was just trying to get by, I couldn't see that then,
he was just as big a mess as anyone, and *nobody'd* fucking
help him . . ."

I stood watching Tim wrestle with his conscience, wondering how I could use this. Wondering how I could ever
bring myself to spill this guy's story across a front page.
And knowing that somehow I *would* find a way. As always.
I'd gone to a lot of trouble to find him, hadn't I?

Remember that tidbit of Chinese wisdom? Be careful
what you wish for, for you may get it.

I never learn.

The sound of bootheels thudding steadily down the hall
knocked Tim from his bleak reverie. "I gotta get back on-
stage, but you pay me, I can tell you what I know, I remember that morning, I remember it real good. You *are* gonna
pay me, aren't you, you said you could make it worth my
time, that means money, doesn't it?"

He sat on that bucket clutching a bottle as empty as his
eyes, only the bottle didn't plead. He looked sadder than
Judas.

"Yeah," I finally said. "I'll pay you." Some quick calcula-
tions in my head, some quick reductions, too. It wouldn't
take much to hook this one. "I'll pay you a thousand dollars cash for exclusive rights. Contract and everything."

And Tim smiled with the sick hope of a cancer patient,

waking up to one more day of life. Tomorrow, his place, and
he told me where he lived. But make it afternoon, give him
time to sleep, okay?

Sure. I could wait. I'd been hoping for it anyway, a
chance to sit him down with a tape recorder, and a list of
more incisive questions than I was able to come up with on
the spot.

When I rejoined Joyce and the limo, to return at last to
my hotel, I rode the rest of the way in the back.

That afternoon I took a cab to Tim's west Hollywood
apartment. Someone other than Joyce doing the driving
felt odd. We had dissolved our impromptu partnership for
good last night, as I left her sitting behind her wheel in
bewilderment over just what I had found inside Nine-One-
One. She wanted to know, I honestly believe she did. But I
couldn't tell her, and she could never ask.

Tim lived in the dingy squalor of some fifth-floor walkup.
In this building's halls it was always dusk. I stood knocking
at his door and got no answer. No sound from within, either, at least nothing to carry over the building's ambi-
ence. The crying babies and blaring TV's and radios and
domestic turmoil leaking from other lives, behind other
doors.

His door was unlocked. I needed no more invitation.

It was hot inside, with a subtle stuffy reek of aged laundry and sheets too long without changing. And beneath it,
worse, the stink of emptied bowels. I knew Tim was dead
even before I saw him stretched diagonal across his iron-
frame bed. The loose tourniquet still around his bicep and
the spike still in that battered vein. On a rickety bedside
table sat a spoon with the impromptu cotton filter balled
up, and a candle had burned into a stub.

Oddly enough, he didn't look much more dead now than
he had when he was still upright at the club.

And in a strange way, I think I actually felt a measure of
relief.

The gentle footsteps came from off to my right, and the
guy walked evenly out from what I presumed was the bath-

room. Startled, oh yes I was, but I don't think I was afraid at first because of how utterly benign the man looked. A simple slacks, shirt, and tie combo, of obvious label quality. Neat sandy hair, thinning at the temples, and his face had that taut smoothness of one or two trips under the knife for cosmetic tucks.

He stopped a few feet before me and we stared, and there was no doubt but that he was in charge. And if I tried to run, well, so much for me. His eyes were that cold and hard.

"In some South American rain forest rivers," he said, "there lives a tiny little fish. And the Indians know better than to piss in the river, because those fish can home in on a stream of urine, and they're so powerful and fast, *they can swim up the stream of urine.*" He looked quite delighted to be sharing this with me. "The fish lodges inside the urinary tract, with these barbs. It's supposed to be quite excruciating. The fish can only be removed by surgery."

He looked at me a long time, measuring me up. The longer he stared, the more I felt myself dwindling. At last he nodded sadly.

"You have been pissing in the wrong river." He spread his hands and fingers wide, it's showtime. "And here I am."

"How about—" My voice was trembling a bit and I didn't like that at all. "—I zip right up and go back where I came from."

He appeared to consider this at great length. Cracking his knuckles, and I saw just how truly strong his hands looked. With long fingers, all bone and sinew, and I didn't want to see this man with his shirt off.

"Your name is Michael Lancer, you live in Delray Beach, Florida, and you've worked for a supermarket rag called *The Vanguard* since April of 1983. You have no savings account, no CD's, no money markets or mutual funds, only a checking account with the First National Bank of Miami, and as of ninety minutes ago, it had a balance of four hundred sixteen dollars and eighty-one cents. Have I . . . made my point?"

I nodded. Whoever had sent this guy up five floors to silence my one and only witness had long arms indeed.

He walked closer and laid one firm hand on my shoulder, and while I wouldn't give him the satisfaction of shaking, I still felt about ten years old in his presence. He steered me to a chair and sat me down, facing a window and Hollywood by day. He stood behind me with a hand on either shoulder and I wondered if it would be a bullet in the back of the head or a quick snapped neck. And why I couldn't muster up enough courage to at least go down fighting.

"This is a huge city, Mr. Lancer. But if you ask enough questions to enough people about the wrong subject . . . you still attract the kind of attention you'd rather not have. But that's all right. That's why troubleshooters are paid so well. Your bank balance? Why, I've made that much just standing here talking to you."

The pressure on my shoulders grew stronger as he kneaded the bunched muscles for a moment.

"I'm not going to kill you," he finally said. "Because I know why you're here, and so do your editors, I'm sure, and if you were to turn up dead, even if it looked like an accident, well, the way you people work and think, it would only validate your reason for being here . . .

"So what you're going to do is, you're going to fly home and say nothing of me, nothing of Tiny Tim over there, nor will you write a word about us. Because I'll be buying your piece of shit tabloid from now on, every week, and if I see anything I don't like, anything at all that hits too close to home as I see it . . . then someday, someone's going to walk into your apartment and they'll find that I've been there. And that your heart is missing."

I think it lost a beat or two hearing that one.

"So you be the judge, Michael Lancer. You decide whether it's worth it or not."

The grip on my shoulders suddenly eased off, and I heard footsteps pacing away from me, and in no way would I turn around to check on this cultured apparition. I sat facing the window, eyes shut, hearing auto horns drifting up five floors, hands rigid as they clenched the edge of the chair beneath my thighs. I think he stopped somewhere near the door.

"There are planes leaving for Miami all the time. Find one of them by tonight. And in the meantime . . . if you don't have anything to do . . . go see a movie."

Gone.

It was a long time before I could move. Some crusader for the sordid truth I made, no? Sitting there on the verge of losing sphincter control, keeping company with a corpse who already had. Top of the world, Ma.

And when I finally readied to leave, I thought I could at least call in an anonymous tip. Somebody please run by and clean up this dead junkie. He wasn't much, but he doesn't deserve to lie around in his own wastes. I found a scrappy little towel and used it to lift the phone receiver. And put it down.

Disconnected.

Once upon a time, years ago, director John Landis, who was at the helm of *Animal House*, the only profitable, hit movie that John Belushi was ever in, had an argument with Belushi's manager. Get him off the drugs, Landis argued. "You can't make money off a corpse."

I figure that one should be carved on the tombstone.

That's what it's really all about out there: the bottom line. Black ink versus red.

In flight between L.A. and Miami, I had plenty of time to put things together to my own satisfaction. To contemplate those calming drinks on my drop-down tray. No George Dickel on the flight, but I made do just fine.

Kingpin? Moon Over Miami? I'd been looking too far afield for motives to kill the man. The best one was right there in his own celluloid world.

John Belushi was the wrong guy in the wrong place in the wrong time, with limitless access to all the wrong chemicals. But he made us laugh for all the right reasons. He was a man who didn't know how to compromise, and who could absolutely not be controlled. By anyone. The same quality that made him such a brilliant comedian was

the same thing that made him such a terror to work with
at times.

So what happens, I had to wonder, when you have a guy
like that, out of control on a personal level? Whose movies
are declining in quality because of poor judgment, whatever, and who can not be brought up short on a leash?

How do the power brokers react, the *real* players, the
financiers and comptrollers who handle the purse? They
who pay closest attention to that bottom line. When do
they decide that enough is enough, that someone involved
in a project insured against loss in case of noncompletion is
worth more dead than alive?

I think I know, at least in one instance.

Hollywood has never been kind to the renegades in its
midst. Genius requires a singular vision, whereas films are
group effort. There's a long, ugly tradition of that Hollywood system breaking the backs of giant renegade talent.
Erich Von Stroheim, Orson Welles, Frances Farmer, Den-
nis Hopper . . . they found out the hard way. Only four of
many.

I'm sure the methods employed over the years are as
varied as the reasons why. But it all distills down to the
same fundamental: Someone doesn't play the game the
way they're supposed to.

Enough time has passed since John Belushi's death to
notice the difference in his contemporaries. Those with
whom he made razored moments of dangerous comedy,
with an edge, without rules. Live on a studio stage in New
York. But look at them now, those who can still be seen. A
few gems scattered here and there in their careers, but it's
mostly been downhill in terms of quality. From mediocre to
dismally unfunny. But they play the game, take no risks.

It's safe.

Is it any wonder the best work nowadays tends to come
from unknowns, working in independent corners, or other
countries, with budgets the size of a simple Hollywood ca-
tering bill?

Maybe it's just as well. In the long run, I don't think
anybody really wins the game out there. You either lose

money, or your soul. Maybe your life is the cheapest of all, in a town where everything's for sale.

Shit. What was I going to give Janice back at Taco Hell in return for her expectations and cash allocation? Because she would most definitely demand a return on her investment. I felt sure I could whip up a rough outline before touchdown in Miami. It's a long flight, and I tend to work well under pressure.

So. The *Kingpin* angle or the *Moon Over Miami* angle, which was it going to be? Either one would be just as fictitious.

And, so far as I was concerned, safe.

Once upon a time, I used to think I had ideals. That I would never allow *myself* to get caught up in playing those games where all I was was a spinning cog in some larger machine. I used to think I knew how to avoid a life like that.

But noooooo.

NON-SKID JACKS:*
THE D.C.–SAIGON CONNECTION
by Rex Miller

Why did the United States become so deeply involved in the civil war in South Vietnam? Why was it so difficult for us to disengage? Read on.

**ULTRA TOP SECRET SENSITIVE
YOUR EYES ONLY**

Summary of the President's decisions regarding U.S. troop deployment, 1 April:

Subject to modifications, coordination, and direction both in country and in Washington, the President approved the March Covert Action Memorandum.

The President approved the urgent exploration of the specific suggestions for covert and other actions submitted by Clandestine Services under date of 1 March.

The President approved the program of military actions submitted and reemphasized his desire that this program be accelerated.

The President approved a twenty-five-thousand-man increase in U.S. military support forces to fill existing units and logistic personnel needs.

The President approved the urgent exploration of the rapid deployment of significant combat elements from

* *National Security Council Directive / Joint Chiefs of Staff Summary*

those forces so stipulated in the March 6 Memorandum of
Presidential Recommendations by the Joint Chiefs.

Subject to ongoing monitor and review, the President approved the ascending of action against Vietnam and Laos.

The President desires that with respect to these actions,
premature publicity be avoided by all precautionary mea-
sures. Recommended actions should be taken in a manner
consistent with existing action frameworks, and every possible effort should be made to minimize any appearance
that might suggest sudden changes in official policy.

I CTZ/Quang Tin/Chu Lai Taor/Northern Sector:
"COME ON, LADIES," Gunny screams over the noise,
"LET'S GET HER DONE NOW." Black Huey slicks, un-
marked. Blackbirds from the armed chopper company, cobra gunships, joining them for escort, and the air is a madness of turbine and rotor noise.

The fireteams comprising the strike force element of Operation Green River climb aboard their baking bubbles of
high tech transport.

USMACV. The Army. Navy. The Crotch. The Air Force.
The intelligence community. Even the private sector is represented in this weird lash-up. Every unit, group, or agency
involved with the prosecution of the war effort seems to
have a dirty thumb in this pie. Elite special forces people.
Mercs. Headhunters. SEALs. A combined-forces/JCS op
run out of the big spook complex on Magic Mountain.

A controller spits radio talk into the pilot's headset in a
sawblade screech of metal whine. Whirl. Roar. The lead
ship is aloft, a covey of blackbirds is airborne now, airmo-
bile, that is, and in the jaws of a running mission.

The early sun comes up shooting pieces of itself into the
South China Sea, into waterways and rice paddies, into the
wetness that is everywhere below, breaking into fragments
of tracer green and blood red, earthtone burnt sienna and
glittering Buddha-head gold. The colors of light on water
reflect like the spill of coins at altitude, washing the varie-
gated green hues with illum white, fire blue, and shrapnel
silver. The fireteams lock and load.

Washington, District of Columbia
U.S.A.

In a sound-swept room many thousands of miles from the Republic of Vietnam, a small war-torn S of hardscrabble along the curved coastline of Southeast Asia, a man of fame and fortune reads aloud from one of his own memoranda, which are tedious, winding affairs that have made him the target of a few wonderfully wicked upper-crust impressions.

But these impressions are performed in secret, by lesser luminaries in the pol stratosphere. He is a serious man, who speaks often of such things as "internal security," "oppositionists," "casualty numbers," and other subject matter of a decidedly grim nature.

"—see those kinds of remedial changes. Point four deals with morale. Morale generated within his own bureaucracy and the military clique in general is poor. If the V.C. could pull off a substantive operation against him, or if another coup would eventuate, or—" A gray haze of words fills the room like smoke.

As he speaks a stretch limo glides through the hysterical D.C. traffic. In the rear seat, momentarily separated from his chauffeur by a double thickness of shatterproof privacy glass, the man whose Secret Service designation is "Eagle" adjusts a crease in the crossed leg of his meticulously tailored Savile Row blue pinstripe and removes a yellow notepad from the open case beside him. He begins to make notes. Forming the text of the message that he will soon impart to the President of the United States of America.

"—he could be removed or terminated in place, whether by coup, political process benign or malevolent, death by natural or prejudicial causes, said removal being—"

A man from Clandestine Services follows his guide down a long expanse of lush carpet, his burnished oxfords leaving indentations like a blood trail. He carries a cumbersome, extra-large leather briefcase of the kind favored by artists, advertising agency personnel, and others who show-and-tell. It is an ungainly, zippered affair full of

charts, graphs, overlays, and the visuals of his traveling
dog-and-pony side show.

"—polarization of the GVN leadership. It is my view
that the overriding concerns are those of national unity,
stability, the ongoing campaign, and the preservation of
some semblance of cohesion—" Hot air rises.

"Camel with Charcoal coming topside," a hidden
watcher intones into Secret Service earpieces. The man
from Clandestine Services feels tiny beads of perspiration
on his freshly barbered temples.

"Camel" and "Charcoal" enter a small elevator, and the
man acting as escort jabs one of the three buttons with a
manicured finger. Being a professional observer, the Clandestine Services man takes note of the manicure, the sauna
skin, and the subtle but visible lifts. The elevator stops.
They get out in a beautifully appointed waiting area. They
wait.

Within moments another famous face appears in the
doorway and smiles, whispering in a down-home drawl

"Ahm gonna take ya in. He's got some people, but jes
have a seat and he'll get around to ya directly." The man
beams his celebrated smile and about fifteen thousand dollars worth of Georgetown orthodontia sparkle and vanish.
The man with the big presentation case is guided into an
imposing sanctum sanctorum with one hand on his left
arm and another around his shoulder. The manipulator's
half nelson, a further variation on the Washington two-
hander.

"—if they exploit what they perceive to be the contradic-
tions within our internal situation—" He carefully rests
the big case, which he has come to hate, beside the chair to
which he has been gently but firmly guided. No one has
recognized his presence in the room in any way. "—they'll
be able to generate insurmountable difficulties using the
bloc to escalate the war. Exact language being—" the man
of fame and fortune pushes his bifocals back, glancing
down at an open dossier, "—difficulties in using the aggres-
sive force of the Southeast Asian bloc." The man does not
appear to be addressing the room so much as he is speaking

in the direction of a door that stands ajar on the other side of the conference room, from which a liquid splashing noise can distinctly be heard.

"And the Lao Dong Party Central Committee—" the man from Clandestine Services, code-named "Charcoal" in Secret Service lexicon, tunes completely out for a moment, unwilling to let himself understand the ludicrousness of his situation.

"Diplomatic strategy"—he hears.

"Heavily concentrated efforts within those areas. It's the same tired containment strategy—" Charcoal blots his sweaty temples which are chilling in the freezing room. It dawns on him that he . . . is . . . "with respect to Pacification"—listening—"and Vietnamization" to something quite incredible. His mind works to grasp it.

"It's going to be viewed—"

Yes. There is no doubt about it.

"—as a political disaster."

They are listening to someone urinating.

"If this concentration-camp philosophy of his—"

They are listening to the President urinating. There is something so irrational and crazy about it, he rebels at the thought. Embarrassed for the woman he now realizes is seated to his left he can feel redness suffuse his face as he glances at her, but she is oblivious to the peeing and seems enraptured by the speaker, "—into a free fire zone geographically."

The thing drones on. More pontificating about the land reform program as the door is finally pushed all the way open and the jowly, wrinkled face of The Man with its all-too-familiar hang-dog expression fills the doorway as he glances back over his shoulder to see who is in the room. He appears to be wearing about $675 of his $900 wardrobe, the remaining $225 worth of sartorial perfection being down around his ankles as he stands peeing into a porcelain commode, the audience taking note of him from the orchestrated positions around the table.

"—linear regression of tables of probability—" Charcoal just catches with the edge of his mind, fighting back a burst of nervous laughter. The splashing noise has stopped and now the stern-looking man at the end of the table is speaking.

"Well, the gov'ment just isn't that much of an obvious improvement over the Diem Nhu regime, but you know the old line about he's a son of a bitch but he's our son of a bitch and that's applicable here. Viet Cong support from the north only seems to be increasing," The Man is washing his hands from the sound of it, "and the concept of curtailing the supply lines is covered in the JCS paper, but the bottom line is there is just too much coastline involved, too many waterways, too much area to seal off. The trail strategy is clearly not going to hold water as we've discussed, but for security purposes we should retain that posture in any speeches, news releases, or interviews." Charcoal wonders if he really heard him say "hold water."

"As I've told the President privately, I think that the kinds of ideas we've been coming up with to sabotage the supply lines from the north are grossly inadequate to the situation." The man with the slicked-back hair turns a page of his notes as The Man comes into the room and walks toward a silver coffeepot that sits on a table against the wall. "The instability of the new gov'ment under the PRC is highly sensitive. Policy differences are already causing some serious fissures, and other conflict-of-interest developments have arisen to help bring about what appears to be a total lack of substantive morale and a climate that could be quite detrimental to our existing programs."

"May I say something here, Bobby?" The man with the expensive smile interrupts.

"Certainly."

"I think one of the bigges' areas we need to discuss is this basic strategic thing. Ya' know organizationally I believe that it ties right in to what you've been sayin'. Because what I think we must do, and I see this as absolutely vital, is to become maneuverable and organizationally conscious instead of so tactical and static.

"Now I know there is a widespread area of controversy here, especially among our military brethren, but we are clearly not fightin' that kind of a war nor is our military mindset in that camp. This whole thing of behavin' in a reactional mode, observin' the enemy and analyzin' his weaknesses, and pittin' your strongest point against his most vulnerable, is just completely negated by this attritional mindset."

"Yeah, I agree as you well know. Let's get into this in depth after a while. We have the gentleman from Clandestine Services with us today for a special briefing the Plans people have put together against the black communications centers." The hard eyes turn toward him. *Christ,* he thinks, *that's me.* Charcoal unzips his ungainly case, hoping that it doesn't sound like the zipper on his pants, but before he can get so much as a thank-you out he hears that voice say from across the room,

"Ah hope this isn't gonna' be another of them goddamn hair-brained schemes to put mah pecker back in the wringer again." Charcoal looks up nervously, but the famous countenance is smiling benignly. Charcoal, who has never seen the man with the most famous initials in the world up this close before, is electrified by his overpowering presence. Magnetism and all the other clichés come to mind. The Man picks up the thick leather-bound, gold-stamped book in front of him as he speaks in his rich Texas accent,

"Ya know," he sighs tiredly, "ah ask for a report on the status quo and this is typical." He waves the dossier in the air. "Listen to this. We uh gonna' build a fence . . . all . . . across the fucking . . . Ho . . . Chi . . . Minh . . . *TRAIL,*" he levels eyes like lasers at Charcoal, "outta' *BOB*-wahr, and mines, and cover . . . one . . . hunnert . . . kilometers. . . . with about 47 trillion seismic and accoustic sensor devices shaped like . . ." he glances at a page, "little bam*BOO* shoots . . . *CAMOUFLAGED,* you understand. . . . This is gonna' cost the taxpayers of this great Democratic Republic somewhere in the neighborhood of—oh, less' call it two billion dollahs?"

"Ridiculous!" explodes the man with the slicked-back hair.

Charcoal feels his own head nodding in the affirmative, as if it had a life of its own, scowling at the thought. Telling The Man *he'd* never come up with any goddamned harebrained scheme like that. No, sir!

"Would you want to hazard a guess as to who gets the inordinate pleasure of sellin' a piece of crap like this to my esteemed colleagues over on the Hill and our worthy adversaries in the media?" He smiles paternally. He drops the bound book and turns to a hundred-twenty-dollar potted dracena.

Charcoal is center stage.

"Mister President," he says, "gentlemen, ma'am," he nods stupidly, "the radio operations are primarily across-the-fence jobs. The primary targets are the one in the Zone, one about a hundred miles north and one in Laos. There are two island-based transmitters and a base relay station.

"The plan, OPERATION GREEN RIVER, is a tripodal attack of covert paramilitary units to liaise through MACV under totally sanitized cover. These star-rated XP's will be independently contracted outside the company, utilizing professional mercenaries, and commando/PT crews for the island ops. The big three targets are the relay near the de-milled zone, the DRVN op on Hon Ngu across the fence, and the radar station on Hon Me. The plan—"

A double-stretch Lincoln, fourteen hand-rubbed coats of Obsidian Diamond Eggshell shining with the approximate luster of an angel's halo, purrs to a stop and its distinguished passenger emerges with his bodyguard. Although he has never so much as held a public office for one day, he is the single most powerful man in American government.

The briefing upstairs is being held in Eagle's conference room, and is taking place at Eagle's suggestion to our C.E.O. Eagle knows, as always, precisely how the briefing will go. That is why *he* is Eagle, and not someone else. He diffuses prescience.

"Central," a voice squawks. "Eagle and Serpent headed topside." Eagle is The Man behind The Man. Bearing—

upper class. Aura—velvet over tempered steel; a mace sheathed in noblesse oblige and sprinkled with Chanel. A paragon of suavity in a toadstool world.

His is the greater vision for the global good. His picture is the big picture. Aspiring to the finest precepts of public conduct, maintaining as he does that man's highest achievements are those that enoble the human spirit, his outward image is a careful sculpture. He presents himself as a scintillant fountainhead of probity, wisdom, conservatism, restraint, and great wit.

Privately? Ah. He is something else again. The powers that be reside, you see, therein. Eagle is our secret monarch.

He speaks the language of Executive Mandarin, a practiced elliptical obliquity of verbiage hardened in the lofty echelons of the military, private, and public service sectors, where a certain mannered ambivalence of spoken/written word is now as admired as grace under pressure once was.

Serpent and Eagle have reached the conference room access area. He opens the door and softly speaks the President's first name and The Man pushes himself away from the table, standing heavily as he tells the charcoal suiter from Clandestine Services

"Okay. Let's do it. But I don't want to see or hear another word about it."

"Right. Yes, sir."

"Complete deniability," he emphasizes as he walks out of the room.

There is no greeting. The President leans close, his massive left ear close to Eagle's mouth. There is a brief whispered message, a horrible combination of sentences which end with the words "—the same generals you made your deal with. The top guns. National Minister of Defense, Vice Chairman of the AFC,"—he ticks them off on his fingers.

"The Saigon black market boys," the President says. "In other words."

"You should be so lucky. This is the economic tie between the generals and the ones who financed the coup. The thing in there—" he tilts his handsome head slightly in the direction of the conference room, "—that's their common link to the general staff's private heroin export franchise. That's their *rice bowl* you just ordered destroyed." He smiles without a trace of good humor. "You can't do it. It's central to our understanding with the big man."

"Then why in *hell* did you let me put it in motion?"

"You know you always do better when you don't have to act—you've told me that how many times? I want it remembered that you did precisely what you did in there. You sent a penetration mission in. If it gets into trouble—that's not *our* dilemma, is it? Whatever happens, I would say the office of the President is insulated, wouldn't you?"

The President, who does not know a dangling participle from a glottal stop, knows the nuances of manipulation as few men do, and the reaffirmation of his own speech patterns and inflections is a subtlety that does not go unnoticed.

"So y'all gonna finesse this thing then," he says, and it is not a question.

And it does not receive a spoken answer.

I CTZ / L Z Blacktop:
"Dragon Two to King Six."

"King Six. Wait One."

"DRAGON TWO TO KING SIX, WE'RE TAKING FIRE OVER THE EL ZEE! WE'RE TA-" the voice explodes in a crackle of intercom static.

"—arty, goddamnit, you're short! YOU'RE FIRING SHORT! CORRECT YOUR GODDAMN FIRE KING SIX (STATIC) "YOU'RE RIGHT ON TOP OF—"

"Transmission breaking up, Dragon Two. Repeat your message, over."

"YOU'RE FIRING ON TOP OF US YOU SON OF A—"
(STATIC.)

Classification: Ultra Top Secret
THIS DOCUMENT IS NOT TO BE
COPIED IN ANY FORM OR RE-

MOVED FROM THIS FACILITY
WITHOUT EXPRESS WRITTEN
PERMISSION OF THE UNDER-
SIGNED.

From: Brigade G-2
To: CommUSMACV/(1)

Pursuant to NON-SKID JACKS five APC s (2/4), a platoon of five M-48 tanks from the 1st Armored Cav, and two
M-67 flame tanks attached to 1/3 were deployed as an anti-
tank strike force mounted against VC/NVA regs and armored support elements massing in the vicinity of LZ
Blacktop. Significant to these deployments was the presidential decision to lift the restriction on the Army and
Marine infantry battalions operating in the northern sector of the Chu Lai TAOR, in Quang Tin Province, in I Corps
Tactical Zone, and permit troops to engage in counterin-
surgency operations.

A strike mission had also been undertaken from
Firebase King, involving a force of "Cobra" gunships and
"Huey slicks," which had been assigned to lift a covert action troop unit from the vicinity of FBK, and CA to a clandestine target approximately twenty-two klicks due North
of the firebase. This mission was flown in support of a penetration search and Combat Assault code-named OPERA-
TION GREEN RIVER.

Led by Lieutenant Colonel Trask, the helicopters encountered massive antiaircraft fire in the target area, forc-
ing them to divert. The ships which were "sheep-dipped" of
insignia and observing radio silence, attempted to land in
the vicinity of LZ Blacktop, where they were destroyed by
friendly fire from the armored elements who believed them
to be the spearhead of an enemy assault force.

Given the hazards of such operations, perhaps it is impossible to completely avoid tragedies of this scope, but a
more complete and horrible "snafu" cannot be conceived.
The terrible climax of this operation, from which no covert
action troops survived, will surely remain a textbook case

of the sort of catastrophe that can result from "one hand not knowing what the other is doing," as one observer remarked.

Classification: ULTRA TOP SECRET

THE WINTER MEN
by Brian Harper

*Do you remember those two guys who ruled the Soviet
Union for a short time before Gorby? Here's why their
time in office was so short.*

Dr. Viktor Shatrov sat at the wheel of his idling Lada
sedan, watching the motorcade speed east along Kalinina
Prospekt in the chill mist of a February morning. He permitted himself a tired smile as he noticed the pedestrians
and other drivers gawking at the line of motorcycles,
Chaika security cars, and black armor-plated ZIL limousines.

He knew what they were thinking. The motorcade was
headed for the Kremlin. Inside one of those limousines—
that one there, probably, the one with the curtains drawn
behind its green-tinted windows—must be a member of the
Politburo. Perhaps the General Secretary of the Party himself.

Shatrov watched the procession disappear into the gray
drizzle. Once traffic started moving again, he turned onto
Kalinina. He drove west, away from the Kremlin, out of
Moscow.

His fellow citizens were wrong, of course. The motorcade
was merely a ruse, a charade. None of the limousines carried passengers. The General Secretary was not on his way
to the Kremlin. He had not passed through the Kremlin's
gates for over six months.

And, Shatrov thought as his grip on the steering wheel tightened, he will never pass through those gates again.

He reached Kutuzovsky Prospekt and bore left. A few minutes later, his sluggish, rattling car reached Kuntsevo, Moscow's most exclusive suburb. He turned down a side street and pulled up before the entrance to a walled and gated compound. The guards confirmed his identity and let him in.

The road led through a park, past a dead brown lawn and rows of skeletal, leafless trees huddled under a leaden sky. Shatrov thought of winter, of cold, of death. He thought of the warm spring sunlight that seemed so very far away.

Sudden tears blurred his vision. He was dabbing at his eyes with a handkerchief as he parked outside Kuntsevo Hospital.

The building was big and grim and old. Stalin had died here. Now it was time for another tyrant to join him.

If Shatrov had the nerve.

And he did. He had to. There was not much more time. His patient was rapidly improving. Before long the old man would leave the hospital and return to his office in the Kremlin. Then the opportunity would be lost.

Shatrov tried to draw a deep breath, couldn't. He needed courage. From his pants pocket he removed a well-worn photograph. He studied it for a long moment, then pocketed it once more.

Calm again, or nearly so, he got out of the car. He walked toward the hospital's front door, carrying his medical bag and trailing plumes of frosted breath.

Two more security officers checked his ID, examined the contents of the bag, and frisked him thoroughly. Shatrov endured the procedure in silence. One would think he had never visited the hospital before, when in fact he had been working the day shift, from nine in the morning to nine at night, since last August.

Finally the guards were satisfied. The door swung open, then banged shut behind him. He thought of the closing of a coffin lid.

Stop it, he ordered.

He was not afraid, not really. Soon he would die, yes; but what did that matter? He had no desire to go on living. His life, all fifty-two years of it, had given him little joy. The world he knew was a sad gray place run by gray men with souls as clammy and chill as the Moscow winter. Men like vampires, who leeched on the living while dead inside. Shatrov knew all about those men; he had been forced to serve them all his life, trapped in the prison they had made, with no hope of escape. Despair had broken him, as it had broken so many others. He had retreated from the world, hiding inside himself, living alone, seldom socializing, performing the motions of his job like an automaton, until he was no more alive than his soulless masters.

Shatrov sighed. Perhaps, he thought, it was best that way. If he had lived differently, he might not enjoy the peculiar freedom that was now his. Because he *was* free; of course he was—the freest man in the U.S.S.R. He had no wife, no children, no close friends or relatives; his parents were long dead, buried in a windswept, untended graveyard in the North Caucasus. He had forged no ties to anyone still alive. He could do as he pleased, asking no one but himself to suffer the consequences.

The hospital smelled of disinfectant and echoed with distant footsteps. Shatrov hurried through a maze of corridors and stairways, stopping twice at security checkpoints, and at last reached an upper-story ward.

Two more KGB officers were seated in an anteroom near the nurses' station. One of the men was trying to impress a nurse by telling stories of his service in the border patrol; she listened in feigned indifference, making occasional derisory remarks that only prompted a new anecdote. This little drama had been going on for weeks. Shatrov thought it was too bad the KGB man had not proceeded a little faster in his courtship. He would surely be reassigned—or imprisoned—after today.

The two dark-suited agents rose as Shatrov entered. The ritual of the search was repeated. One man frisked Shatrov, while the other rummaged through his medical bag. Then both nodded, and Shatrov was free to proceed.

Beyond the anteroom was a small, dingy, overheated office. Dr. Kondakov sat at a battered desk, drinking the strong tea he favored and rubbing his bleary eyes.

"Good morning, Misha," Shatrov said briskly. He shrugged off his fur-collared jacket, hung it on a rack, and slipped into his white lab coat. "God, you look tired."

"These twelve-hour shifts are killing me," Kondakov muttered. "They work us like dogs. Although, of course," he added hastily, "no one could object to hard work in the service of the General Secretary's health." He directed his voice at a large light fixture, which had always seemed a likely location for an eavesdropping device.

"Of course not," Shatrov agreed with a smile. "And what exactly is the state of our patient's health today?"

"He continues to show marked improvement. His strength is clearly returning. Earlier this morning he was ambulated nearly the length of the hallway and managed the trip without undue exertion. The cardiograph displays a steady pattern, with no arrhythmia; the cardiotonics are working. He still refuses Demerol—he insists he must stay alert—and I'm afraid his pain is worse than he admits. The echocardiogram showed a great deal of infarcted tissue, as you know. But considering his condition only three weeks ago, I must say I feel pleased with his prognosis."

"It's all very good news."

"Yes. Obviously. Barring a relapse or other unforeseen developments, the General Secretary should be making public appearances by spring."

"Or even before then," Shatrov said. "I predict you will see him on the dais of the Hall of Columns very soon." In an open casket, he added silently.

Kondakov nodded, looking at the light fixture with a frozen grin. "You may well be right. Our President's powers of recovery are indeed extraordinary."

"As befits an extraordinary man."

"Precisely. Precisely."

Shatrov clapped his hands. "Everything sounds most en-

couraging. Now I believe I'll check on the patient myself.
And as for you, Misha—why don't you go home and get a
good eight hours' sleep?"

"I'll try, Viktor Ivanovich. It is reassuring to know I'm
leaving our beloved General Secretary in your care."

Kondakov bustled out of the office, waving gaily to the
KGB guards. Shatrov stared after him. He could not de-
spise the man. Kondakov had a pretty wife with a taste for
foreign merchandise, the kind that could be obtained only
on the black market at a gigantic markup. He had a son
who had recently applied for admission to a top university.
He could afford no stain on his reputation. Unlike Shatrov,
he had something to lose.

While I have already lost the one thing that mattered, he
thought.

Spring bloomed in his mind again, blue skies crowning
the onion-top domes of the Kremlin's churches, a pleasant
breeze skimming the placid waters of the Moskva River. In
the assembly hall of the Metropole Hotel, the vast, glittering room where Lenin had spoken many times, a conference was in progress. Experts on the treatment of cardiac
disorders had gathered from around the world to share
their knowledge and celebrate the new spirit of détente.

He supposed it was a cliché to have seen her across a
crowded room, but he had. Even today he did not know if
she was beautiful. But there was something in her bearing,
in the way she moved and stood and tilted her head as she
listened—a quality of simply being alive, so rare and miraculous in this drab country—alive and vital and free.

He still had no idea how he had found the courage to
introduce himself. It was the one brave act of his life, before today.

"Hello, I am Viktor Shatrov of U.S.S.R. I apologize for
my English which is very terrible."

"Oh, it's not so very terrible, Dr. Shatrov."

"Viktor. Please. And you are . . . ?"

"Elizabeth Holland. U.S.A."

"Yes"—eagerly—"I knew you were U.S.A."

"You read my name tag."

"No, even from a distance I knew. Women in America, they are different, they are—how do I say this? They are at home in their own bodies." Frustration at the inadequate words competed with embarrassment at what she must be thinking. Helplessly he shrugged, feeling heat in his face. "This is not making any senses, I know."

"At home in my body." She looked thoughtful, her eyes half shut. "I hadn't thought of it that way."

Hesitantly: "Have I insulted you?"

"No, Dr. Sha—Viktor. Not at all." She gifted him with a smile. "Just the opposite, in fact. You've charmed me."

"Truly?" He took a breath, then rushed the words out. "I would like to charm you again."

Silvery laughter. "You may get the opportunity. After all, we are here to learn about the human heart. Aren't we?"

Shatrov smiled at the memory, the conversation so often replayed in his thoughts. With an effort he shook free of his reminiscence. He had a job to do.

He moved to the rear of the office, where he could not be seen from the anteroom. Quickly now. He opened a drawer filled with supplies and took out a glass syringe. Elizabeth had told him that Western doctors used plastic disposables, but he found it hard to believe that story. No society could be so obscenely productive as to make possible such extravagant waste.

Carefully he removed the hypodermic's plastic sheath, then found an empty vial in the supply cabinet and uncapped it. Next he pulled the stethoscope out of his medical bag. He studied the two rubber tubes that connected the binauruls with the diaphragm. The tubes were hollow and normally quite lightweight; today they were slightly heavier than usual. But none of the KGB thugs had noticed that.

Shatrov twisted the binauruls free of the tubes, then poured the contents of the tubes into the vial. Clear liquid climbed up the scale markings.

He filled the syringe from the vial. Put the syringe in the pocket of his lab coat. Stuck the vial at the back of the supply cabinet, where it would not be noticed. Repaired the stethoscope and returned it to his bag.

So far, so good.

He dug the photograph out of his pants pocket again. For the last time he looked at it. In the photo Elizabeth was smiling, her head thrown back, face lifted to the May sun, silver-streaked hair falling around her shoulders like tumbled smoke.

She had smiled often when she was with him. He remembered their first dinner together at the best restaurant he knew. They dined on Siberian whitefish and toasted each other in the dancing candlelight. Afterward he took her to his apartment, feeling mildly ashamed of its shabbiness. Their lovemaking was alternately passionate and tender, her energy intoxicating, like a drug.

In the morning, when they returned to the conference, he noticed two men following them. KGB. Perhaps his affair with a foreigner would put a black mark against his name in a file somewhere. He didn't care.

For four days they spent every free moment together. They took a river-boat ride on the Moskva, shared a dish of ice cream in Hermitage Park, wandered among the paintings and sculptures in the Tretyakov Art Gallery. They explored the city by day, and at night they explored each other's bodies with the same enthusiasm.

To Shatrov, their affair was an entrance into another world, a world that was not gray and narrow and hopeless, a world where people casually crossed borders and debated ideas and did bold, outrageous, shocking things without fear of punishment. He did not know if he loved Elizabeth or only what she represented to him, or if he could draw a distinction between the two.

He was alive. He knew that much. For four days of his life, he was alive.

And then she was gone. He saw her off at Sheremetyevo Airport. Intourist did not permit him to accompany her to the gate. At the last security checkpoint Elizabeth kissed him—dampness glittered at the corners of her eyes—and whispered, *"Do svidahniya."* Then she was hurrying through the crowd, turning once to wave, then vanishing among the anonymous travelers.

He had loitered outside the airport, watching the Aeroflot jets take off and wondering which was hers, until a uniformed man ordered him to move on.

The return to his ordinary life, the dreary routine of his days, suffocated him. Often he felt he literally could not breathe.

For a while he wrote to her, and she returned his letters, but her replies were brief and soon stopped altogether. The affair had not meant much to her, he supposed. It had been a fling, an adventure, nothing more. From what she had told him, he gathered that she attended many medical conferences in many parts of the world. Perhaps she had enjoyed numerous liaisons. Oddly, he almost hoped so; he wanted her to be alive, to enjoy her freedom, to pursue pleasure without the constraints that bound him.

He had kept her few letters for years. Last night he had burned them. Now only the photograph was left.

She had mailed it to him after getting the film developed in the U.S. The snapshot was one he had taken, using her camera, on the final day of the conference, their final afternoon together.

In the ten years since he'd last seen her, he had studied that photograph many times. On lonely nights he had held whispered conversations with it. At bedtime, alone in his dusty apartment, he would kiss it, imagining that he tasted her mouth against his. Then he would slip the photo under his pillow before switching off the light.

He followed her career as best he could. Occasional references were made to her in the American medical journals he received. She was often noted to have spoken at an international conference in one foreign capital or another. Her last appearance had been scheduled for a meeting in Seoul last September.

Shatrov shook his head slowly. He supposed a man like the General Secretary would find his little story of unrequited love quite amusing and pitiable. And perhaps it was. Yet his affair with Elizabeth Holland had been the one sweet thing in his life, the single bright spot in the gray procession of his days. So perhaps it was the rest of his life that was to be pitied and scorned.

Smiling sadly, he raised the photograph to his lips one final time.

Do svidahniya, Elizabeth.

Then he placed the picture in the sink, lit a match, and touched the flame to the faded image. He watched as the snapshot curled and blackened. In seconds there was nothing left but ash. He washed it down the drain, then dried his hands.

Now the KGB would find no photos, no letters, no evidence by which they might trace his connection to Elizabeth or grasp the motive of his act. He did not think they would dare to carry out revenge against her family in the United States, but anything was possible.

One last preparation had yet to be made. Shatrov removed his left shoe and shook it gently, dislodging the small white capsule in the toe. He picked a piece of lint off the capsule, then placed it carefully in his mouth, wedging it behind a wisdom tooth, above the gumline.

Picking up his medical bag, his heart beating fast, he left the office. Swiftly he walked down the hall and turned a corner. At the far end of the intersecting corridor a single KGB man, one of the General Secretary's two personal bodyguards, sat in a straight-backed chair outside a closed door.

The bodyguard stood up as Shatrov approached.

"Good morning, Doctor. Your bag, please."

Once again the bag was submitted for examination. This was routine. The danger lay in what happened next. On most mornings the bodyguard did not bother to frisk Shatrov's person, apparently assuming that this detail had been amply covered in the previous security checks. Occasionally, however, he felt an urge to be thorough.

Shatrov could not permit the syringe to be found in his pocket. There was no possible explanation for it that he could invent. If he were frisked, he would have to grab the hypodermic and use it on the KGB man. Then burst into the room—swing the heavy medical bag like a club, take down the second bodyguard with a blow to the head—strangle or smother the General Secretary before help arrived.

A bad plan, unlikely to succeed. He might dispatch the first bodyguard, but probably not the second. Then he would have to swallow the capsule and die, leaving the General Secretary unharmed, his greatest crime unavenged.

He waited tensely, his heart drumming in his chest, his right hand hovering near the pocket of his lab coat.

Finally the bodyguard gave back the bag. "Very well, Doctor. Let us visit your esteemed patient."

Shatrov kept his face neutral. There would be no frisking today.

The bodyguard opened the door without knocking and ushered Shatrov inside.

As he entered, he was greeted by the sweet strains of Beethoven's *Pathétique* Sonata, rising from a pair of large speakers wired to a Sony cassette player in a corner of the room. The composition was the General Secretary's favorite piece, and he played it often, usually in the mornings.

"Good morning, sir," Shatrov said, smiling.

Yuri Andropov—General Secretary of the Central Committee of the Communist Party of the Soviet Union, Chairman of the Defense Council, and, since June, President of the Presidium of the Supreme Soviet—looked up from the sheaf of documents he was reading. The light from a bedside lamp flashed on the thick lenses of his rimless spectacles.

He grunted an acknowledgment. To say hello in return, to smile, to display a human emotion or even a normal courtesy, would have been beyond him. He was a machine, a computer. A robot programmed to kill. He was the grayest of the gray men, the bloodless essence of his world.

"Dr. Kondakov tells me you're making excellent progress," Shatrov said conversationally as he glanced around the room, noting the locations of the first bodyguard, who had positioned himself near the open door, and the second, who sat in a chair a few feet from the bed. "You walked down the hall, he says."

"I dislike small talk, Shatrov." Andropov had already returned to his reading. "Get on with it."

"Very well, sir."

Shatrov removed the clipboard from its peg behind the door, checked the Intake & Output Record, and scanned the page for any recent notations. A summary of Andropov's medical history was attached to the clipboard, as well, but Shatrov had no need to review it. He knew the General Secretary's history of ill health. He had given much thought to it over the past two weeks, ever since he learned the news.

To look at Yuri Vladimirovich Andropov, one would not think he could survive another day. His skin was ashen, contrasting sharply with the gray hair swept back from his high forehead; his hands trembled uncontrollably as he leafed through the report he was studying. He looked at least ten years older than his true age, sixty-nine.

Wires ran from the electrodes on his chest to a cardiograph machine; the oscilloscope displayed the pattern of his heartbeat in time with a winking red light and a low, steady beeping sound. The cardiograph was linked with a console at the nurses' station, providing continuous monitoring of Andropov's condition from both locations. Near the heart monitor was a closed-circuit television camera, its lens trained on the bed.

IV lines ran from an overhead rack to Andropov's left arm, feeding him potassium and packed cells. A central venous pressure line had been inserted in a vein in his arm and guided into the vena cava, permitting blood-pressure readings from the interior of his heart. In his left nostril there was a nasogastic tube; from his groin ran a Foley catheter. Until recently he had worn an oxygen mask for a good part of each day.

He was an old and very sick man. Why, then, was it necessary to kill him? Why not let nature take its course?

But that question could be asked only by one who did not know what obstacles Andropov had already overcome. Cardiac arrhythmia first diagnosed in 1957. A cardiac arrest in 1966. Two more heart attacks in the decade of the seventies. A pacemaker—American-made, of course—installed in 1978. It was this pacemaker, along with regular trips to a sanatorium in Kislovodsk, that had kept Andropov alive despite recurring weakness and an acute susceptibility to infection. Yet with all his health problems, he had risen steadily, first as ambassador, then as a Secretary of the Central Committee, then as Chairman of the Committee for State Security, the KGB.

In 1980 his body betrayed him again, this time with failing vision. He underwent cataract surgery on both eyes. There were whispers that Andropov, seemingly enfeebled, would be forced to retire. Yet incredibly, he regained his strength, held on to his job, even succeeded in engineering a promotion to a key post on the Central Committee. From there, following Brezhnev's death, he became leader of the Party and the nation.

Then, last March, he suffered a fourth myocardial infarction, followed by a fifth, in August, which put him in this hospital, where he had remained ever since. Finally, only three weeks ago, his heart arrested for the sixth time, bringing on a state of cardiogenic shock that nearly killed him.

But once again he had survived. And, as Kondakov had observed, his strength was rapidly returning. Already he was working, albeit in bed; already he was planning his return to the Kremlin to resume a full schedule of duties; already he was discussing the orchestration of the May Day celebration in which he meant to play an active and highly visible role.

He might very well recover. He had a powerful incentive. All his life he had struggled for power, struggled as viciously as a clawing, snarling animal. Blackmail, extortion, and assassination had been his means of climbing ever higher in the Party. Now at last he had what he wanted. He would not be cheated of his prize. He would not die after only fifteen months in office. To savor the fruits of victory for so brief a time after such a long and joyless harvest would be, to him, unspeakably unfair.

That was why Shatrov concurred in Kondakov's prognosis. Andropov would continue to regain his strength. He would not permit himself to die.

But Shatrov would no longer permit him to live.

The thought made him stiffen. A sudden vivid awareness of what he was about to do—the reality of it, and the frightening finality—struck him like a fist. His stomach clenched. He drew a shallow, nervous breath and told himself not to think about it. The time for thinking was past.

Replacing the clipboard, he walked to the bed and made a show of checking the IV infusions. Then he shook down a thermometer and took Andropov's temperature.

The two bodyguards watched him carefully. He did not think they were suspicious of him. It was their job to scrutinize anyone in close proximity to the General Secretary. To observe and, when necessary, to react.

How fast could they draw their guns and fire? Fast enough to kill him before he had made the lethal injection? Possibly. Then it would all have been for nothing, his death —like his life—a meaningless waste.

Andropov continued reading with the thermometer in his mouth. His hazel eyes, cold and unblinking and reptilian, gazed at the document before him. Beethoven's sonata went on, the sparkling notes somehow obscene in this monster's den. Shatrov wished someone would turn off the music. Suddenly it seemed too loud, painfully loud.

Fear squirmed in his belly. He had not expected to be so afraid. He had thought fear, like joy, had been bled out of him long ago. But perhaps no man could ever be completely reconciled with his own death.

He remembered the thermometer. Quickly he removed it and held it up to the light. His eyes were not working properly, and he had trouble reading the column of mercury.

"Your temperature is normal, sir," he said, hearing a flutter in his voice.

Andropov grunted.

Do it now? Get it over with? Yes—no, not yet. The bodyguards—they could see him too clearly from this angle. He needed to get around to the other side of the bed, where he could remove the syringe from his pocket without immediately giving himself away. That extra fraction of a second might make the difference between success and failure.

How to accomplish the maneuver? Think of something.

"Excuse me, sir," Shatrov heard himself say, "but I must examine your fingernails."

"My fingernails?" Andropov glared at him. "What are you, my manicurist?"

One of the bodyguards emitted a bark of laughter.

Shatrov showed no expression. "I must look for indications of cyanosis. Insufficient oxygenation of the tissues—"

"Yes, yes, all right. Get on with it."

Andropov put down the document and extended his hands. Shatrov bent close, then shook his head.

"I'm sorry, sir. I need to get closer to the lamp." He was already moving around the bed. "This will take only another few seconds."

His terror was mounting. As he reached the opposite side of the bed, his heart kicked, and suddenly he was dizzy, trembling, his head filled with a sourceless rushing noise. A train. That was what it was. He was on a train pounding through a tunnel, the engine roaring, the interior lights flickering on and off, his body swaying as the train car lurched and wobbled on the track.

He reached for Andropov's hand, but his own hands were shaking now, worse than the old man's.

The General Secretary's gaze ticked to Shatrov's face. "Are you all right, Shatrov?"

"Yes, sir. Of course."

"You're trembling."

The first bodyguard took a step toward him. The second one rose from his chair. Their hands slipped under their jackets, fingering the grips of the guns in their shoulder holsters.

This had gone wrong, completely wrong. They were all watching him now.

"I . . . I seem to be a little light-headed, sir," Shatrov said.

Andropov's mouth was a flat line, his eyes hooded. "Indeed."

"Yes." Do it. *Do it.* "Yes, I'm afraid I . . ." He fumbled at his lab coat. "I have some medicine I sometimes take . . ." His hand in his coat pocket, closing over the syringe. "Pills—"

"Did you search his clothes?" Andropov snapped at the first bodyguard.

"No, General Secretary, I—

"Stop him! *Shoot him!*"

Shatrov tried to pull the hypodermic out of his pocket, but the needle caught on a loose thread, and then the room roared in time with twin muzzle flashes. Pain exploded in his chest. He staggered back, certain he was dead.

But he was not dead. Not yet.

With his last strength he ripped the syringe free. Lurched forward. Slammed the needle into Andropov's neck. Depressed the plunger. Injected its contents into the carotid artery.

A gift for you, Yuri, Shatrov thought wildly. *A gift of strychnine.*

He had time to see Andropov's eyes widen in terror and pain, and then the guns boomed again, and Shatrov staggered, toppled, fell down on his knees. He made a hoarse, choking sound that in his ears was triumphant laughter.

Beethoven poured from the imported speakers. Drumming footsteps pounded down the hall. The bodyguards were shouting for help. Andropov began to convulse on the bed, his back arching, his head whipsawing wildly. His glasses snapped off at the stem. His hands jerked and his legs kicked crazily at the sheets and blankets, spilling the sheaf of papers onto the floor.

Shatrov's tongue searched his mouth and found the capsule, two hundred milligrams of cyanide. He did not swallow it. Soon he would. Soon there would be an end to pain.

I love you, Elizabeth, he said voicelessly, the words solemn in his mind. *Yah lyubyu vih.*

Nurses and orderlies crowded the room. One of the nurses prepped Andropov for an injection of barbiturates, and another shook Shatrov by the shoulders, screaming hysterically in his face—*"What did you do to him? What the hell did you do, you traitor?"*—and meanwhile Andropov kept on thrashing and sunfishing and jackknifing, his nerve impulses fatally disrupted, the cardiograph shrilling an alarm as his heart pattern broke up into the agonal rhythm that preceded death.

"What did you do to him?"

But that is not the question, Shatrov thought. *The question is: What did he do to me?*

They would never know, none of them. They would not know the pain he had felt, a pain equal to that which the General Secretary was experiencing now. They would not know about the day, two weeks ago, when he looked through his mail and found one of the American medical journals he subscribed to.

The delivery of foreign magazines was always delayed, often by months. This one, which arrived on January 26, was an October issue, long out of date. He opened it and saw Elizabeth Holland gazing up at him. He stared at the picture, stunned. She was older, her hair more gray than he remembered, but still lovely. So lovely.

Under her picture was an obituary.

Now Andropov's head was thrown back on the pillow, his lips skinned back from his teeth in a sardonic leer, strychnine's signature. He was fighting for breath, as he had always fought for survival; his hands, now claws, tore at the air as if in a desperate attempt to grab hold of life and hang on. But he would not make it. Not this time.

The obituary should have been torn out by the censors, but they had overlooked it somehow. Shatrov read the words through a mist of tears and a red haze of anger.

Dr. Elizabeth Holland had died on September 1, 1983, while en route to a medical conference in Seoul, South Korea. Died when her plane was shot out of the sky by an air-to-air missile. A missile fired by a Soviet SU-15 jet fighter.

A missile that had sent her and two hundred sixty-eight others to their deaths in the icy waters of the Sea of Japan.

The gray men had murdered her. The men with winter in their souls had snuffed out the only springtime he had known.

Shatrov did not know if Andropov himself had given the order to shoot down the Korean Air Lines passenger plane that had strayed over Soviet territory. It was possible he had; even though he had been hospitalized at the time, he had remained in firm command of the apparatus of government. But perhaps the decision had been made elsewhere, at some military command post. To Shatrov, it made no difference. The General Secretary ran the system. He had instituted the climate of terror and ruthlessness that made such things possible. He was responsible.

And now he had paid.

Two of the nurses were frantically wrestling with Andropov, struggling to restrain his spasming body long enough to slap an oxygen mask on his face. "Bag him!" Bag him!" screamed a doctor who had just wheeled a crash cart into the room. "We're trying!" one of them shot back, and the other one yelled something about an anticonvulsant, and then suddenly Andropov shuddered with a final spasm and lay still.

The heart pattern on the oscilloscope was now an unbroken horizontal line.

"Epinephrine, one cc!"

"What did you *do* to him, traitor?"

"Defib, stat, three-sixty!"

"Murderer! Assassin! What did you *do?"*

The pain of the bullet wounds had gotten very bad. Shatrov was tired of the pain. He wanted to rest. The cyanide would take him quickly, without the agonies of strychnine.

His mouth was dry, and it was difficult to swallow. But with a little effort he managed.

He shut his eyes, taking himself away from this room and this hospital, away from this world of winter men whose touch had frozen everything around them. The shouts and the loud blatting sounds of the defibrillator re-ceded, as did his own body. Then the last of the world he had known faded out, and Viktor Shatrov found himself in another place, a place that smelled of spring flowers, where a woman waited for him, posing for her picture, smiling at the sun.

SHADOW
by Matthew J. Costello

The search for living ex-Nazis continues—it must continue. The hardest-to-find still-thought-to-be-alive Nazi monster is Martin Bormann. Until now.

* 1

The hum—the cars, the buses, the cabs—from First Avenue was incessant.

There were two windows in his studio apartment, each shut tight. Locking in the sick wheeze of the dripping air conditioner.

But the roar of the traffic never stopped. It lessened slightly in the early-morning hours. But then there were the terrible sirens, the police, the fire trucks. Night brought them out.

Still, he had a chair positioned by the window. Right by the dusty, dirty venetian blinds. There were spots where he had made a trail, running a finger through a filthy white blind. Sitting there, looking out at the street.

Looking for what, he thought?

Someone to stop? Someone to look up. Perhaps light a cigarette—in the melodramatic fashion of a cheap spy movie. Stop on a corner, light up a cigarette. And during that first long, slow drag, look up at his window.

Sometimes he left the TV on. What he heard didn't concern him.

There was a lot about this weekend. Lots of red, white, and blue. All this talk about the American Bicentennial.

Two hundred years. Just think of it! Two hundred years.

Which is *nothing*. A country filled with self-importance, too much money, and lazy people. *I see trouble here,* he thought. *Not today, not tomorrow, but coming. So much pride can only lead one place . . .*

There were news stories about the ships. The Tall Ships. The announcers sounded so excited! Like children. The Tall Ships! Filling the harbor.

The man didn't detect any changes in the traffic outside.

No holiday crush up First Avenue, heading toward the Willis Avenue Bridge. Not yet.

No one stopped at his corner, right next to the Orange Julius place, next to the battered payphone. No one came and looked up.

Orange Julius, he thought . . .

What's an Orange Julius?

That place used to be called the Berlin House. It sold hot dogs, frankfurters, and real sausages—bratwurst, and blutwurst.

A landmark in Germantown.

But Germantown was slipping away, vanishing.

Most of the Germans were gone.

The man stood up.

Most of the Germans were leaving New York City, running to the Island, to the leafy suburbs of Westchester.

Most of them were gone.

But not all.

* 2

He took the pot off the small stove. Everything was so handy in this studio apartment; it was just there, at his elbow.

Like a cell.

Though the bathroom had a door. Yes, that was convenient. *Very necessary for all my entertaining. A nice touch of privacy.*

The gala parties I hold here. Right above the Orange Julius store on First Avenue.

He poured the hot, bubbling milk into a chipped cup. And then he tipped in some Tobbler powdered cocoa and stirred the cup with a fork. There was half of a bottle of Barenjager, maybe less—under the sink. The yellow liqueur would taste good. Its sweet sting in the dark cocoa would feel so good.

But no. He couldn't allow it. Not today, he thought. Today was the day. He couldn't risk screwing up. Not today.

He sipped the scalding mixture. And he looked around the room, at the walls, all covered . . .

There were the subway maps, maps that he finally understood. The A line, the H line. Where they intersected, where one could change from the IRT to the IND. How you could make your way from Eighty-sixth Street all the way to Battery Park.

He had traveled the route many times. He had practiced, rehearsed.

Why—I'm almost a commuter, he thought.

Still, he worried about people seeing him, people looking at him, curious, wondering—

He took another sip of the cocoa.

Then there were the other things, things that would certainly be hard to explain if anyone ever came into the cramped apartment. The photographs ripped out of books and old magazines.

They curled against the faded yellow wallpaper wall, uncomfortable, the pages growing brittle, the pieces of tape losing their stickiness.

Sometimes, at night, he'd hear one of the pictures hit the floor.

A leaf falling.

There were group photos, and head shots, and candid photos.

He took another sip.

He chewed at his lip.

Today.
Was the day.

* 3

An SS officer with slicked-down hair and birdlike eyes
held a pair of tattered, torn trousers. Clown pants, they
looked like.

But there was nothing funny about these pants cut into
streamers. The young Wehrmacht officer was holding the
Führer's pants. And—hard to believe—the madman, Uncle
Adi, *lived* after that. He was able to stagger away from his
war meeting, from the bomb, needing just a bandage for
his hand.

Fate! Once again wondrous *fate* intervened to save the
beloved German Führer.

Another sip.

And then there was a photo of the Führer, surrounded
by all his cronies, his gang. Himmler, an accountant, a
bookkeeper, an actuary, a ghoul. Goebbels, looking embarrassed, dwarfed by the others, mortified by his twisted club
foot. And Herman Göring, Luftwaffe ace turned piggish
buffoon, all painted nails, perfume, and blubber. Whatever
Hitler wanted Göring's Luftwaffe to do, the ex-ace said,
"Jawohl!"

Even when there were no planes left to fly.

And there—in the back—

Was Martin Bormann.

Bormann was undistinguished compared to the rest. He
wasn't fat, or owlish, or deformed, or particularly mad-
looking. The face was common, even a bit coarse. But he
looked impassive in every photo, whether standing with
Frau Gerda Bormann and some of their nine children, or
huddled near his Führer's elbow.

Martin Bormann. "The Secretary," who came to control
all access to the drug-addled leader of the thousand-year
Reich, while the Americans and Russians chewed their

way to Berlin, to the bunker, to the funeral pyre of Germany.

And now the man could smell it. In his tiny apartment. Of course he could. The gasoline. He heard the grunts, the labored breathing as Linge and Stumpfegger carried the bodies outside. Hitler's head banged against the stone in the stairwell. It made such a loud crack. Such a *dishonor*, such a disgrace. Then Eva Braun was carried out, one of her shoes dangling, finally rocking off.

He remembered thinking. It's almost over.

Almost.

Whatever happens after this—it can't be worse.

The war should have ended months earlier.

But no one could get to the Führer—to make him stop. Not his generals, not Himmler. No one could get past the Secretary in the end.

The flesh smell, the stench of burning skin, made its way down to the bunker. Throats went tight, stomachs clenched.

There were yells, calls for more petrol. It had to be siphoned from abandoned, wrecked trucks. The fabled German war supplies were at an end.

The bodies didn't burn easily. The skin shriveled, turning them into black mummies.

Then the carnage continued, with Goebbels, his wife, their children.

Everyone thought of running then.

Run west. To the Americans.

But Bormann quickly took charge.

Anyone fleeing was to be shot. In the head. There was to be an *organized* withdrawal to the West. Before the Russians came to the bunker, the last stronghold of the Reich. They'd find only cinder blocks and shredded documents.

And the burnt bodies.

The man took a last sip of cocoa. It had turned cold. He tasted grit from the bottom of the cup. He licked his lips.

It was almost time.

He touched the photo, the bullet-shaped head of Bormann, standing in the back, always in the back.

There were three groups.

And, he thought. *What luck—I went with Bormann, to the Fredrichstrasse Station, through the subway tunnel. The shelling cannonaded through the empty tubes. Squeaking rats cheered us on.*

Days later, everyone had surrendered to the allies or the Russians. The ones who went East never returned.

I was lucky . . .

The man turned and walked back to his sink, to his small refrigerator that hid under the counter. Above the sink there was a photo. He had enlarged the photo from a book, enlarging it, cutting it into sections, and then enlarging it again—until, when he taped it together, it completely covered the wall above the sink.

Lest I forget, he thought.

It looked like a puzzle picture. A jumble that needed unscrambling. It was so grainy from all the enlarging, losing definition, reality.

But he knew what it was.

He had been there the day it had been taken. The American corporal made him watch, made him stand there while the picture was taken, while the bulldozer pushed the bodies into a pile.

Bones and heads and stick legs and arms. A few children, if you looked closely. Impossible to count the quilt of bodies. Impossible. They were all piled together, killed hurriedly, last orders of the Reich.

From the Führer to the concentration camp commandants.

Through the Secretary . . .

The black-and-white TV was still on.

The man turned to it.

Oberleutnant Heinrich Wunsche turned to the tiny TV screen.

Boats—tugboats—were spraying water in the air, welcoming the ships for the weekend celebration.

It was Friday afternoon.

People were going home for the great celebration.

Wunsche turned off his TV.

There was just the hum of the traffic now.

He walked to the door, undid the locks, the dead bolt, the door lock, then the chain. He opened the door, walked out, and then shut the door behind him. Leaving it unlocked.

And he started down the stairs . . .

* 4

Wunsche looked up and down the Eighty-sixth Street station. It was still early for the weekend rush hour, and the station was quiet. He heard a click, as a switch moved into place down the dark tunnel. There were steps, the exaggerated footfall of someone walking down to the station, the sound echoing.

It was cool down here. Cooler even than in his apartment.

He looked at his watch. Plenty of time, he thought. Too much time, perhaps, too much time to think, to wonder about this, to worry . . .

Then there was that great subterranean roar, an angry sound. Hundreds of sounds really, blending into one terrible cacophony. The screech of the wheels, screaming to leap off the rail. The sputtering of electrical sparks. The Doppler effect of the whistling train. The steady clackety-clack of the track rattling as the behemoth crossed it.

So loud.

Wunsche looked down to the other person waiting. A woman, young, nicely dressed. She looked to him, and then quickly turned away.

The rattling of the train continued.

When Wunsche looked back, the woman had moved down to the other end of the station. The subway was growing dangerous. There were stories . . . Bad things happened in the subway.

Then—too quickly—the train was there, rushing past the station, surely unable to stop, cars filled with people, looking pasty-white under the lights.

Then the howling of the brakes, desperately grabbing, trying to hold on.

The train stopped with a relieved whoosh, and the doors slid open.

I sense every detail of this, Wunsche thought. *All so clear, no—stronger than that. Exaggerated.*

It's only natural, he thought. Only to be expected.

He walked into the open car.

* 5

He had to stand, but at least people weren't packed together like a cattle car. The hot air wasn't so full of the smell of humans.

A large black woman—the size of two people—was looking at him. Her milky eyes watched Wunsche, unblinking. Wunsche looked away. It felt as if she could see more than just a middle-aged man holding on to a plastic subway strap. She could see everything—the past, and what was to come.

The air grew thin. Wunsche gulped at it. It was stifling hot now. The train rattled south, shaking like an amusement park ride, this way and that, trying to shake loose the human fleas.

This express sailed past some stations, the supporting pillars looking like bars, keeping the people on the stations away from the speeding train.

Wunsche looked at his watch.

Plenty of time.

A door slid open . . . a door leading from a car to the rear.

Wunsche looked up. Quickly, with the smallest amount of interest. *Ja,* the way New Yorkers do. Keeping the eyes away. It wasn't good to look at people for too long.

Three kids came in, one lanky black kid, two smaller white kids. They were laughing.

No one else was laughing in the train. This was something to be endured.

They had high-pitched laughs, giggling, falling into each other. The people in their seats looked away, even when the kids hung from the plastic straps, dangling in front of the people, looking at them. Making faces.

They moved closer to Wunsche. He shifted around, holding the plastic strap with one hand and then shifting to the other.

He looked at one of the boys. He wore a T-shirt with a big tongue on it, a big red licking tongue. Except the colors were faded. The tongue looked cracked, diseased.

"Hey, Pops. What da fuck you looking at?"

The kid saw him looking, and Wunsche heard the kid, clearly, sharply above the rattling of the train.

The express roared on to Fifty-seventh street. Seconds away. Or minutes. Maybe a long time . . .

Wunsche kept looking away. Even when he felt the kids come close.

"You like my goddamn T-shirt—?"

The other kids laughed. They cheer for each other, Wunsche knew. That's how it happens. You need one bully. And the rest just to cheer, to urge him on.

The kid touched his shoulder.

"You fuckin' deaf? Wots a matter? Can't you fuckin' hear?"

More giggles. And Wunsche—feeling trapped—turned.

He was a boy.

With a big grin. A clear shining face, deep blue eyes. Long black hair, hanging down the side of his face, Jesuslike.

The boy's eyes sparkled, so clear, so untroubled.

They were eyes that Wunsche knew.

Wunsche shook his head. An answer. He started to turn away.

"Oops!" the kid said exaggeratedly, laughing, whooping. He fell into Wunsche, nearly knocking him down.

And then they moved on.

Wunsche didn't look up until he heard the sliding door open, signaling that another car was about to be visited by the three boys.

Then Wunsche had a bad thought.

His back hand flapped back to where he kept his wallet.

The pocket was empty.

He looked around at his fellow riders. The train started to slow, the brakes howling.

Did any of them see?

He patted both back pockets now, just to be sure. But they were empty.

Wunsche licked his lips.

It didn't matter. Not really.

A young man in a suit got up to get off at Fifty-seventh Street, and Wunsche sat down.

Thirty-third Street was ahead. He'd change lines and then continue downtown.

The lost wallet didn't matter . . .

* 6

After he changed lines, he fell asleep.

His dream started in a subway car, a car filled with punks, laughing at him, pushing him down on the ground, laughing at him.

Until—one time—they pushed him down and he fell onto a pile of bones, arms, legs, skulls, a floor of bones. And he couldn't get any footing.

He smelled the gasoline. The crispy bacon smell.

He heard the Goebbels children screaming, crying. *No, Daddy.* The loving mother and father reassuring them. That they'd all be together.

Then more bodies were carried outside, and everyone was running around the bunker, deciding who was going with whom.

The dream was like that children's book, Alice. In Wonderland. A terrible place.

They had to escape the Russians. The Russians were almost there. Just a block away.

Bormann came up to Wunsche—standing guard in the bunker.

"Oberleutnant—you will come with me, and Hein, and Krebs. The rest—"

Wunsche nodded.

In his dream, he stood in the bunker, only now the stone floor was awash with bones.

And he had the thought.

Bormann is no longer in the shadow.

He's no longer the invisible man, the man who issues the orders, the promulgations . . . to destroy factories, to destroy women and children . . .

They ran down into the station, Heim in the lead, Bormann just behind him. Skeleton soldiers, skeleton Russians chased them, the rattling of their bones loud in Wunsche's dream-ears.

Shells exploded. Dust fell down from above, into the black pit, into the darkness of the subway station.

They ran, the rats' squeaks urging them on.

A loud squeak . . .

The train stopped.

And Wunsche woke up.

He looked at the station, the letters blurry, unreal, slowly coming into focus. He had passed his station, passed Worth Street. He was at Battery Park . . .

He looked at his watch. And suddenly there wasn't so much time left. And he had allowed a lot of time. The platforms were filling with people now, ready to begin the great American Bicentennial, the holiday weekend. At beaches and picnics, at cookouts and vacation houses.

Wunsche hurried to the other side of the station, pushing past the people, a human tide he struggled against, whispering, hissing, "Excuse me . . . pardon me."

He saw a train on the other side, waiting, ready to move north. He pushed even harder, stepping on people's feet, barking at them now . . .

"Excuse me . . . pardon me . . . I—"

But the train waited for him—and he took the train two stops.

To Worth Street . . .

The Worth Street station was filled, barely any room to move. It had always been crowded, all the other times Wunsche had come to see . . . to look.

But not like this.

He moved to a pillar, to a gum machine, just as a train arrived. It would look odd that he didn't get on when the near-empty train arrived. He dug in his pocket and found a coin.

Yes. I'll buy some gum. That's what I'm doing. Buying Wrigley's gum.

He dropped the quarter in the slot.

The train stopped. The crowd on the platform forced their way onto the train. The doors slid shut, gobbling them up.

The train left. And more people streamed down from the hot sun above to the stifling air below.

Wunsche looked at the posters, the advertisements on the walls of the station, always making his eyes dart left to check the stairs.

Ya Gotta Believe!

He read the words. It was about the baseball team. The Mets.

Ya Gotta Believe!

There was an ad for a film next to it. *Marathon Man.* Laurence Olivier. A good actor, Wunsche believed. A movie about running . . .

He didn't know.

He looked left. Women in heels. Men in suits. More people filled the platform. Some holding their sport coats, their brows dotted with pearls of sweat.

Another ad urged, *Come Out to the Big A—Aqueduct.*

The photo of the horses was grainy, Wunsche stood so close.

He looked left again.

He saw shoes, black broughams, a shuffling step.

Wunsche's heart began to beat a bit faster. He saw the shoes, a gray suit . . .

It was him.

The man's gray suit was rumpled. Not a wealthy man's suit, nothing to call attention to itself.

Who took care of him? Wunsche wondered.

Who were the people who kept his secret . . . who protected him?

Then the man was there.

The old man. The head nearly completely bald, sweat covering the shiny dome on top.

Wunsche sidled away from the billboards.

Following now, just behind the old man.

But there were so many people between them. More than Wunsche expected, more than any other Friday. This might have been a mistake. After all the planning. Wunsche would have to get closer . . .

Then Wunsche felt feverish. There were all these sounds, the chattering of the people on the station—excited about their holiday. And—in the distance—the sound of a train coming. He felt dizzy.

But Wunsche, looking at the back of the old man's head, heard other things.

Voices from forty years ago . . . in another subway tunnel.

Bormann ordering everyone to split up.

Telling Heim and Krebs to go *up* now, *now!* At this station, while he and Wunsche—yes, Oberleutnant Wunsche —continue farther west, away from the Russians . . .

Wunsche stepped closer.

The old man moved to the edge of the platform, peering down the black tunnel. If you didn't move to the edge, you didn't get a seat.

Wunsche had seen him do this before.

He watched the old man take a kerchief out of his pocket and dab at his brow.

The train was coming. A minute away. Maybe less.

And Wunsche spoke . . .

For the first time.

"Herr Sekretar . . . Herr—"

The man stopped wiping. *"Mein herr,"* Wunsche said loudly, his voice gaining in strength, force. He knew people were watching him now. He moved a step closer.

The man lowered the kerchief.

"Herr Secretary . . ."

The big head turned.

Their eyes met.

And for a second—for just a moment—Wunsche thought that he was wrong. This wasn't him. It looked like him. That's all. Just some German burgermeister, living in the New World.

The West Germans had found a skull. Just three years ago. In 1973. Maybe—maybe it was Bormann's, they said.

And then, three months after that, a maxillary incisor bridge was found by Dr. Soggnaes—so conveniently—and it matched Bormann's almost perfectly.

Bormann had died emerging from the tunnel, they announced. There was no mystery. He never escaped.

Except—

Wunsche saw Bormann run away, through the empty streets of the Berlin suburb. Wunsche watched. Bormann knew people.

Shadows disappear in the light.

Three months later, nearly a perfect match . . .

Anything can be arranged . . .

"Herr—"

Their eyes locked. And Wunsche knew. The recognition was total, instantaneous. Bormann's lip curled back from his teeth. He nodded.

Where had the Secretary vanished? Bolzano, Italy, Wunsche learned that from others who hunted Bormann. Then to Egypt. The Israelis, the Mossad, were on to him . . . even after the masterful dental work was discovered. There were immigration records, photographs . . .

People on the platform pressed closer together.

There was no honor left for Germany, for Germans. The country had been turned into a slaughterhouse. Forever the charnel house, the gassings, the crematoria.

There was no honor left, only blood and guilt, endless guilt.

He spoke. The Secretary . . . the shadow . . .

"What do—"

He knew. Bormann recognized him.

Old friends from another subway station.

"What? What do you—"

The train was nearly there. Entering the station, screaming, roaring toward them.

Wunsche pushed himself forward some more, bumping people, making them look at him.

"Herr—"

Bormann's eyes—old man's rheumy eyes—picked up a different glint.

He was smart. One doesn't get to be Party Chancellor by being stupid.

Wunsche had rehearsed this many times, his eyes closed, listening, listening for the rhythm, the sound of the wheels, the track, clues to the proper time, the moment—

Now.

He looked up and pushed Bormann. Hard, with his full might.

Bormann staggered backward. One foot went off the platform. The old man's arms flew up in the air.

In Wunsche's mind—there was the gasoline smell, and screaming. The slats of the track were bones.

People tried to grab at Bormann, to stop the old man's fall. But it happened too fast. And they had to step back to avoid the wave of air pushed by the train.

Bormann fell to the tracks. He was able to kneel and look up.

Wunsche stood there, and watched.

Bormann had used a word. Wunsche had heard Bormann use it . . .

Disinfection. That's all he and the rest of the gangsters were doing. The woman, the children, the scarecrow men, the babies who just wouldn't stop crying.

Yes.

Disinfection . . .

The train was there.

Wunsche didn't bother to look up to see the horrified expression of the conductor, pulling the brakes tight, making them scream their loudest.

Instead, he watched Bormann look up, watched his eyes. Looking for pity.

There was none.

Judgment was late.

But the train wasn't . . .

There was just this tiny fragment of justice.

And then it was gone, Bormann's scream lost, carried down the tunnel.

People grabbed Wunsche. He heard screaming, crying.

But it didn't matter.

Wunsche nodded. He didn't know whether he'd tell them the truth.

It was enough that it was over.

SABOTAGE
by William L. DeAndrea

All crimes are tragedies, but are all tragedies crimes? There is something in the human psyche, which, when faced with catastrophe, looks for someone or something to blame. In this case, the real life tragedy was enormous, and the culprit, the author implies, was an attitude.

Mother Gaia, he wrote, *the being that is the Living Earth Herself, is the most beautiful of the Universe's Wonders.*

The computer screen reflected his frown. He rubbed his lip for a moment, then moved the cursor to change "Universe's Wonders" to "Wonders of the Universe." What the hell. It was trite, but it flowed better.

But She is not perfect, he went on, *for She harbors within Herself a virus, a poison, a parasite that, left unchecked, will destroy Her and all Her Beauty. That parasite is the evil and arrogant creature called Man.*

He smiled at that. He always referred to the human race as "Man" when he was talking about what a bunch of scumbags they were. It subliminally let the feminists off the hook; he got a lot of support from feminists.

Man, the destroyer of Mother Gaia's other helpless children. Man, burner of forests, polluter of waters, befouler of air. If any species deserved extinction it is this insane ape. Unfortunately, there is as yet no way to be rid of pestiferous Man without doing irreperable harm to Mother Gaia Herself.

*Therefore, Man, like the idiot-genius he is, must be kept
in check. He and the plague he pleases to call "progress"
must be slowed down and scaled back, he must be forced, if
necessary, to take his proper, humble place at Mother Gaia's
generous banquet until that happy (if unlikely) day when
ungrateful Man repents and learns to properly love his
Mother.*

Allen Prince read over the last few words again. He was
pleased. He hit the save button, then ordered the computer
to tell the laser printer to make a hard copy to be faxed to
the magazine that had commissioned the article. If the idiots' modem had been compatible with his, they could have
had the thing already.

Prince went to the thermostat and lowered the temperature. He liked the place extra cool when he came out of the
shower. Prince exulted in the shower, letting the clean,
perfectly heated mountain water wash the work and fa-
tigue off him. Carefully, he shampooed his graying hair
and beard. He would have liked to shave the thing off—it
did get to be a nuisance—but he didn't dare. A "clean-cut"
look, as his father, the bookkeeper, would have called it,
would have clashed with his image, and his image was all
the leverage he had.

Prince smiled. Right, he thought, like all the leverage
J.P. Morgan had had was a billion dollars. There were
levers and levers.

He stepped out of the shower and dried himself off. He
put on a set of sweats and a pair of wooden shoes, and
headed for the secret kitchen. The shoes made muffled
clops on the thickly carpeted floor.

He really liked wooden shoes. When he'd first started
wearing them, they had been a gimmick, a way to get a
message in the press to the animal rights folks that he was
One Of Them, No Foolin'. He had suspected, and rightly so,
that there was a lot of zeal among the animal rights movement that could be useful to him.

The fringe benefit was the wooden shoes. Amazingly,
they weren't uncomfortable at all, and you could slip in
and out of them with no fuss. They also added about an

inch and a half to his height without exposing him to the stigma of wearing lifts. And they gave him a trademark the press could always talk about, like Ralph Nader's rumpled suits.

Prince opened the stainless-steel, restaurant-style refrigerator, and took out a can of Diet Coke. He'd just popped the tab and taken the first pull at the soda when, surprise of surprises, there was a knock at the door.

Prince smiled ruefully, took another swig of soda, and stuck the can back in the fridge. He slid the door to the secret kitchen shut, and locked it. Then he went to answer the door.

It didn't happen often, but every once in a while some intrepid soul ignored the KEEP OUT signs (and the bears and the mountain lions) and made his way up the twisting dirt road to Allen Prince's retreat, on the bare top of a wooded plateau. Usually, though, Prince heard them coming—it took a powerful four-wheel-drive vehicle like the one in the garage to make it up that hill. Whatever their virtues, such vehicles weren't known for quiet motors.

Of course, his visitor (or visitors) might have driven up while he was in the shower, but he'd been out for a while now. Had they been there, gawking at the house, since before he'd gotten out of the shower? All the better. The awestruck ones were the easiest to deal with. He'd bring them in, give them a gentle lecture about the no-trespassing signs being there to protect the habitat, not humble Allen Prince, pour them a cup of herb tea (sun brewed), then see them on their way full of the warm fuzzies for Allen Prince and all his works in defense of the planet. It was a pain in the ass, but once or twice a year, he could stand it for the sake of the good PR.

Prince went to open the door. The closed-circuit monitor assured him that it wasn't a lawyer, or somebody else in a suit, come to make trouble for him. Allen Prince *sent* suing lawyers; he did not receive them.

However, it wasn't one of the awestruck gapers, either. This one had the look of a mountain man; at least the weekend variety thereof. His hair was shaggy and covered his ears; his beard grew down to where his neck joined his torso. His eyes were set and determined. Though his mouth was invisible behind the beard, the eyes would have gone with a grim line of lip and a set jaw.

Prince had this kind of visitor, too, though more rarely. This was the kind who came and wanted him to stop the city folks from pulling all the trout out of Peapack River. Prince gave them the tea, told him he'd look into it, and sent them on their way. There wasn't enough ink in fighting recreational fisherman to make it worth Prince's while. He'd get around to them, but way later.

Prince swung the door open, thereby learning that the mountain man's plaid flannel shirt was red, his corduroy pants were green, his backpack was blue, his hair and eyes dark brown.

"Hello," the mountain man said. The voice was calm and cultured. It didn't go with the look, and it certainly didn't go with the expression Prince had seen on the TV monitor. "My name is Peter Knox. Of course, I recognize you from TV. I've come a long way to talk to you. May I come in?"

"I didn't hear you drive up," Prince said. He craned his neck into the warm mountain air. "Where's your car?"

The mountain man smiled and showed a mouthful of even white teeth. Something else that didn't fit the image. "I came on foot. I knew you didn't like cars on the freeway; I figured you wouldn't allow them on your mountain."

"Ordinarily, I don't," Prince said, joining quite involuntarily in the smile. "But I don't want my visitors to get heart attacks, either."

"Let them," Knox said. "What's a couple fewer pollution-spewing Man-creatures, right?"

"Ahh, right. Right. The mountain is posted against trespassing, you know. For the sake of the environment, you realize."

"Oh, naturally. It's just that what I wanted to tell you is so important, I took the liberty. I came up the south face of the mountain."

"Through the array?"

"Yeah. Very impressive."

"Very dangerous," Prince told him. "You could have been fried."

"The mirrors were too bright to look at," Knox conceded. "Like looking at the sun."

"At the peak, they reflect a beam of almost six hundred degrees."

Prince's retreat was once a millionaire's home. Prince had caused his foundation to buy it in order to conduct an experiment: Was it possible to run a home on solar power alone? To find out, Prince had had engineers come in and put in the array. This was a group of focused mirrors on motorized mounts. The motors would keep them focused in synchronization with the sun, reflecting concentrated beams of sunlight to an egg-shaped water tower at the top of a long shaft. The heat from the mirrors boiled the water and sent it down the shaft under pressure where it spun a turbine and generated electricity—plenty of electricity, it turned out, to run Prince's computer, his air conditioner, anything he wanted, including the mirror-motors themselves.

So the experiment was a success—you *could* maintain a twentieth-century lifestyle on solar power—if you had twenty acres of land to put up an array to power one house, and about two million in capital to get the thing built. No, Prince sometimes told his followers not quite sadly *(they* weren't sad about it, after all), the only way out was to march backward, to give up electricity and live as our ancestors did, in harmony with nature. He was always applauded warmly for this.

He continued to use the retreat, he told them, because, alas, the monster of progress has to be fought with the weapons of progress—computers and mass media. At least he wasn't ripping off the planet to do it, he told them to more cheers.

Except in the winter, when he had to fire up the gas generator to keep things going after a few short, overcast days. He didn't tell people about that.

"May I come in?" Knox said again.

Prince looked down on his visitor's feet. "I don't allow

leather in my house," he said. "Or meat. It's a symbolic
gesture, but one that is very important to me. If you'll take
off your boots, I'll go and get you some wooden shoes."

"Oh," Knox said. "I have my own." He slid the blue ny-
lon backpack to the ground and opened it.

Allen Prince couldn't tell *what* all was in there—papers,
books, something that looked like a large tool kit, the usual
socks and underwear—and at last, one large wooden shoe.

"Damn," Knox said. "I must have lost the other one."

"Never mind," Prince said. "I'm touched that you made
the effort. I'll get you a pair. About an eleven for you? I
keep them in all sizes."

"Eleven is perfect," Knox said. "I'll take off my boots out
here, like you said."

Knox was wiggling stockinged toes when Prince came
back. He slid into the wooden shoes and joined his host in
clomping across the lush rug to the vast living room.
Prince settled down on his favorite armchair; his guest
perched on the edge of the sofa. They chatted politely
about weather until the herb tea was done. Prince waited
until his visitor took a sip, then said, "Now, Mr. Knox, how
can I help you?"

The mountain man reached into his pocket. For one horrible instant, Prince thought he was going after the mak-
ings of a hand-rolled cigarette or something equally dangerous to the rug. When he saw the small white rectangle
of a business card come out instead, he was relieved, but no
less puzzled.

"Actually," the man said as he handed over the card,
"it's *Doctor* Knox. I'm a psychiatrist."

And not just a psychiatrist, Prince saw, but one with a
fancy Park Avenue address.

"You have me at a loss, Doctor," Prince said. "I'm sane. I
don't mean to sound immodest, but I believe my work
makes me one of the sanest men on earth."

"I suppose you're right," Dr. Knox said. A strange smile
played on his lips. "*I* would say so. Of course, 'sanity' is a
legal term regarding degree of responsibility for one's own

actions. It has no medical or moral significance whatsoever."

Knox waved the thought away with the back of his hand. He no longer looked like a mountain man. He looked like a professor who'd been roughing it for a while. For a purpose.

"It's not important. We'll talk about that later, if at all. Right now, I want to consult you about a patient of mine."

"Ah," said Prince. "I see."

"Do you?"

"Oh, yes. This has happened one or two times before. You have a patient who is in severe anxiety over the state of the world; is thrown into panic at the thought of nuclear power, and global warming, and acid rain. You want me to tell you how to reassure this person, keep your patient from being paralyzed with fear."

Prince leaned back and took a deep breath. He was enjoying this. "I'm afraid I can't do it."

"You can't?"

"I won't. Anxiety and panic are the *proper* responses in the face of the world situation. Those of us who can calmly go about their business—even a business such as mine, fighting the criminal society that causes the problems—are the ones who are insane. Sorry, let me say *unhealthy.*"

"You are aware, aren't you," Knox said, "that even factoring in Chernobyl, nuclear power is the cleanest, safest, and most efficient source of power in the history of mankind? That there is no scientific evidence of any global warming whatever? That a five-year study failed to find a single—even *one*—organism that was harmed by so-called acid rain?"

"I have heard lies," Prince said with dignity.

"Well," Knox said wryly. *"Somebody's* lying."

Allen Prince was accustomed to being spoken to with more respect, especially here. He was about to put Knox in his place, but the psychiatrist didn't give him a chance. He grinned and waved this matter away, too.

"But that's not important, either," Knox said. "That's not the kind of patient I have in mind."

"Then why *are* you here?" Prince could feel his impatience rising. It was something he'd discovered in the early days of building his movement—it wasn't worth the effort to be polite to the opposition. Treat them with contempt, and you reinforce the beliefs of your own followers. An open mind on your part simply raises the danger that the minds of those you've already convinced might open as well. It was a tactic well learned by the associate professor he'd once been, and one that had proven invaluable ever since.

"I'm a busy man, and you are trespassing. Perhaps you should go now. I can't help you with your patient."

"How do you know? You don't even know who it is yet."

"What difference does it make?"

"It's Dwight Noring," Knox said.

Prince was silent for a few moments. He stared hard at Knox. The psychiatrist had no trouble meeting the stare.

"Dwight Noring," Prince said quietly, "is dead."

"So many people are," Knox said. "Including Dwight. But a person's death doesn't end his significance, does it?"

"Depends on the person. Poor Dwight had unlimited potential, but he was . . . misguided. I don't know if it's sad or fortunate he died before he accomplished anything."

Dr. Knox rubbed his nose. "Oh," he said. "Well, *Dwight* thought he'd accomplished something. He thought he'd accomplished something so big he couldn't figure out how to live with it."

Peter Knox remembered sitting at his desk before his first appointment with Dwight Noring. As he read the file, he kept thinking that the boy was too good to be true. First of all, he was a genius, the child of parents who themselves had been gifted children. They had taken care to try to keep their son's childhood as normal as possible, while not neglecting the appetite of a giant intellect.

Dwight spoke six human languages, and all computer languages. He had built (with a little soldering help from his father) his first computer at the age of six, and programmed it himself from scratch.

("I made a lot of mistakes doing that," he was to tell Knox. "I learned a lot before I got it running right.")

He played piano, guitar, and trumpet. He composed music, and wrote science fiction stories. In Knox's admittedly inexpert opinion, the music was excellent; the stories suffered because the science they hinged on was insufficiently simplified for the lay reader (like Peter Knox, for instance) to understand.

Dwight played soccer (All-State prep) and basketball ("I wasn't really tall enough, but I was a good passer.")

Dwight was the shining light of the gifted students program at a local university. Or rather, he had been.

Because two years ago, he had dropped out of the program; had dropped out of his whole life. He now spent virtually all his time in his room, watching old movies on his VCR. He wasn't angry, or violent, or defiant. He just brooded.

Attached to the file was a note from Allen Prince, Ph.D., professor at the University, and director of the Gifted Students Program. Knox had heard of him—he was getting a lot of ink lately because of some militant environmental stands he had recently taken.

The note said that Dwight had showed no signs of "burnout" prior to his dropping out of the program, that he had been eager and energetic right until the end of the previous January. Dr. Prince went on to say that in his experience, the most brilliant young people *did* have periods in which they let their talents lie fallow. Under no circumstances, in his opinion, should Dwight be "pushed," or made to feel as if he were letting anyone down.

Dwight's parents were inclined to agree, having had their share of being pushed during their own gifted childhoods. So for a little over two years, they let their son be, and did nothing.

Until the morning their son, now sixteen, took a razor and cut his wrists.

He had been discovered in time and rushed to the hospital. The M.D. in charge of the case, as well as the psychiatric resident, recommended Dwight be sent to Knox, who'd treated gifted children successfully in the past. Everything Knox had heard or read said that this was a kid worth helping.

Then Dwight Noring came into the office. His wrists were still bandaged. Other than that, he looked like a healthy, handsome kid of medium height. The first thing he said when he sat down was, "You can't help me."

Knox got a look at the boy's eyes. They were old and sad and beaten.

It was in his tone of voice, too. Nothing belligerent, or even challenging. Just hopelessly matter of fact. "You can't help me. I wish somebody could."

"That's a good start," Knox said. "I spend about seventy-five percent of my time trying to get patients to admit there's something wrong to need help about."

"I don't *need* help," Dwight insisted. "Anyway, the term is meaningless, with all due respect."

"I don't understand."

" 'Help' for me doesn't exist. Can't. It would involve time travel. Violation of free will and causality. All sorts of impossibilities. How can you 'need' something that has never been and never will be?"

"Good point," Knox said. "A bit of a sophistry, perhaps, but nicely done."

"I thought you guys were never supposed to argue with your patients," Dwight said.

"Is that what I'm doing?"

"An accusation of sophistry implies disagreement. And disparagement. Is that wise? I mean, they made me come here because I tried to kill myself. You shouldn't call me a sophist and break down my self-esteem any more than it is."

"A couple of things. You may not believe this, but you do want to be helped."

Dwight clenched his jaw. "Don't pretend to read my mind, Doctor, okay?"

"I'm not reading your mind. All I have to do is read your record. I'm supposed to believe somebody with a brain like yours doesn't know or can't find out fifteen quicker and less painful ways to commit suicide than by cutting his wrists? Or, if he were determined to cut his wrists, he'd know not to cut them across?

"I know you know how to research. You've read some psychiatry texts in preparation for coming here—that much is obvious. You could have checked up on anatomy just as easily. Believe me, Dwight, if you'd really wanted to die, you would be dead."

The boy stared at him.

"To answer your other question," Knox said, "now that you've read the books, and know what I'm *supposed* to be doing, you'll have nice walls built up to keep me out. I'll have to improvise. What do you want to argue about?"

Dwight gave him a crooked smile. "That was good," he said. "It might even turn out to be interesting. You come on more like a cop than a doctor."

"Is that appropriate?"

"How do I know what's appropriate?"

"I mean, is it appropriate to what's troubling you? You might as well have a neon sign over your head flashing GUILT. Did you do something bad? Something criminal."

Dwight laughed, but there was no mirth to it. "Something bad. Oh, God, yes. I can't think of anything worse than what I did. Criminal? Well, no policeman would arrest me. Wouldn't believe me if I confessed. Even if he did, a court wouldn't try me and a jury wouldn't convict me."

"But who needs them, right?"

Dwight looked unblinking into Knox's eyes. "Right. I know I'm guilty. That's enough."

"What did you do? Care to tell me?"

"No."

"Sure?"

"Are you serious? Yes, I'm damned sure, Doctor."

"Why don't you want to tell me?"

"I can't even stand to think about it, for God's sake!"

"You're thinking about it now, aren't you?"

Again, the crooked smile. "Uh uh. You're not going to get me that way. Drop it, Doc. If we do these sessions for fifty years, I won't tell you. Just drop it."

"All right, let's change the subject. Why did you cut your wrists."

Dwight shook his head. "Well, gee, Doc, when I walked in here, I thought I knew the answer to that one. Now I'm all confused. According to you, it was a cry for help. Which doesn't exist and will never come."

"No," Knox said. "I mean, why did you cut your *wrists,* as opposed to say, your throat? Or, going with the cry-for-help theory, take a not-quite-fatal overdose of some chemical you cooked up in the lab?"

There was silence for a few long seconds, then Dwight said, "I'm having a strange experience, Doc. I think I may have run into someone too smart for me."

"I thank you for the compliment, but let's cut the bullshit, shall we? Will you answer my question?"

"I can't."

"Can't or won't?"

"All right, I won't. Let's just say it seemed 'appropriate.' "

"Appropriate?" Knox asked.

Dwight Noring wasn't listening. He was looking at his hands as if they were some sort of slimy creatures he'd found under a rock. Tears came to his eyes, and he muttered something.

Knox let it go on for a full minute, then gently said, "What are you saying?"

No luck. Dwight snapped out of it. "What? Oh, nothing. Nothing."

"Something about the future, right?"

"Forget it," Dwight said.

"You wanted me to know, or you wouldn't have mumbled it in front of me."

Dwight got to his feet. Seeing the near-tears look on the boy's face, Knox realized that no one was a genius when it came to dealing with his own emotions.

"I told you I won't talk about it!"

"Okay, okay. Don't talk about it. Think about it."

"All I do is think about it!"

"All you do is think about the guilt and fear it causes you

—whatever 'it' is. I want you to think about the thing or event itself. I want you to realize that you are breaking your back, staggering around under the weight of it. I also want you to remember that your parents are paying me a whole lot of money, maybe more than they can afford, so I can help you shoulder this and get on with your life."

"Get on with my life. Somehow it doesn't sound very attractive, Doctor."

"Just promise me you'll see me one more time before you do anything drastic, okay? Just show up next week. Call me if things get particularly tough."

Dwight said he would, and kept his word. He showed up the next week, and for many weeks after that.

Many in Knox's profession measured progress in terms of getting the patient to tell you things he's hidden from himself. In the case of Dwight Noring, that didn't really apply. He wasn't hiding all that much from himself. He was so immersed in self-loathing, he was hiding everything from the rest of the world.

There were moments when he'd let something slip. Once Knox had asked, "What do you want to *do?* 'Genius' is not something you can put on your income tax return."

"I used to want to be an astronaut," he said. "How's that for a laugh, now? They don't recruit nut cases who've tried to kill themselves, do they?" Dwight laughed bitterly. When Knox suggested he might still do something for the space program, Dwight became hysterical. He laughed un- til he sobbed; sobbed until he had to stumble to the bath- room to throw up. He came out wiping his chin. He wore a sick grin on his face. "I touch the future, huh, Doc?"

Every few weeks, Knox came back to the central ques- tion. He asked it in many different ways; he hid it in a maze of other questions, or disguised it as case histories or parables.

But the heart of the question was always the same: "What in the name of God do you think you did?"

A couple of times, Knox even got answers. Once, Dwight exploded, "You want to know what I did? I did my *home- work.* I was a good little boy, and I did my fucking *home-*

work!" Another time, much more calmly, with a sort of laughter of despair, he said, "I saved the Earth, Doc. I made it possible to save Our One Earth." Generally, after such an outburst, the rest of the session would be spent in silence.

And on it went. Knox grew to like Dwight (an indulgence not really good for a psychiatrist's own mental health), but he never came close to really helping him. He used to like to tell himself he was functioning as a safety valve for the boy's emotions, that if he just kept Dwight hanging in there long enough, his own brainpower would pull him through.

He was wrong. At the end of the next January, the twenty-eighth, to be precise, a year to the day after he'd slashed his wrists, Dwight Noring, now seventeen, succeeded in killing himself.

Prince's face was bland. "So how can I possibly help you, Doctor? It seems your failure is complete."

Knox nodded. "As far as Dwight's concerned. But there's always the future, isn't there?"

Prince smiled. "My entire life is dedicated to ensuring that there is one."

Knox returned the smile. "I disagree. Your entire life is dedicated to marching humanity triumphantly back to the past, where every day was a backbreaking struggle to get enough to eat; where woman's life was in peril with every pregnancy; where filth and terror were the only release from the mind-destroying boredom of unending physical labor."

"A lot of people call those the good old days."

"Some," Knox agreed. "Even some people who lived that kind of life. Understandable. The human mind has an almost miraculous capacity for blotting out past pain. There'd be no second children, otherwise. And there's no denying the present has its problems."

"Hmph. Kind of you to admit it. But what about the young? Almost all of my followers are young people."

"That's easy. I was the same way in the seventies. I did

my sit-ins and my shouting. Vietnam was the 'cause' then. It was all a young jerk could desire—the opportunity to feel really virtuous without doing anything to earn it except make trouble for people who are really dealing with the problems of the day. You declare the moral equivalent of war, Mr. Prince, then demand that the human race do the moral equivalent of surrender. You offer these kids a chance at feeling warm and toasty about themselves as they're driving some poor schmuck out of business because he can't afford to spend a quarter of his time filling out EPA forms. You take legitimate concerns about progress and the environment, blow them completely out of proportion, and sell doomsday to a bunch of people who won't check facts or think for themselves."

"Are you done?" Prince asked.

"Except to tell you that you make me sick, yes."

"Fine. You came here to tell me I make you sick. You've told me. Will you go now?"

"Not yet. I'm just done with my *tirade*. It felt good, by the way. I want to tell you that I know why Dwight killed himself."

"How? Did it come to you in a dream?"

"It came to me in Dwight's will."

"He left a will?"

"Well, not a legal one. Holograph wills aren't legal in New York, but Dwight had left a note saying he wanted me to have something."

"What was it?"

"I'm not sure. The note called it the 'red metal toolkit on my desk.'"

"You saw the note?"

"Yes. Dwight's parents called the police, then me. My apartment was just in the next block. I got there first. I saw the note. I saw the toolkit. I saw the body."

"He shot himself, didn't he? Must have been a terrible mess."

"That was the interesting thing. No mess at all. There was a small black hole about the size of a pencil point in the middle of his forehead. If he shot himself, he didn't use a bullet."

Knox started rummaging in his backpack.

"Be careful, Doctor," Prince said.

Knox looked up to see himself looking into the barrel of a .38 caliber revolver.

He grinned. " 'Appropriate technology,' right, Prince?"

"I don't know what you've got in the bag. I'm being prudent."

"I'm not armed. Or bugged, either, if you're interested." He kept talking as he looked. "Neither Dwight's parents nor I touched anything, you know. When the cops came, they took a look at the note, then they looked inside the box. They closed it up, sent us all to another room, and called the bomb squad. And that was the last I heard of the box I was supposed to get. Ah, here it is."

Knox pulled a red metal toolkit from the knapsack. "Look familiar?" he asked.

"Never seen it before in my life," Prince said.

"Not this one, of course. Yours might have been a different color. Or maybe it was a lunch box. Something you could carry unobtrusively."

"If you never heard of the box, where did that come from?" Prince asked.

"Glad you're still paying attention. That was the last I heard . . . until about six months ago. It showed up in the mail, with a photocopy of the note. The return address was the Department of Defense, Arlington, Virginia."

Prince's eyes opened wide. "They wouldn't!"

"Wouldn't what?"

"Wouldn't just send you . . . in the mail . . ." His voice petered out. He seemed to forget he had the gun. He drew back in his chair, as if to get away from the toolbox.

"I don't see why not," Knox said. He flipped open the lid. "It's empty, see? An ordinary tool box, just a couple of extra holes drilled in it. Like wire-size holes."

Knox scratched his nose. "Of course, I knew the New York Police hadn't called the bomb squad over an empty box. I got curious about the contents, and I started calling and writing the Pentagon. I got a royal runaround—bureaucracy—but eventually, I would up talking to a lawyer attached to the research department. That's when I learned three things—the phrase "classified information" is no joke; holograph wills are not valid in the state of New York, and even if they were, all I'd been left was the *box*, which I now had, and not the contents; and three (unofficially), that somebody working for the Pentagon had so much respect for the late Dwight Noring that he directed the kid's last request to be honored to the extent possible, and that's why they sent me the box in the first place.

"Then they told me to shut up and not to bother them anymore."

Allen Prince was back to his old self now that the box had proved to be empty. "I admire the sentiment."

Knox grinned at him. "So? You've heard enough? Maybe I should go now?" He bent over and began to remove the wooden shoes.

"Stay, stay," Prince said. "There's a certain pulpish ingenuity to your hallucination. I'd like to see how it turned out."

Knox sat up and grinned. "I knew you would. Anyway, I didn't bother the Pentagon anymore, but I was plenty bothered myself. I started doing what I should have done after my first session with Dwight."

"Go ahead, I know you're going to tell me."

"I listened to the boy. I started acting like a cop instead of a shrink." Knox sighed. "Unethical. We're not supposed to pry into anything but the patient; we're not even supposed to try real hard to ascertain whether what he tells us is fantasy or reality, on the theory that the emotions are the same. Sometimes theory should take a hike.

"So I decided to treat every hint Dwight had given me as gospel. Of course I had help in reaching that conclusion. I don't expect the Pentagon's research department spends a couple of years examining a fantasy it found in a toolkit. Or bends procedure to honor the fantasist's last wish, do you?"

"I wouldn't presume to guess what goes on in someone's mind. That's your profession, Doctor, not mine."

Knox looked at him. "Don't sell yourself short, Mr. Prince. You're a master at guessing what's in other people's minds. That's how you manipulate them so well."

Knox shrugged and went on. "I'll give you this. From what I could tell, you were an excellent teacher for these kids. I tracked down a few of your former students. I especially liked your practice of having each kid at the beginning of the term pick something they felt would be impossible for them to accomplish, then assigning them to accomplish it as well as they could by Christmas break. That's exactly the kind of challenge a gifted student needs."

"I've always thought so."

"You don't have any of your former geniuses working for your organization, though, do you?"

"As a matter of fact, no. What of it?"

"Just interesting. Are smarter people somehow more selfish about the resources of Mother Gaia, do you think, or are they just better at sifting facts from propaganda? Where was I? Oh, yes, the assignments. For Janey Chang, it was to write a cantata in the manner of Bach. She's first cello with the Phoenix Symphony these days, you know. For Arnie Barheim, it was a novel. He has his own PR firm, now. Works for Mammoth Oil."

"Pity."

"They were good friends of Dwight's before he dropped out. They seem to recall that Dwight's impossible project was to build a laser small enough and powerful enough for a soldier to use in combat. They finished their assignments, but they didn't know if Dwight ever managed to complete his. But we do, don't we? I know because Dwight told me he did his homework; you know because he handed it in to him."

Knox leaned back with his hands behind his head. "What did you do, tell him it was dangerous and should be kept a secret? Until what? I can't see your turning it over to the Pentagon—not with your track record. On the other hand, you couldn't flunk Dwight, either. He'd make a stink, and build *another* one for the Pentagon. So that was one annoyance you were facing."

"Have you found more? In the course of your imagining, I mean?"

"I certainly have. I've found out where you were at the end of January the year Mark dropped out of school."

Allen Prince was a True Believer in those days. The evening before the launch, he sat on the patio swatting bugs and sweating in the Florida sun while he wondered what he was going to do with young Mr. Dwight Noring. There was no denying the boy's brainpower. Dwight was undoubtedly the most brilliant student who'd ever passed through the program. But that mind had been saddled with the most disgustingly bourgeois values and attitudes. One of the reasons Prince had taken this job was to try to stem the flow of the greatest minds to the profit-market beast that was oppressing the masses and eating up the planet's resources.

Young Mr. Noring treated everything wrong with the world as an opportunity for someone to be great. Pollution? Cars that run on hydrogen gas, and make fresh water as exhaust. Overpopulation? Not a problem for thousands of years, yet all long-term famines in this century deliberately caused by totalitarian governments, here are the figures to prove it. He always had the figures to prove it, and Prince just wasn't mathematically sophisticated enough to find the mistakes that must be there. It was a constant irritation.

Then there was the class trip. The university budgeted a certain amount of money to take the participants in the gifted-students program away somewhere between terms. Students usually voted, but the vote was almost always a rubber-stamp approval of Prince's recommendation. This year he had arranged for the students to spend a month at the Dawn of Man Commune in Idaho, where the participants lived life at a technology level of the late Stone Age. It was a magnificent way to gain an appreciation of nature.

Dwight Noring would have none of it. He led a revolt, and insisted that the class have a chance to vote to go to Florida to watch the launch of the space shuttle Challenger.

This was to be the one with that woman on board, the civilian. The schoolteacher. The one who said her job let her "touch the future." Allen Prince hoped she had more effect on her students than he had on these ungrateful snots. They backed Dwight enthusiastically.

Prince hated the space program. Usually, he echoed the standard line, and decried the waste of sending all the money into space to take pretty pictures and to bring back a few rocks when there were people starving on earth.

When he'd tried that on the class, Dwight had raised his hand and said, "Excuse me, Mr. Prince, but nobody ever sent a penny into space. The money remained on earth, creating jobs and stimulating the economy. Furthermore, the space program has more than paid for itself with the development of minicircuits, plastics, new medical technologies . . ."

And on and on. As usual, Dwight had the figures to prove it.

None of that mattered of course, because of the *real* reason he hated the space program. In fact, all these so-called miracles were *themselves* the reason. Allen Prince hated the space program because it allowed the bourgeois to delude themselves into believing there was *hope*. People who were convinced there was a Universe to explore and conquer and be learned from were unable to focus on the severity of the problems here on Earth. They kept pushing for *progress,* when it was progress that was killing the helpless snail darters and the owls; they wanted more technology instead of less. They wanted to continue to make their parasitical lives *easier* and longer, instead of harder and shorter, as an all-wise Nature intended.

The space program was the symbol of all this insane looking forward, and Allen Prince hated it. And here was Dwight Noring, ready to devote his amazing brain to that nonsense.

And now what had the boy done? He had delivered to him, all smiles, a powerful laser with a nearly invisible beam. The whole thing fit in a tool box. He had had Dwight show him how it worked the weekend before they left. Prince had watched in horrified fascination as Dwight burned his initials a half-inch deep in a boulder two miles away. The letters were two inches high; the lines that made them up about a quarter-inch thick. If this could be done to a rock at half a mile, what could it do to a human body at close range? What was Allen going to do with the thing? Dwight wouldn't let him suppress it, and he couldn't reveal it. He hadn't even dared leave it back in New York. He'd thrown it in the suitcase and brought it along.

Allen Prince thought. He had a few drinks, then thought some more. An idea came to him, and made him laugh. He had another drink and laughed some more.

What the hell, he'd do it. Pitting one of his problems against the other wouldn't destroy them both completely, but it would pass the time and make Prince feel a little better.

He drove his rented car a few miles to a nearly deserted beach that had a clear view of the launch pad. He grabbed the toolkit from the beach beside him, placed it on the roof of the car, aimed it as well as you can aim a toolbox, and pushed the button on top. A thin line of light was visible for about a pencil's length in front of the opening in the front of the toolbox as the beam hit some dust. That was all. Prince gave it about five seconds.

Combined with the drinks in him, it felt good. "Take that," he said, then, laughing, got back in the car and drove back to the hotel.

The next morning, he had a better vantage point. He and his group watched from a NASA-approved viewing site as the Challenger took off. Prince was disappointed as it cleared the launch pad. He'd been hoping his little prank last night would have screwed something up enough so that the launch would have to be delayed past the time they'd budgeted to stay in Florida. Serve young Mr. Dwight Noring right.

Then the ship blew up. Six astronauts and a civilian plunged to their deaths; a whole nation went into shock.

Including Allen Prince, though his reason was slightly different. It didn't last very long, either. Before he'd even gotten his stunned little geniuses back to the motel, Prince had realized that this incident was his step up to the big time in media awareness. The loudest and most extreme voices would make it into print and on the air. He made sure his was among them. He started with a statement accusing NASA of murder, and went on from there. That gave him the notoriety he needed to build a local organization into the vast movement it was today.

There were two flies in the ointment. One was his guilt over seven human lives. He soothed himself with the knowledge that what they were doing was harmful, a crime against the Nature of Things, and that they had served the world much better in death than they would have in life. Besides, when the official investigation blamed O-ring malfunction for the disaster, he was off the hook.

The other was Dwight Noring. He wanted his laser back. And he wanted a grade.

"You can't have it," he said. "I destroyed it. I smashed it and threw it in the ocean."

"You can't do that! It's my work, and the material wasn't cheap, either! I'll build another one! My father will go to the chancellor about this."

Prince grabbed the boy by the shirt. "Listen, you little bastard, you say one word about this, and I'll testify to the authorities you were down there in Florida with your little laser weapon. They'll love that."

The kid turned white. He went limp in Prince's hands. His face wore a look of horror. "You," he said. "You had it. You—"

"No, Dwight. *You. You're* the genius. *You* built it. Everyone will know *I* couldn't have. And you're a frustrated spaceboy, aren't you? Everybody knows that. They'll remember that John Lennon was shot by somebody who called himself his 'Number One Fan.' So you just keep your mouth shut and your parents happy, and have a nice life."

It was a risk, but it worked. Prince left the university to run his movement full-time, and Dwight dropped out, accompanied by a concerned note from his former teacher, suggesting oh-so-subtly that Dwight had burnt out on his own brainpower.

Aside from the news of Dwight's suicide, which reached the busy Allen Prince months after the fact, he hadn't heard another word about it.

Until today.

"Do you know where the word 'sabotage' comes from?" Peter Knox asked.

"Huh? Oh, from French, I think."

Knox chuckled. "So it *was* unintentional. 'Sabotage' comes from French, all right. At the beginning of the Industrial Revolution, when weaving machines were first brought to France, the weavers stormed the factories, destroying the machines by throwing their *sabots* into them. Do you know what a *sabot* is?"

"I studied German."

"A *sabot* is a wooden shoe."

Prince started to laugh. "Does it really? Oh, marvelous! I wish someone had told me sooner."

"I accuse you of sabotage, Mr. Prince. I accuse you of damaging the space shuttle *Challenger*. I accuse you of sabotaging the promising young life of Dwight Noring. Even more, I accuse you of trying to destroy the human race's entire reason for living."

"Damn! I must be a terrible person. What is this reason?"

"To learn. To grow. To build. To face problems as they come up, and *defeat* them, damn you, not run away like a puppy who's been slapped on the nose. But you're just like the original saboteurs. You might delay progress, but you'll never stop it."

Prince rubbed his chin. "No, it usually takes a war to do that."

"War's a lot less likely than it used to be."

Prince was silent for a few minutes, thinking. "I'm going to tell you a few things that may surprise you, Dr. Knox."

"Like you're not going to kill me?"

"This gun is for defense only. I have better methods of attack. Take off all your clothes, please." He smiled at the look on Knox's face. "You see, I *did* surprise you. Relax. I just want to make sure you're not concealing any recording or transmitting device. I know you said you weren't, but you might be lying now, mightn't you?"

Knox complied. As he stood there naked, Prince walked behind him and tugged at Knox's hair and beard. "Can't be too careful, you know."

"I just grew them in order to look like somebody you might let in up here."

"Well, it worked. Sit down, Doctor." Prince went through the clothes Knox had taken off, then threw them back. "Get dressed now. Your knapsack stays here when you go. Oh, and I'll take your watch, as well."

Knox took a look at the dial before handing it over. "I ought to be going soon," he said.

"This won't take long. I'm going to confess. You see, I did fire the laser at the rocket." He went on to tell the whole story. "Of course, when they found out about the defect in the O-ring," he concluded, "I slept better. No one will ever know whether it was my tipsy escapade that did the damage or the O-ring as all the experts said."

Knox snorted. "Dwight didn't have any doubts. And it would have been better for you if they'd *never* found any defect in the O-rings."

"Why do you say that?"

"Because they would never have launched another human into space before they found the cause of the disaster. And how would they have found a little pinhole, especially after it had been the focus of an explosion? You would have destroyed manned space flight permanently. As it is, you may have saved future disasters by inadvertently bringing the O-ring problem to light."

"I'd never thought of it that way. I don't suppose that earns me any credit with you."

"None."

"Good. I don't want any mixed feelings here. You may be wondering why I told you all this."

"It's crossed my mind."

"It's because I hate you, Mr. Knox. I hate you most of all because on your last point, I have come to know you are right. The human race *is* a pack of greedy gluttons who won't rest content until they exterminate everything on the planet, and then themselves with their *progress*.

"So be it. Let them have their suicide party. But I have arranged things so that it's being held in *my hall*. Any of your precious so-called progress will have to pass through *me*. I'll collect what I can from the spoiling bastards, and I'll drive out of business those I can. I'll drive them to suicide, if I can manage it. You call me a saboteur. I want to tell you it is my intention to be the greatest saboteur in the history of economics—before the end comes."

"And you want me to know that."

"I want just one of you smug, destructive bastards to know that. And you're the perfect one, Dr. Knox, because no one will be able to prove we ever met. You have no evidence of *anything*. And if you take this to the media, who do you think the media will believe?"

"You can be fought, you know. You can be fought the same way you fight."

"Go ahead, Doctor Knox. Try to speed your inevitable victory. Fight. I'm not going anywhere, except back to my writing."

"I'm counting on that," Knox said.

Peter Knox finished lacing up his boots, then walked away from the house, moving quickly but not running. He went back the way he came, through the solar array. All the mirrors had moved with the sun, in order to keep their burning rays trained on the water tower.

All but one. This one hadn't moved since Knox had walked by here before. It was still angled for the morning sun, and it shot its afternoon beam in the direction Knox had calculated during the days he'd spent on Prince's

mountain, scouting and figuring. He could see the brightness now, slashing across the house, leaving a trail of fire,
sealing off the study wing. Knox could see Prince now,
banging against the windows of his study. Within a minute, the beam hit the window itself. It wasn't quite a laser,
just five or six hundred degrees of concentrated heat. Knox
thought he could hear a scream.

A puff of smoke obscured the window. When it cleared,
Prince was gone. Knox shuddered. It was, he had to remind
himself, probably an easier death than that suffered by the
Challenger crew.

This would be, he reflected, a perfect opportunity to
make a fuss, call a press conference, denounce solar energy
as dangerous, and call for its banishment. He could see the
NO SOLAR buttons, and the picketers.

But he wouldn't do it. Someday, someone, maybe someone like Dwight Noring, would figure out how to use solar
power economically. *That* would be progress. *That* would
be how humanity is supposed to work.

In the meantime Knox bent, and with an effort, pulled
loose the object with which he'd jammed the movement of
the mirror.

It was a wooden shoe.

JACK BE QUICK
by Barbara Paul

Who was Jack the Ripper? More people have addressed this question than have sought the solution to any other murder case in human history.

30 September 1888, St. Jude's Vicarage, Whitechapel
He took two, this time, and within the same hour, Inspector Abberline told us. The first victim was found this morning less than an hour after midnight, in a small court off Berner Street. The second woman was killed in Mitre Square forty-five minutes later. He did his hideous deed and then escaped undetected, as he always does. Inspector Abberline believes he was interrupted in Berner Street, because he did not . . . do to that woman what he'd done to his other victims. My husband threw the Inspector a warning look, not wanting me exposed to such distressing matters more than necessary. "But the second woman was severely mutilated," Inspector Abberline concluded, offering no details. "He finished in Mitre Square what he'd begun in Berner Street."

My husband and I knew nothing of the double murder, not having left the vicarage all day. When no one appeared for morning services, Edward was angry. Customarily we can count on a Sunday congregation of a dozen or so; we should have suspected something was amiss. "Do you know who the women were, Inspector?" I asked.

"One of them," he said. "His Mitre Square victim was

named Catherine Eddowes. We have yet to establish the identity of the Berner Street victim."

Inspector Abberline looked exhausted; I poured him another cup of tea. He undoubtedly would have preferred something stronger, but Edward permitted no spirits in the house, not even sherry. I waited until the Inspector had taken a sip before I put my next question to him. "Did he cut out Catherine Eddowes's womb the way he did Annie Chapman's?"

Edward looked shocked that I should know about that, but the police investigator was beyond shock. "Yes, Mrs. Wickham, he did. But this time he did not take it away with him."

It was one of the many concerns that baffled and horrified me about the series of grisly murders haunting London. Annie Chapman's disemboweled body had been found in Hanbury Street three weeks earlier; all the entrails had been piled above her shoulder except the womb. Why had he stolen her womb? "And the intestines?"

"Heaped over the left shoulder, as before."

Edward cleared his throat. "This Eddowes woman . . . she was a prostitute?"

Inspector Abberline said she was. "And I have no doubt that the Berner Street victim will prove to have been on the game as well. That's the only common ground among his victims—they were all prostitutes."

"Evil combating evil," Edward said with a shake of his head. "When will it end?"

Inspector Abberline put down his cup. "The end, alas, is not yet in sight. We are still conducting door-to-door searches, and the populace are beginning to panic. We have our hands full dispersing the mobs."

"Mobs?" Edward asked. "Has there been trouble?"

"I regret to say there has. Everyone is so desperate to find someone to blame . . ." The Inspector allowed the unfinished sentence to linger a moment. "Earlier today a constable was chasing a petty thief through the streets, and someone who saw them called out, 'It's the Ripper!' Several men joined in the chase, and then others, as the word spread that it was the Ripper the constable was pursuing. That mob was thirsting for blood—nothing less than a lynching would have satisfied them. The thief and the constable ended up barricading themselves in a building together until help could arrive."

Edward shook his head sadly. "The world has gone mad."

"It's why I have come to you, Vicar," Inspector Abberline said. "You can help calm them down. You could speak to them, persuade them to compose themselves. Your presence in the streets will offer a measure of reassurance."

"Of course," Edward said quickly. "Shall we leave now? I'll get my coat."

The Inspector turned to me. "Mrs. Wickham, thank you for the tea. Now we must be going." I saw both men to the door.

The Inspector did not know he had interrupted a disagreement between my husband and me, one that was recurring with increasing frequency of late. But I had no wish to revive the dispute when Edward returned; the shadow of these two new murders lay like a shroud over all other concerns. I retired to my sewing closet, where I tried to calm my spirit through prayer. One could not think dispassionately of this unknown man wandering the streets of London's East End, a man who hated women so profoundly that he cut away those parts of the bodies that proclaimed his victims to be female. I tried to pray for *him*, lost soul that he is; God forgive me, I could not.

1 October 1888, St. Jude's Vicarage
Early the next morning the fog lay so thick about the vicarage that the street gaslights were still on. They performed their usual efficient function of lighting the *tops* of the poles; looking down from our bedroom window, I could not see the street below.

Following our morning reading from the Scriptures, Edward called my attention to an additional passage. "Since you are aware of what the Ripper does to his victims, Beatrice, it will be to your benefit to hear this. Attend. 'Let the breast be torn open and the heart and vitals be taken from hence and thrown over the shoulder.' "

A moment of nausea overtook me. "The same way Annie Chapman and the others were killed."

"Exactly," Edward said with a hint of triumph in his voice. "Those are Solomon's words, ordering the execution of three murderers. I wonder if anyone has pointed this passage out to Inspector Abberline? It could be of assistance in ascertaining the rationale behind these murders, perhaps revealing something of the killer's mental disposition . . ." He continued in this speculative vein for a while longer.

I was folding linen as I listened. When he paused for breath, I asked Edward about his chambray shirt. "I've not seen it these two weeks."

"Eh? It will turn up. I'm certain you have put it away somewhere."

I was equally certain I had not. Then, with some trepidation, I reintroduced the subject of our disagreement the night before. "Edward, let me urge you to reconsider your position concerning charitable donations. If parishioners can't turn to their church for help—"

"Allow me to interrupt you, my dear," he said. "I am convinced that suffering *cannot* be reduced by indiscriminately passing out money but only through the realistic appraisal of each man's problems. So long as the lower classes depend upon charity to see them through hard times, they will never learn thrift and the most propitious manner of spending what money they have."

Edward's "realistic appraisal" of individual problems always ended the same way, with little lectures on how to economize. "But surely in cases of extreme hardship, a small donation would not be detrimental to their future well-being."

"Ah, but how are we to determine who are those in true need? They will tell any lie to get their hands on a few coins which they promptly spend on hard drink. And then they threaten us when those coins are not forthcoming!

This is the legacy my predecessor at St. Jude's has left us, this expectancy that the church *owes* them charity!"

That was true; the vicarage had been stoned more than once when Edward had turned petitioners away. "But the children, Edward—surely we can help the children! They are not to blame for their parents' wastrel ways."

Edward sat down next to me and took my hand. "You have a soft heart and a generous nature, Beatrice, and I venerate those qualities in you. Your natural instinct for charity is one of your most admirable traits." He smiled sadly. "Nevertheless, how will these poor, desperate creatures ever learn to care for their own children if we do it for them? And there is this. Has it not occurred to you that God may be testing *us?* How simple it would be, to hand out a few coins and convince ourselves we have done our Christian duty! No, Beatrice, God is asking more of us than that. We must hold firm in our resolve."

I acquiesced, seeing no chance of prevailing against such unshakable certitude that God's will was dictating our course of action. Furthermore, Edward Wickham was my husband and I owed him obedience, even when my heart was troubled and filled with uncertainty. It was his decision to make, not mine.

"Do not expect me until teatime," Edward said as he rose and went to fetch his greatcoat. "Mr. Lusk has asked me to attend a meeting of the Whitechapel Vigilance Committee, and I then have my regular calls to make. Best you not go out today, my dear, at least until Inspector Abberline has these riots under control." Edward's duties were keeping him away from the vicarage more and more. He sometimes would return in the early hours of the morning, melancholy and exhausted from trying to help a man find night work or from locating shelter for a homeless widow and her children. At times he seemed not to remember where he'd been; I was concerned for his health and his spirit.

The fog was beginning to lift by the time he departed, but I still could not see very far—except in my mind's eye. If one were to proceed down Commercial Street and then follow Aldgate to Leadenhall and Cornhill on to the point where six roads meet at a statue of the Duke of Wellington, one would find oneself in front of the imposing Royal Exchange, its rich interior murals and Turkish floor paving a proper setting for the transactions undertaken there. Across Threadneedle Street, the Bank of England, with its windowless lower stories, and the rocklike Stock Exchange both raise their impressive façades. Then one could turn to the opposite direction and behold several other banking establishments clustered around Mansion House, the Lord Mayor's residence. It still dumbfounds me to realize that the wealth of the nation is concentrated there, in so small an area . . . all within walking distance of the worst slums in the nation.

Do wealthy bankers ever spare a thought for the *appalling* poverty of Whitechapel and Spitalfields? The people living within the boundaries of St. Jude's parish are crowded like animals into a labyrinth of courts and alleys, none of which intersect major streets. The crumbling, hazardous buildings fronting the courts house complete families in each room, sometimes numbering as many as eleven people; in such circumstances, incest is common . . . and, some say, inevitable. The buildings reek from the liquid sewage accumulated in the basements, while the courts themselves stink of garbage that attracts vermin, dogs, and other scavengers. Often one standing pipe in the courtyard serves as the sole source of water for all the inhabitants of three or four buildings, an outdoor pipe that freezes with unremitting regularity during the winter. Once Edward and I were called out in the middle of the night to succor a woman suffering from scarlet fever; we found her in a foul-smelling single room with three children and four pigs. Her husband, a cabman, had committed suicide the month before; and it wasn't until we were leaving that we discovered one of the children had been lying there dead for thirteen days.

The common lodging houses are even worse—filthy and infested and reservoirs of disease. In such doss houses a bed can be rented for fourpence for the night, strangers often sharing a bed because neither has the full price alone.

There is no such thing as privacy, since the beds are lined up in crowded rows in the manner of dormitories. Beds are rented indiscriminately to men and women alike; consequently many of the doss houses are in truth brothels, and even those that are not have no compunction about renting a bed to a prostitute when she brings a paying customer with her. Inspector Abberline once told us the police estimate there are twelve hundred prostitutes in Whitechapel alone, fertile hunting grounds for the man who pleasures himself with the butchering of ladies of the night.

Ever since the Ripper began stalking the East End, Edward has been campaigning for more police to patrol the back alleys and for better street lighting. The problem is that Whitechapel is so poor it cannot afford the rates to pay for these needed improvements. If there is to be help, it must come from outside. Therefore I have undertaken a campaign of my own. Every day I write to philanthropists, charitable establishments, government officials. I petition every personage of authority and goodwill with whose name I am conversant, pleading the cause of the *children* of Whitechapel, especially those ragged, dirty street Arabs who sleep wherever they can, eat whatever they can scavenge or steal, and perform every unspeakable act demanded of them in exchange for a coin they can call their own.

12 October 1888, Golden Lane Mortuary, City of London
Today I did something I have never done before: I willfully disobeyed my husband. Edward had forbidden me to attend the inquest of Catherine Eddowes, saying I should not expose myself to such unsavory disclosures as were bound to be made. Also, he said it was unseemly for the vicar's wife to venture abroad unaccompanied, a dictum that impresses me as more appropriately belonging to another time and place. I waited until Edward left the vicarage and then hurried on my way. My path took me past one of the larger slaughterhouses in the area; with my handkerchief covering my mouth and nose to keep out the stench, I had to cross the road to avoid the blood and urine flooding the

pavement. Once I had left Whitechapel, however, the way was unencumbered.

Outside the Golden Lane Mortuary I was pleased to encounter Inspector Abberline; he was surprised to see me there and immediately offered himself as my protector. "Is the Reverend Mr. Wickham not with you?"

"He has business in Shoreditch," I answered truthfully, not adding that Edward found inquests distasteful and would not have attended in any event.

"This crowd could turn ugly, Mrs. Wickham," Inspector Abberline said. "Let me see if I can obtain us two chairs near the door."

That he did, with the result that I had to stretch in a most unladylike manner to see over other people's heads. "Inspector," I said, "have you learned the identity of the other woman who was killed the same night as Catherine Eddowes?"

"Yes, it was Elizabeth Stride—Long Liz, they called her. About forty-five years of age and homely as sin, if you'll pardon my speaking ill of the dead. They were all unattractive, all the Ripper's victims. One thing is certain, he didn't choose them for their beauty."

"Elizabeth Stride was a prostitute?"

"That she was, Mrs. Wickham, I'm sorry to say. She had nine children somewhere, and a husband, until he could tolerate her drunkenness no longer and turned her out. A woman with a nice big family like that and a husband who supported them—what reasons could she have had to turn to drink?"

I could think of nine or ten. "What about Catherine Eddowes? Did she have children, too?"

Inspector Abberline rubbed the side of his nose. "Well, she had a daughter, that much we know. We haven't located her yet, though."

The inquest was ready to begin. The small room was crowded, with observers standing along the walls and even outside in the passageway. The presiding coroner called the first witness, the police constable who found Catherine Eddowes's body.

The remarkable point to emerge from the constable's testimony was that his patrol took him through Mitre Square, where he'd found the body, every fourteen or fifteen minutes. The Ripper had only fifteen minutes to inflict so much damage? How swift he was, how sure of what he was doing!

It came out during the inquest that the Eddowes woman had been strangled before her killer had cut her throat, thus explaining why she had not cried out. In response to my whispered question, Inspector Abberline said yes, the other victims had also been strangled first. When the physicians present at the post mortem testified, they were agreed that the killer had sound anatomical knowledge but they were not in accord as to the extent of his actual skill in removing the organs. Their reports of what had been done to the body were disturbing; I grew slightly faint during the description of how the flaps of the abdomen had been peeled back to expose the intestines.

Inspector Abberline's sworn statement was succinct and free of speculation; he testified as to the course of action pursued by the police following the discovery of the body. There were other witnesses, people who had encountered Catherine Eddowes on the night she was killed. At one time she had been seen speaking to a middle-aged man wearing a black coat of good quality which was now slightly shabby; it was the same description that had emerged during the investigation of one of the Ripper's earlier murders. But at the end of it all we were no nearer to knowing the Ripper's identity than ever; the verdict was "willful murder by some person unknown."

I refused Inspector Abberline's offer to have one of his assistants escort me home. "That makes six women he's killed now, this Ripper," I said. "You need all of your men for your investigation."

The Inspector rubbed the side of his nose, a mannerism I was coming to recognize indicated uncertainty. "As a matter of fact, Mrs. Wickham, I am of the opinion that only four were killed by the same man. You are thinking of the woman murdered near St. Jude's Church? And the one in

Osborn Street?" He shook his head. "Not the Ripper's work, I'm convinced of it."

"What makes you think so, Inspector?"

"Because while those two women did have their throats cut, they weren't cut in the same manner as the later victims'. There is a *viciousness* in the way the Ripper slashes his victims' throats . . . he is left-handed, we know, and he slashes twice, once each way. The cuts are deep, brutal . . . he almost took Annie Chapman's head off. No, Polly Nichols was his first victim, then Chapman. And now this double murder, Elizabeth Stride and Catherine Eddowes. Those four are all the work of the same man."

I shuddered. "Did the four women know one another?"

"Not that we can determine," Inspector Abberline replied. "Evidently they had nothing in common except the fact that they were all four prostitutes."

More questions occurred to me, but I had detained the Inspector long enough. I bade him farewell and started back to St. Jude's, a long walk from Golden Lane. The daylight was beginning to fail, but I had no money for a hansom cab. I pulled my shawl tight about my shoulders and hurried my step, not wishing to be caught out of doors after dark. It was my husband's opinion that since the Ripper killed only prostitutes, respectable married women had nothing to fear. It was my opinion that my husband put altogether too much faith in the Ripper's ability to tell the difference.

I was almost home when a most unhappy incident ensued. A distraught woman approached me in Middlesex Street, carrying what looked like a bundle of rags which she thrust into my arms. Inside the rags was a dead baby. I cried out and almost dropped the cold little body.

"All he needed were a bit o' milk," the mother said, tears running down her cheeks.

"Oh, I am so sorry!" I gasped helplessly. The poor woman looked half starved herself.

"They said it was no use a-sending to the church," she sobbed, "for you didn't never give nothing though you spoke kind."

I was so ashamed I had to lower my head. Even then I didn't have tuppence in my pocket to give her. I slipped off my shawl and wrapped it around the tiny corpse. "Bury him in this."

She mumbled something as she took the bundle from me and staggered away. She would prepare to bury her child in the shawl, but at the last moment she would snatch back the shawl's warmth for herself. She would cry over her dead baby as she did it, but she would do it. I prayed that she would do it.

16 October 1888, St. Jude's Vicarage
This morning I paid an out-of-work bricklayer fourpence to clean out our fireplaces. In the big fireplace in the kitchen, he made a surprising discovery: soot-blackened buttons from my husband's missing chambray shirt turned up. When later I asked Edward why he had burned his best shirt, he looked at me in utter astonishment and demanded to know why *I* had burned it. Yet we two are the only ones living at the vicarage.

22 October 1888, Spitalfields Market
The chemist regretfully informed me that the price of arsenic had risen, so of necessity I purchased less than the usual quantity, hoping Edward would find the diminished volume sufficient. Keeping the vicarage free of rats was costly. When first we took up residence at St. Jude's, we believed the rats were coming from the warehouses farther along Commercial Street; but then we came to understand that every structure in Whitechapel was plagued with vermin. As fast as one killed them, others appeared to take their place.

A newspaper posted outside an ale house caught my eye; I had made it a point to read every word published about the Ripper. The only new thing was that all efforts to locate the family of Catherine Eddowes, the Ripper's last victim, had failed. A front-page editorial demanded the resignation of the Commissioner of Police and various other men in authority. Three weeks had passed since the Ripper had taken two victims on the same night, and the police still had no helpful clues and no idea of who the Ripper was or when he would strike next. That he would strike again, no one doubted; that the police could protect the women of Whitechapel, no one believed.

In the next street I came upon a posted bill requesting anyone with information concerning the identity of the murderer to step forward and convey that information to the police. The request saddened me; the police could not have formulated a clearer admission of failure.

25 October 1888, St. Jude's Vicarage
Edward is ill. When he had not appeared at the vicarage by teatime yesterday, I began to worry. I spent an anxious evening awaiting his return; it was well after midnight before I heard his key in the lock.

He looked like a stranger. His eyes were glistening and his clothes in disarray; his usual proud bearing had degenerated into a stoop, his shoulders hunched as if he were cold. The moment he caught sight of me he began berating me for failing to purchase the arsenic he needed to kill the rats; it was only when I led him to the pantry where he himself had spread the noxious powder around the rat holes did his reprimands cease. His skin was hot and dry, and with difficulty I persuaded him into bed.

But sleep would not come. I sat by the bed and watched him thrashing among the covers, throwing off the cool cloth I had placed on his forehead. Edward kept waving his hands as if trying to fend someone off; what nightmares was he seeing behind those closed lids? In his delirium he began to cry out. At first the words were not clear, but then I understood my husband to be saying, "Whores! Whores! All whores!"

When by two in the morning his fever had not broken, I knew I had to seek help. I wrapped my cloak about me and set forth, not permitting myself to dwell on what could be hiding in the shadows. I do not like admitting it, but I was terrified; nothing less than Edward's illness could have driven me into the streets of Whitechapel at night. But I reached my destination with nothing untoward happening; I roused Dr. Phelps from a sound sleep and rode back to the vicarage with him in his carriage.

When Dr. Phelps bent over the bed, Edward's eyes flew open; he seized the doctor's upper arm in a grip that made the man wince. "They must be stopped!" my husband whispered hoarsely. "They . . . must be stopped!"

"We will stop them," Dr. Phelps replied gently and eased Edward's hand away. Edward's eyes closed and his body resumed its thrashing.

The doctor's examination was brief. "The fever is making him hallucinate," he told me. "Sleep is the best cure, followed by a period of bed rest." He took a small vial from his bag and asked me to bring a glass of water. He tapped a few drops of liquid into the water, which he then poured into Edward's mouth as I held his head.

"What did you give him?" I asked.

"Laudanum, to make him sleep. I will leave the vial with you." Dr. Phelps rubbed his right arm where Edward had gripped him. "Strange, I do not recall Mr. Wickham as being left-handed."

"He is ambidextrous. This fever . . . will he recover?"

"The next few hours will tell. Give him more laudanum only if he awakes in this same disturbed condition, and then only one drop in a glass of water. I will be back later to see how he is."

When Dr. Phelps had gone, I replaced the cool cloth on Edward's forehead and resumed my seat by the bed. Edward did seem calmer now, the wild thrashing at an end and only the occasional twitching of the hands betraying his inner turmoil. By dawn he was in a deep sleep and seemed less feverish.

My spirit was too disturbed to permit me to sleep. I decided to busy myself with household chores. Edward's black greatcoat was in need of a good brushing, so that came first. It was then that I discovered the rust-colored stains on the cuffs; they did not look fresh, but I could not be certain. Removing them was a delicate matter. The coat had seen better days and the cloth would not withstand vigorous handling. But eventually I got the worst of the stains out and hung the coat in the armoire.

Then I knelt by the bedroom window and prayed. I asked God to vanquish the dark suspicions that had begun to cloud my mind.

Whitechapel had changed Edward. Since he had accepted the appointment to St. Jude's, he had become more distant, more aloof. He had always been a reserved man, speaking rarely of himself and never of his past. I knew nothing of his childhood, only that he had been born in London; he had always discouraged my inquiring about the years before we met. If my parents had still been living when Edward first began to pay court, they would never have permitted me to entertain a man with no background, no family, and no connections. But by then I had passed what was generally agreed to be a marriageable age, and I was enchanted by the appearance out of nowhere of a gentleman of compatible spirit who desired me to spend my life with him. All I knew of Edward was that he was a little older than most new curates were, suggesting that he had started in some other profession, or had at least studied for one, before joining the clergy. Our twelve years together had been peaceful ones, and I had never regretted my choice.

But try as he might to disguise the fact, Edward's perspective had grown harsher during our tenure in Whitechapel. Sadly, he held no respect for the people whose needs he was here to minister to. I once heard him say to a fellow vicar, "The lower classes render no useful service. They create no wealth—more often they destroy it. They degrade whatever they touch, and as individuals are most probably incapable of improvement. Thrift and good management mean nothing to them. I resist terming them hopeless, but perhaps that is what they are." The Edward Wickham I married would never have spoken so.

"Beatrice."

I glanced toward the bed; Edward was awake and watching me. I rose from my knees and went to his side. "How do you feel, Edward?"

"Weak, as if I've lost a lot of blood." He looked confused. "Am I ill?"

I explained about the fever. "Dr. Phelps says you need a great deal of rest."

"Dr. Phelps? He was here?" Edward remembered nothing of the doctor's visit. Nor did he remember where he'd been the night before or even coming home. "This is frightening," he said shakily. His speech was slurred, an effect of the laudanum. "Hours of my life missing and no memory of them?"

"We will worry about that later. Right now you must try to sleep some more."

"Sleep . . . yes." I sat and held his hand until he drifted off again.

When he awoke a second time a few hours later, I brought him a bowl of broth, which he consumed with reawakening appetite. My husband was clearly on the mend; he was considering getting out of bed when Dr. Phelps stopped by.

The doctor was pleased with Edward's progress. "Spend the rest of the day resting," he said, "and then tomorrow you may be allowed up. You must be careful not to overtax yourself or the fever may recur."

Edward put up a show of protesting, but I think he was secretly relieved that nothing was required of him except that he lie in bed all day. I escorted the doctor to the door.

"Make sure he eats," he said to me. "He needs to rebuild his strength."

I said I'd see to it. Then I hesitated; I could not go on without knowing. "Dr. Phelps, did anything happen last night?"

"I beg your pardon?"

He didn't know what I meant. "Did the Ripper strike again?"

Dr. Phelps smiled. "I am happy to say he did not. Perhaps we've seen an end of these dreadful killings, hmm?"

My relief was so great it was all I could do not to burst into tears. When the doctor had gone, I again fell to my knees and prayed, this time asking God to forgive me for entertaining such treacherous thoughts about my own husband.

1 November 1888, Leman Street Police Station, Whitechapel

It was with a light heart that I left the vicarage this bright, crisp Tuesday morning. My husband was recovered from his recent indisposition and busy with his daily duties. I had received two encouraging replies to my petitions for charitable assistance for Whitechapel's children. And London had survived the entire month of October without another Ripper killing.

I was on my way to post two letters, my responses to the philanthropists who seemed inclined to listen to my plea. In my letters I had pointed out that over half the children born in Whitechapel die before they reach the age of five. The ones who do not die are mentally and physically underdeveloped; many of them who are taken into pauper schools are adjudged abnormally dull if not actual mental defectives. Children frequently arrive at school crying from hunger and then collapse at their benches. In winter they are too cold to think about learning their letters or doing their sums. The schools themselves are shamefully mismanaged and the children sometimes mistreated; there are school directors who pocket most of the budget and hire out the children to sweatshop owners as cheap labor.

What I proposed was the establishment of a boarding school for the children of Whitechapel, a place where the young would be provided with hygienic living conditions, healthful food to eat, and warm clothing to wear—all before they ever set foot in a classroom. Then when their physical needs had been attended to, they would be given proper educational and moral instruction. The school was to be administered by an honest and conscientious director who could be depended upon never to exploit the downtrodden. All this would cost a great deal of money.

My letters went into the post accompanied by a silent prayer. I was then in Leman Street, not far from the police

station. I stopped in and asked if Inspector Abberline was
there.

He was; he greeted me warmly and offered me a chair.
After inquiring after my husband's health, he sat back and
looked at me expectantly.

Now that I was there, I felt a tinge of embarrassment. "It
is presumptuous of me, I know," I said, "but may I make a
suggestion? Concerning the Ripper, I mean. You've undoubtedly thought of every possible approach, but . . ." I
didn't finish my sentence because he was laughing.

"Forgive me, Mrs. Wickham," he said, still smiling. "I
would like to show you something." He went into another
room and returned shortly carrying a large box filled with
papers. "These are letters," he explained, "from concerned
citizens like yourself. Each one offers a plan for capturing
the Ripper. And we have two more boxes just like this
one."

I flushed and rose to leave. "Then I'll not impose—"

"Please, Mrs. Wickham, take your seat. We read every
letter that comes to us and give serious consideration to
every suggestion made. I show you the box only to convince
you we welcome suggestions."

I resumed my seat, not fully convinced but nevertheless
encouraged by the Inspector's courtesy. "Very well." I tried
to gather my thoughts. "The Ripper's first victim, you are
convinced, was Polly Nichols?"

"Correct. Buck's Row, the last day of August."

"The *Illustrated Times* said that she was forty-two years
old and separated from her husband, to whom she had
borne five children. The cause of their separation was her
propensity for strong drink. Mr. Nichols made his wife an
allowance, according to the *Times,* until he learned of her
prostitution—at which time he discontinued all pecuniary
assistance. Is this account essentially correct?"

"Yes, it is."

"The Ripper's next victim was Annie Chapman, about
forty, who was murdered early in September?"

"The night of the eighth," Inspector Abberline said, "although her body wasn't found until six the next morning.

She was killed in Hanbury Street, less than half a mile from the Buck's Row site of Polly Nichols's murder."

I nodded. "Annie Chapman also ended on the streets because of drunkenness. She learned her husband had died only when her allowance stopped. When she tried to find her two children, she discovered they had been separated and sent to different schools, one of them abroad."

Inspector Abberline raised an eyebrow. "How did you ascertain that, Mrs. Wickham?"

"One of our parishioners knew her," I said. "Next came the double murder of Elizabeth Stride and Catherine Eddowes, during the small hours of the thirtieth of September. Berner Street and Mitre Square, a fifteen-minute walk from each other. The Stride woman was Swedish by birth and claimed to be a widow, but I have heard that may not be true. She was a notorious inebriate, according to one of the constables patroling Fairclough Street, and she may simply have been ashamed to admit her husband would not allow her near the children—the *nine* children. Is this also correct?"

The Inspector was looking bemused. "It is."

"Of Catherine Eddowes I know very little. But the *Times* said she had spent the night before her death locked up in the Cloak Lane Police Station, because she'd been found lying drunk in the street somewhere in Aldgate. And you yourself told me she had a daughter. Did she also have a husband, Inspector?"

He nodded slowly. "A man named Conway. We've been unable to trace him."

The same pattern in each case. "You've said on more than one occasion that the four victims had only their prostitution in common. But in truth, Inspector, they had a great deal in common. They were all in their forties. They were all lacking in beauty. They had all been married. They all lost their homes through a weakness for the bottle." I took a breath. "And they were all mothers."

Inspector Abberline looked at me quizzically.

"They were all mothers *who abandoned their children.*"

He considered it. "You think the Ripper had been abandoned?"

"Is it not possible? Or perhaps he, too, had a wife he turned out because of drunkenness. I don't know where he fits into the pattern. But consider. The nature of the murders makes it quite clear that these women are not just killed the way the unfortunate victim of a highwayman is killed—the women are being *punished.*" I was uncomfortable speaking of such matters, but speak I must. "The manner of their deaths, one might say, is a grotesque version of the way they earned their livings."

The Inspector was also uncomfortable. "They were not raped, Mrs. Wickham."

"But of course they were, Inspector," I said softly. "They were raped with a knife."

I had embarrassed him. "We should not be speaking of this," he said, further chagrined at seeming to rebuke the vicar's wife. "These are not matters that concern you."

"All I ask is that you consider what I have said."

"Oh, I can promise you that," he answered wryly, and I believed him. "I do have some encouraging news," he continued, desirous of changing the subject. "We have been given more men to patrol the streets—more than have ever before been concentrated in one section of London! The next time the Ripper strikes, we'll be ready for him."

"Then you think he will strike again."

"I fear so. He's not done yet."

It was the same opinion that was held by everyone else, but it was more ominous coming from the mouth of a police investigator. I thanked Inspector Abberline for his time and left.

The one thing that had long troubled me about the investigation of the Ripper murders was the refusal of the investigators to acknowledge that there was anything carnal about these violent acts. The killings were the work of a madman, the police and the newspapers agreed . . . as if that explained everything. But unless Inspector Abberline and the rest of those in authority could see the fierce hatred of women that drove the Ripper, I despaired of his ever being caught.

10 November 1888, Miller's Court, Spitalfields
At three in the morning, I was still fully dressed, awaiting Edward's return to the vicarage. It had been hours since I'd made my last excuse to myself for his absence; his duties frequently kept him out late, but never this late. I was trying to decide whether I should go to Dr. Phelps for help when a frantic knocking started at the door.

It was a young market porter named Macklin who occasionally attended services at St. Jude's, and he was in a frantic state. "It's the missus," he gasped. " 'Er time is come and the midwife's too drunk to stand up. Will you come?"

I said I would. "Let me get a few things." I was distracted, wanting to send him away; but this was the Macklins' first child and I couldn't turn down his plea for help.

We hurried off in the direction of Spitalfields; the couple had recently rented a room in a slum building facing on Miller's Court. I knew the area slightly. Edward and I had once been called to a doss house there to minister to a dying man. That was the first time I'd ever been inside one of the common lodging houses; it was a big place, over three hundred beds and every one of them rented for the night.

Miller's Court was right across the street from the doss house. As we went into the court, a girl of about twelve unfolded herself from the doorway where she had been huddled and tugged at my skirt. "Fourpence for a doss, lady?"

"Get out of 'ere!" Macklin yelled. "Go on!"

"Just a moment," I stopped him. I asked the girl if she had no home to go to.

"Mum turned me out," the girl answered sullenly. "Says don't come back 'til light."

I understood; frequently the women here put their children out on the street while they rented their room for immoral purposes. "I have no money," I told the girl, "but you may come inside."

"Not in my room, she don't!" Macklin shouted.

"She can be of help, Mr. Macklin," I said firmly.

He gave in ungraciously. The girl, who said her name was Rose Howe, followed us inside. Straightaway I started to sneeze; the air was filled with particles of fur. Someone in the building worked at plucking hair from dogs, rabbits, and perhaps even rats for sale to a furrier. There were other odors as well; the building held at least one fish that had not been caught yesterday. I could smell paste, from drying match boxes, most likely. It was all rather overpowering.

Macklin led us up a flight of stairs from which the banisters had been removed—for firewood, no doubt. Vermin-infested wallpaper was hanging in strips above our heads. Macklin opened a door upon a small room where his wife lay in labor. Mrs. Macklin was still a girl herself, only a few years older than Rose Howe. She was lying on a straw mattress, undoubtedly infested with fleas, on a broken-down bedstead. A few boxes were stacked against one wall; the only other piece of furniture was a plank laid across two stacks of bricks. I sent Macklin down to fill a bucket from the water pipe in the courtyard, and then I put Rose Howe to washing some rags I found in a corner.

It was a long labor. Rose curled up on the floor and went to sleep. Macklin wandered out for a few pints.

Day had broken before the baby came. Macklin was back, sobriety returning with each cry of pain from his young wife. Since it was daylight, Rose Howe could have returned to her own room but instead stayed and helped; she stood like a rock, letting Mrs. Macklin grip her thin wrists during the final bearing down. The baby was under-size; but as I cleared out her mouth and nose, she voiced a howl that announced her arrival to the world in no uncertain terms. I watched a smile light the faces of both girls as Rose cleaned the baby and placed her in her mother's arms. Then Rose held the cord as I tied it off with thread in two places and cut it through with my sewing scissors.

Macklin was a true loving husband. "Don't you worry none, love," he said to his wife. "Next 'un'll be a boy."

I told Rose Howe I'd finish cleaning up and for her to go home. Then I told Macklin to bring his daughter to St. Jude's for christening. When at last I was ready to leave, the morning sun was high in the sky.

To my surprise the small courtyard was crowded with people, one of whom was a police constable. I tried to work my way through to the street, but no one would yield a passage for me; I'm not certain they even knew I was there. They were all trying to peer through the broken window of a ground-floor room. "Constable?" I called out. "What has happened here?"

He knew me; he blocked the window with his body and said, "You don't want to look in there, Mrs. Wickham."

A fist of ice closed around my heart; the constable's facial expression already told me, but I had to ask nonetheless. I swallowed and said, "Is it the Ripper?"

He nodded slowly. "It appears so, ma'am. I've sent for Inspector Abberline—you there, stand back!" Then, to me again: "He's not never killed indoors afore. This is new for him."

I was having trouble catching my breath. "That means . . . he didn't have to be quick this time. That means he could take as much time as he liked."

The constable was clenching and unclenching his jaw. "Yes'm. He took his time."

Oh dear God. "Who is she, do you know?"

"The rent-collector found her. Here, Thomas, what's her name again?"

A small, frightened-looking man spoke up. "Mary . . . Mary Kelly. Three months behind in 'er rent, she was. I thought she was hidin' from me."

The constable scowled. "So you broke the window to try to get in?"

" 'Ere, now, that winder's been broke these past six weeks! I pulled out the bit o' rag she'd stuffed in the hole so I could reach through and push back the curtain—just like you done, guv'ner, when you wanted to see in!" The rent-collector had more to say, but his words were drowned out by the growing noise of the crowd, which by now had so multiplied in its numbers that it overflowed from Miller's Court into a passageway leading to the street. A few women were sobbing, one of them close to screaming.

Inspector Abberline arrived with two other men, all three of them looking grim. The Inspector immediately tried the door and found it locked. "Break out the rest of the window," he ordered. "The rest of you, stand back. Mrs. Wickham, what are you doing here? Break in the window, I say!"

One of his men broke out the rest of the glass and crawled over the sill. We heard a brief, muffled cry, and then the door was opened from the inside. Inspector Abberline and his other man pushed into the room . . . and the latter abruptly rushed back out again, retching. The constable hastened to his aid, and without stopping to think about it, I stepped into the room.

What was left of Mary Kelly was lying on a cot next to a small table. Her throat had been cut so savagely that her head was nearly severed. Her left shoulder had been chopped through so that her arm remained attached to the body only by a flap of skin. Her face had been slashed and disfigured, and her nose had been hacked away . . . and carefully laid on the small table beside the cot. Her breasts had been sliced off and placed on the same table. The skin had been peeled from her forehead; her thighs had also been stripped of their skin. The legs themselves had been spread in an indecent posture and then slashed to the bone. And Mary Kelly's abdomen had been ripped open, and between her feet lay one of her internal organs . . . possibly the liver. On the table lay a piece of the victim's brown plaid woolen petticoat half wrapped around still another organ; it looked like a kidney. The missing skin had been carefully mounded on the table next to the other body parts, as if the Ripper were rebuilding his victim. But this time the killer had not piled the intestines above his victim's shoulder as he'd done before; this time, he had taken them away with him. Then as a final embellishment, he had pushed Mary Kelly's right hand into her ripped-open stomach.

Have you punished her enough, Jack? Don't you want to hurt her some more?

I felt a hand grip my arm and steer me firmly outside. "You shouldn't be in here, Mrs. Wickham," Inspector Abberline said. He left me leaning against the wall of the building as he went back inside; a hand touched my shoulder and Thomas the rent-collector said, "There's a place to sit, over 'ere." He led me to an upended wooden crate, where I sank down gratefully. I sat with my head bent over my knees for some time before I could collect myself enough to utter a prayer for Mary Kelly's soul.

Inspector Abberline's men were asking questions of everyone in the crowd. When one of them approached me, I explained I'd never known Mary Kelly and was here only because of the birth of the Macklin baby in the same building. The Inspector himself came over and commanded me to go home; I was not inclined to dispute the order.

"It appears this latest victim does not fit your pattern," the Inspector said as I was leaving. "Mary Kelly was a prostitute, but she was still in her early twenties. And from what we've learned so far, she had no husband and no children."

So the last victim had been neither middle-aged, nor married, nor a mother. It was impossible to tell whether poor Mary Kelly had been homely or not. But the Ripper had clearly chosen a woman this time who was markedly different from his earlier victims, deviating from his customary pattern. I wondered what it meant; had some change taken place in his warped, evil mind? Had he progressed one step deeper into madness?

I thought about that on the way home from Miller's Court. I thought about that, and about Edward.

10 November 1888, St. Jude's Vicarage
It was almost noon by the time I reached the vicarage. Edward was there, fast asleep. Normally he never slept during the day, but the small vial of laudanum Dr. Phelps

had left was on the bedside table; Edward had drugged himself into a state of oblivion.

I picked up his clothes from the floor where he'd dropped them and went over every piece carefully; not a drop of blood anywhere. But the butchering of Mary Kelly had taken place indoors; the butcher could simply have removed his clothing before beginning his "work." Next I checked all the fireplaces, but none of them had been used to burn anything. It *could* be happenstance, I told myself. I didn't know how long Edward had been blacking out; it was probably not as singular as it seemed that one of his spells should coincide with a Ripper slaying. That's what I told myself.

The night had exhausted me. I had no appetite, but a cup of fresh tea would be welcome. I was on my way to the kitchen when a knock at the door stopped me. It was the constable I'd spoken to at Miller's Court.

He handed me an envelope. "Inspector Abberline said to give you this." He touched his cap and was gone.

I went to stand by the window where the light was better. Inside the envelope was a hastily scrawled note.

My dear Mrs. Wickham,

Further information has come to light that makes it appear that your theory of a pattern in the Ripper murders may not be erroneous after all. Although Mary Kelly currently had no husband, she had at one time been married. At the age of sixteen she wed a collier who died less than a year later. During her widowhood she found a series of men to support her for brief periods until she ended on the streets. And she was given to strong drink, as the other four victims were. But the most cogent revelation is the fact that Mary Kelly was pregnant. That would explain why she was so much younger than the Ripper's earlier victims: he was stopping her before she could abandon her children.

Yrs,
Frederick Abberline

So. Last night the Ripper had taken two lives instead of one, assuring that a fertile young woman would never bear

children to suffer the risk of being forsaken. It was not in
the Ripper's nature to consider that his victims had themselves been abandoned in their time of need. Polly Nichols,
Annie Chapman, Elizabeth Stride, and Catherine Eddowes
had all taken to drink for reasons no one would ever know
and had subsequently been turned out of their homes. And
now there was Mary Kelly, widowed while little more than
a child and with no livelihood—undoubtedly she lacked the
education and resources to support herself honorably.
Polly, Annie, Elizabeth, Catherine, and Mary . . . they
had all led immoral and degraded lives, every one of them.
But in not one case had it been a matter of choice.

I put Inspector Abberline's note in a drawer in the writing table and returned to the kitchen; I'd need to start a
fire to make the tea. The wood box had recently been filled,
necessitating my moving the larger pieces to get at the
twigs underneath. Something else was underneath as well.
I pulled out a long strip of brown plaid wool cloth with
brown stains on it. Brown plaid wool. Mary Kelly's petticoat. Mary Kelly's blood.

The room began to whirl. There it was. No more making
of excuses. No more denying the truth. I was married to
the Ripper.

For twelve years Edward had kept the odious secret of
what he was, hiding behind a mask of gentility and even
godliness. He had kept his secret well. But no more. The
masquerade was ended. I sank to my knees and prayed for
guidance. More than anything in the world I wanted to
send for Inspector Abberline and have him take away the
monster who was asleep upstairs. But if the laudanum-in-
duced sleep had the same effect this time as when he was
ill, Edward would awake as his familiar rational self. If I
could speak to him, make him understand what he'd done,
give him the opportunity to surrender voluntarily to the
police, surely that would be the most charitable act I could
perform under these hideous circumstances. If Edward
were to have any chance at all for redemption, he must beg
both God and man for forgiveness.

With shaking hands I tucked the strip of cloth away in

my pocket and forced myself to concentrate on the routine of making tea. The big kettle was already out, but when I went to fill it with water, it felt heavy. I lifted the lid and found myself looking at a pile of human intestines.

I did not faint . . . most probably because I was past all feeling by then. I tried to think. The piece of cloth Edward could have used to wipe off the knife; then he would have put the cloth in the wood box with the intention of burning it later. But why wait? And the viscera in the teakettle . . . was I meant to find that? Was this Edward's way of asking for help? And where was the knife? Systematically I began to look for it, but after nearly two hours' intensive search, I found nothing. He could have disposed of the knife on his way home. He could have hidden it in the church. He could have it under his pillow.

I went into the front parlor and forced myself to sit down. I was frightened; I didn't want to stay under the same roof with him, I didn't want to fight for his soul. Did he even have a soul anymore? The Edward Wickham I had lain beside every night for twelve years was a counterfeit person, one whose carefully fabricated personality and demeanor had been devised to control and constrain the demon imprisoned inside. The deception had worked well until we came to Whitechapel, when the constraints began to weaken and the demon escaped. What had caused the change—was it the place itself? The constant presence of prostitutes in the streets? It was beyond my comprehension.

The stresses of the past twenty-four hours eventually proved too much for me; my head fell forward, and I slept.

Edward's hand on my shoulder awoke me. I started, and gazed at him with apprehension, but his face showed only gentle concern. "Is something wrong, Beatrice? Why are you sleeping in the afternoon?"

I pressed my fingertips against my eyes. "I did not sleep last night. The Macklin baby was born early this morning."

"Ah! Both mother and child doing well, I trust? I hope

you impressed upon young Macklin the importance of an
early christening. But Beatrice, the next time you are
called out, I would be most grateful if you could find a way
to send me word. When you had not returned by midnight,
I began to grow worried."

That was the first falsehood Edward had ever told me
that I could recognize as such; it was I who had been waiting for him at midnight. His face was so open, so seemingly
free of guile . . . did he honestly have no memory of the
night before, or was he simply exceptionally skilled in the
art of deception? I stood up and began to pace. "Edward, we
must talk about last night . . . about what you did last
night."

His eyebrow shot up. "I?"

I couldn't look at him. "I found her intestines in the teakettle. Mary Kelly's intestines."

"Intestines?" I could hear the distaste in his voice.
"What is this, Beatrice? And who is Mary Kelly?"

"She's the woman you killed last night!" I cried. "Surely
you knew her name!" I turned to confront him . . . and
saw a look of such loathing on his face that I took a step
back. "Oh!" I gasped involuntarily. "Please don't . . ." Edward? Jack?

The look disappeared immediately—he knew, he knew
what he was doing! "I killed someone last night, you say?"
he asked, his rational manner quickly restored. "And then
I put her intestines . . . in the teakettle? Why don't you
show me, Beatrice?"

Distrustful of his suggestion, I nevertheless led the way
to the kitchen. As I'd half expected, the teakettle was
empty and spotlessly clean. With a heavy heart I pulled
the piece of brown plaid cloth out of my pocket. "But here
is something you neglected to destroy."

He scowled. "A dirty rag?"

"Oh, Edward, stop professing you know nothing of this!
It is a strip from Mary Kelly's petticoat, as you well realize!
Edward, you must go to the police. Confess all, make your
peace with God. No one else can stop your nocturnal expe-

ditions—you must stop yourself! Go to Inspector Abberline."

He held out one hand. "Give me the rag," he said expressionlessly.

"Think of your soul, Edward! This is your one chance for salvation! You *must* confess!"

"The rag, Beatrice."

"I cannot! Edward, do you not understand? You are accursed—your own actions have damned you! You must go down on your knees and beg for forgiveness!"

Edward lowered his hand. "You are ill, my dear. This delusion of yours that I am the Ripper—that is the crux of your accusation, is it not? This distraction is most unbefitting the wife of the vicar of St. Jude's. I cannot tolerate the thought that before long you may be found raving in the street. We will pray together, we will ask God to send you self-discipline."

I thought I understood what that meant. "Very well . . . if you will not turn yourself over to the police, there is only one alternate course of action open to you. You must kill yourself."

"Beatrice!" He was shocked. "Suicide is a *sin!*"

His reaction was so absurd that I had to choke down a hysterical laugh. But it made me understand that further pleading would be fruitless. He was hopelessly insane; I would never be able to reach him.

Edward was shaking his head. "I am most disturbed, Beatrice. This dementia of yours is more profound than I realized. I must tell you I am unsure of my capacity to care for you while you are subject to delusions. Perhaps an institution is the rightful solution."

I was stunned. "You would put me in an asylum?"

He sighed. "Where else will we find physicians qualified to treat dementia? But if you cannot control these delusions of yours, I see no other recourse. You must pray, Beatrice, you must pray for the ability to discipline your thoughts."

He *could* have me locked away; he could have me locked away and then continue unimpeded with his ghastly killings, never having to worry about a wife who noticed too much. It was a moment before I could speak. "I will do as you say, Edward. I will pray."

"Excellent! I will pray with you. But first—the rag, please."

Slowly, reluctantly, I handed him the strip of Mary Kelly's petticoat. Edward took a fireplace match and struck it, and the evidence linking him to murder dissolved into thin black smoke that spiraled up the chimney. Then we prayed; we asked God to give me the mental and spiritual willpower I lacked.

Following that act of hypocrisy, Edward suggested that I prepare our tea; I put the big teakettle aside and used my smaller one. Talk during tea was about several church duties Edward still needed to perform. I spoke only when spoken to and was careful to give no offense. I did everything I could to assure my husband that I deferred to his authority.

Shortly before six Edward announced he was expected at a meeting of the Whitechapel Vigilance Committee. I waited until he was out of sight and went first to the cupboard for a table knife and then to the writing table for a sheet of foolscap. Then I stepped into the pantry and began to scrape up as much of the arsenic from the rat holes as I could.

23 February 1892, Whitechapel Educational Institute for Indigent Children

Inspector Abberline sat in my office, nodding approval at everything he'd seen. "It's difficult to believe," he said, "that these are the same thin and dirty children who only months ago used to sleep in doorways and under wooden crates. You have worked wonders, Mrs. Wickham. The board of trustees could not have found a better director. Are the children learning to read and write? *Can* they learn?"

"Some can," I answered. "Others are slower. The youngest are the quickest, it seems. I have great hopes for them."

"I wonder if they understand how fortunate they are. What a pity the Reverend Mr. Wickham didn't live to see this. He would have been so pleased with what you've accomplished."

"Yes." Would he have? Edward always believed the poor should care for their own.

The Inspector was still thinking of my late husband. "I had an aunt who succumbed to gastric fever," he said. "Dreadful way to die, dreadful." He suddenly realized I might not care to be reminded of the painful method of Edward's passing. "I do beg your pardon—that was thoughtless of me."

I told him not to be concerned. "I am reconciled to his death now, as much as I can ever be. My life is here now, in the school, and it is a most rewarding way to spend my days."

He smiled. "I can see you are in your element." Then he sobered. "I came not only to see your school but also to tell you something." He leaned forward in his chair. "The file on the Ripper is officially closed. It's been more than two years since his last murder. For whatever reason he stopped, he *did* stop. That particular reign of terror is over. The case is closed."

My heart lifted. Keeping up my end of the conversation, I asked, "Why do you think he stopped, Inspector?"

He rubbed the side of his nose. "He stopped either because he's dead or because he's locked up somewhere, in an asylum or perhaps in prison for some other crime. Forgive my bluntness, Mrs. Wickham, but I earnestly hope it is the former. Inmates have been known to escape from asylums and prisons."

"I understand. Do you think the file will ever be reopened?"

"Not for one hundred years. Once a murder case is marked closed, the files are sealed and the date is written on the outside when they can be made public. It will be a full century before anyone looks at those papers again."

It couldn't be more official than that; the case was indeed closed. "A century . . . why so long a time?"

"Well, the hundred-year rule was put into effect to guarantee the anonymity of all those making confidential statements to the police during the course of their investigations. It's best that way. Now no one will be prying into our reports on the Ripper until the year 1992. It is over."

"Thank heaven for that."

"Amen."

Inspector Abberline chatted a little longer and then took his leave. I strolled through the halls of my school, a former church building adapted to its present needs. I stopped in one of the classrooms. Some of the children were paying attention to the teacher, others were daydreaming, a few were drawing pictures. Just like children everywhere.

Not all the children who pass through here will be helped; some will go on to better themselves, but others will slide back into the life of the streets. I can save none of them. I must not add arrogance to my other offenses by assuming the role of deliverer; God does not entrust the work of salvation to one such as I. But I am permitted to offer the children a chance, to give them the opportunity to lift themselves above the life of squalor and crime that is all they have ever known. I do most earnestly thank God for granting me this privilege.

Periodically I return to Miller's Court. I go there not because it is the site of Edward's final murder, but because it is where I last saw Rose Howe, the young girl who helped me deliver the Macklin baby. There is a place for Rose in my school. I have not found her yet, but I will keep searching.

My life belongs to the children of Whitechapel now. My prayers are for them; those prayers are the only ones of mine ever likely to be answered. When I do pray for myself, it is always and only to ask for an easier place in Hell.

DIESEL DREAM
by Alan Dean Foster

Why did Marilyn Monroe die? What really happened to her?

Whatthehell. I mean, I know I was wired. Too many white crosses, too long on the road. But a guy's gotta make a living, and everybody *else* does it. Everybody who runs alone, anyway. You got a partner, you don't have to rely on stimulants. You half a married team, that's even better. But you own, operate, and drive your own rig, you gotta compete somehow. That means always making sure you finish your run on time, especially if you're hauling perishables. Oh sure, they bring their own problems with 'em, but I'd rather run cucumbers than cordite any day.

Elaine (that's my missus), she worries about me all the time. No less so than any trucker's wife, I guess. Goes with the territory. I try to hide the pills from her, but she knows I pop the stuff. I make good money, though. Better'n most independents. Least I'm not stuck in some stuffy little office listening to some scrawny bald-headed dude chew my ass day after day for misfiling some damn piece of paper.

Elaine and I had a burning ceremony two years ago. Mortgage officer from the bank brought over the paper personal and stayed for the burgers and beer. Now there's a bank that *understands*. Holds the paper on our place, too. One of these days we'll have another ceremony and burn that sucker, too.

So I own my rig free and clear now. Worked plenty hard for it. I'm sure as hell not ready to retire. Not so long as I can work for myself. Besides which I got two kids in college and a third thinking about it. Yep, me. The big guy with the green baseball cap and the beard you keep seein' in your rearview mirrors. Sometimes I can't believe it myself.

So what if I use the crosses sometimes to keep going? So what if my eyesight's not 20/20 every hour of every day? Sure my safety record's not perfect, but it's a damnsight better than most of these young honchos think they can drive San Diego–Miami nonstop. Half their trucks end up as scrap, and so do half of them.

I know when I'm getting shaky, when it's time to lay off the little mothers.

Anyway, like I was gonna tell you, I don't usually stop in Lee Vining. It's just a flyspot on the atlas, not even a real truck stop there. Too far north of Mammoth to be fashionable and too far south of Tahoe to be worth a sidetrip for the gamblers. A bunch of overinsulated mobile homes not much bigger than the woodpiles stacked outside 'em. Some log homes, some rock. Six gas stations, five restaurants, and one little mountain grocery. Imagine; a market with a porch and chairs. Lee Vining just kind of clings to the east slope of the Sierra Nevada. Wouldn't surprise anyone if the whole shebang up and slid into Mono Lake some hard winter. The whole town. The market sells more salmon eggs than salmon. Damn fine trout country, though, and a great place to take kids hiking.

Friendly, too. Small-town mountain people always are, no matter what part of the country you're haulin' through. They live nearer nature than the rest of us and it keeps 'em respectful of their humanity. The bigger the country, the bigger the hearts. Smarter than you'd think, too.

Like I was saying, I don't usually stop there. Bridgeport's cheaper for diesel. But I'd just driven nonstop up from L.A. with a quick load of lettuce, tomatoes, and other produce for the casinos at Reno and I was running on empty. Not Slewfoot: she was near full. I topped off her tanks in Bishop. Slewfoot's my rig, lest you think I was cheatin' on

Elaine. I don't go in for that, no matter what you see in those cheap films. Most truckers ain't that good-lookin', and neither are the gals you meet along the highway. Most of them are married, anyway.

Since diesel broke a buck a gallon I'm pretty careful about where I fill up. Slewfoot's a big Peterbilt, black with yellow and red striping, and she can get mighty thirsty.

So I was the one running on empty, and with all those crosses floating around in my gut, not to mention my head, I needed about fourteen cups of coffee and something to eat. It was starting to get evening and I like to push the light, but after thirty years plus on the road I know when to stop. Eat now, let the crosses settle some, drive later. Live longer.

It was just after Thanksgiving. The tourists were long gone from the mountains. So were the fishermen, since the high country lakes were already frozen. Ten feet of snow on the ground (yeah, feet), but I'd left nearly all the ski traffic back down near Mammoth. U.S. 395's easier when you don't have to dodge the idiots from L.A. who never see snow except when it comes time for 'em to drive through it.

The Department of Transportation had the road pretty clear and it hadn't snowed much in a couple of days, which is why I picked that day to make the fast run north. After Smokeys, weather's a trucker's major devilment. It was plenty cold outside; cold enough to freeze your bvd's to your crotch, but nothing like what it would be in another month or so. It was early and the real Sierra winter was just handing out calling cards.

Thanks to the crosses I kind of floated onto the front porch of a little place called the Prospector's Roost (almost as much gold left in those mountains as trout), twenty percent of the town's restaurant industry, and slumped gratefully into a booth lined with scored Naugahyde. The window behind me gave me something besides blacktop to focus on, and the sun's last rays were just sliding off old Mono Lake. Frigid pretty. The waitress gave me a big smile, which was nice. Soon she brought me a steak, hash browns, green beans, warm rolls with butter, and more coffee, which was better. I started to mellow as my stomach filled up, let my eyes wander as I ate.

It's tough to make a living at any one thing in a town the size of Lee Vining. If it don't take up too much floor space, some folks can generate an extra couple of bucks by operating a second business in the same building.

So the north quarter of the Prospector's Roost had been given over to a little gift shop. The market carried trinkets and so did the gas stations, so it didn't surprise me to see the same kind of stuff in a restaurant. There were a couple of racks of postcards, film, bare necessity fishing supplies at outrageous prices, Minnetonka moccasins, rubber tomahawks for the kids, risk-kay joke gifts built around gags older than my uncle Steve, Indian turquoise jewelry made in the Philippines. That sort of thing.

Plus the usual assortment of local handicrafts: rocks painted to look like owls, cheap ashtrays that screamed MONO LAKE or LEE VINING, GATEWAY TO YOSEMITE. T-shirts that said the same (no mediums left, plenty of extra-large).

There was also a small selection of better-quality stuff. Some nice watercolors of the lake and its famous tufa formations, one or two little hand-chased bronzes you wouldn't be ashamed to set out on your coffee table, locally strung necklaces of turquoise and silver, and some wood-carvings of Sierra animals. Small, but nicely turned. Looked like ironwood to me. Birds and fish mostly, but also one nice little bobcat I considered picking up for Elaine. She'd crucify me if I did, though. Two kids in college, a third considering. And tomorrow Slewfoot would be thirsty again.

The tarnished gold bell over the gift-shop entrance tinkled as somebody entered. The owner broke away from his kitchen and walked over to chat. He was a young fellow with a short beard and he looked tired.

The woman who'd come in had a small box under one arm which she set gently on the counter. She opened it and started taking out some more of those woodcarvings. I imagined she was the artist. She was dressed for the weather and I thought she must be a local.

She left the scarf on her head when she slipped out of her heavy high-collared jacket. I tried to look a little closer. All those white crosses kept my eyes bopping, but I wasn't as sure about my brain. She was older than I was in any case, even if I'd been so inclined. Sure I looked. It was pitch black out now and starting to snow lightly. Elaine wouldn't have minded . . . much. A man's got to look once in a while.

I guessed her to be in her midfifties. She could've been older, but if anything she looked younger. I tried to get a good look at her eyes. The eyes always tell you the truth. Whatever her age, she was still a damn handsome woman. Besides the scarf and coat she wore jeans and a flannel shirt. That's like uniform in this kind of country. She wore 'em loose, but you could still see some spectacular countryside. Brown hair, though I thought it might be lighter at the roots. Not gray, either. Not yet.

I squeezed my eyes shut until they started to hurt and downed another swallow of coffee. A man must be beginnin' to go when he starts thinking that way about grandmotherly types.

Except that this woman wasn't near being what any man in his right mind would call grandmotherly, her actual age notwithstanding. Oh, she didn't do nothin' to enhance it, maybe even tried hiding it under all those clothes. But she couldn't quite do it. Even now I thought she was pretty enough to be on TV. Like Barbara Stanwyck, but younger and even prettier. Maybe it was all those white crosses makin' gumbo of my thoughts, but I couldn't take my eyes off her.

The only light outside now came from gas stations and storefronts. Not many of the latter stayed open after dark. A few tourists sped through town, fighting the urge to tromp their accelerators. I could imagine 'em cursing small towns like this one that put speed limits in their way just to keep 'em from the crap tables at Reno a little longer.

I considered the snow. Drifting down easy, but that could

change. No way did I need that tonight. I finished the last of my steak and paid up, leaving the usual good tip, and started out to warm up Slewfoot.

The woman was leaving at the same time and we sort of ended up at the door together, accidental-like. Like fun we did.

"After you," she said to me.

Now I was at least ten years younger than this lady, but when she spoke to me I just got real quivery all through my body, and it wasn't from the heavy-duty pharmaceuticals I'd been gulping, either. She'd whispered, but it wasn't whispering. I knew it was her normal speaking voice. Now I've had sexier things whispered to me than "After you," but none of 'em made me feel the way I did right then, not even those spoken on my fourth date with Elaine which ended up in the back of my old pickup truck with her telling me, "Whatever you want, Dave."

Somebody real special has to be able to make "After you" sound like "Whatever you want." My initial curiosity doubled up on me. It was none of my business, of course. Here I was a married man and all, two kids in college and a third thinkin', and I oughtn't to be having the kinds of thoughts I was having. But I was running half an hour ahead of my schedule, and the snow was staying easy, and I thought, well, hell, it don't hurt nothing to be friendly.

"You local?"

She smiled slightly, not looking up at me. It got darker fast when we stepped outside and those damn crosses were making like a xylophone in my head, but damned if I didn't think she was so pretty she'd crack, despite the fine lines that had begun to work their way across her face. She pushed her jacket up higher on her body and turned up the sheepskin collar.

"It's cold, and I've got to go." I shivered slightly, and it wasn't from the snow. "Nothing personal. I just don't believe in talking to strangers."

What could I say, how could I reassure her? "Heck, I don't mean no harm, ma'am." I think maybe that got to her. Not many folks these days say heck and ma'am, especially truckers. She glanced up at me curiously. Suddenly I wasn't cold anymore.

"Where are you from?"

"I asked you first."

"All right. I live here, yes. You?"

"L.A. right now, but me and my wife are from Texas. West Texas. The back o' beyond." Funny how Elaine had slipped into the conversation. I hadn't intended her to. But I wasn't sorry.

"Nice of you to mention your wife." She'd picked up on that right away. "Most men don't. That's why I try to come into town around dark. You'd think an old lady like me wouldn't have that kind of trouble."

"No disrespect intended, ma'am, but I've never set eyes on an old lady looked like you do." I nodded toward the cafe/gift shop. "You do those woodcarvings?"

"Yes. Do you like them?"

"I've seen a lot of that kind of stuff all over the country, and I think yours stack up real well against the best. Real nice. Good enough to show in a big gallery somewhere."

"Willie's place is good enough for me." Her voice was honey and promise. "This is my home now. The people up here leave you alone and let you be what you want to be. I'm happy."

"You married?"

"No, but I have friends. It's enough that they like me for what I am. I've been married before, more than once. It never worked for me."

The snow was coming down heavier.

"I'm sorry." She must have seen the concern on my face. "Got far to go?"

"Reno and on to Tahoe. Groceries for them folks that are trying to make it the easy way. Can't let the high rollers go hungry." Her smile widened slightly. It made me feel like I'd just won a new rig or something.

"No, I guess you can't." She tossed her head slightly to her left, kind of bounced a little on her feet. "It's been nice talking to you. Really."

"My name's Dave."

"Good meeting you, Dave."

"You?"

She blinked away a snowflake. "Me what?"

"What's your name?"

"Jill," she said instantly. "Jill Kramer." It was a nice name, but I knew it was hollow.

"Nice meeting you, too, Jill. See you 'round, maybe."

"See you, too, Dave."

That's what did it. She didn't so much say my name as sort of pucker her lips and let it ooze out, like a little hot cloud. She wore no lipstick. She didn't have to.

White crosses. White crosses and bennies and snow. Damn it all for a clear head for two lousy minutes!

I tried to think of something to say, knowing that I had to glue my eyes to the blacktop real soon or forget about driving any more that night altogether. I couldn't afford that. Nobody pays a bonus for brown lettuce and soft tomatoes.

"I thought you were dead," I finally blurted out. I said it easy, matter-of-fact, not wanting to startle her or me. Maybe the crosses made me do it; I don't know. She started to back away, but my country calm held her.

"I knew I shouldn't have talked to you this long. I try not to talk to anyone I don't know for very long. I thought by now. . . ." She shrugged sadly. "I've done pretty well, hiding everything."

"Real well." I smiled reassuringly. "Hey, chill out. What you've done is no skin off my nose. Personally I think it's great. Let 'em all think you're dead. Serves 'em all right, you ask me. Bunch of phonies, the lot of 'em."

She still looked as if she wanted to run. Then she smiled afresh and nodded. "That's right. Bunch of phonies. They all just wanted one thing. I spent all my time torn up inside and confused, and nobody tried to help. Nobody cared as long as they were making money or getting what they wanted. I was just a machine to them, a thing. I didn't know what to do. I got in real deep with some guys and that's when I knew that one way or another, I had to get out, get away.

"Up here nobody cares where you come from or what you did before you got here. Nice people. And I like doing my carvings. I got out of it with a little money nobody could trace. I'm doing fine."

"Glad to hear it. I always did think you were *it,* you know."

"That wasn't me, Dave. That was never me. That was always the problem. I'm happy now, and that's what counts. If you live long enough, you come to know what's really important."

"That's what me and Elaine always say."

She glanced at the sky and the light from the cafe fully illuminated her face. "You'd better get going."

"How'd you work it, anyway? How'd you fool everybody?"

"I had some friends. True friends. Not many, but enough. They understood. They helped me get out. Once in a while they come up here and we laugh about how we fooled everyone. We go fishing. I always did like to fish. You'd better get moving."

"Reckon I'd better. You keep doing those carvings. I really liked your bobcat."

"Thanks. That one was a lot of work. Merry Christmas, Dave."

"Yeah. You, too . . . Jill."

She turned away from me, knowing that I'd keep her secret. Hell, what did I have to gain from giving her away? I knew how she must feel, or thought I did. About the best thing you can do in this mean world is not step on somebody else's happiness, and I wasn't about to step on hers. It's too damn hard to come by and you might need somebody else to do you a similar favor sometime. It doesn't hurt to establish a line of credit with the Almighty.

I watched her walk away in the falling snow, all bundled up and hidden inside that big western jacket, and I felt real good with myself. I'd still make Reno in plenty of time, then pop over to Tahoe, maybe get lucky and pick up a return load. My eyes followed her through the dark and white wet and she seemed to wink in and out of my sight, dreamlike.

White crosses. Damn, I thought. Was she real or wasn't she? Not that it really mattered. I still felt good. I sucked in the sharp, damp air and made ready to get back to business.

That's when she sort of hesitated, stopped, and glanced back at me. Or at least, whatever I saw there in the Sierra night glanced back at me. When she resumed her walk it wasn't the stiff, horsey stride she'd been using before but a rolling, rocking, impossibly fluid gait that would've blasted the knob off a frozen thermometer. I think she did it just for me. Maybe it was because of the season, but I tell you, it was one helluva present.

Not knowing what else to do I waved. I think she waved back as I called out, "Merry Christmas, Norma Jean." Then hurried across the street to the parking lot to fire up Slewfoot.

THE LINCOLN-KENNEDY CONNECTION
by Rex Miller and Dr. Fred L. King

Is it possible that the assassinations of Presidents Lincoln and Kennedy are somehow connected? They occurred almost one hundred years apart—how can this be?

PRESIDENTS LINCOLN AND KENNEDY . . .

* were assassinated on a Friday, each shot in the head, from behind, in the presence of their wives.
* Lincoln's secretary, whose name was Kennedy, advised him not to go to the Ford Theatre. Kennedy's secretary, whose name was Lincoln, asked him not to participate in a motorcade in which he rode in a Lincoln, made by Ford Motor Co.
* Their respective assassins, John Wilkes Booth and Lee Harvey Oswald, Southerners supporting unpopular political causes, each had fifteen-letter names. Lincoln and Kennedy were seven-letter names.
* Each man was succeeded by a vice president named Johnson.
* Each assassin was murdered before he could be brought to trial.
* Each assassinated President's successor had six-letter first names, Andrew and Lyndon, and seven-letter last names.
* The first President elected to office following Lincoln's

death and the first after Kennedy's each had nineteen-
letter names: Ulysses Simpson Grant and Lyndon Baines
Johnson.
* Lincoln was first elected in 1860—Kennedy in 1960.
* Andrew Johnson was born in 1808, Lyndon Baines John-
son in 1908.
* John W. Booth was born in 1839, Lee H. Oswald in 1939.
* Lincoln was the first of our Presidents to be assassinated,
Kennedy the last, though there was at least one bungled
attempt on a President in each subsequent period.
* Rex Miller and Fred L. King each have nine-letter
names.

This is true fiction. Stay tuned. You'll get the picture.

In 1957, I was a kid radio jock on the air in Oklahoma
City, a street kid who had stars in his eyes, and like so
many people in broadcasting, advertising, show biz, and
the related glamour (snort, guffaw) industries, I had a
small problem. What they call an "obsessive/compulsive"
personality.

It made me vulnerable to a set-up, and again, for both
reasons of space limitations and the lack of my desire to do
a public mea culpa and fall on my literary sword—so to
speak—I will jump over a lot of details. (Jeezus. I realize
even as I prepare to write this how it will look on paper.
Nothing sounds more like bullshit than the unadulterated
truth.) I did bad things—folks—for money.

To put it as succinctly as possible, in 1957 certain en-
forcement agencies still seriously surveilled North Americans with known Communist ties. I was dating a lady who
was high up in the Party, back in the days when it was
Them vs. Us. "Dawn," (no—not the ones who sang with
Tony Orlando), my lady of the moment, may or may not
have been what she appeared. The point is that if you were
around her a lot you got watched.

I was forced into a tragic situation in the winter of 1957,
and had no choice but to commit a terrible act, which was
done in self-defense, but which happened to be witnessed
by those surveilling me.

A big Hispanic fellow went gunny fruit over something so trivial it isn't worth talking about, and he ended up planted and I ended up in a local station house.

I remember only two things about this period of hours when I was (supposedly) booked and interviewed: they kept talking about the two pieces I happened to have in the front seat of my '53 Chevy, a .22 and a .32, both loaded. I was and am a "gun nut," and thank God I wasn't packing when they took me down or I might have gone for one. I was a *whole* bunch crazier than I am now, back in 1957, and you wouldn't want me to marry your sister *now*— capeesh?

"Are you in a gang?" one cop would say.

"No, sir."

"Are you or have you ever been a Communist?" the other would ask. No, sir. Back and forth. This was bad cop/bad cop. Finally the Good Cop came in and asked me if I knew what was going to happen to me? No, sir.

"You're going away for a long time, sonny boy," he said.

Now we cut to a different situation. Never mind how I managed to get out of that one. But by the next morning I was back on the air at the local station, and a meeting was arranged with certain people about "Dawn." They wanted me to set her up. Get her to talk about certain things. I was to learn the etiquette of wearing "a wire," which back then was a horrible torture device that only did one thing dependably, and that was malfunction. This was back in the Mylar tape years, when state of the art was a Wollensak reel-to-reel recorder.

Cut to the you-know-what. I did what I had to do, ratted out Dawn like a good snitch, and chomped down firmly on the hook. I was eighteen, integrity fans, and what did I know? All I knew was that I wasn't going up the river.

I can't detail the next decade as much as I'd love to, and God willing it will never happen, but I ended up putting in seven years of active service with the Good Guys. Let me lay my résumé on you, replete with call letters of actual stations:

1957   KOCY, Oklahoma City
1958   KILT, Houston
1959   KLIF, Dallas
1960   WNOE, New Orleans
1961   WQXI, Atlanta
1962   floater status—Miami, New Orleans
1963   KLIF again, Dallas

As you can see I relocated once a year, and was always "duked in" to whatever market area where my services were needed.

I can't discuss the work I did while I was on the air, but I was given a fully sanctioned target and "access," what the wiseguys call a contract on TV, in 1962. He had a workname, as opposed to a real name, an official "jacket," and all that usually goes with that sort of situation: "Mr. Lee," as in the song "I Shot Mr. Lee," by the Bobbettes.

This was something that occupied a full year of my time as a floater, (sleeper to you CIA buffs), and it was a royal pain in the ass—the guy not always in-country, etc. These things don't happen the way they do in the films, set-ups take TIME, TIME, TIME. Lots of work; unpleasant work. Expensive, too. The Good Guys were not sugar daddies, but it was there to draw from, so we were surprised when the target was aborted, early in 1963, with such an investment.

They shot me up to Big D again, and I did my second trick on the air there, working with the Good Guys, and the Other Guys, and doing my thing. (I know, I know.)

In the winter of '63, I was doin' exactly what you were doin', when I saw my bud Jack, one of the "buffs" where we hung out, plant my aborted target, the focus of a costly and time-consuming year's float. It was Live—right there for all of us to see on television—and made a convenient way to dispose of a potentially explosive loose cannon.

None of us snuffies, not even the head snuffie, had a clue as to what it was all about, Alphie. Nobody was real *surprised* by it, of course, seeing as how these boys do everything but draw concentric bull's-eyes on their own backs, but we pretty much figured Jack's part to be just the way it was run down on the tube. He always was one of those emotional cats and he just went off and did the thing.

The fact that Mr. Lee was suddenly cut loose in the early months of 1963, and in November he takes The Man off the count, that looked a tad strange. But that wasn't the weirdest part about my connection with the hit.

In my role—not with the Good Guys, but with the RADIO STATION, I now became a figure in the scene: got interviewed by agents, did press schtick, hung out with the Carousel people, traded newsroom stories about Jack, watched one buddy snuggle up to Mr. Lee's lady, another regale my wife and I with tales about the Commission, for whom he was a primary witness. It was all bull, but such a rich load of humus that everybody in the country was hip to it. So much for that cover-up. It would go down in history as a muddied, but almost certain, conspiracy. I can't shed any light on it beyond the aborted sanction. Maybe the people who make these things happen saw he was a type who'd be useful. Maybe they set *him* up the way they set *me* up. I promise you one thing, Li'l Ranger, if they ever want to do it to *you,* you'll bend over and grab your ankles just the way we all do. Hope you never find out.

When I got out of the life, in the 1960's, and entered a new and gentler career—the wonderfully dull mail-order business—I met a collector. We became good friends. He confessed to one of the most bizarre secrets imaginable. He said, and I was later to learn that it was true, that he had obtained, back in the 1940's, the remains of a former President of the United States. He claimed that while a serviceman stationed in Europe during World War II, he had purchased the remains of Abraham Lincoln.

I was granted access to the provenance attached to this sale and I think it is legit. Every previous owner has signed an extraordinary document, a kind of genealogy of the presidential remains as the body passed down through modern hands. All the owners, male but for one, have been affluent professional men. Collectors of course. I have a good deal of document expertise and I doubt if there's any way this one is spurious, and I've seen plenty of dandy fakes.

Former collectors, by the way, include a *major* eastern gallery—which I would think was a fairly outrageous gamble on their part. Obviously, there has been no publicity about this. But so much time has passed, and—finally—the remains were destroyed, out of a sense of honoring the man who our government claims is buried ten feet under concrete and marble at his tomb, and out of fear. The man my friend sold it to swears the remains have been scattered to the winds, and perhaps it's just as well, both for the nation and the owners. Recent plans to run DNA tests on the remains might have exposed an empty tomb. (The idea of exhumation was eventually scotched in favor of tests on hair and fiber samples extant from the 1800's.)

There are over thirty photographs which date back to the time of Lincoln's assassination and they show his slow de-evolution through blackened face with rouged mortician's chalk, through embalming and cosmetic restoration of the completely blackened corpse (still with the chin whiskers intact), through eviscerated remains. Unquestionably, this series of photographs is the same cadaver in progressive stages of atrophy beginning in 1865.

The first owners, Big Jim Kinealy, a man named Boyd, and others who stole the corpse for ransom, ended up selling him to a collector named Swegles, who kept framed scrapbooks on the incident. To say that the remains were "well documented" would be an understatement.

The highest price paid for the remains was in the 1970's, when a foreign national bought the Lincoln cadaver for a reported sum of $365,000, less than the recent paperback advance received by a best-selling genre writer.

The Lincoln-Kennedy connection is one that has always fascinated researchers because of all the common coincidences surrounding these two infamous presidential assassinations, but the real connection is not the number of letters in their respective assassin's names or that Kennedy was killed in a Lincoln made by Ford and that Lincoln was killed in the Ford Theatre—or any of that.

The connection is that the people of the U.S., the world for that matter, were never told the facts surrounding the deaths of our two most beloved assassinated Presidents. (And that my friend and I are dust specks on the footnotes of history: each of us knows a part of a secret nobody would believe!)

DOWN ON ME
by Nancy A. Collins

Janis Joplin was a legend in her own time. Why did she throw it all away? Or did she?

Man, I knew her when.

Yeah, I can tell by lookin' at you; you think I'm jerkin' your chain. Can't says I blame you none. Folks round here tend to be full of shit when it comes to Janis. But I ain't one of 'em.

Not that I'm the type to brag, but I'm the one who made her what she is today.

Don't get up. Stay. Here, have another shot of Southern Comfort. It's on me. Hell, it's the only thing I'll touch. That's better.

Yeah, I bet you're wondering who this old hippy asshole is, right? The name's Bobby. Like Bobby McGee. And me and Janis went way, way back. All the way to 1948. That's when my folks moved to Port Arthur from Mud Creek.

I was five at the time—same age as Janis. Hell, it's hard to believe she'd be close to fifty by now! In my mind she's always twenty-seven. Guess that's how most folks see her: eternally young, never gettin' any older, never losin' any of that lust for life she always had.

We was in the same Sunday school class. Our teacher was Miz Hardesty, a real vinegar bottle of a spinster. They had this game where all the kids was supposed to march clockwise, but me an' Janis would march counterclockwise

and laugh! Boy, that really got Old Lady Hardesty's pant-
ies in a wad! Me and Janis was friends ever since then.

Port Arthur ain't much now, so you can imagine what it
was like growin' up there in the fifties! At least back then
the oil fields were still hirin' regular. But it's never been
what you'd call a hotbed of radical ideas. Although Janis's
folks were educated and progressive, leastwise by East
Texas standards, it's still a miracle someone like her came
outta a hole like this in the first place!

By Port Arthur's standards, the Joplins was decent, mid-
dle-class folks; Janis's daddy worked for the oil company,
while her mama sang in the choir. Mine, however, were
not nearly so upstandin'.

My daddy drew a check after losin' a leg in the oil field,
and he and Mama spent most of it on beer and cigarettes.
Most times all I had in the way of food, morning-noon-and-
night, was cheap baloney sandwiches. Miz Joplin, bless
her, felt sorry for me and let me eat dinner with her family
just so's I'd have a hot meal now and again.

Hmm? Oh, yeah. Janis always had a way with the boys.
No, not the way you're thinkin'. Not the way *anyone*
thinks! She had this ability to, I dunno, become "one of the
boys." She was always a tomboy; runnin' round gettin' into
things and havin' adventures with the other kids on the
block. Wasn't anything Janis wouldn't do on a dare!
'Course, that attitude got her in trouble when she got older.

When she was thirteen, about the time she was gettin'
into junior high school, things began to change. All the
other "good" girls in Port Arthur started wearin' dresses
and puttin' on makeup and started actin' the way their
mamas and grandmas told 'em ladies is supposed to act if
they want to have a good reputation and land themselves a
husband.

By then it was pretty obvious that Janis wasn't gonna be
what you'd call beautiful. Not that she was ugly, mind you.
When I hear folks talk about how she was a dog it really
gripes my ass! Janis might not have been Miss America,
but she had *soul*, damnit! You can look at the pictures—the
ones taken when she didn't know nobody was lookin'—and

you can *see* the beauty and energy inside her. It leaked out of her eyes like sunshine!

Like I said, Janis wasn't the prettiest gal in town, but I'll bet the farm she was the most *passionate*. No, and I don't mean *that way,* either! Janis was a virgin until she graduated high school. I know that for a fact. But she had—I dunno, call it a lust for living. A taste for adventure. A wild hair up her ass. Something. She was always up for a good time, which usually meant going across the river in Louisiana and hangin' out in the Cajun honkytonks.

Lord, them places was tough! When I think back on all the times me and her and the others used to set out barhoppin' after midnight and head back home come sunup . . . it's a miracle we never wrapped ourselves around a telephone pole or ended up in the Sabine River! I guess the good Lord looks after fools, drunkards . . . and angels.

And she *was* an angel! She might have had dirty wings and a dirtier mouth, but she *was* divine! I knew she was meant for bigger things than Port Arthur, even back when we was kids! She had talent, and not just for singin'. Before she got into music she used to paint. I got a couple of her old canvases back at the house. They're pretty damn good for a teenage girl.

She used to write poetry, too, back then. She always had a head on her shoulders, but in the end it wasn't what you had *inside* yourself that was important to people in Port Arthur, it was how you looked and how you acted. And that was Janis's biggest stumbling block.

She was rambunctious, I'll give you that! But no more than most kids her age. But such curiosity about life was considered unseemly in a girl. Word started going around that she was "wild," "boy crazy," and a "bad girl." Parents told their daughters not to associate with her. The "in" kids at school—you know the ones I'm talking about; the football players and cheerleaders—started calling her a "weirdo" and "kook" to her face.

It hurt Janis. Hurt her more than anyone realized—especially her folks. They just couldn't see how anyone couldn't love their little girl. She was miserable the last

three years of high school. Her grades were good, but the
teachers didn't seem to care about that. They were always
raggin' her for lookin' "unladylike" and "not living up to
her potential"; meaning she wasn't interested in taking
Home-Ec.

By her senior year Janis had taken to hangin' out with
some of the rebel-without-a-cause kids. They smoked,
drank, cussed, and drove their cars real fast, but they
weren't hoodlums or nothin'. Leastwise not by today's standards. But for the 1950's they were a pretty tough crowd, I
guess. I wasn't really a part of that scene—I'd dropped out
of school my sophomore year and I didn't see Janis that
much anymore.

Janis graduated from high school in 1960. Me, I joined
the Marines and was off bustin' my hump in boot camp
come that spring. I didn't see or hear from Janis for several
years—I was off in Vietnam.

In 1966 I got my ass out of the service. I could see that
things were only gonna get worse over there and I didn't
want to hang around for the show. Still, I kept connections
with some of my South Vietnamese buddies, which is how I
set myself up for my civilian occupation. Yeah, that's right.
I was a dealer. Thai sticks, china white, hashish, raw
opium . . . If you could get fucked up on it, I could get it!
No prob with Bobby!

I set up shop on the West Coast, working out of El Lay
mostly. In 1967 I spent some time in the Bay Area, checking out what's going down in Berkeley and the Haight. The
Summer of Love was on the horizon and I meant to make
some bread off it.

There was this straight I knew at the time who was an
ad exec during the week and a freak on weekends. Anyway, this guy calls me up out of blue, asking if I can help
him with a party he's throwin'. So I show up and this guy's
all over me like a dog that needs to go shit. Seems he'd
promised candy to some of his more important guests and
his usual connection stiffed him. So he's *real* happy to see
me!

The suit leads me into the kitchen, which is where all

the "hip" people at the party are hangin', right? The Grateful Dead was there, as well as guys from Big Brother and the Holding Company, and Country Joe and the Fish! No wonder the suit was shittin' bricks! 'Course, it would be a year or two before they'd become national superstars, but they were pretty famous already on the West Coast.

Before the suit can introduce me proper, there's this gawdawful yowl, like someone slammed the door on the cat.

"Jesus H. Christ on th' fuckin' cross! I thought you said there'd be *smack* at this fuckin' party!?!"

I turn around, not believing my ears, and there she is! Leanin' against the sink, an open bottle of Southern Comfort cocked on one hip like a sawed-off shotgun! She's wearing a pair of bell-bottom flares and a macramé top and no bra underneath, looking down her nose at me over a pair of rose-tinted granny glasses, but I can tell it's her.

"Janis?"

That hell-bent-for-party smile of hers fades and she squints at me harder.

"It's me, babe! Bobby! From Port Arthur!"

She spins around and hurries out of the kitchen into the living room. I go after her, grabbin' her before she has a chance to put on her coat and leave.

"Hey, wait a minute! What's the matter? Ain't ya glad to see me, honey?"

"Bobby, what in hell are *you* doin' here?" She has this panicked look in her eyes, like a little kid caught smokin' behind the barn. I remember lookin' down at her arms and seein' the tracks. She was just startin' to use back then and wasn't good about coverin' up yet.

"Babe, I'm the man!"

She looks at me funny for a second, then cracks this crooked grin, like she used to give me in Miz Hardesty's Bible school class. "I guess we've both come a long ways from Port Arthur, man!"

A couple of months later she and Big Brother appeared at the Monterey Pop Festival and took the fucker home in a bag! I was in the audience for that one. While the Who and Hendrix weren't nothing to sneeze at, Janis was the one who *made* that concert!

That was the first time I heard her sing, to tell the truth. She didn't get into music until she was at the University of Texas in Austin, and by then I was sloggin' through rice paddies lookin' for gooks in black pajamas. But the moment I heard that glorious voice, felt the pain behind her songs, I knew that my belief in her had not been misplaced!

Janis was destined to be *great*. Not just a star but a *superstar!* The First Lady of Rock 'n' Roll! When she was onstage she stopped bein' the plain-lookin' fat gal with the bad complexion the popular kids voted "the Ugliest Man on Campus" and she became sexual energy personified! It was like watchin' someone be possessed by a demon or a god! And the kids loved it and wanted more!

I saw Janis every now and again, my business bein' what it was. Sure, I sold to her. Always quality stuff, though. I'd never rip her off with milk sugar or baby powder, like some of the others did.

I remember going over to her place one night in '68 and she's sittin' up in bed with one of her pretty young boys, starkers except for this lynx coat!

"How y'like m'coat, Bobby?"

"Where'd it come from? Did he give it to you?" When I pointed at the boy passed out next to her, she busts out with this drunken mule-laugh, spraying me with liquor.

"Hell, no! Southern Comfort give it to me! On account of me bein' so good at promotin' their product!" She thought that was pretty damn funny.

Nineteen sixty-nine was a busy year for me. I spent most of my time in Hollywood, keepin' the people who run the Great American Dream Machine stoked. I was makin' good money. Lot better than I'd ever see bustin' my hump in an East Texas oil field.

I had me a firetruck red Ferrari, a four-bedroom house in Beverly Hills, not to mention more sex than two men could handle! Yep, them was good days!

I didn't see much of Janis that year—she spent most of it in New York, hanging out at the Chelsea and ironing out the kinks with her new band, the Kozmic Blues. I knew she was doing well because she called me up to tell me she was buying a place over in Marin County. No more Geary Street flats for Janis! From now on she was goin' first class, all the way!

I lost touch with her for a while when she and the band went on tour in Europe. The next thing I hear she's performing at Woodstock. When she comes back from the East Coast she's bummed out because one of her girlfriends has up and left her on account of her habit. So she decides she's gonna kick it. Just like that!

Janis was never one for half-measures. She lived full-throttle or nothing. When she was up she was *up*, by damn! But when she was down . . . well, she'd convince herself that nobody really loved her and that everyone around her was just into a free ride. She tried to hide it behind all those feathers and bells and freaky outfits she wore, but deep inside she was still a lonely little Southern Baptist gal from East Texas who never got over not bein' asked to the prom.

I tried reachin' her on the phone several times, but she wouldn't take my calls. Then I hear she's takin' the cure in Brazil, shacked up with this lawyer called Niehaus. From what I heard, they really loved one another. It didn't last, though. None of Janis's affairs lasted more than a few weeks. The lady was just too *intense.*

By March of 1970 she's back in the States, this time headin' the Full Tilt Boogie Band. She's off the stuff, but she's drinkin' hard core. We're talkin' start-your-day-with-tequila-over-Wheaties-and-pass-out-before-*Captain Kangaroo* boozin'!

It was about then I start gettin' these weird phone calls from her, all hours of the night and day, complainin' about how Kris Kristofferson won't fuck her. Or love her. I forget which.

Anyway, she goes on and on about this guy for weeks on end. Kris this and Kris that. Blah-blah-blah. I got sick of hearin' about him! I saw that guy in *Heaven's Gate,* and I can tell you he ain't nothin' to write home about!

Once Kristofferson's out of the picture, she starts up bitchin' about how everyone loves Pearl, but no one loves Janis. It took me awhile to figure out she was talkin' about herself. She called herself "Pearl" when she was "on." Pearl wore feather boas and partied like a sailor on three-day leave; Pearl was a hard-drinkin', hard-lovin' honky-tonk woman. And while Janis felt she had to live up to that image, she didn't consider it to be the *real* her.

Sometimes she'd get real wistful and talk about all she really wanted was an old man who'd be there for her at the end of the day. Someone she could cook and fetch slippers for and have babies with. She sounded like a dumb-ass prom queen in Port Arthur! I didn't say anything about it at the time, seein' how it meant so much to her, but listenin' to her spout that crap made my skin crawl!

What really got me worried, though, was the news she was gonna go back to Port Arthur for her high school reunion!

At first I thought it might be a good idea; I pictured her swaggerin' into that tacky old gym with one of her pretty young boys on her arm, reporters buzzin' around her like she was a queen bee, and tellin' all those constipated jerk-offs who wouldn't give her the time of day ten years ago to jump up her ass! Right on, Janis!

But when we talked about her goin' back, I could tell she wasn't gonna be wearin' warpaint and takin' scalps. She was going back there because she wanted those good-for-nothing shits to *like* her! She wanted their fuckin' *approval!* It made me sick that after all they'd done, all the hell she'd gone through at the hands of those dickless assholes, she would come crawlin' back . . .

Well, it was a disaster! Janis was clean that weekend. She didn't even drink! She showed up at the reunion, acted proper and respectable, and got treated like shit. Nobody would talk to her! They shunned her, just like she was still a homely, geeky weirdo instead of the First Lady of Rock! And to make matters worse, after she left for California, folks started lyin' about how she showed up shit-faced with her titties hangin' out an' comin' on to anything with two legs! It was disgustin'! They called her a pig in high school; they were callin' her a pig at the height of her career, too!

It broke her heart. It really did. And it did something to her. Within weeks of returnin' from Texas she was shacked up with this Berkeley student, a guy named Seth. Well, that wasn't nothin' new. But now I'm gettin' phone calls again. She's in love! For real this time! She and Seth were gonna get married!

She was so excited about the whole thing. She wanted to see me the next time she was El Lay, so she could tell me all about her wedding plans. Hearin' her talk like that made me queasy. It was like listenin' to someone chatter on about slittin' their throat with a straight razor.

In October Janis and Full Tilt Boogie are working on the *Pearl* album in El Lay. Janis is stayin' at the Landmark Hotel, but Seth isn't with her.

I get a call from Janis on the Second. She wants to see me. I show up at her hotel, thinkin' she wants to make a connection. But no; all she wants is to talk.

She tells me that she wants me to be the first to know: she called City hall and made arrangements for her and Seth to get hitched! She was babblin' on about how she was gonna stop tourin' and settle down and raise herself a passel of kids! She was kickin' smack and cuttin' back on her drinkin'. She'd had enough of wakin' up drunk. She wanted to be a good mother to Seth's babies.

I couldn't believe it! She was really fallin' for that house-in-suburbia, two-car garage bullshit! Here she was, the Love Goddess of Rock, cheerfully plannin' on throwin' away her career—her goddamn *life*—just so she could live like those brain-dead cheerleaders who snubbed her!

I tell her I think she's makin' a big mistake, that she should be satisfied with what she's got and leave the straight shit to the dumbfucks she left behind in Port Arthur. She starts cussin' me out, accusin' me of being like all the rest; that I don't want her to be happy because all I'm interested in is watchin' the show!

She starts rantin' about how she *deserves* to be happy, how she's worked *hard* for it, and nobody's gonna tell her she can't have what she wants! She's screechin' like a barn owl and throwin' shit at me, so I split. But I know what's gotta be done, even if Janis don't.

You see, she weren't meant to be happy. She just weren't built that way. That's not what made her Janis, or Pearl, or whatever the hell you want to call her. Bein' miserable was what turned her from a pimply-faced bookworm into the queen of honky-tonk blues. It was the core of her greatness. Bein' happy would destroy her. How can you sing the blues when you ain't got nothin' t'be blue *about?*

The bad thing about it, though, was that *she* couldn't understand the nature of her karma, or didn't want to admit to it. She was being given a chance at becoming part of history—of being a *god on earth,* and she was ready to chuck it in favor washin' diapers and livin' in a double-wide with an asshole who'd beat her twice a day!

I spent the next day following her around El Lay, drivin' a rented car so she wouldn't recognize me. That evening she drove over to the studio with Nick Gravenites and Bobby Womack to listen to the instrumental mixes on the album. Later she and Ken Pearson drove her Porsche over to Barney's Beanery.

I managed to sneak in and watch her from one of the booths and I could tell she was stickin' to her promise about cuttin' back on the booze. I was hopin' mebbe she'd just been full of hot air about her plans, but I should have known better. When Janis set her cap to do something, she usually did it. That was the way she was.

I follow her back to the Landmark. By this time it's around midnight-thirty. She goes up to her room but is only in there for a few minutes before she goes back to the lobby to buy some cigarettes—she might have given up on smack and hard liquor, but she still had to have her cancer sticks! Then she went back to her room. That was the last time anyone saw her alive. Except for me.

I was waitin' for her. I don't think she knew it was me. I'm also pretty sure she never knew what hit her. I caught her across the bridge of her nose, breakin' it and knockin' her unconscious instantly. Yep, havin' been in the Marines certainly has its advantages!

I knew she kept her works in a little Chinese box she usually left on her nightstand. I cooked up a shot and pulled it into the needle. I knew the stuff was too pure, but that's why I gave it to her in the first place.

I sent her to glory riding a white tiger. I'm sure there was no pain. I'd never hurt her.

The minute she stopped breathin' I tossed the balloon in the wastebasket and put her works back in their box, stashing it in a drawer. I wanted it to look like she'd done up first *then* gone out to the lobby for cigarettes. Then I left her.

I knew the pigs would come lookin' for me—not on account of what I'd done, but because I was one of her connections and they'd want to know about the shit I'd sold her. I'd made a point of distributin' random packets of pure smack amongst my mules, makin' sure there'd be more than one o.d. in the city that weekend. I didn't want Janis's death to stick out like a sore thumb. Better the pigs think a stronger than usual shipment was on the street rather than Janis was a victim of foul play. So I blew town and never went back.

I read all about it in the papers. No one doubted Janis administered the hot shot herself. She'd worked hard to create the image of a self-destructive party girl on the road to hell and, in the end, that's what folks chose to believe. There was even a rumor goin' round that she'd committed suicide over that Kristofferson jerk.

The coroner ruled it as death by overdose, although some of her junkie friends were kinda suspicious. They knew there was no way on earth Janis could have shot up something that potent and strolled down to the lobby and back for a pack of cigarettes. But junkies aren't real eager when it comes to talkin' to the cops, so most of 'em kept their opinions to themselves.

As for me, I lived in New York City for a while, cozyin' up with the Velvet Underground and the rest of the Factory hangers-on. I didn't know it, though, but the writin' was already on the wall.

When the U.S. pulled out of 'Nam, my livelihood disappeared. Suddenly I wasn't Mr. Hot Shit Connection anymore. I was shut out big time, with the local Mafia breathin' heavy down my neck. So, you guessed it, I ended up back in East Texas with nothin' to show for my time away than a shitload of memories I didn't dare share with no one.

After driftin' for a while, I landed back in Port Arthur, workin' in the oil fields like my daddy before me. I saved up enough money to buy me a double-wide—one of your finer mobile homes—and even had myself a wife and a rug-rat for a while. They're gone, now. Then in '82 I hurt my back workin' on one of the rigs, and I been drawin' a check ever since. Funny how things go, ain't it?

Folks hereabout think I'm a crazy drunk. I don't care. They thought Janis was crazy, too. I don't mind if they point me out to their young'uns as an example of what too many drugs and too much liquor will do to a man. Suits me just fine. 'Cause no matter what anyone else thinks, *I* know I've done somethin' worthwhile with my life.

Like I told you; I made her what she is today. I stopped her from betrayin' everything she stood for. She was going to sell out, man! I couldn't let her do that to herself! I made sure she would stay young and full of life *forever.* Yeah, I killed her. But I made her *immortal!* I made her a *god,* man! I figgered it was the least I could do, for old time's sake.

Here, have another shot of Southern Comfort.

It's on Janis.

THE INTRANSIGENTS
by Barry N. Malzberg

Here, Barry Malzberg, who has examined the Kennedy assassination in more works of fiction than any other writer, wraps up three mysteries in twenty-five hundred stunning words.

Rifka stared at the Director. I don't believe it, he said.

You'd better believe it, the Director said. We've been running the tapes all morning and the words come out the same. She's crying, she's screaming, she's going to call the press. She's got Hopper on the string, Winchell. She's going to let the whole thing out. You shouldn't have pushed her, the Director said. You and that Jeptha, you took her over the line. I warned you, didn't I? I was in the Oval Office with all of the files a year ago and I told you to quit. But would you listen?

Rifka looked at the Director as if for the first time and thought how much he hated him. He really hated the Director, more maybe than anyone else he had found in place when they got there and the Director was an untouchable. It was a son of a bitch, that was all there was to it. Some-day the Director would fold up, probably at Pimlico, and keel upside down on the black-eyed Susans, a fat, puffing, ugly man with secrets and coarse arteries. But not in enough time, Rifka knew, for it to help anyone around here. The good ones or those you didn't mind hanging around for a while blew out early but the bastards went on

and on and their power never got broke, it just got transferred. Jeptha quit, Rifka said. You have the tapes, you
know everything? Then you know he quit. We listened.

The Director looked at his fingernails. Too late, he said.
And you didn't quit. So what the hell is the point? Now
she's going to take the roof off everything and leave you
nowhere to go. Anything you boys look at you feel is yours
if you want it. But it doesn't work that way.

It was different with me, Rifka said. He wanted to smash
the Director, pound his head into the sleek desk, watch it
pulp and explode, watch the blood arc like the files; the
tapes, the hidden secrets in the Director's lair would explode if he could only lay a bomb in it. There was no point
in thinking that way. The Director was only trying to help.
Besides, the Director could destroy them with one phone
call, a few careful releases. So what do you want to do?
Rifka said.

You learned that from your old man, the Director said.
He took a nail buffer from his inside jacket pocket, rubbed
it idly over his old nails, then buffed vigorously so that
small embers of nail poured into the thin light. But your
old man could have learned a thing or two. There were
holes in his technique. We go way back, your old man and
me. Of course, the Director said, there ain't but a lettuce
leaf left there now, is there?

I've had enough of this, Rifka said. The chair squeaked
back, he stood. I don't have to listen to this.

Oh yes you do, the Director said, because the way your
actress is going, I figure you and your brother and a lot of
your friends have maybe forty-eight hours before it's all
over. You'd have to go to war with the Commies to push it
off the front pages. Sit down, the Director said, I'm not
finished talking to you.

I don't have to sit, Rifka said. His voice took on a whin-
ing tone, he could hear the pleading within the hollows of
his head. I'm your technical superior, he wanted to say, I'm
the head of the Justice Department. Don't order me
around. Go away. Drop dead. Jeptha will back me up on
this. Fuck you, you've terrorized your last politician, you

bastard. Rifka said none of this. He sat. The Director worked the buffer on his nails, sighed, leaned toward Rifka. We're going to have to take her out, the Director said. It's the only way. She's hysterical, full of poisons, angry and gut-shot by you boys. It's a bad combination. Don't say anything, you don't have to talk. This is our play. You don't have to order it, you don't even have to not get in the way. But you're going to know beforehand what's happening. That's what is happening.

How do you take her out? Rifka said. It was going too quickly for him, but then all of it had always gone too quickly. Thirty-eight years old, sitting in the Department of Justice, listening to the Director, his nominal subordinate. Two years ago he had been on the road from Los Angeles, spreading the word, ten years before that he and Jeptha had been laughing while the Brahmin staggered around. The Senate seat was theirs. He had had the actress in a hundred ways after Jeptha had gotten rid of her and there had been moments so pure, so vaulting, so pornographic and yet spiritual in their content that he had gasped. People like Rifka grew up thinking about things like this, never getting to do them. But he had gotten to do them. He and Jeptha, standing on the beach together election night, waiting for Daley to report and making their plans. And here he was.

I won't condone it, he said, I won't have a thing to do with it.

No you won't, the Director said. You never did. People like you and Jeptha just powered ahead and figured that people like me would come behind as the clean-up crew. We're going to do it again and we don't even have to ask permission. It won't be too hard.

I don't want to know about it, Rifka said. You don't have to tell me anything.

That's the way you would want it, the Director said. Show but don't tell. But it's not going to be that clean. You'll know, all right. We have hold of everything there, it won't be difficult. We're going to save your bacon for the

last time, though, Rifka. This is the end. You tell Jeptha
that, you hear me?

The Director stood suddenly, wavering in the room. Not
a tall man, not imposing, either, but he was threat, pure
threat, the secret knife of terror wavering over Rifka in
the empty room. He had the files. He had everything, wires
running here, wires there, secrets, contents, documents,
dossiers. Once with Jeptha a year and a half ago, the Director and the two of them had been laughing over some of the
files, the Director's standard greeting, the Director said.
Everybody new in office got a good look at them for laughs,
could see anything on request. Of course the implication
was that your files were back there, too, and could turn up
just as quickly. That was a long time ago, before Rifka even
knew the actress, before Jeptha had started in with her,
before the steel crisis. Before anything. I told him to lay off,
the Director said, shouting at Rifka. You get that message
back to him. We have cleaned it up for the last time, do you
hear? You go and tell your brother that and more. This
isn't your playpen and you'd better face that.

Don't ask any questions, the Director said after a pause.
The reports will come into you, you just sit and listen. I'd
save any official statements of regret, though, for the funeral, you understand? Just some friendly advice. The Director turned and walked slowly out of the office. Rifka
looked at him moving through the door, then looked away
as the door quietly closed. The insane impulse to call the
actress, to warn her, to tell her to leave the house immediately and get out of the country crossed his consciousness,
but then whisked away. No line was secure, least of all his.
The actress was calling and calling now, he had had everything blocked, he could hardly turn around now and reach
out for her. It was the calls that had brought the Director
here anyway. Rifka sighed. It really was a mess, he had no
idea that it would go this far. That was the thing, matters
went out of control. There was no accounting for people,
particularly a woman as unstable and pained as the actress. Rifka more than most knew of the pain there.

He called Jeptha instead. Jeptha tried to sound casual

but it was obvious that he had been waiting, waiting. Was it fixed? Jeptha wanted to know, was it what he thought it was. Come over and talk to him right now. Rifka said that anything he had to say better be said face-to-face in a secure facility. Was it fixed, was it being worked on? Jeptha shouted. Rifka said he guessed so. That was the problem, they were over their heads, but if *they* couldn't control this kind of thing, who could?

Rifka had a bad feeling about it. It all had the look of a set-up of some kind. Stevenson had warned how things were down there and Jeptha had seemed to really waver for a little while, but then Johnson and Yarborough and Connally and the rest of them had become insistent. You've got to go, they said, you'd make fools of us if you don't. Heal the party, Johnson said. Johnson was a big party man as long as it was *his* party. Rifka had told Jeptha flatly no, don't do it, but Jeptha had after this and that amount of wavering decided that he was committed, he would have to do. There was no way out at this time and there was already the matter of sixty-four. If he were going to dump Lyndon, not going would have been too much of a signal, would have given Lyndon too much lead time to move around and angle. So you had to protect your plans, you had to go. Rifka let himself be persuaded, but he thought the situation was dangerous. Someone could get hurt down there.

They never talked about the actress. After that one conversation in Jeptha's office she had never been mentioned again. There was a big hole in Rifka's life and sometimes when he thought about her he wanted to cry, but of course there was no point to any of that. For Jeptha it seemed to make no difference, Rifka suspected that the actress had been erased from Jeptha's mind months before it happened, leaving the Director—as the Director had rightly said—to deal with the situation. That was the point and the Director was right there, too, Jeptha had always had someone to take care of matters for him. Rifka, too, mostly, but sometimes Rifka was doing the taking care. Anyway, there was nothing to be done about it now and talking about her would only have made things more complicated for the two of them. There was some unease, real lacunae between them anyway.

Rifka summoned the Director. It was not the kind of thing which he would have done usually, and there had been no one-on-one contact with the Director since that August afternoon over a year ago, only a few collisions at ceremonial affairs, but he felt now that he had to talk to him. The Director had his secretary put Rifka off several times, but then Rifka, stunned, had lost his temper and used a direct line and told the Director to get the hell over. Which the man had done, looking even older and more corrupt than he had a year and a couple of months ago, but then what would he have expected? Rifka said, I don't like the situation in Dallas. It's an ugly one. I want Jeptha watched and protected at all times.

What the hell you think we're here for? the Director said, and the Secret Service. What kind of shit is this? We protect him all the time, every time, that's our job. That's why we did that little number for you, remember? Well? Do you remember?

Rifka clasped his hands and said, Just shut up. Shut up about that other job, it's all over. This is '63 and we're talking about Dallas. I want Jeptha protected, you understand? Just make sure that no one gets to him.

This is '62 and it's Los Angeles, the Director said. We worked it then, why shouldn't we work it out now? You're a real shit, the Director said. You go ahead and fire me, you don't like it, Rifka, but that's what you are. You and your protected brother. You leave the stuff lying around and we clean it up. Now you're suddenly afraid of his life. Maybe you should have worried about his life a long time ago? He's got Addison's, the Director said, and he's a self-destructive bastard, too. You don't think we do know that, Rifka? We know everything. You don't like it? Well, what's your suggestion?

There's no suggestion, Rifka said. He could see it now, the swirling, distant chasm, the waters below, he was on the perch, not falling, suspended. He had ventured onto that ledge and that was where he had lived. There was nothing, nothing else to be done, nowhere to go, nowhere to be moved. Just make sure that nothing bad happens, Rifka said. You think I'm a shit, that's on your own time. Civil Service pension rules permit that. Put in for compensated hours.

You're a real funny guy, Rifka, the Director said. Is that all?

That's enough, all right. You heard me. You don't protect him, you'll hear from me. I don't want anyone breaking through the lines.

You liked that stuff, didn't you? the Director said. You Catholic boys with your upbringing, she must have been Gloria Swanson for you. Rockets and pinwheels. You sort of really miss her, don't you?

Rifka stood. He wanted to kill the Director, but then the Director had all of the tapes and files, likewise methods which could be put to any kind of use. The Director knew everyone and everything, had connections at every level, you couldn't fuck with him, that was the sum of it. You just couldn't do that. Maybe you could play him even, but not without terrible risk. Good-bye, he said.

You look real mad, Rifka, the Director said. Real mad and upset. You called *me* over here, remember? What do you think of that? But don't worry about it, the Director said, swaying upright, stamping his feet on the carpet. We'll take good care of him just like we always did. The office is beyond the man, right? And after I'm gone there will still be an office. The Director walked by Rifka, went to the door, turned, seemed about to say something, said nothing, went out. Rifka unfurled a handkerchief and wiped his forehead. You Catholic boys, right. Yes, that was the way it was for Catholic boys. The Director would know all right.

Much later, almost at the end, Rifka saw how it all came together, saw the way it must have been. The Director had been given a nasty job, he did it like he did all of the others, but this had been *personal*, difficult in ways which Rifka could not quite fathom but which definitely had been there. Jeptha, after the job was done, had to be taken out of the way because Jeptha had been the real cause of the job in the first place.

So that left Rifka. Rifka was still around, had potential, but he was paralyzed, grief-stricken. Out of power, out of Washington. How much damage could a junior senator do, one with plenty of his own agenda, his own grief, and Lyndon who knew the truth hovering over him?

Rifka could figure all of this out, almost at the very end, too late for it to make any difference. He was no threat, he represented nothing to the Director. But there had been the goddamned excruciating war and the administration had drowned in its blood and then it was Rifka's turn to run, to take Lyndon down. The Director had seen early on, maybe even earlier than Rifka himself that this was a real campaign, a real possibility. Rifka in power without Jeptha to hold him back, Rifka in office with the only real agenda to avenge Jeptha—the war was just an excuse—it would have been dangerous. Very much so to a director who knew too much.

Rifka copped to it all. It came upon him suddenly and in a blaze of clarity exactly what the Director would be bound to do and why. But even as that insight burst upon him with clarity and shimmering force, a force which might have once been his in the actress's arms he was already turning from the podium, moving back toward the kitchen. So it's on to Chicago, he said and waved and turned and then the clattering of the gun and Rifka knew, he *knew* what had necessarily been planned for him just as the actress must have known in the last minutes before the men came in. Too late, though, for both of them, too late for Jeptha, too. The Director, Rifka thought, he hated women, hated women-fuckers, too, and Rifka in power would have known too much. Too late for America, Rifka thought as his brain burst, his brains pouring out in the kitchen. Well, maybe not for America, but a lousy fucking end to one great doomed ride, he thought and then thought no more of this. *The Director had put it in him.*

WINDSOR R.I.P.
by Sean Flannery

The penetration of British Intelligence by Soviet spies, recruited when they were young men at places like Oxford and Cambridge, is well known. What is not known is who helped them, and who else was involved.

It was twilight on a day late in September when Wallace Iver Mahoney watched from the darkness inside his kitchen as the heavyset man climbed out of a dark-blue Chevrolet sedan. He'd heard the car's tires crunching on the gravel driveway, and had come from the front porch to see who his visitor might be. It was so seldom anyone came out to the lake these days; no one from Langley, and only an occasional visitor from Duluth . . . because there were no relatives now, absolutely no one.

In stature Mahoney was an unremarkable man: five feet ten at just under two hundred pounds. His hair was still thick, but absolutely white. Here is a man of great intelligence, evident in the economy of his motions and in the depths of his clear blue eyes. Here is a man who has been places, has seen things, a man who has suffered, as indeed he had.

The car was a rental unit, Mahoney spotted that from the license plate series, and even from inside the cabin he could tell that this was no ordinary visit. Trouble, he guessed. But at seventy-one Mahoney figured he was getting a bit long of tooth for the "game," as it had been

called. Besides, the Wall was down and the Russians, if not
exactly our friends, were too busy starving to death to create much mischief.

His visitor walked around the side of the house, out of
sight. "Hullo?" the man called. His accent was definitely
British. Cockney.

Mahoney moved silently through the kitchen to the
front of the four-room cabin and waited just off the en-
closed front porch for the Brit to show up.

The evening breeze had kicked up small ripples on the
lake. With the full moon this evening, the effect would be
lovely. But already the first hints of autumn and winter
were in the air. Lately the mornings were crisp. But it was
northern Minnesota. Home. Familiar since childhood.

Mahoney reached into the pocket of his button-up
sweater to touch the reassuring weight of the .38 caliber
pistol. Just a precaution, he told himself, because what old
spy is completely unafraid of his past? The faces of all his
(old) enemies came to mind at the speed of light in a sort of
preternatural collage. They weren't all dead, though by
now he supposed he must have outlived most of them.

The Brit came around the corner and mounted the steps
to the porch. He knocked. "Anyone home?" he called.

Mahoney was looking right at the heavy-jowled man.
Greasy was the first thought that came to mind. It was as if
the man had been eating fatty foods all of his life without
ever wiping his chin. And there was something else about
him; about his look, his stance, that was slightly bother-
some. He had a problem, and he'd come here for help.

"Who are you?" Mahoney asked from the darkness.

"Fuckin' hell," the Brit swore, stepping back and stumbling half down the steps.

"I asked who you were?"

"Name is Tom Churchill, and you scared the bleedin'
shit out of me, mate. Is that Wallace Mahoney in there?
Have you got a gun on me, or something?"

"What do you want, Churchill?" Mahoney asked. Dough-
nuts to dollars, he figured the man was from Fleet Street
here to do some fool feature story: Old Spy Who Trained

With SIS In U.K. At Home In America's North Woods. Yet
. . . there was something else.

"I'm a writer for *News Of The World* and I've come because I need your help."

"With what?"

"A pair of my colleagues were murdered seven days ago.
You may have heard of it. At Windsor Castle. They were
gunned down by a Russian. KGB, though the SIS are denying that part. May I talk to you? Will you listen?"

"How'd you get my name?"

"If you agree to hear me out, I'll tell you that and everything else."

"Hold up your press credentials and your passport," Mahoney said. He took a flashlight from the shelf beside him,
aimed it at the screen door, and switched it on.

Again the Brit was startled, but he did as he was told.

Taking his pistol out of his pocket, Mahoney stepped
across the porch stopping two feet away from the man. He
could smell Churchill's body odor; it was not pleasant.

"Flip through your passport, please. I would like to see
the visa pages."

Churchill complied, slowly flipping through the passport's pages, holding each up for Mahoney to inspect. The
passport was nearly filled with visa stamps. The U.S., most
of Europe, though not the Soviet Union, nor Cuba or Communist China. He'd been to Hong Kong a half dozen times
within the past year, though. And Japan.

Mahoney lowered the flashlight and pocketed his pistol.
"Beer or Bourbon whiskey?"

"Both, if you don't mind," the Brit replied. He came inside as Mahoney went back into the kitchen, flipped on a
light, and got the glasses down from the cupboard.

Mahoney had the British journalist lay a fire on the
grate because the evening was getting chilly. Even though
the job was inexpertly done, in ten minutes they had a
pleasantly warm blaze going and they were seated across
from each other with drinks.

"My name?" Mahoney prompted.

Churchill looked up, a slight line of perspiration on his upper lip. In the firelight he looked pale and frightened.

"I'll come to that," he said. "I need your help, as I said, and I'd rather tell this story straight out . . . A to Zed."

Mahoney settled back in his easy chair. It had been a very long time since he'd been in this sort of a position, and like a man who'd lived alone for many years, he wasn't sure he was up to the company, but he was curious just the same.

"They should never have been killed, you know. They went up on a lark. At worst one might have expected the bobbies or maybe even grounds people to nab them and toss them out. But they were gunned down in cold blood."

"We were going to start at the beginning," Mahoney said.

"Yeah," Churchill said, taking a deep pull at his whiskey. "Dice Richards and Amory Fitzpatrick, chums of mine. They got on to this idea about who is buried where. You know: Who's buried in Grant's tomb? They'd got a tip that some hanky-panky was going on with the royal resting places. Switching bodies, maybe. Grave robbing. Coverups. Who knows?"

Mahoney said nothing. Churchill's paper was a British equivalent of the *National Enquirer* tabloid in this country, considered the worst of London's trashy rags.

"They spent a couple of days poking around, and the night they were assassinated, Fitz rang me up. Told me there were on to something. *Really* on to something this time, and wanted to know if I could come up to help out."

"With what, specifically?"

"He didn't say, but he was excited as hell, I can tell you that much. I couldn't get free until the next morning, and in the meantime the Russian killed them."

"How do you know it was a Russian?"

"Because the SIS were there waiting for me. They'd bagged the Russian, and tried to sweat me for whatever I knew . . . which was exactly nothing."

"But some security officer actually told you that it was a

Soviet citizen who'd killed your colleagues? Someone actually said that to you?"

"Yes."

Look for the anomalies, the out-of-step man in the platoon, the apple going bad in the barrel, the out-of-place, out-of-sequence thing, and there you would begin to find the answers. He'd lived by that principle his entire career as a field service officer and then later as an analyst. In the first place Scotland Yard should have been on the scene, not the Secret Service. And whoever had been in charge certainly would never have given out such a statement—especially not to a journalist of Churchill's stripe.

"Was it the . . . Secret Service who gave you my name?" Mahoney asked.

Churchill shook his head. "No, of course not, but they threatened us with a D notice if we didn't keep our yaps shut. Beasley . . . he's the number-two man behind the publisher . . . went along with it, which of course left Dice and Fitz dead for nothing, and me left holding the bleedin' bag."

Mahoney decided to find out just how this scumbag had come up with his name, and then kick him out. This was about nothing more than some sleazy story that would capitalize on the deaths of two men who'd probably stepped on the wrong toes. Very possibly this one would be next, and Mahoney did not want to get mixed up in it, or in British politics.

"The next day they put a tail on me. I spotted three pairs of them right off, but I'm sure there were others. One of the bastards even set up shop in the apartment across the avenue from mine. Took my picture, watched me through a telescope. My phone was tapped, and my mail intercepted. I sent a letter to myself from my office. Usually takes one day, this time it took two. Stuff like that."

Churchill suddenly got up and went to a window. It was fully dark outside now, and except for a few lights across the lake there was nothing to see. The moonrise wasn't until around midnight.

"How close is your nearest neighbor?" he asked.

"This time of the year, across the lake. A mile."

"Day before yesterday they were gone. No one across the way. No one waiting in the gray car. No one on the tube, no one outside the *News.*"

"You must have been relieved," Mahoney said somewhat sarcastically, but Churchill didn't catch the inflection.

"Gave me the creeps. But that night, coming back from work, on the tube, this Russian comes up to me and says there's only one man in the world whom he would trust to help both him and me."

"Russian?"

"He spoke with the accent, looked like a Russian, said he represented a man by the name of Tsyganov. Gave me your name, told me where you lived."

Mahoney looked at the newsman with renewed interest. "Help with what?"

Churchill remained standing by the window, nervously glancing outside as if he suspected someone was out there. "He said you would figure it out from the name, and everything else that had happened."

"Did he give you the first and patronymic?" Mahoney could not recall ever hearing the Russian's name.

"No, just Tsyganov. Said he'd been number five, but now he was in the minority in Moscow. 'One voice in the wilderness,' he said. Those were his exact words."

"Number five at what? The KGB? The Kremlin? Some ministry? What?"

"He didn't say."

"What else?"

A puzzled expression came over Churchill's features. "I made him repeat this, because I didn't understand him at first. He told me that the Kuril Islands would never belong to the Japanese. They must never belong to the Japanese or anyone else, and that it was up to you to see that it never happened."

"That makes no sense," Mahoney said half to himself.

"No."

The Kurils, which had originally belonged to Japan, had been ceded to the Soviet Union at Yalta in 1945 as part of a war reparations package. The heavily forested group of forty-seven volcanic islands stretched more than four hundred miles northeast from the Japanese island of Hokkaido to the Russian peninsula of Kamchatka. The Japanese wanted them back. The Russians refused even to discuss the matter.

"Did your Russian friend make a connection between that and the killings at Windsor?"

"No," Churchill said. "But it was no coincidence, him coming up to me like that."

"Did he say anything else to you?"

"No. He couldn't."

"Why?"

"He collapsed at my feet. Dead."

"Shot, stabbed, what?"

"He just bloody well folded up, stone dead. No blood, not a mark on him that I could see, but then I didn't stick around long enough for a post mortem."

Mahoney sat back. It made no sense whatsoever. Although the KGB was still as active as it had ever been (that was public knowledge even here in rural northern Minnesota) the vast spy organization had mounted a worldwide public relations campaign depicting itself as a benevolent watchdog of peace. In effect, it meant that the Komitet's wet affairs, in which blood was spilled, had been severely restricted. A *mokrie dela* would only be ordered under the most extreme circumstances.

But what did Windsor Castle, and the sensationalism of a pair of yellow journalists have to do with the Russians and the Kuril Islands? And who the hell was Tsyganov?

"Why did you come here?"

"Don't be daft. What else could I do? There's a story, of course. The biggest of my career, if you'll help."

Mahoney rose, took Churchill's glass and went into the kitchen, where he poured them both another drink. "Let's go over this again," he called.

Glass tinkled on the living-room floor, and a moment later something heavy fell. Mahoney stood stock-still for a long second or two, then put down the drinks, took out his pistol, and went back to the living room.

Churchill lay on his face on the floor, the back of his head dark with blood. A small hole had been drilled in the window glass where he'd been standing. He'd been shot, probably from a distance, by a high-power rifle.

Washington was like a dream after Mahoney's self-imposed exile in the hinterland, and coming by cab in from Dulles International Airport he felt as if he were returning home after too long an absence. Yet everything was different: No fool like an old fool, Marge, his wife of four decades, would have said to him.

Everything was different now. He had changed and the city had changed. Coming across the river on the Key Bridge into Georgetown he was aware of the increased traffic, much of it seemingly old junky cars belching blue smoke; increased pedestrian traffic, every street corner, it seemed, held a contingent of young people, mostly blacks; and everywhere there seemed to be litter, paper, styrofoam cups, abandoned cars, trash. The city, in his absence, had noticeably deteriorated, and it saddened him.

His memories of World War II and postwar Washington were still very fresh. He and Marge lived in a small apartment, in a very neat section of the city (though the exact street name now escaped him), while he worked first with the Office of Strategic Services under Allen Dulles, and then in '53 with the newly formed Central Intelligence Agency.

His postings had taken him and Marge around the world; Berlin, Moscow, Vienna, London. But always between assignments they would return to Washington so that it had become home to them. The only real home, in fact, that either of them knew until his retirement when they'd set up at Shultz Lake outside of Duluth, Minnesota, his home as a boy.

In a way, then, coming into Washington like this *was* like coming home, made sad by the neglect the city seemed to have suffered and the fact that he no longer had Marge at his side.

Yet he felt a certain excitement, too. A stirring of his blood now that he was back in the fray, now that he had a purpose again.

Flying out this morning he had tried to make some sense out of what Churchill had come to tell him. Find some possible connection between Windsor Castle and who was or was not buried there, with the Soviet-Japanese dispute over the Kurils. But there was no evident connection. Not yet.

He'd spent much of the night replacing the glass in the windowframe, and cleaning up the living room. He'd managed to drag Churchill's body out to the rental car and lock it in the trunk.

At first he'd thought about reporting the killing to the local police and letting them handle it, or calling Larry Danielle at Langley and reporting the incident to him, including the British journalist's fantastic story. But some inner sense of precaution (call it survival) made him hold back. If Churchill was to be believed, four people were already dead because of whatever was going on, and he didn't think the killings would stop simply because the incident went public. Before he said anything to anybody, he wanted to establish a few facts; what intelligence officer went into the field without first establishing a clear background for his case?

By noon he was checked into a room at the Four Seasons Hotel in Georgetown, and after a light lunch in the grillroom, took a cab over to *The Washington Post* on 15th Street, N.W.

Upstairs in the reference library he filled out three request slips and turned them in at the counter. One concerned the recent murders of Dice Richards and Amory Fitzpatrick at or near Windsor Castle; the second concerned the death of a Soviet man on the London subway three days ago; and the last was a request for information about a man by the name of Tsyganov, who possibly was a Soviet intelligence officer.

A few minutes later he was assigned one of the carrels in
the public section of the newspaper's library and a clerk
brought him a single microfilm canister.

"Sorry, sir, but this is all we have," the young man apolo-
gized. The microfilm contained the *Post's* local edition for
all of last week. "It's on page thirteen-F, the Foreign Section, Wednesday the twenty-eighth."

"Thanks," Mahoney said.

When the clerk left, he threaded the film on the reader,
flipped on the light, and turned the crank to that page. It
took him a moment or two before he found the article in
the lower right-hand corner. The entire piece was less than
two column inches under the headline: MURDERS AT
WINDSOR CASTLE.

LONDON—A pair of British journalists were killed Tuesday outside the grounds of Windsor Castle west of the city.

Authorities said Dice Richards and Amory Fitzpatrick, reporters for the London Sunday newspaper *News Of The
World,* were shot and killed by an unknown assailant or
assailants sometime between 10 P.M. and midnight.

No motive had been established, nor would the newspaper
confirm or deny if the two men were on assignment at the
time of their deaths.

There was no mention of any Russian connection, but at
least the story did confirm some of what Churchill had told
him; that two reporters had been killed at Windsor Castle.
Searching the journalist's body, he had come up with no
notes or anything else that would corroborate it, except
that the man did work for the *News.*

Nor had Mahoney found an overnight bag or suitcase in
Churchill's car. The man had either checked his bag somewhere and hidden the key or had checked in at a local
motel and left his room key at the desk. In any case, Mahoney had not wanted to take the time to find out, deciding
instead to leave the rental car with Churchill's body in the
long-term parking lot at the airport. It would be a few days,

he figured, before the car was discovered, and even longer before it was connected to him.

Time enough, he wondered leaving *The Washington Post* building and heading across the busy street to a pay phone, for him to unravel the mystery?

Deputy Director of Central Intelligence Lawrence Danielle was one of the very few people left at Langley whom Mahoney had worked with. The soft-spoken, diffident-appearing man had worked his way up through the Intelligence section, rather than Operations. But he'd always had a very firm grasp on every one of the Agency's directorates, offices, and staffs. For a time he'd worked as acting director, but had gladly stepped down to the number-two slot when former Army general Roland Murphy had been appointed head man.

He came down to the lobby when Mahoney signed in, his face lighting up in genuine pleasure.

"My God, Wallace, how long has it been?" he said, and they shook hands.

"It sometimes seems like years and years, but you look fit, Lawrence."

"Thanks for the white lie, but retirement seems to have been kind to you." Danielle took Mahoney's arm and they went across the lobby to the elevators.

Mahoney looked up at the inscription on the marble wall as he always did passing this way. It read: AND YE SHALL KNOW THE TRUTH/ AND THE TRUTH SHALL MAKE YOU FREE/ John, VIII:32.

A fine principle, he'd always thought. Yet he was not alone in having lived through betrayal. In fact he doubted if there were many in this business whose hands were completely clean. "It's the nature of the beast, Wallace," Dulles had told him in London after they'd betrayed the SIS. "And it won't get any better."

Upstairs on the seventh floor, Mahoney was subjected to a full body search with an electronic wand by the contract guards on duty just off the elevator before he was allowed to proceed through the glass doors and then right to Danielle's office.

Large windows overlooked the new building addition and beyond, the rolling green Virginia countryside. Only a few puffy clouds marred an otherwise clear blue sky. Again Mahoney was brought back to his past. How many times had he sat in this office, or offices downstairs? Beyond count.

"Coffee?" Danielle asked, motioning Mahoney to the couch and chairs. The meeting was to be kept on an informal level for the moment.

"No thanks," Mahoney said, settling into one of the thick chairs.

"Bourbon?"

Mahoney had to laugh. "You know me too well."

Danielle poured them both a stiff measure of whiskey, neat, at the sideboard, and brought them over. "Well enough to believe that your being here is not a social occasion." He sat down on the couch, raised his glass in a toast, and took a drink.

"No it's not, Lawrence. At least not entirely."

"You're retired," Danielle said flatly.

"It's nothing like that, either. But I do need the Agency's help. Archives."

"Special Registry," Danielle said. "What sort of information do you need, and for what purpose?"

Danielle had always been a straight-to-the-point man, and Mahoney appreciated it now. He didn't want to screw around here.

"I'm getting old, I need my memory jogged," Mahoney said. "I'd like to have access to the Russian Desk's historical registry, specifically for a half dozen names."

He'd jotted the names of five former KGB officers he'd come in contact with at various times in his career, to act as a screen on Tsyganov's name. In two other cases he'd written only the last names. He took the list out of his pocket and handed it across to the Deputy Director.

"Matveyev and Velichko worked out of Berlin in the late

fifties, early sixties," Danielle said, studying the list. "I don't know about the others."

"I'm writing my memoirs and I got stuck," Mahoney said.

Danielle looked up. "We'll have to pass on it before you show it around."

"Naturally. But in the meantime I'll need some help."

Danielle eyed him for a long time, the expression on his face unfathomable, except that it was not friendly. "Nothing goes out of here without my personal approval."

Mahoney shrugged.

Again Danielle held his silence for a moment or two. "We generally don't like this sort of thing, Wallace. The Agency has been burned before. You know the history as well as I do. We definitely do not want to become embroiled in another lengthy legal battle."

Mahoney's eyes narrowed slightly. He sat forward and placed his glass on the coffee table. "You know what I have done for this organization, Lawrence, so save the lecture. You'll either authorize my access to records, or you won't. I came directly to you, rather than apply under the Freedom of Information Act, because we go back a long way together, and I have respect for the business, especially in these unsettled times."

Danielle put his glass down, then got up and went over to his desk where he picked up the telephone. He dialed an in-house number.

"Jack, it's me. Wallace Mahoney dropped by for a chat. As a matter of fact he's here in my office now. I'm sending him down to see you. He needs some help with some old files."

Danielle avoided looking Mahoney's way.

"No, old Russian desk stuff. He has a list of a half dozen names he'd like to review. I'd like you to give him a hand."

Mahoney stood up and retrieved the list of names the Deputy Director had laid on the table and stuffed it in his pocket. It really didn't matter, of course, because a record of his inquiries would be automatically kept in the computer, but old habits died hardest.

"He takes nothing out of the building, Jack. Do you understand?"

Jack Costeau, chief of Special Registry, was a Cajun who spoke with a thick Louisiana-French accent. He was a small, olive-complected intense man with thick black hair and deeply hooded black eyes.

"My secretary is gone for the day, so you may use her desk," he told Mahoney. "Do you need help entering the system?"

"If you please," Mahoney said. "I'm afraid I'm one of the last computer illiterates anywhere."

Costeau smiled faintly as he went around his secretary's desk, and quickly entered the Special Registry's Russian Desk archives.

"You have brought with you a list of names for which you need information?" the Special Registry chief asked, looking up.

"Antonov, no first or patronymic."

Costeau entered the name, and pushed an instruction key. "All you have to do is type in the name, and press the F3 key; the machine will do the rest."

Three names appeared on the screen: ANTONOV, GEORGI PAVLOVICH: ITALY 66-71 ANTONOV, SERGEI N.: AUSTRIA 65-67 ANTONOV, VIKTOR NIKOLAEVICH: AUSTRALIA 52-54.

"Since in this case you have three choices, you will have to move the cursor to the name that you would like to learn about."

"Let's try Sergei N.," Mahoney said. "I believe I met him in Austria in '66."

Costeau pushed a button bringing the cursor down to the second Antonov, and again pressed the F3 key. After a very slight delay, the screen filled with information about that man, beginning with his birth in October of 1931 in Odessa.

"Use the scroll key to bring up more information, and when you're finished with this file, touch return to start over."

"Thanks," Mahoney said.

"I've locked out the print function, Mr. Mahoney. And I've been instructed to request that you make no notes."

"I understand."

"Very well. If you need any assistance, I'll be in my office."

When the man was gone, Mahoney sat down at the computer terminal, studied the keyboard for a second or two, and began his search, starting with the Antonov file already on the screen.

The architecture of this program was about what he'd expected it to be and presented no undue complications. With only a small bit of manipulation he was able to instruct the machine to conduct a simultaneous search of three or more files, only one of which would be recorded in a security program, allowing him to range freely through the system without detection. He'd been in retirement, not dead.

When he was set he brought Tsyganov up on his screen and touched the F3 key. A moment later the information began to appear.

TSYGANOV, VLADIMIR ILICH: (GRU) AUSTRIA 61-63; BEIRUT 63-65; WEST GERMANY 65-68; EXPELLED 68.

According to Agency records, the man had been born in 1921 in Moscow, had attended university there studying electrical engineering, and during the war had distinguished himself fighting Nazis. He'd joined the NKVD briefly, switching to the GRU less than a year later.

Following the biographical data several photographs of the man came up on the screen one at a time; most of them taken years ago, showing him as a young man in uniform. One shot, however, was taken in London, the Tower Bridge behind him. The picture had evidently been taken by a long-range hidden camera, and it showed Tsyganov in civilian clothes talking with a blond-haired man who stood in a slouch. The computer-enhanced photos were of a reasonably high quality, even represented on a CRT, so that Mahoney was able to recognize the second man as Kim Philby, the infamous British spy who'd worked for the Russians through his long, distinguished career.

Mahoney sat back. Philby had disappeared from his posting in Beirut in '63 even though a British Secret Service investigation had supposedly cleared him of any suspicion. There were, of course, people in London and in Washington who figured Philby was the mole code-named "Stanley" but there was no hard evidence.

But someone must have tipped him off that Washington was sending over a special team to reopen the investigation.

Tsyganov? The GRU officer had been stationed in Beirut in '63. And he and Philby had met in London. There was no date accompanying the photograph, but Mahoney got the impression that it had been taken in early fifties, perhaps even the late forties. Both men looked very young, the cut of their suits from that era.

Was it possible, Mahoney wondered, that Tsyganov was Philby's real control officer all those years, apparently unbeknownst, or at least unpublished in the West?

But in addition to Philby, there were others working for the Soviets: Guy Burgess, Donald Maclean, Anthony Blunt, and a fifth, still-unknown, man.

The man who'd spoken to Churchill on the subway had made a curious statement: He'd apparently been instructed to say that Tsyganov had been number five. Five, as in the control officer for the still-unknown fifth man?

And he'd also said that Tsyganov was now a minority in Moscow. A minority at what? "One voice in the wilderness," the Russian had told Churchill.

Mahoney stared at the photograph of Tsyganov and Philby as he let his thoughts drift where they would; making and rejecting free associations. Playing the "what if" game, as he called it. Connections within connections. Links hidden within smokescreen associations.

Tsyganov knew Philby. They'd met on at least one occasion in London, a fact also known to whomever had ordered the surveillance photograph taken.

Presumably there was a second connection between Tsyganov and Philby, this time in 1963 in Beirut at the time of Philby's sudden flight to the Soviet Union.

But Tsyganov, evidently still alive, sent an emissary to London to tell a yellow tabloid journalist not only that he's number five and now in a minority in Moscow but that the Kuril Islands can never be given up by the Russians and that the only man in the world to solve their problem was a very old spy retired from the CIA and living on an obscure little lake in northern Minnesota.

Mahoney had to shake his head with the thought of it. Anomalies were blossoming all over the place, like ornaments on a Christmas tree—pretty and eye-catching, but not very substantial.

And what the hell did a pair of murders at Windsor Castle have to do with anything?

He brought up the section of Tsyganov's file that dealt with his assignment in Beirut. There was, of course, nothing, not even speculation that the Russian was connected with Philby, but Mahoney didn't think he'd find that in the files. Instead he took mental note of Tsyganov's former residence on Lord Nelson Boulevard, which, if he remembered Beirut, was above the city, overlooking the harbor.

Again Mahoney sat back a moment to think it out. Tsyganov had, in effect, sent him a message through Churchill, confident that the message would be understood for what it was.

"He said you would figure it out from the name, and everything else that had happened."

Mahoney hit the return key, sending Tsyganov's file back to archives, then pulled himself out of his search and seize program, bringing the computer back to one of the other files, before blanking that out as well and shutting down the terminal.

Costeau came out of his office as Mahoney was getting up.

"Finished?"

"Just now," Mahoney said. "Thanks."

"Will you be going back up to Mr. Danielle's office?" the chief of Special Registry asked.

Mahoney shook his head. "No, I don't think that'll be necessary. I'll just sign myself out downstairs."

Costeau glanced at the computer terminal, then nodded curtly. "Glad to have been of some help."

The mountainous coast of Lebanon gradually rose up out of the mist that seemed to permanently hang over the Mediterranean as the Middle East Air jetliner made its approach into Beirut's beleaguered airspace.

Mahoney had in no way tried to mask his movements after taking a cab back from CIA Headquarters in Langley to his hotel in Georgetown. Neither had he advertised what he was doing, nor did he make it obvious that he was maintaining a careful watch over his shoulder.

Tsyganov's messengers—both the Russian in London and Churchill in Minnesota—had been murdered. Sooner or later Mahoney would become a target as well, if he wasn't already one, so he was being careful. To this point he had been unable to detect the presence of any tail. For the moment no one seemed to be watching him.

It had taken the remainder of that day to book a flight out of Dulles Airport on United's nonstop service to Charles de Gaulle in Paris. He stayed the day in a hotel nearby Orly Airport until it was time to board for the overnight flight to Beirut. And coming now into the country of perpetual civil war he girded himself for what he might find . . . or not find.

All of this could be some sort of an elaborate plot to embroil him in something that would potentially embarrass the United States. Or it could be a plot to lure him out of the country, where he would be killed.

But somehow he didn't think either case was fact. There was something about this business, something about the connection between who was buried at Windsor and the dispute over the Kurils that was just beyond his ken. Churchill's story had the ring of authenticity to it. The truth was always filled with holes, whereas a carefully contrived story was usually pat. This time Mahoney had the eerie feeling that however this turned out, the revelations would be stunning . . . perhaps so much so they would be unacceptable.

The airport was temporarily in the hands of a Christian faction led by an obscure colonel, and from what he'd picked up in Paris, was reasonably safe for the moment. Or at least as safe as anyplace could be in the region.

The terminal was very busy when Mahoney worked his way through passport control and customs with his fellow passengers, most of whom were middle eastern. Armed guards were stationed everywhere, carefully scrutinizing everyone who passed.

When it was his turn the passport official stamped his entry visa without comment, and he went tiredly down a short corridor into the customs hall, where fifteen minutes later he retrieved his single bag and presented it at one of the counters for inspection.

"Have you anything to declare?" the uniformed official asked. An armed soldier stood at his elbow.

"No," Mahoney replied, although he'd brought his pistol and an extra SpeedLoader of ammunition. He could only imagine what the penalty would be for trying to bring a weapon into the country.

"The purpose of your visit?"

Mahoney leaned forward confidentially. "I've come unofficially from Washington to discuss the . . . hostage situation. My President is very interested in settling the business."

"He stands for reelection soon, isn't it so?" the official asked with a smirk.

Mahoney nodded.

The official held his gaze for a moment, then made a chalk mark on the side of Mahoney's bag. "Good luck," he said, obviously not meaning it, and Mahoney took his bag and walked out.

Beirut smelled like plaster dust and rotting garbage. The city that had once been called the "Paris of the Mediterranean" had the look of the capital of any country at war. Burned-out derelicts of cars and trucks were scattered here and there along the roads. Many buildings were nothing

but bombed-out, burned-out shells, and in some cases entire blocks had been destroyed, rubble everywhere. And
there seemed to be very little new construction going on.
The city was being destroyed bit by bit and nothing was
being done to restore it.

Mahoney's cabbie was an old man, his face weathered
and deeply lined, most of his front teeth missing. His clothing was filthy dirty and ragged, but he had a thick gold
chain around his neck, and every time he looked over his
shoulder at his passenger in the backseat his grin got
wider.

He kept up a running commentary all the way through
the city and into the foothills to the number on Lord Nelson Boulevard that Mahoney had gotten from the Agency's
files on Tsyganov. Tsyganov had used this place as his residence when he'd been stationed here in the midsixties.
That was more than twenty-five years ago, and it was
likely that the house might not even be standing after all
that time.

But Tsyganov's message was that Mahoney would figure
out what to do simply from his name. The Russian GRU
officer had laid out a puzzle: Find me if you can. This was
the only logical place, although, coming out of the city, he
asked himself again what the hell he was doing here like
this. He was seventy-one years old, a has-been, over the
hill, out of contact with the real world as it was today. He
had been a soldier of the Cold War. Now the politicians
were calling the struggle, the Invisible War. The President's "New World Order."

Yet, some inner sense that had always directed him was
telling him that this was necessary. For some reason he
was needed. Four people had lost their lives, which meant
this business was very important to someone.

The old address turned out to be a nondescript house
hidden behind a tall white wall on a narrow, tree-lined
street. The rear of the property faced downhill, toward the
city, the harbor, and the hazy Med. Up here the air smelled
sweetly clear and fragrant from some flower blossom. Almost like oranges, Mahoney thought.

It was quiet, too. Coming through the city he'd heard gunshots in the distance, but here they were far enough away so that the war seemed safely afar. Peaceful.

He paid off his garrulous driver and when the cab was gone went up to the door and pulled the bell chain. It was opened almost immediately, and Mahoney was face-to-face with a much older, frail-looking version of the man with Philby in the photograph.

"Vladimir Ilich Tsyganov?" Mahoney asked.

The old man nodded, a faint smile creasing his thin mouth. "I am sincerely glad that you came, Wallace Mahoney. Sincerely glad."

The Russian was alone in the big house, and had been waiting for six days for Mahoney to show up, fending for himself.

"I'm not much of a cook," Tsyganov said. "But then old men do not eat much."

They were seated on a veranda overlooking the city. The morning was very pleasant, still, cool, and fresh. The Russian offered no food or drink, and Mahoney got the impression that the man was in a hurry.

"I have a lot of questions for you," Mahoney said.

"I'm sure you do, and I shall answer them all. But first you must explain to me why you came here."

"It was your message . . ."

"No." Tsyganov waved him off impatiently. "I mean, what did you hope to learn. What do you think is going on?"

"Whatever is going on is very important," Mahoney began. "Four people have given their lives already. By the way, who was your messenger on the London subway?"

Tsyganov shook his head sadly. "Poor Arkasha," he said. "He was my son. He was a GRU lieutenant colonel."

"I'm sorry. Who killed him?"

"The KGB," Tsyganov answered sharply. "The old men who are still afraid of change. Afraid of the West. Of new ideas, capitalism, free enterprise . . . call it what you will because the label means nothing." Tsyganov glanced toward the city. "You must understand the Russian spirit, Wallace Mahoney. We are a people who do not suffer embarrassment well. Face, as you say, means very much. So much, in fact, that certain elements in Moscow wish *perestroika* and especially *glasnost* to fail. They understand that we can never return to the old ways, but they desperately want to cover up some of their . . . *our* excesses of the past."

"You were control officer for the fifth man."

Tsyganov nodded. "Yes, but I worked with the others as well. Philby, Burgess, Maclean, Blunt. I knew them all. The Philbys became close personal friends of mine and my wife's in Moscow. It was a sad day when we buried him."

"The fifth man has never been identified."

"No. And for all the newspaper and magazine articles, and all the books that have been written, your people have not even come close."

Mahoney's eyes narrowed. "Is that what it's all about? Four murders including your son's merely to hide the identity of some Brit who betrayed his country a half century ago?"

Tsyganov didn't reply.

"Nobody cares any longer. It doesn't matter. It's become nothing but grist for the occasional writer. Whoever that fifth man was, he's either dead by now or very very old."

For a long time Tsyganov held his silence. It was clear that he was trying to come to a decision that was causing him some distress. Yet it had been his call to action that had brought Mahoney this far, so it was equally as clear from the expression in his eyes, and from the set of his shoulders, that he would not hold back now.

"You're wrong," he said finally. "It's more important than you can possibly imagine."

"Then tell me: who was the fifth man?"

"I'll show you, and then you'll understand everything. And maybe you will be able to help us."

"Show me?" Mahoney asked. "What?"

"His grave."

"Where?"

"Urup," Tsyganov said softly. "On an island in the Kurils, where we thought he would be safe."

A full eighteen hours later, and ten time zones to the east, Mahoney hunched up his coat collar against the raw north Pacific wind and made his way down the steep boarding stairs that had been pushed up to the small Ilyushin jetliner.

It was very dark, the sky obscured by a thick blanket of clouds, and although it was still early in the season, it felt and smelled like snow was on its way.

The only lights to be seen in any direction, besides those of the jetliner, were the airport beacon (the runway and taxi lights had already been extinguished) and a single light over the door of a small building that apparently served as airport operations.

Tsyganov had gone ahead, and stopped a few meters away as a Zil limousine materialized out of the darkness, its headlights off, and pulled up.

The driver, when he jumped out, seemed very nervous and he kept glancing at something across the field.

"If you will please hurry, Comrade General, there isn't much time," the driver said.

"Come," Tsyganov beckoned to Mahoney and he climbed into the backseat of the limo, Mahoney crawling in after him.

Moments later they were headed away from the airstrip, down an extremely bumpy dirt road. But not until they were completely out of sight of the field did the driver dare switch on the car's headlights, and when he and Tsyganov spoke, it was in hushed tones.

"Has there been trouble, Yurii?" Tsyganov asked.

"Borodin and his pricks are on their way. Valentin radioed from Moscow two hours ago."

"When are they due?"

"They should have been here by now, Comrade General. Viktor is watching the docks in case they come over on a patrol vessel."

"In this weather?" Tsyganov asked, surprised.

"Anything to catch you here," the driver replied. "Thank God the Air Force is remaining neutral."

All of their conversation was in Russian, most of which Mahoney was able to catch. "Are we in some danger here?"

Tsyganov turned to him and nodded. "Yes. If Constantin Borodin shows up with his troops they will not hesitate to kill us."

"Who is he?"

"KGB. You need not know anything else about him."

"High ranking?"

"A general," Tsyganov answered after a moment's hesitation. "A true patriot, Mr. Mahoney, do not get that wrong. But he is of the old school."

"He is opposed to you being here, and opposed to you revealing to the outside world who is buried here?"

"Violently opposed. You see, he and I are in agreement. The situation is intolerable, and if it gets out, the Soviet Union will suffer for a very long time to come. So Borodin believes that the status quo must remain . . . at all costs. But I believe that is no longer possible, though for the life of me I cannot imagine how you will be able to help us."

"Did Borodin's people kill your son, and those others?"

"Yes."

"Including Churchill while he was visiting my home?"

Tsyganov nodded again.

"If you don't have any idea how I can help, why did you involve me? My life is in danger now because of your actions."

"Because I couldn't think of anything else, Mr. Mahoney."

"But why me, specifically?"

"Because of your reputation. Even now you are extremely well thought of at Dzerzhinsky as well as Langley. And because you have friends in Whitehall. If anyone can find a way out for us, it might be you."

They passed a small stone hut, and their driver turned off the dirt track, down a narrower, rocky path through the thick woods. A hundred meters farther, he stopped the car and switched off the headlights.

"Here," he said softly, and he handed a flashlight back to Tsyganov. "Please hurry, Comrade General."

"Now you will see," Tsyganov told Mahoney, and he got out of the car.

Mahoney hesitated for a moment or two, not at all sure he wanted to know who was buried here. But then he climbed out of the car and hurried after Tsyganov, who had stepped off the path and stood holding the light on a small headstone.

Joining the Russian, Mahoney looked at the inscription on the stone. It was written in English. ARTHUR 1894–1972 R.I.P.

"I don't understand," Mahoney said, looking up. "Who was Arthur?"

"It was his code name. You know. Stanley was Kim Philby, this one was Arthur."

"The fifth man?"

"Yes."

"The man you're so worried about?"

Tsyganov nodded.

"Well, who was he?"

Tsyganov looked at Mahoney for a very long time before he took a slip of paper out of his pocket and handed it over. When Mahoney opened it, Tsyganov turned the beam of his flashlight on what was written.

For at least a full half minute Mahoney could do nothing more than stare at the name. The wind seemed to have stopped, and the cold had turned neutral somehow. It was 1939 and he had gone to Lisbon for the O.S.S. The meeting had been a chance one at some sort of party being held by the British Embassy. He remembered that at the time he had been struck by the sheer tragedy of the man, and yet he'd been dazzled by the man's charisma.

The fact that he was buried here, though, was nothing short of stunning.

Mahoney looked up. Tsyganov was watching him. "I see," Mahoney said.

"Then you agree to help?"

"Why not just leave sleeping . . . Leave him here? Obliterate the marker, and simply forget about it?"

"No," Tsyganov answered. "Someday it would come out. The historians would find the records."

"You don't want that on your conscience."

"On the conscience of the Soviet people. We have enough to be ashamed of without this. Will you help?"

"I don't know if I can . . . or should," Mahoney said. "It's still hard to believe. Why him? What possessed him to work for you?"

"He'd had contacts with the Nazis . . . with Hitler himself before the war, so he knew them for what they were. We were fighting Nazis, so he agreed to use his . . . connections and influence to help us. Maybe it was an intellectual game for him later. I don't know. But at some point it was too late for him to back out. Considering everything else that had happened in his life, this would have done no one any good if it had been found out." Tsyganov smiled sadly. "Fact is, he never did do much for us during the war, and absolutely nothing afterward. He was being saved for a propaganda coup that thankfully no one in Moscow had guts enough to attempt."

Their driver jumped out of the limo. "Comrade General, we must go now!" he called. "An aircraft is incoming."

"Will you help?" Tsyganov asked urgently.

"I don't know if I can," Mahoney answered, as he and Tsyganov hurried back up the path and clambered into the car.

Their driver backed up to the dirt road, spun the big car around, and headed back to the field, his foot to the floor.

Five minutes later they reached the airfield and shot across the apron directly toward the Ilyushin. The pilot had already started the jetliner's engines, and the big plane was ready to take off immediately.

Their driver pulled up beneath the port-side wing and helped Tsyganov and Mahoney get out. Together they rushed up the boarding stairs and into the aircraft.

The crew, including the flight deck crew, were all seated

in the first-class section, the expressions on their faces completely neutral.

Tsyganov pulled up short, Mahoney right behind him, as a tall, well-built man stepped from behind the curtains separating tourist class. He wore a KGB uniform, general's insignia and braid on his shoulder boards. He was holding a pistol, his face livid with rage.

"You have told him," he said in Russian.

"Yes, Constantin Konstanovich, but if you kill him now the crime will be compounded because he has come to help."

"With what? How?" Borodin demanded menacingly. He was clearly on the edge of losing control.

Tsyganov turned to Mahoney. "Tell him," he said.

Mahoney's hand had gone to the pistol in his pocket. Borodin had apparently come aboard alone. If it came to a shoot-out, Mahoney at least wanted a chance . . . but then he had it, and he took his hand out of his pocket.

"General Borodin, do you know of me?" Mahoney asked in Russian.

The general's eyes flicked to him, and he nodded hesitantly. "You should not have become involved."

"I have a solution that will get you and the Soviet Union out of trouble."

Borodin started to protest, but Tsyganov held him off. "Hear the man out."

"These islands will be given back to Japan in return for the monetary help that your country so desperately needs."

"Impossible . . ."

"The British will go along with it. They don't have the money to help, and they'd just as soon see the Japanese do it."

Borodin's eyes narrowed. "How?"

"I have a friend in London. Retired now, but he was a senior officer in the SIS. A very senior officer."

"All the more reason for you never to leave this island," Borodin said.

"I'm going to die tonight. A heart attack, whatever, and

you are going to transport my body back to the United States."

"What are you talking about?"

"Via London, where unfortunately this aircraft will have to remain grounded for a full twenty-hours because of mechanical difficulties."

Understanding began to dawn on Borodin's face, and he looked to Tsyganov. "How can he be trusted?"

"What other options do we have?"

"If it gets out, it will be the end for us."

"It won't get out," Mahoney said. "And General Tsyganov is right: What other choice do you have?"

Retired General Sir Howe Richardson came down the stairs into the crypt and joined Mahoney, who stood staring at the tablets marking the two interred bodies.

"Extraordinary, isn't it," the general said.

Mahoney looked up at him. They'd been friends for a great many years, their careers almost parallel except that Richardson had risen to briefly head the SIS for a short period before his retirement, whereas Mahoney had never had such ambitions.

"I'm glad you could help, Howe."

"Nothing else we could have done. Would have been unthinkable to raise a stink at this late date. Never kick the bastard while he's down, what? Even though he might deserve it."

"This might help," Mahoney said. "Getting it off their conscience."

"Nobody will know."

"Let's hope not," Mahoney said.

The general turned to leave, but before Mahoney followed him, he took one last long look at the two tablets: the old one to the left was marked with the name DUCHESS OF WINDSOR, WALLIS WARFIELD SIMPSON.

The one on the right, the newly replaced tablet, was marked: HRH EDWARD VIII.

Home at last to Windsor, Mahoney thought. The fifth man was finally at rest where he belonged.

MEET ME AT THE GRAVE
by William H. Hallahan

*Who kidnapped and murdered the Lindbergh baby?
The law says Bruno Richard Hauptmann did. And he
was duly executed for the crime. Not so, say many people.
The real culprit was never found. Herewith Bill Hallahan unmasks him for all the world to see.*

On the twentieth of May in 1927, an engagingly modest
and handsome twenty-five-year-old American stepped into
a small single-engine airplane at Roosevelt Field in New
York City and, with the pockets of his leather flight jacket
loaded with sandwiches and his fuel tanks overloaded with
gasoline, just barely managed to take off. It was 7:52 A.M.
He was attempting a flight most people regarded as sui-
cidal. His tiny plane would surely crash into the sea with
empty fuel tanks far short of his avowed goal—Paris,
France.

He was last seen flying northeast into a thick cloud bank.
The world waited. As the hours wore on, hope paled. People shook their heads. Alas.

Incredibly, impossibly, wonderfully, thirty-three and a
half hours later the little aircraft swooped down from the
French sky and landed at Le Bourget Field outside Paris.

He stood there on that French airfield beside his plane,
in that vast sea of wildly cheering Frenchmen, relaxed,
casual, golden youth, with a crooked grin, tousle-headed,
the very hero that most people dream of being, the man

who made every other man's dream come true. He was the perfect hero, making the perfect accomplishment at the perfect time.

Charles Augustus Lindbergh, piloting the Spirit of Saint Louis, became the most well-known man on earth and the world's hero.

All men and women felt better, walked straighter, dared more. There was nothing man could not do. Ask the Lone Eagle. Charles Augustus Lindbergh.

The world was never the same again thereafter.

Five years later, twenty-month-old Charles Augustus Lindbergh Junior, golden-haired, dimple-chinned like his father, and just learning to talk, the world's favorite baby, was kidnapped from his crib, ransomed for fifty thousand dollars and then found dead facedown in a shallow grave a few miles from his nursery. The entire world was outraged, furious, spluttering with indignation. The kidnappers had to be found and boiled in oil, drawn and quartered, peeled with a dull knife.

In time a man was arrested and brought to trial in a hysterical circus atmosphere. The howling newspapers tried and convicted him on the day he was arrested for questioning. With all the world watching, he was found guilty and executed in New Jersey's electric chair.

And thereafter, the world quarreled about the trial and about the guilt or innocence of the convicted Bruno Richard Hauptmann.

More than sixty years later there is still a stubborn band of people that claims that the prosecution suppressed key evidence, that Hauptmann's defense was so incompetently handled by his attorney Reilly that he should have been granted a new trial, that in sum the prosecution had failed to make its case and that Richard Hauptmann was innocent. And a few who have had access to the long-sealed New Jersey State Police files say bluntly they believe there's ample proof he was framed.

Dance Hills believed it, and he also liked to believe, sixty years after the fact, that with his exceptional investigative skills, if ever he had the time, he could uncover evidence that would point unequivocally to the true kidnapper. He said so one day at the wrong time, in the wrong place and to the wrong person.

And thereafter, his life was never the same.

It was Friday, March 17, Saint Patrick's Day, and he was to meet Peg Katzenborn for dinner at Killibrew's on Fordham Road, which billed itself as the oldest Irish pub in the Bronx.

Everyone in the Bronx with an Irish name or an Irish grandmother seemed to be there, wearing a knitted Irish sweater and a green cardboard derby, while singing Irish songs and drinking green-dyed beer. The special of the day of course was corned beef and cabbage.

When Hills, who didn't have a drop of Irish blood in him, stepped out of the rain into Killibrew's, he found that he didn't have a drop of Irish luck, either, that night, for lo, there in the booth with Peg sat Morgan. Karl Morgan. His nemesis.

Trapped. In an Irish saloon. On a sodden Saint Patrick's Night. With the mightiest mouth in the Bronx—who sat there surrounding a pitcher of green beer. And Morgan the mouth didn't waste any time using it.

"So how's the book coming?" Morgan asked, a classic Morgan opener.

"Which book?" Hills asked, fencing.

"There's always a book with you guys," Morgan said. "I never met a reporter yet who wasn't lugging around a half-finished book. So what's yours? The Al Capone story?"

There was no book. He thought of something to say. "Lindbergh," Hills said flippantly. But Fate had struck. He'd opened his mouth and out had come the wrong word.

"Lindbergh?" Morgan looked offended. "Not that old chestnut. The guy was guilty."

"Unjustly convicted," Hills said.

"Get out," Morgan said. "Bruno Richard Hauptmann was guilty."

"Railroaded," Hills blundered on, "by the flimsiest stuck-together collection of improbable circumstantial evidence you've ever seen." And so the battle was joined.

"Is that a fact?" Morgan said.

"Even the governor of New Jersey condemned the trial," Hills said. "In fact, he informed the head of the New Jersey State Police who conducted the investigation that it was the most incompetent police investigation he had ever seen. And to make his point, after the Lindbergh trial was over, he personally fired the man."

"So?" said Morgan. "Even if it was the most botched-up prosecution in history it doesn't mean your guy was innocent. Just that the state couldn't prove it. And you can't prove the opposite—that he wasn't guilty."

It was that smirk, Morgan's infuriating wise-ass know-it-all smirk, that goaded Hills into making his gaff. Anything to wipe that supercilious smirk off his face just once.

"Of course I can," Hills answered. There: he'd said it. And Morgan's eyebrows shot straight up.

There was nothing else to do except to pour more beer and wait for Morgan's attack. Wishfully, Hills looked out at the dark rainwet street. Still trapped by the rain.

"You can?" Morgan asked.

"Sure," Hills said not so surely. "What put Richard Hauptmann in the electric chair? Two unbelievable witnesses, and Hauptmann's missing work records for March 1, the day the baby was kidnapped."

"So? Go on." Morgan waited to pounce.

Hills went on. Why was he so shaky when he was absolutely sure of his facts? "Neither one of those two witnesses would have been allowed on the stand today," Hills insisted. "Without them the prosecution's whole case goes out the window. And Hauptmann walks."

Morgan hunched his shoulders and spread his hands. "So? That doesn't prove he was innocent."

"Yes, it does," Hills insisted. "When you include vital evidence that was suppressed. Evidence that would have cleared him."

"Come on, Hills. They caught Hauptmann with the

money. What was it—twenty thousand dollars in the ransom bills?"

"Now wait," Hills said. "Stay on the kidnapping charge. The only way the prosecution could put Hauptmann in the electric chair was to put him in New Jersey on the day of the kidnapping."

"March first?"

"March first, 1932. The only way they placed him in Jersey was two ridiculous witnesses. An eighty-seven-year-old welfare recipient named Hochmuth who had cataracts and was nearly blind and another man—Whited—who first said he didn't see anyone that day in the area then later changed his story after he was told he could share in the reward money and then on the stand unequivocally identified Hauptmann. How would you like to be sentenced to the electric chair on the testimony of two guys like that?"

"Come on—" said Morgan.

"Come on, my left foot," Hills said. "After the trial, Hochmuth was brought to the office of the governor of New Jersey—"

"Yeah, yeah," Morgan said. "Hoffman."

"Right," Hills said. "Governor Hoffman. And there in front of a number of witnesses this old man identified a silver cup filled with flowers not six feet from him as a woman wearing a hat. And Whited—let me tell you about Whited. He was branded the village liar and a cheat by three of his neighbors on the stand under oath. And it was those two witnesses that put Hauptmann in the electric chair. And to make matters more disgraceful, Hauptmann's alibi—the daily work sheet from the Majestic apartment construction job—was impounded by the police, then conveniently lost. They lost his alibi, but mysteriously it turns up fifty years later in the State Police Archives in West Trenton, New Jersey, along with all the evidence that was used in the trial. And when the work record does turn up, someone had very clumsily tried to alter it."

"This is all leftover soup," Morgan said. "It all comes down to one thing. This case will never be settled to everyone's satisfaction until the real kidnapper is produced with unshakable proof. Can your new book do that?"

"Oh come on," Hills protested.

"What do you mean—come on? Prove it. What the world doesn't need is another Lindbergh book unless you come up with new material. If Bruno Richard Hauptmann didn't do it, produce the guy who did. Find the real kidnapper. Can you do that?"

"Sixty years later?"

"Can you do that? Can you produce the real kidnapper?"

"You're ticking me off, Morgan."

"So. Tick. Can you or can't you find him?"

"Stop pushing."

"So. Push back. Can you produce the proof?"

Out of Hills's mouth came tumbling angrily the words: "Yes, I can." And that was that.

Morgan hooted. "Go on. How many professionals worked on this case over the years? Dozens? Hundreds? New Jersey alone spent a bloody fortune over two years trying to find him. How many books have been written about this case? This ground has been gone over and over. And now, more than sixty years later, little old you, all by yourself, you're going to find the kidnapper? Get out of here."

"I will."

"You will?" Morgan rose up and rapped the tabletop with his knuckle. "Come on, Hills. Last chance to get off the hook. Admit that no one will ever solve this case—not in a million years."

"I can."

"OK," Morgan said. "I'm going to hold you to it, Hills. I'll give you—let's see . . . a year. How's that? A whole year."

"That's fine," Hills said.

"It is, ha? How much are you betting here?"

"Fifty bucks."

"Fifty! Come on, Hills. Let's make it a grand. A grand by next Saint Patrick's Day. Done?"

Hills hesitated.

"Come on, Hills. Either you can or you can't. Are you going to put your money where your mouth is?"

"Done," Hills said. He shook Morgan's hand. Morgan exited hooting. "You'll never do it."

Watching Morgan step through the crowd at the bar, past all those men in cardboard green derbies singing the "Green on Green Boys" and out into the rainy streets, Hills shook his head at himself.

"Don't say it, Peg," he said to her.

"Mirror, mirror on the wall," she murmured, "who's got the biggest mouth of all?" She watched Morgan skip down the rainy street. "They're all dead," she said to Hills. "Lindbergh and Wilenz and Condon and whoever it was who kidnapped that baby and all the rest of them. All dead."

She knew the whole cast of characters by heart—from too many nights in bars with Hills. They were real enough —the politically ambitious prosecutor Wilenz with both eyes on the governor's chair, and that foolish middleman Condon and that alcoholic defense attorney Reilly swaying before the jury drunk and already psychotic from the encroaching syphilis in his brain, and the mysterious Isador Fisch who died back in Germany trying and failing to whisper a secret message into his brother's ear to tell to Richard Hauptmann.

"A year from now," she said, "you're going to have to hand over to that man one thousand dollars and then you'll never hear the end of it. He's going to ride you for years. Forever."

"Ummm," he groaned.

"There's only one way out of this," she said.

"Tell me," he said. "Quick."

"Find the real kidnapper."

Dance Hills lived with Peg Katzenborn. They got along OK, slept in the same bed, and shared expenses—a not-so-successful investigative reporter who needed a little more hustle and a psychiatric nurse who still, improbably, liked her job after thirty years.

At home she looked at Hills thoughtfully. "Any ideas?" she asked, pulling off her white nurse's blouse.

"Maybe," he said.

"You'd better," she said. "Or you're going to lose more than a thousand dollars."

He looked sharply at her.

"I mean it," she said. She stepped out of her white nurse's pants and dropped them into the laundry hamper. "I'm not going to put up with that man's braying up and down every bar on Fordham Avenue for the rest of my life. How dumb can you get, Hills?" She pulled off her brassiere and shut the bathroom door behind her. He heard her turn on the shower.

Peg Katzenborn reached for a bath towel in the linen closet. She'd heard all of Hills's arguments about finding the "true" Lindbergh kidnapper many times. But somehow it all missed the point. Men in bars arguing endlessly over the wrong points. It wasn't the kidnapping of the baby that was so significant. It was his murder.

Katzenborn looked at herself in the bathroom mirror and saw the stretch marks on her belly from two rough births. Still visible after thirty years. And she thought about her daughter's stretch marks from her firstborn. The union card that women pass along, one to the other. In the mirror stands Peg Katzenborn looking back at Peg Katzenborn, a mother with stretch marks looking in the mirror at a grandmother with stretch marks.

She thought about Anne Morrow Lindbergh, mother of five, or was it six? She could not ever have gotten over it: her firstborn child found dead facedown in the mud a scant mile or so from his crib.

Katzenborn thought about her grandson who was coming for a visit. He, too, was just twenty months old and just learning to talk. The thought of having him kidnapped made the flesh on her arms look like plucked chicken skin.

There was something about this case that had always bothered her, and now she tried anew to identify it.

This man—whoever—came to the Lindbergh house at night and climbed that absurdly inept excuse for a ladder into the nursery window and, probably while standing there right beside the crib, raised something deadly in his hand and with one blow to the head killed the still half-asleep baby.

And she felt again, yet again, forever again, that old unslakable anger, like a fist in her belly.

Baby killer.

How do you go about finding a kidnapper? Hills got out all his charts and notes on the Lindbergh case and began pinning them on the wall over his desk.

Hills studied his map of the Bronx. A very large borough of New York City, embracing some forty square miles, and, even in 1932, containing a population of one and a half million, one of whom kidnapped the Lindbergh baby. But which one?

"Follow the money," he said when she came out of the shower.

"Follow the money?" She looked back at him thoughtfully. "Are you sure?"

Tanya arrived in the evening in the rain with her baby and the rucksack filled with toys and diapers and milk bottles. Proudly. Two new teeth. And the three of them watched him stand and stagger and fist up everything reachable, liftable, mouthable. Then he climbed up onto Peg's lap, happily, trustingly, safely.

Peg Katzenborn watched the child, looked at his fingernails, his hands, his head scarcely covered with hair, then into his eyes which looked into hers, and she wondered anew how a man could kill a baby. A cold, calculating man, climbing in a window and picking up a sleeping child he has never seen before and, to silence him during the climb back down the ladder, kills him with a blow to the back of the head as casually as one drives a bung into a barrel.

She looked at Hills. "Stretch marks," she said.

"What?"

"I'll tell you later."

Later, in bed, she said, "Manfred, right?"

"What?"

"Wasn't his name Manfred—Hauptmann's child?"

"Yes."

"I recall reading how fond he was of his son, how he played with him and played songs on his mandolin for him and sang to him. Now listen, Hills. The money's the wrong way to go. That's what the police did and the prosecution and the newspapers and everyone else who has ever gotten involved—following the money."

"So?"

"So that's the wrong trail."

"So what's the right way?"

"Follow him."

"What are you saying?"

"I'm saying tomorrow is Saturday."

"Yeah."

"And I'm not on duty tomorrow."

"Yeah."

"So you not only have a big mouth; you have a small brain. We'll spend tomorrow correcting a sixty-year-old mistake."

"Which is what?"

"For sixty years, people have been looking for the wrong man."

The next morning, Hills said to her, "OK. What are we going to do?"

"We're going to do what any good specialist in abnormal psychology would do. Forget the money and look for the man. He left behind a great deal of information about himself, willy nilly, and I think it will be enough to find him."

"A psychograph?"

"Precisely. What do we know about this person?"

"Not much."

"Hills, I've been working with nut cases for thirty years and I can tell you that not even in 1932 were there many men in the Bronx who had the kind of mind that could pull an infant from a crib, kill him with a blow to the head, scuff open a half grave with the heel of his shoe, and indifferently throw the body into it. Because that's the kind of man you have to find. You know what's wrong with following the money? The kidnapper really didn't care about the money. That's not why he kidnapped that baby."

"Get out. That's why people kidnap babies. Money."

"Really?" she said. "I bet I can prove you wrong. Let's start with Dr. Shoenfeld's profile from 1932. That's what the police used. Right? Where is it?" He pulled it down from the wall.

Based on a study of the handwriting in the ransom notes Dr. Dudley Shoenfeld, a noted psychiatrist of the day, had provided police in the spring of 1932 with a list of the kidnapper's characteristics, a basic psychograph.

"There it is," she said, "a portrait of the man who kidnapped the Lindbergh baby." Her finger ran down the list:

[ ] In a low station in the world. Poorly educated. Not very skilled.

[ ] Felt ill used by the world, believed he had been deprived of his rightful status by others who were crowding him out of the limelight. And resentful of the successful, the exalted. The kidnapping was a way of striking at them, of humbling Lindbergh in the world's eyes.

[ ] Greatly overvalued his own worth. Harbored a compelling need to feel important, to get the attention of the whole world. *Make me feel important* was his one burning desire. He therefore might have had a string of failures behind him.

[ ] Misanthropic and psychotic, capable of killing a child without hesitation.

[ ] May have been a repressed homosexual.

[ ] Filled with bitterness. Anger.

[ ] Exhibits handwriting characteristic of schizophrenics. Overly decorated letters.

[ ] Arrogant self-confidence. But very secretive. He doesn't trust anyone on earth, not even his mother, maybe especially his mother.

[ ] With such overweening self-confidence in his own ability, he would take great risks.

[ ] About forty at the time of the kidnapping.

[ ] May have had a prison record.

[ ] Would never confess willingly, even under great coercion.

[ ] Most probably a German immigrant.

"One last thing," Hills said. "Shoenfeld believed that the kidnapper would keep some token of the kidnapping—some proof that would remind him of his power and conquest over Lindbergh. He thought it would be one of the old gold certificates that were in the ransom money. He even said it would be folded in half long ways then folded twice shortways since that was the way the early bills were passed. He said the folding had some symbolic meaning to the kidnapper."

"So I'm right," she said. "It wasn't the money. It was status. With one blow to the head of that little baby a sick little Mr. Nobody became a Mr. Somebody."

He looked at her. A sick Mr. Somebody.

"OK," she said, looking at the list. "Shoenfeld's profile is fine as far as it goes. Now what else can we learn about this man?"

"He was a terrible carpenter," Hills said. "A real wood butcher. The ladder he made was so bad it nearly broke under his weight. The fact that it didn't indicates that he was probably very slight—less than 140 pounds. Perhaps shorter than five feet ten."

"Just as you would expect from Shoenfeld's profile. An incompetent who had probably failed at many things. A real klutz who couldn't even make a decent ladder. What else?"

"The handwriting experts say his handwriting was a product of either South German or Austrian schools. He spoke English very poorly, was not a good speller, and wrote English phonetically."

"What else?" Katzenborn asked.

Hills shrugged. "The odds are he lived in the Bronx. He met with Condon in Woodlawn Cemetery; he received the ransom money here in Saint Raymond's Cemetery; and most of the ransom bills were passed here in the Bronx."

"What else?"

Hills smiled. "He probably read the Bronx *Home News*.

"Why do you say that?"

"Because that's the only paper that carried Condon's offer to be a go-between."

"Any more?"

"He may have been in the German infantry in World War I. The symbol he signed the ransom notes with had three interlocking circles which was similar to the German Army rifle target. If so, then he might have entered the U.S. sometime in the 1920's or even the early thirties."

"So he would be in the immigration files?"

"Unless he entered illegally. And he may have done just that if he had a prison record in Germany."

Katzenborn studied the list. "Sounds like a full-blown psychotic. In fact—" She looked thoughtfully at Hills. "He may have crossed the line once or twice."

"You mean he may have been committed?"

"On Monday I'm going to show this stuff to Dr. Budke. And I bet she says this guy had a definite inclination for violence. Self-destruction even."

"That means he might have been in a psychiatric ward."

She nodded again. "I'm sure he was. Maybe he even died there. How old would he be?"

"Shoenfeld said he was around forty."

"In 1932?" Katzenborn asked. "Sixty years ago? Forty years old? So he'd be over a hundred. The odds are he's dead."

"What else?" Hills asked.

"Judging from Dr. Shoenfeld's description I'd say your kidnapper was a loner. Very antisocial. A malcontent. Hater of the establishment. Definitely an outsider. Probably strong criminal tendencies. I'll bet he was a Communist or a Socialist or even a wild-eyed anarchist."

"Go on," Hills said. "You're doing great."

"How many men in 1932 lived in the Bronx who were a German immigrant, about 140 pounds, five ten, semiliterate, semiskilled with psychotic tendencies, an antisocial loner, a brooding failure, and who probably had a history of mental illness? It certainly narrows your search, Hills."

"Why didn't the police do this?"

"Because they followed the money."

"Somebody," he said.

"Mr. Somebody," she echoed. "Does any of this fit Richard Hauptmann?"

"Hardly any," Hills said. "Hauptmann was a skilled carpenter and the ladder was made by a total tool incompetent. The handwriting wasn't his—"

"Forget the evidence. Look at the profile that emerges. This is the picture of a psychotic. A sociopath. Was Hauptmann?"

"No. He was no loner. He was very popular and outgoing. Had many friends. If anything he was too trusting."

"The point is this man is always called a kidnapper. He wasn't. He was a very sick cat who killed another man's infant son to aggrandize himself, then made his murder look like a kidnapping. You see what I'm saying, Hills? For sixty years people have been looking for the wrong man."

He looked thoughtfully at his notes.

"So when do you start?" she asked.

"What?" Hills looked trapped.

"Nice bright Saturday afternoon."

"So?"

"Oh, come on, Hills."

"Hell, I can't do that, Peggy."

"Why not?"

"Go through all the schizoid mental cases in the psychiatric hospitals in the area? That's what you're talking about, isn't it? Going back through the psychiatric files twenty or thirty years—sixty years—after the kidnapping?"

"And you have until next Saint Patrick's Day," Katzenborn said. "You've got a lot riding on this, Hills. You'd better get your butt moving or I get a new bunkie."

Hills started with one of the most likely psychiatric institutions, the Long Shore Mental Hospital. With a note from

Peg Katzenborn's boss, Dr. Budke, Hills was admitted to an old wing of the hospital, no longer used, and there in slanting March sunlight that came through the barred windows, on the floor of what had once been the main receiving room lay strewn about cardboard cartons holding old psychiatric records. They were in alphabetical order.

"How do I find the admissions for the early 1930's?" he asked the guard.

"You have to go through them one at a time."

Hills looked with dismay at the cartons scattered helter-skelter around his feet. "How many dossiers are here?"

"Looks like thousands to me, mate." The guard left him there with an old wooden chair, a rickety old folding table, and a long shaft of sunlight. Hills looked around and thought about the mad, the psychotic, the catatonic, the screaming, violent, suffering souls who had come into this room over the years.

There were forty-one cartons and he started through them, opening each file and checking the admission dates. "Mirror, mirror on the wall," he murmured.

Some patients had been admitted, released, and admitted again, some as many as ten times. It took days to go through all the files to select only those patients who were admitted between May of 1932 and Pearl Harbor Day, December 7, 1941, an arbitrary cut-off date he selected because it was easy to remember.

Outside his barred window, while he passed the days with his head bowed over the cartons, spring arrived. The gum tree branches that rubbed against the windowpanes sprouted star-shaped leaves.

Finally he had reduced the cartons of files to just 137 that bracketed those two dates. Now he sat with his chin on his fist and browsed through them one at a time.

Male, with a German name, speaking with a heavy German accent, about forty in 1932, slightly built, about 140 pounds, under five feet ten, from the Bronx, working in an unskilled job and suffering from paranoia and schizophrenia.

He found many paranoid schizoids but they were the wrong nationality, the wrong sex, the wrong age. Three dossiers that looked promising he photocopied and turned over to Kazenborn.

She returned, shaking her head. "Dr. Budke shot all three down."

"Happy day."

"Start on the next nut house."

The spring wore into the summer, and the summer—the usual brutally hot New York summer when the vast city lay panting under that unforgivable, unforgettable humid heat—dogged him.

He was glad that he was busy with freelance assignments—magazine articles mainly. The thought of sitting in a superheated records room with nothing but a small fan was enough to make him give up the search. A thousand dollars to Morgan seemed a small price to be freed of his task.

But in October the last great heat wave broke on an assault from a massive Canadian cold front, and suddenly it was autumn in New York. The leaves changed and the city streets bloomed with the latest autumn outfits. The kidnapper seemed as elusive as ever.

"No excuses, Hills," she said. "Up and at 'em. Find him."

So he turned his attention to another collection of psychiatric records, this time at the Queensbury Hospital for Psychiatric Disorders.

"Never thought life had undone so many," he murmured to the clerk who opened the file room for him. Before him stacked one atop another were seventy-five large cartons bulging with old patient files.

She nodded and said, "Sooner or later, you realize all the world is nuts."

He sat there in the semidarkness, choking on old paper dust and reading through the unrelieved horrors of the mentally ill, hearing the screams, hearing the clink of the straitjacket buckles, the scuffles in the hallway, the thrown dishes, the terrifying unmoving silence of the catatonics—until one afternoon during an unexpected snowfall, he stood and fled.

He spent the afternoon in Killibrew's, talking postseason baseball and drinking beer and getting sozzled. "No more," he told himself. "No more." He would pay Morgan the grand.

That night, he slurred out his feelings to her.

"How do you stand it?" he demanded. "Year after year, working with wackos and fullmoonies and those infuriating, arrogant schizoids? You're just storing nuts in cages with no hope of ever helping them. You must like nuts."

"Sure," Katzenborn said. "I even live with one."

Christmas came and went. He wrote several pieces for a Chicago magazine which enabled him to pay Peg his share of the last two months' rent. He thought about getting a full-time newspaper job once more. He avoided the psychiatric files.

New Year's Eve was bad. Morgan came uninvited, talking, and taunted Hills at his own party. His raucous sneering voice hooted at Hills the entire evening. He was the first to arrive and the last to go, still braying about Hills's foolish boast as he stepped out of the door at 3 A.M.

"One thousand clam shells, baby" was his exit line. "Very soon now."

"That man has the most obnoxious characteristics of anyone I know," Katzenborn said, "but the worst is he never knows when to go home."

"Monday morning," Hills said, "I'm going back to those psychiatric files."

He was working, he always remembered the date, on January 18, feeling depressed by the clinical reports, nightmarish biographic data, psychiatric evaluations, drug summaries, and not believing that he would ever actually find the man he was looking for when he picked up a file on one Henry Boris Renner.

Born in Germany, 1899. Weight 149. Height 5′ 9″. Residence: the Bronx. Occupation: artist, then, in a later hospital admission, wall washer.

First admitted by court order on April 8, 1936, in a straitjacket. April 8: that was just five days after Bruno Richard Hauptmann was executed. Released two years later, May 1938.

Readmitted in May of 1953 again by court order. Released in six months.

Admitted again by court order on April 3, 1961—the twenty-fifth anniversary to the day of the 1936 Hauptmann execution.

Hills scanned the psychiatric summary on the patient. Original case notes by Dr. Henri Brule, psychiatrist.

The word Lindbergh struck him. "The patient seems obsessed with the Lindbergh case."

Coincidences and striking parallels piled up. According to his dossier, Henry Boris Renner was born in Kamenz, Germany, Hauptmann's hometown, in 1899, the same year Hauptmann was born. And if he was to be believed, Renner served as a machine gunner in the German Army in World War I just as Hauptmann had done. And to cap the coincidences, he was probably an illegal immigrant, although for reasons unrevealed, the hospital and the courts chose not to bounce this dangerous psychiatric problem back to Germany.

The first commitment, in 1936, followed a court hearing, during which one Martin Lewis, a court-appointed attorney represented Renner, and became Renner's custodian of incompetent properties. But Renner's property value was listed as zero. Renner was a psychotic public pauper.

Police record showed that Renner's arrest followed a series of violent acts against neighbors. He was bound over for psychiatric evaluation, which led to his commitment.

Renner's address was just five blocks from Hauptmann's and not very far from Condon's.

Hills took the subway to Renner's old neighborhood. And then walked through the streets. It was largely Hispanic now, and he began ringing apartment doorbells. Most of the people were all sullenly suspicious of him and answered in low monosyllables. Sí. No. No. Sí. None of them had ever heard of Henry Bruno Renner.

Hills shrugged. He hadn't expected to roll a seven with the first pass of the dice. But he did hit it lucky. A woman perhaps in her midfifties answered one door.

Hills told her he was looking for someone—related to a missing heir case.

She shook her head. "I don't live here," she said. "I'm just getting some things for my mother in the hospital."

Hills guessed her mother would be in her seventies or eighties—old enough. "Is she nearby?"

"Oh, yes," said the woman, "she's in a permanent-care nursing home."

"Can you tell me how long she lived here?"

"Yes. Let me think. Since 1931."

"Then you must have lived here at some time."

"Oh, yes, but not for many years. More than twenty-five years I would say."

"Did you ever hear of Henry Boris Renner?"

She drew back. "Renner? You're interested in Renner?"

"Yes. Did you know him?"

"I was a very small child when he lived here. But there were many stories about him. He was a mental case. They put him away. My mother could tell you more. She knew him. She talked about him a lot in the old days."

"Perhaps I could see her now?"

She hesitated. "Well, yes. I'll be going there shortly. It— my mother is not from this country."

"She came from Germany?"

"Yes. How did you know?"

"A guess. There were many Germans in this neighborhood in the thirties."

"My mother's mind isn't—she's begun to forget some English words. I think it would help if I was there—I speak German."

"Of course."

Her name was Helga. Helga Zorn. She was eighty-four
and had come to the United States in 1925 at the age of
seventeen. Even now, after more than sixty-five years in
the United States, she still spoke with a hint of a German
accent. In October 1931, she was married to Otto Zorn and
moved to that one apartment and never moved out. With
rent control, she just stayed year after year, even after her
husband died, her daughter married, and the neighborhood
changed. Stubbornly she wouldn't move, even though her
daughter urged her to many times.

She remembered Henry Bruno Renner well—and Nellie.

"Who was Nellie?" Hills asked.

"She lived with him. Actually he moved in with her one
day. Neighbors told her to stay away from him."

"Why?"

"He was a bad man. A terrible temper. He beat her. And
they had no money. And after he moved in, she started to
take men visitors. She and that Renner—they lived on
what she earned from those men. But sometimes she
wouldn't do it. And then they would fight and he would hit
her."

"What did Renner do?"

"He told everyone he was an artist. But his crazy sick
paintings, no one would buy them. He would tell everyone
that someday he would be a world-famous artist. Sometimes to get money for drink he would work as a wallpaper
remover. He had no skills, and for a German that was un-
usual. We always believed that he was an illegal alien."

"What was Renner's reputation in the neighborhood?"

Mrs. Zorn spoke to her daughter in German.

"The neighbors there they"—she leaned close—"Oh."
The daughter looked at Hills. "They called him a—her
pimp."

"What happened to her?"

"She disappeared," Mrs. Zorn said.

"When?"

"Just before the Hauptmann execution. I remember because they had a fight—they had been fighting all that
week—and then he went out and got drunk the night of the

execution. A lot of us stayed up to hear the news. Richard Hauptmann was executed I think at eight o'clock at night and Renner was drunk and he stayed drunk for three days then he got into a terrible fight when someone asked where Nellie was."

"She was never seen again?"

"I always thought he did something to her."

Hills stood in the hallway of the nursing home, pondering his copy of Renner's psychiatric file. He had decided on his next move.

Hills found Martin Lewis in New Jersey, an old man in an old house, a nurse feeding him.

"Don't get old," he said to Hills. "And don't get sick." He shifted in his chair with effort. "If I were a hand grenade, I would pull the pin. That wunderkind who comes here dangling his stethoscope. What a laugh. I tell him, 'Give me an embolism. A little bubble of air. Who's to know?' And he says, 'You'll feel better tomorrow.' Asinine child. Tomorrow is always worse than today."

Nineteen thirty-six was his first year out of law school, he told Hills. It was a bad Depression, long bread lines still, and he was doing a lot of pro bonum stuff. Free law.

"I was chosen because I spoke German," he said. "But it was cut and dried. Renner was a raving lunatic. In a straitjacket. I represented him when they drew up the commitment papers."

"I'm looking for a sample of his handwriting," Hills said.

"Ha. Good luck. He wasn't allowed anything sharp like a writing instrument. It was a straightforward case of commitment I forget where. Creedmore perhaps. Kings Park Psychiatric. But samples of his handwriting—never."

"Did he ever say anything about the Lindbergh case?"

"Lindbergh? Oh my God. So long ago. Hauptmann. He got a terrible defense. Reilly, his defense lawyer, ended up in a psychiatric ward himself a few months after the trial. How would you like to have as your defense attorney a staggering alcoholic with an advanced case of syphilis of the brain who's telling people privately that he thinks

you're guilty? If Renner said anything about Lindbergh I
don't remember it now. Perhaps he and Reilly met in the
looney bin somewhere. Wouldn't that be a tale?"

As Hills was leaving, the old lawyer called to him. "He
had consumption."

"Who."

"Renner. He had TB. I can still hear the cough. I don't
suppose he lived very long."

As Hills was getting into his car, and remembering that
Condon had said that "Cemetery John" had a hacking
cough, the old man's nurse hurried up. "Mr. Lewis says his
old files are in the garage. He says you're welcome to look."
She held out the garage key.

In Martin Lewis's legal folder there were file copies of all
the commitment papers that Hills had found in Renner's
hospital files. Plus the lawyer's handwritten notes and
other miscellaneous documents. But the most astonishing
find in the file was the notebook—a handwritten notebook.
Even Hills could see that it was the writing of a psychotic.
The handwriting was haywire, every which way. And the
word Nellie on some pages was written two inches high.
Enormous. Megalomaniacal. Other pages were written
with very small writing in some kind of code.

And on one page in huge block letters was written: Margaret Schlatter.

The next morning the handwriting expert called him.

"OK," he said. "This is pretty wild. This handwriting is
all over the place, but I'll compare it with the original ransom notes and get back to you in a day or two."

The hospital's Director of Human Resources said, "Mr.
Renner worked here as a wall washer at various times covering a twenty-year period. He retired on June 1, 1969, at
age seventy, disabled from rheumatoid arthritis. And
that's about all I'm allowed to tell you."

"Is this his last address you have?" Hills asked her, holding up his notepad. She compared it with her files.

"No," she said. "But even the one I have is getting on to

twenty-five years ago. He'd be well into his nineties if he were alive today. I'm sure he died some time ago."

She let him copy Renner's retirement address.

"When did his pension stop?"

"I have no idea. That is handled by a private agency."

Hills looked at the twenty-five-year-old address. It was a pretty cold trail. He wondered if there would be some record of his death in the probate court.

On a hunch, he went to Renner's last address to talk to the neighbors. Maybe he'd turn up another Mrs. Zorn. He tried the apartment janitor first.

The man had a remarkably thin face, almost bladelike with two huge eyeglass lenses that in total made him seem like a political cartoonist's satirical rendering of the President.

"Renner? Sure. What did you want to know?"

"When did he die?"

"My God. Did he die?"

"You mean he's alive?"

"Well, he was the last I heard. But not for long. He's in the hospital dying from cancer. You from the Welfare Board? My God, you people don't even let the corpse get cold, do you?"

"You have a key to his apartment?"

The janitor hauled on a lanyard attached to his belt and brought forth a large brass ring with dozens of keys on it. "You ain't going to find nothing there. Why'n't you let him die in peace? He's just a crazy old man crippled with arthritis. Living on a fish cake from Welfare and Social Security. He must be ninety-five or more."

Hills followed the man up the brownstone steps.

"It's a pigsty," the janitor said.

"I'll be here a while," Hills said.

"Be my guest." Exiting, the janitor paused at the door. "If a mouse came here, he'd have to bring his own lunch."

It was a one-room efficiency and it was jammed with trash. Hills spent an hour sorting through it—old papers, empty cornflakes boxes, discarded milk cartons, soup cans, and everywhere the sour smell of unwashed old age. The bed sheets hadn't been laundered in weeks—months. And on several hooks, old man's clothes hung, pants with knees, limp shirts and, below, several pairs of curled, rainstained old shoes. A dying old man's final possessions—a broken toaster, a disconnected radio, an old razor and a brush, no toothbrush or toothpaste and a small very dried-out piece of soap. The bathtub had a layer of city soot at the bottom and a torn shower curtain. He found one towel under the bed. No phone.

Under the chair he found a cracked, very old hat box, an antique from an age when men wore hats and kept them in boxes. He pulled off the top. It was stuffed with papers, old yellowed papers and several candy bar wrappers and, on top, newer papers.

He found old work records, pay stubs as a wall washer in the hospital, letters from Social Security, disability and welfare correspondence, records from psychiatric hospitals, and at the very bottom, work records from the 1930's, incomplete with many gaps.

Intermittently, in the early 1930's, Renner had worked as a wallpaper stripper. And in the late winter of 1932, according to his pay stubs, during February, he worked on "The Johnson job, Hopewell." Nearly six weeks of stripping wallpaper. In Hopewell, New Jersey, where Charles Lindbergh had built his new home from which his son was kidnapped.

Hills sat down on the floor staring at the pay records. Six weeks stripping wallpaper meant a large estate, and right next to the Lindbergh estate during February 1933. Charles Augustus Lindbergh Junior was kidnapped March 1, 1933, while Henry Boris Renner was working right next door.

Hills found a receipt for flowers. Renner had sent memorial flowers to Margaret Schlatter on April 3 past, the anniversary of Hauptmann's execution. Who in the world was Margaret Schlatter?

The florist said, "A basket of grave flowers for the grave of Margaret Schlatter. He sends them every year."

"Where is she buried?" Hills asked.

The man glanced at his records. "St. Raymond's. It's in the Bronx."

"Yes," Hills said. "I know exactly where it is."

The man at the gate house at Saint Raymond's Cemetery was quickly helpful. He took out a map of the cemetery grounds and drew a pencil line from the gate house to the Schlatter plot.

"They're all in there," he said. "Margaret and Herman, two sisters and their husbands and several grandchildren. Go right out the door here and follow the path to the right."

"When was Margaret buried?"

"Interment took place April 4, 1936."

Hills walked up the path. A cold wind flapped his coat-tails, and he pushed his hands into his coat pockets and stood looking at Margaret Schlatter's gravestone. At last, after nearly a year, the end of the trail.

At two in the afternoon as prearranged, he called the handwriting expert. "You got a pretty good case here. I'm not ready to go to court with it yet—I'd have to have the actual ransom notes—but I'm almost prepared to swear that this handwriting, while very psychotic, is the same handwriting in the ransom notes."

Hills needed just one more piece. The key piece. It was time to go see Henry Boris Renner in the hospital.

Renner was suffering and moved constantly, half off his head from the pain, half off his head from the morphine and half mad to begin with, constantly watching the door for the nurse with his next shot of painkiller.

Wasted, small as a boy, he fixed on Hills a pair of eyes that Hills had seen before. Those same eyes he had once seen on a revivalist preacher in Damascus, Georgia, and those same eyes he had seen on a man who had just shot and killed his entire family—wife, two children, and mother. El Greco had painted those eyes in his portrait of Saint Jerome as a cardinal. Eyes of a fanatic. Single-focused for a lifetime. Mad. Eyes that now looked directly at death.

"Hauptmann?" Renner asked furiously in a croupy voice. "Who are you? Why do you want to know about Richard Hauptmann?"

"Name's Hills. I'm doing a story on the Lindbergh kidnapping."

"Ha. Lindbergh." He squirmed again in his pain. His eyes fluttered and he floated off momentarily. Then he stirred, struggling to concentrate.

"Hauptmann." Yes, he knew Hauptmann. They came from the same town in Germany. Kamenz. Knew quite a bit about him. But that's all.

"What became of Nellie?" Hills asked.

"Ran away." Renner tried to rouse himself. "Never saw her again."

"Did you kill her?"

For a moment, Renner gathered himself and looked with those furious eyes at Hills. Ninety-three, almost dead and still very dangerous.

"You buried her under Margaret Schlatter's coffin. The day after Hauptmann was executed."

Renner rolled in pain. "Go away."

"She wanted to call the police and save Hauptmann's life."

"You'll never prove it."

"She was going to tell the police that you killed that baby."

"Go away." Renner found the strength to raise his head off the pillow and stare at Hills with drugged eyes. A man terrified of death.

"What are you doing?" Renner demanded. He watched Hills open the drawer of the table next to the bed. He watched him take out the battered, seam-split pocket-worn wallet and open it. Social Security Card. Medicare Card. Medicaid Card. Pharmacy identity card. Two singles and a five. And in a side pouch a folded piece of paper.

Hills pulled it out. An oversize twenty-dollar bill. A

United States Treasury Gold Certificate, folded in half longwise, then folded twice the other way.

"You carried it all these years," Hills said. "The token of your victory." The proof that he was somebody. Something that he could take out of his wallet every day to reassure himself, to exult over.

Renner looked at the bill in Hills's hands, then lay back. He managed to raise an unrepentant clenched fist. A moment later, the nurse came in with a hypodermic syringe. Blessed release from pain.

Somebody.

ABOUT THE AUTHORS

DAVID EVERSON knows more than anybody should about state politics (Illinois) and uses this knowledge to write dead-on books about the world's second oldest profession. Everson is working on other types of novels as well these days, and one assumes that he will do just as well by them as he has by pols.

RICK HAUTALA's novel *Nightstone* was a million-copy bestseller that established him as one of horror fiction's strongest voices. Hautala is presently working on a massive novel that will likely enhance his reputation even more.

WILLIAM J. REYNOLDS writes the Nebraska series of private detective novels, books that manage to be fully realized adventures while very gently poking fun at some of the genre's more shopworn conventions. He is stylish without being self-indulgent, and fun without being silly.

JOHN LUTZ's latest novel, *SFW Seeks Same*, is in the process of becoming one of next year's biggest motion pictures. It's hoped that the film will bring Lutz the belated fame he deserves because he's one of the best writers in suspense fiction today. He is a winner of the Edgar Award and President of Mystery Writers of America.

BRIAN HODGE has written several novels, each more intense than the previous one. His books combine a Conradian sense of the jungle (though this jungle is usually urban America) and eerie vision of the everyday.

REX MILLER is often mentioned, favorably, with Thomas Harris as this country's best teller of serial killer tales. Miller's style is all his own, and though it's filled with darkness, there is always a tender if fragile humanity at work. He will likely be one of the major voices of this decade. Dr. King is an associate of Rex Miller.

BRIAN HARPER is a pseudonym for an established suspense writer.

MATTHEW J. COSTELLO is a dark suspense novelist just now beginning to be celebrated by press and public alike. His most recent novel, *Wurm,* is a roller-coaster ride of suspense, eeriness, mordant humor and first-rate craftsmanship. His next novel, *Manhattan Beach,* may well bring him the even wider audience he deserves.

WILLIAM L. DeANDREA has won no less than two Edgar Awards, sired two very popular series, written an extremely wry and readable historical novel about New York called *The Lunatic Fringe,* and gone on to write three extremely popular espionage novels. And he's accomplished all this quickly. Still a young man, his future appears blessed.

BARBARA PAUL has written so many classic mysteries, including *First Gravedigger* and *Kill Fee,* that she is sometimes taken for granted. Finally, however, her publisher seems to be preparing her for bigger things. This should be Barbara's decade, one launched auspiciously with the publication of *In-laws and Out-laws.*

ALAN DEAN FOSTER has written so many bestsellers it's difficult to know which to list here. While he's concentrated on science fiction and science fantasy, his best novel may be *Slipt,* a glimpse of the near future told in an especially intense and occasionally poetic manner that makes it nearly impossible to forget.

NANCY A. COLLINS's first two novels about vampires won international praise so quickly that she was a star within six months of publication. She does her own kind of work, and does it extremely well.

BARRY N. MALZBERG is one of science fiction's poets. Never mind that he wrote such novels as *Guernica Nights* (justly praised by Joyce Carol Oates) or the brilliant *Herovit's World,* he also wrote *Engines of The Night,* which is a sacred and profound critical study of science fiction. After a long hiatus, Malzberg seems to be writing more these days.

DAVID HAGBERG, here writing as SEAN FLANNERY, has

written in virtually every genre but it is in espionage and techno-thrillers that he has begun, both under his own name and that of his pseudonym, to make a serious mark as a best seller. His novel *Countdown* recently won the American Mystery Award as best espionage novel of the year.

WILLIAM H. HALLAHAN has won the Edgar Award for his novel *Catch Me, Kill Me* and written several bestsellers in addition. His first four novels have long been cult classics, especially *The Search For Joseph Tully,* which Dean R. Koontz has called "one of the finest and most original occult novels of the past twenty years."